Mother Knows

Mother Knows

24 Tales of Motherhood

Edited by Susan Burmeister-Brown and
Linda B. Swanson-Davies of
Glimmer Train Stories

A GLIMMER TRAIN PRESS BOOK

WASHINGTON SQUARE PRESS
New York London Toronto Sydney

Washington Square Press
1230 Avenue of the Americas
New York, NY 10020

Library of Congress Cataloguing-in-Publication Data is available.

ISBN: 0-7434-8878-4

First Washington Square Press trade paperback edition April 2004

10 9 8 7 6 5 4 3 2 1

Manufactured in the United States of America

Book design by Helene Berinsky

COPYRIGHT NOTICES

The stories contained herein are works of fiction. Names, characters, places and incidents either are products of the authors' imaginations or are used fictitiously. These stories were first published in *Glimmer Train Stories;* we thank the authors for allowing us to reprint them in *Mother Knows.*

FOR MOM

Love

Contents

Foreword xi

Karen Outen • WHAT'S LEFT BEHIND 1

Dianne King Akers • SMALL SPEAKING PARTS 30

Monica Wood • FROST: A LOVE STORY 48

H. G. Carrillo • LECHE 54

Susanna Bullock • 4149A 67

Diane Chang • MOTHER KNOWS 80

Richard Bausch • WEATHER 91

Michael Frank • IN THE BED OF FORGETTING 112

Ayşe Papatya Bucak • HITCH 133

George Makana Clark • BACKMILK 150

Ronald F. Currie Jr. • VISITING YOUR GRAVE 159

Jennifer Seoyuen Oh • JANUARY 165

Junot Díaz • INVIERNO 176

Nancy Reisman • THE GOOD LIFE 193

Karenmary Penn • RIFT 215

J. Patrice Whetsell • THE COCONUT LADY 230

Nathan Long • TRACKING 237

Margo Rabb • HOW TO FIND LOVE 243
Joyce Carol Oates • THE MISSING PERSON 256
Doug Crandell • COLORED GLASS 272
Lee Martin • LOVE FIELD 284
Ioanna Carlsen • GOING HOME 301
Robin Bradford • BOB MARLEY IS DEAD 311
Ann Beattie • SOLITUDE 333

The Writers 345

Foreword

Susan and I tend to converse with our faces rather than our voices. We're sisters. And we've worked side by side since February 8, 1982, and have made a point of having at least a little hole in the wall—literally—between us so we could communicate this way.

Now we have a wavy glass divider between our two desks, just up to the tops of our noses, so we have complete privacy and focus until we both look up—or until one of us snorts, usually Susan. (Hahahahah! That's what you get for making *me* write this!)

In 1957, our parents decided to switch paths—moving from city life to farming—and, being romantics, conceived Susan, a new life in celebration of a new life. I became a serious farm girl, and Susan became a happily voracious reader by the time she was three. When she was ten, the eye doctor delivered the frightful news that Susan would go blind within a couple of years. Mom, also an unstoppable reader, said simply, *No.* And she was right, I believe, because she said so. Mom, a powerful woman, loved us, and we knew it.

In 1969, our big sister, Dabby, and her husband, Art, took us on a two-month, cross-country road trip. It was grand, but Susan, still only ten, was heartbroken with missing our mom. When we were reunited with our parents, Mom promised Susan that she would never be gone so long from her again.

As Susan recalls, "It was the recent memory of that painful separation that first came to me when she told me the next early spring that she was dying. I could not imagine how I would survive it. And to make matters more complicated, as mother matters often are, I was going through the age-eleven rebellion against her at the time. I was embarrassed that she could no longer speak; I was embarrassed that her head was shaved and that she had lost some of her propriety; I was embarrassed to bring friends home. On the night before she died at home, she waved each of us over to her separately and said the first word she'd been able to speak since that spring. *Love,* she said. When she looked at me, she somehow absolved me of my guilt. I knew she understood, that all was all right with us. She never awoke the next morning. And yet, she has kept her promise. I have never felt she has been far away."

I married in 1971, divorced in 1990, remarried him in 1999. Great guy, both times and still. We have one wonderful daughter, Erin, already striking out on her own. Susan and her husband had their son, a sweet boy named Henry (after our father), in 1995. And life goes on.

Mothers. We have them, we lose them, we shun them, we need them, we become them or we don't. There is always love and loss. And there are stories.

—LINDA B. SWANSON-DAVIES

Karen Outen

What's Left Behind

He sweeps by me. My husband, Dizzy, rushes past me with his arms outstretched like a preacher at altar call. He sweeps by nearly on his back. His lower body is invisible beneath the water. I'll never forget his face: raging against this sudden tide. He is stunned to leave me this way. Take my hand, he screams to me. He sweeps by. I will never know if he meant so that I could save him or follow the flow. My family is driftwood floating by: daughter, daughter, husband. I hold tight to the car. I am strapped into the backseat, held in place by the water that rises against my chest. Trying so hard to recount: how did we get here?

Moments ago, in what I see now as a past life: we are in the car. Dizzy drives us home from Keisha's music lesson, Geena's ballet class, a trip to the hardware store. He says: Look at Main Street. It's all crowded. A little rain and folks act too scared to take their known roads. So we take our usual road, an old back road that is unusually deserted, even considering how small this town is—small and quiet, tucked beneath the mountains that lend a kind of awe and benevolence to our lives. We are insignificant in the world. We know it, and go about our small business easy as you please. We drive pretty slow here. By and large, Sundays are for morning church and afternoon visiting. This town, Ladyslipper, knows her limits, I believe. No fast food, no high rises. Only 2,000 people live here, half of them driving ten-, fifteen-year-old cars.

So in our old car we take our old road because the rain has stopped finally after four days, and the kids have stopped bugging me to read about Noah's Ark. I sit on the backseat behind Dizzy, as usual. Keisha's up front and Geena's beside me. We bump on the soggy road. The baby inside my womb kicks a swift protest. Then we hear the hard "Bang!" loud and shocking as a cannon, as we lurch forward and down into a deep pothole. We bounce and jerk there a minute. My forehead slams the headrest in front of me and tunnels of pain shoot through my head. My girls scream. I feel sick. Our front tires are stuck so deep that the back tires don't touch the ground. We're rutted midway up the hubcaps.

Goddamn! Dizzy says, It's a wonder we didn't flip! His nose is bloody. He holds his chin. See? See, girls? he says. That's why Mommy and Daddy make you wear seat belts. He reaches for Keisha, who's beside him: You'da gone right through the windshield without that seat belt. Damn. That's the axle gone, I'll bet.

I throw up in my lap, into my maternity pants and thin sweater. I hardly hear them get out of the car, the girls running behind Dizzy, anxious to see a broken axle, whatever that is. My seat belt loose but still buckled, I swing my legs out of the car. Hold tight to the door and put my head near as I can between my knees. My feet swing above the ground.

Look, look, Daddy! The car's off the ground. Wow! The girls run to the back of the car, peer under the tires; it's so unusual to see them off the ground. I remember Dizzy was driving slow over the potholes, fifteen miles an hour. Maybe we'd all be dead now if he'd gone faster.

Dizzy says: Listen. What's that? I listen but my head aches too much to hear anything. I shrug: I don't hear a thing. A few minutes later, still inspecting the back of the car and pinching the bridge of his nose to stop the bleeding, he says it again: What's that roar? Listen. I hold tight to the door to steady myself. I'm still shaken. Look up and catch his eyes, the two gray lashes on his left eyelid, that spidery brown mole in the white of his eye. This look I remember now as a caress.

I hear a roar, and the world explodes. Not a warning drop, but a solid wall of water hits us. The car tilts forward. My legs and crotch get soaked. I hold tight to the car doorjamb as the water grabs at my legs. The car door slams wide open. Dizzy is screaming to my children. Screaming with the conviction that his voice could be a life raft.

Geena goes first—six years old and tiny, even as an infant too thin for Pampers. She flows off backward, mouth open wide and speechless. Facing me. Her braids are soaked. Quickly, she's just a head bobbing on the water. I think how hard a time I'll have combing her hair now that it's wet and nappy. Water around my pregnant belly. Grip the inside door handle. My brown knuckles nearly white from strain. Can't remember: can she swim? Was it Geena I took to the Water Babies swim class or Keisha?

Keisha: Dizzy grabs her collar with one hand and the car bumper with the other. Water pulls her away, a great tug-of-war and Keisha's eyes are squinted tight. Dizzy bites his lip and holds on, trembling . . . one, two, three . . . It goes so slowly, so fast . . . four, five, six . . . I kick my legs up and fight with the water. I rise, my legs pulled straight out and splayed open . . . seven, eight, nine . . . She glides to me, arms first. Dizzy grips a purple scrap of her shirt. He holds it fierce as she grabs for me: Hold Mommy's leg. Keisha pulls tight, and I stretch long and rubbery. One hand down to her around my swollen belly. Our eyes lock. She is my determined child. The one who learned to throw herself out of the crib when she did not want to nap. I stare into her eyes. Reaching. The baby in my womb is in the way. I cannot bend, only pull myself lopsided. Come to Mommy, Keisha. The seat belt remains tight. Dizzy put in an extension last month to fit around my high, round belly. Keisha slides. My pantyhose rip. I slap at the water. We hold hold hold our eyes. She slides, grabs my shoe. I grip my toes. But the shoe comes off and she sets sail, whirling away. Holding my shoe, a makeshift steering wheel, she zigzags side to side. And he sweeps by me. Calling me to him. How can I not follow? I hold tight to the door frame. Slammed hard by the water. My legs are sucked beneath the surface. The water rises quickly against my chest. I am still strapped in. The car is rutted deep, the rear of it pushed ever higher by the water. While its joints sigh and moan, the car door hangs open, an unhinged mouth. The baby in my womb closes itself as a fist.

Open my eyes at the hospital. The ambulance stops and out I pour. Cameras pointed at me. I lie still, though I am jostled on the stretcher. Cameras lean over me, hot and bright. I hear them say: This is a good one. Feed it through to the networks. Get the shots of her in the water. An ambulance attendant runs beside my stretcher and tells the doctor about me, about what has happened to me—*what has happened to me. what has. happened. to me.* The doctor looks deep into my face, retrieving my girls, my man. He talks to me but he asks nonsense: Do you know where you are? What's your name? Is there anyone we can call? Are you in any pain? I answer in order. Yes. Mommy. No. Yes. He looks back at the ambulance attendant: Flattened affect. Shock, he nods, and pats my arm.

In high school, before Dizzy, I dated a guy who had been flattened. Run over at a slight diagonal up the center of his body: through the crotch, over his stocky torso and his collarbone, and just missing his head. The school-bus tire left ugly tracks, three serrated rows like a zipper. But he lived, after five months of traction. He came back to school slightly taller, crooked, and very thin. I think of Mose Job like I saw him then: on the blacktop in front of our school, lying there inanimate and sticky with blood. And stunned—why is that? Why aren't we ever prepared? That sometimes it's us.

AMERICA TODAY

FATHER, 2 CHILDREN DROWN IN SWOLLEN RIVER

Ladyslipper—As a pregnant 31-year-old woman watched in horror, her husband and their two young daughters were swept away as the Mehosehannock River spilled over its banks. The family's car had apparently stalled in the path of the oncoming flood. The woman, identified as Maggie Barnes, was rescued by helicopter an estimated 10 minutes after the accident. Flooding caused widespread property damage over a 15-mile area. The Barneses are the only known fatalities.

Day. Night. Day. Night. I think I am awake continually, but the time flashes so quick between light and dark that I suppose I sleep. It is light and a cluster of nurses stands at my door, huddled close to one another. In the dark, someone holds my hand. Light. A nurse says: Sheriff's here. Can he come in? How 'bout your pastor? Dizzy's aunt? No, no, no. I hear her say later that in my sleep I tremble and gulp like I'm choking. Two old women stand at the head of my bed on either side of me, day and night. They are sentinels in pale blue aprons and white uniforms and old-fashioned nurse's caps, stiff and pointed. They coo to me and stroke my brow. Their skin is the color of mahogany wood and finely textured with lines and spidery veins. I stare at them, picking a new wrinkle or crease to follow each day.

When I dream, I see these women wearing angels' wings. They have come to steal me away to my family. But mostly I dream of Mose on the blacktop. I see rescuers peel him off like PlayDoh. On TV, they show pictures of my empty house, the newspeople camped out around it. One night I hear the big nurse who cries over me say that they'll release me the next day. So when it is dark and my sentinels doze, I rise and dress quietly. I slip past the nurse at her station, glued to the local TV news and the endless interviews with my children's teachers, my husband's boss. I'm the one you see on TV. *Look-look-look—oh my God, that poor woman.*

THE STATE CAPITOL TIMES
FLOODING HITS HOME IN LADYSLIPPER

Ladyslipper—Each year scores of Americans are killed in flash floods. But it's never happened here, until now. Since the tragic drowning of Keisha Barnes, 8, her sister Geena, 6, and their father, Dizzy, the town of Ladyslipper has grieved openly for the first children it has lost in eight years. Tucked west of a range of mountains known simply as Bobb's, this sheltered hamlet is working class and close knit with a nearly equal number of black and white residents. Their grief for the Barnes family, who was black, crosses racial and gender lines—"Tragedy ain't just doled out according to skin color," Delilah Pyles admonishes a reporter.

"It's a shock," says Norma McInierney. "Feel just like somebody hit me. Everybody knows them. My husband was Dizzy's high-school coach. The thing is, a warm night like this, those little girls would be playing jump rope in my yard right now." She shakes her head, "I can just see 'em."

"Those are my goddaughters and my best friend," says Sheriff Jonah Kind in a halting voice. "I don't know what to do. I keep going by the house to see if it's not some mistake. Some awful mistake."

Mose answers his door. His face holds a terrified calm. The nurses looked at me frightened, too, as if I were contagious.

Good damn, he says, then shakes his head: Oh, Maggie, Maggie. He holds back awhile, then pulls me to him. We rock back and forth, a pitiful box step. Mose never could dance. You're all over the TV, he says when we part.

I nod: I know. Can't go home. Saw them waiting there.

Inside his house, I dangle on a rope inside his TV. Snatched from the water. I remember the rope around my chest. The rubber-padded man, life vest, helmet. I rose heavy. I look away as my TV self parts the water. I collapse on Mose's couch and sigh.

He sits next to me.

There's nowhere else to go, I say.

I know it, he answers.

This is awkward, or rather it should seem more awkward. I have not really talked to Mose for years and years. But I don't feel it, really. I don't feel much at all.

On TV, a fat woman in her twenties with a Life's a Beach T-shirt takes up the screen: I got two babies of my own. I'm from right here in Ladyslipper. You'da had to shoot me if this was to happen to me. I couldn't take it. I couldn't take it, she wails. She scoops up her toddler, hugs his cheek to her mouth, startling the baby until he cries.

Mose takes my hand. And oddly, I am comforted by his scaly skin, by his dusty smell and the smell of his house, which seems to have been closed tight for years. Old newspapers stand along the walls in dozens of neat, tied stacks. Cardboard boxes with lids are topped with glass or plywood for tables.

Haven't had company, he says, and I know he means forever. And I think about him coming back to school, finally, after his accident. With a cane in his hand and his father at his side—his father who was the oldest man in town, nearly eighty-three when Mose was seventeen, and called Mose by his whole name from birth: Mose Job! Mose Job! Come to supper. Mose Job! Pull my car around front. Mose limped into school. Half of us were silent and scared. The rest of us giggled nervously. His skin seemed taut, and he really was taller. All his pants were highwaters. He walked down that long hallway, and we stood in rows by the lockers, all of us: black and white, underclassmen and seniors, staring like a hearse passed us. Staring at Mose Job and his ancient father. They looked alike for the first time. His father had been set apart by his crooked body—even his fingers bent, with the tips jutting forward. But that day Mose Job and his father both leaned forward on canes like sick, tired trees; they matched. A cold dead air fanned behind them as they passed. Until somebody said: Gumby's back! And we laughed so that the air we expelled pumped into Mose's lungs, heated up that deadly pall around him. Until he laughed, too, then waved his long fingers. We brought him back to us—laugh-two-three, laugh—c'mon back, Mose Job.

Mose is sitting beside me when I wake up. I look long and hard at his face. His lips are full and smooth, his thick eyelids darker than his skin so that they seem shaded. It's an expressive face, full of tenderness and sorrow. I study him. I am sorry I never loved him fully. I feel great sadness at that, something desperate and shameful.

He makes me mush and corned-beef hash and biscuits. Only ever cooked for my pops, he says. He ain't have no teeth left.

I eat it. Because what do I care about taste? And, truth be told, it's not bad. But then I notice it for sure. That it's wet in my seat. Not sopping, but wet. While Mose clears the table, I reach inside my panties. A steady trickle of clear liquid seeps out of me. Fishy liquid. It's not my baby's water breaking—no. Something else.

Mose, I say, I need to go in town. To the drugstore.

We walk down the gravel path leading to Peggy's Neck Road. This path, now muddy and calf-high full of water, is the only place I've glimpsed him since I married and had babies. Sometimes driving by I'll see a skinny man darting through the trees, a hand rising through the branches to wave. I know he's lived here alone since his papa died, and he works at the factory in Slippery, next town over. I remember suddenly, startlingly, being here with him one night fourteen years ago back when we were best friends, and more. Here in his field, I took off my panties, rolled my white knee socks down to my ankles, and pushed my blue plaid skirt above my hips. On a blanket, I sat spread-eagle around him, impatient for him. We were eager to become lovers, but doomed: we took useless turns kneading his crushed penis, and we both fought tears. How angry I was with him.

We cut into town mostly through farmland and people's backyards since the main road, Route 78, is flooded. We walk slow and with purpose. But we can't take shortcuts on the side streets because of the police barricades. And the noise, the noise: the car horns, the hideous rush of water—

Stop walking; I grab Mose's arm. I hear Dizzy say: Listen? What's that roar?

We stand on Side Street in front of Jo-Ellena Fabrics, a two-story whitewashed store that used to be the Pentecostal church. A woman touches me. Clutches my arm. Praying loud. Another one gasps and runs by me to her husband, who stands at his car. She falls into his arms, crying like a baby. I do not recognize Ladyslipper. There's a new attraction: a natural disaster. Main Street, which ought to spread itself out wide two blocks ahead, seems gone. I can't see the Woolworth's, the Baylor's Drug, the Miss June's Ice Cream tucked neatly beside it, or the three-story, fully stocked Kiddie Town on the corner.

We can't cross to Main. Ahead of us, a river rushes down Gulph Street, which is a perfect riverbed. It's a wide street that dips deep in the middle. Police guard it, pushing people back from the brink of the water—all of our police are here, regulars and auxiliary. Even kids from the high-school police club are here, dressed in dark blue shirts and ties and tan pants, and police caps that sometimes swim on their heads. They look solemn and say softly: Please keep back, ma'am. Townspeople stand against the yellow wooden police barricades and dip their hands in the water. Or throw in flowers. I see small placards and big, gaudy funeral flower arrangements: a broken circle, a teddy bear with huge, tiger-lily eyes. All have this message: God bless you, Keisha and Geena. Nobody mentions Dizzy. Women weep over the water. They wear cotton flowered housedresses or dark knit stretch pants. They share the same face, black or white, old or young, the same look of Ladyslipper: loose, fleshy, like well-worked bread dough. They dimple and crease, slide in and out of sorrow. The women lean on the barricades and sob. They throw not only roses and baby's breath into the water, but kiddie bookbags, hair barrettes and bows, Legos, Barbie dolls, baby dolls. And us. Us.

There are pictures everywhere: Keisha and Geena on lapel pins. On black-and-white posters in store windows. On flyers that say, Pray for our girls, Ladyslipper. Or, Remember Keisha and Geena. Drive with care. *They have been in my house, in my things.* I cry out, and they see me. They reach for me, pulling at the hem of my tunic. Grabbing at my arms. Mose holds me. Thin Mose. They seem to reach through him. We look at each other in sorrow. Helpless. I pray for those girls, someone yells. God bless you. Be strong! My sleeve rips as once more I am engulfed. The Lord is my shepherd, I shall not want. Suffer the little children to come unto me.

A woman I don't recognize steps forward swiftly and slaps me hard twice: You bitch! You could've saved them!

I sink back into Mose. She is snatched by people on either side of her. They pull and jostle her, swear at her. Mose and I push out of the crowd. My nose bleeds where she hit me. The police scramble, unprepared. Ladyslipper has had one mugging and three robberies in five years. Never an angry crowd.

Water leaks between my legs in stingy drops. It smells like this makeshift river: angry, briny. The clouds hang low and soiled gray, rising just off Bobb's Mountain to the east. I won't get to see Main Street, Miss Hannah's Studebaker parked below her sign: Hannah's Good Eats. Instead, helicopters circle Gulph Street's river, newscopters that trouble the water with their whirly-burly. My children flow by. First, Geena, her braids a thick raft. Then Keisha, steering by my shoe. And Dizzy, sweet Dizzy, calling my name. I am sane now for one reason: I did not see them go under. Only sweep away wild and sudden, his arms open to me, their tiny girlish heads bobbing above water.

The Times of Ladyslipper
Local Landmark Destroyed

Miss Hannah's 1957 Studebaker was destroyed last night in a collision between two news vans. Vans were racing to Gulph Street where Maggie Barnes was spotted, sparking an uprising among the crowd. Miss Hannah's mint-condition Studebaker has been parked outside the diner since her husband, the late Jenkins Jones, drove it here from the factory in Detroit. As in most of northern Ladyslipper, the diner and car had been spared from flooding.

"It was my daddy's dream to own a car, not just a hauling truck. He was so proud when he come home with it," said Lloyd Jenkins Jones this morning.

Miss Hannah was too distraught for comment.

Mose was some kind of celebrity as Gumby. The newspapers wrote story after story on his progress. No other kid in the state had survived being run over by a bus. In the hallways at school or in town, it was: Hey, Gumby Man, what's happening? I tutored him in English so I was one of the few who knew how changed he was. Something about a damaged optic nerve. He could barely see out of his left eye. And I knew he lost his balance a lot. Sometimes he just fell over for no reason. But when he was Gumby, he had this status he hadn't had before the accident. He had been just this shy, average-looking guy who always wore dusty brown penny loafers and corduroys. But not quite a nerd, because he could set a whole class to laugh with his deadpan humor and blank face. He could joke a teacher out of giving the class detention. Nobody even teased him much about his ancient daddy, even though they could have: Mose Job could never much fight. But as I say, as Gumby, everybody wanted to take a picture with Mose, or invite him to their parties. Or court him. Shy Mose—there he is, at the Superfly party in his flannel shirt with the white T-shirt peeking through. He's standing against the wall, smiling shyly at our polyester double knits and wide lapels. He'd stumble out at some respectably late hour and everybody'd joke that he was so quiet in the corner: Must've been getting high, Cool Mose. So I'd go behind him, lead him by the arm. He'd told me that the strobe lights in these dark cinder-block basements made him night-blind. After a while, he'd just linger near a door 'til I came for him. I'd walk him through the tall alfalfa grass near his home and let him kiss me in the dark. Cold sloppy kisses, nearly swallowing my bottom lip. I was never excited so much as patient and glad. Glad he had somebody to kiss in the dark. I remember his wet, sorry kisses and the breeze in the grass, the way the lower mountains cut a jagged line across the sky. I had some feeling for Mose. Not love. Not pity. Some feeling.

THE HERALD TIMES MAGAZINE
A FLOOD RUNS THROUGH IT

> Ladyslipper—This is normally an ordinary town of winding back roads and farmland. Today, however, a visitor finds those roads transformed into canals, into a stark set from a futuristic science-

fiction movie where dogs paddle by languidly, followed by small chairs and particle-board tables, stuffed bunny rabbits, an occasional dead bird. And where old women gather at the graveyard.

Miss Janice Hoover, 70, the former principal of the Colored Normal School, helps her 89-year-old mother navigate the flood waters. They have visited the grave of Miss Janice's father every day for 23 years. This day will not be an exception. The Hoovers occasionally identify the belongings they pass—"Miss Norrisson's side chair," "Mr. Waples's cane stand"—as they wade in thigh-high water that is cold and nearly still.

At the end of New Deal Street, they reach a plot where the brown water is filled with muddy, half-submerged headstones. Two police deputies sit on the hood of a stalled car, and old women—black and white—are camped out on either side of them. Some sit in the high cabs of pickup trucks with oversize tires. Others sit atop the hoods of stranded cars and recline against the windshields. Some knit, some read from their Bibles, others just "keep company." As the Hoover women approach, the deputies help them climb aboard.

"So many of our porches done flooded or collapsed," says Sudie Nickels, 81. "We don't have no place to gather. Plus, it's sort of keeping watch on our children, those babies and their father what was lost. It's our way to sit a vigil at the wake, and since we got no bodies, we've got to do it this way. I was their great grandmother's best friend, you know, God rest her soul."

I lay on Mose's couch. It's nighttime and the dusty windows absorb the darkness. . . . Next, I am leaning over the creek behind the house, my face inches from the water, my nose touching it. Mose lifts my shoulders, wipes my face, guides me back to his house. It is so dark. I am confused and I long for moonlight. Mose, Mose, I call. Yep, he answers soft.

Again, I must recount: how did I get here? I was on the couch, still soggy and soft between my legs. I concentrated on Mose's house, which smells like Ben-Gay and old newspapers. I thought: I can't sleep here. But I suppose I did.

Back in his house, Mose sits me in a hardback chair and peels the nightshirt from me. He washes my feet and legs, slow, gentle rubbing. My hands smell surprisingly of fish. We both look at them with anger.

Mose went from being Gumby to Mose Job the Fish on a class trip to SeaLand. There we stood in a dimly lit room full of fish swimming behind glass walls. Who saw it first? The blue fish with striped gills, its back arched like a football. And flat as your hand. So odd surrounded by fat fish who swam faster. Who said it? "Look. Look, y'all, it's Mose Job." Flat and blue lying there on the blacktop: CPR, electric shock—how do we get this boy to breathe again? "Look, y'all, Mose the Fish." He looked at it, such a sad startled look. He shuddered. We nudged him: "Say something." But Mose and this fish were locked in, somehow. "Say something clever, Mose Job." He touched the glass and pulled his hand away quick and walked away. Walked out of our lives.

I sob suddenly into my hands. My fishy hands. He takes them, too, soaks them in lemon juice and a little ammonia, then dresses me in a fresh nightshirt. I look down at its old threads, weak and soft.

Papa's, he says.

He makes up the couch again, straightens my sheets, fluffs my pillows, which ooze their stuffing white and silky; they are lost clouds come to make my bed. He stands holding the blanket to put over me. I think of his sweet, messy kisses and shake my head. He mimics me, confused. I point to his bedroom. He drops the blanket and sinks down on the couch.

Not a good plan, he says weakly.

Maybe ten minutes, maybe half an hour, we sit. Nothing happens or moves, except the smell of this house seeps into me. Already there's a layer of dust or sediment that seems to coat my lungs. Sometimes I cough to see what rises from my alluvial soil. Finally he gets up. I feel him before I see him. Leaning over me. He takes my hand and leads me to his bed. Feels like a pile of three or four old mattresses. We sink in and cover ourselves with moth-eaten wool blankets, their satin edges frayed.

He takes my hand and strokes it, wonderful, like these are his first fingers, the first flesh he has known. I kiss him. He lifts my hand and places it on his side: See, he says. Used to be my spleen. Gone.

He moves my hand down to his groin. Moves my fingers under his penis, which is moist, prickly, and cool. Our fingers grope his empty sac.

They're retracted. Pushed inside I don't know where. Maybe where my kidney used to be. Ain't nothing like it was.

My fingers swim in his empty space. I move them over the wide vein of his penis, up to his soft patch of hair. Baby's hair, curly, thick, and strong. I brush my cheek against his shoulder. The skin is scarred where it was grafted. Also, dry and ashy. I sigh and the moist air I exhale softens his skin, makes it tender and almost for a moment like he's fifteen years old again. But he is right. Nothing's as it was. I hold the base of his penis, this delicate, wilted flower.

Later, Mose takes my hand and pulls me from the bed. He helps me put on shoes and an old flannel work shirt over the nightgown. There is still no moonlight as we walk. We step high in the tall grass. Mud oozes into my shoes and chills me. Mose holds my hand so tight. We walk a mile, grass whisking against us—shushh, shushh. The slender grass feels like tiny hands across my thighs, my baby, my arms; it brushes against me and I feel comforted. The blades of grass are small and yielding as babies' hands, old women's hands, patting me, soothing me—shush, shushhh, shushh—my baby folds itself in prayer—shush, shushhh—we find solace, as if all of Ladyslipper hides in this grass, comes to guide me—shush, shushh—it is my people, my Ladyslipper I find here. The tall grass moans and bends to my aid.

Beyond us, the river looms closer as we walk. Closer, louder. I pull back once, but Mose comes for me, his arms around my shoulders; he pushes me on. Eerie now, my comfort gone. The river swallows and gulps. I think of the nurse who said I gulped in my sleep. A stench overtakes Ladyslipper, so strong and sour that my eyes burn. We cross the parking lot for the new Baptist church, the majority of which has peeled away and slid down into the river. The remainder of the church sits sliced clean open, its pews and altar bowing down toward the water. Mose stops walking. I turn to him.

It's a comfort, he says: That it couldn't happen again. You'll see.

He folds his body down, sinks onto the cracked pavement, and stretches full out, arms to the sides, legs apart, head turned hard to the left. So hard that his face presses into the pavement; hard enough to smell the school-bus tires: rubber, sulfur, and traces of manure from the country roads. He closes his eyes.

I walk toward the stagnant water. Glance back at Mose, who watches me now. Straight on to the flow. I feel a deep terror. I stop. I step gingerly to a large rock. A skinny but sturdy tree grows behind it and drapes down over the water. Fearful, then defiant and unflinching, I struggle for balance on the rock—I see myself plunge backward into this open wound of a river, I sink then rise in a long purple robe, belted in gold threads; yes, that was me, twelve years old and baptized here, flung in a sinner and retrieved in salvation. My mother and father were still alive then, and they wept on the shores as I rose, whole and new.

I waddle on this solid rock, squat my knees for balance, and latch on to the tree. Nervous, I sweat and feel chilled. Excited, I am light-headed and mocking disaster. Hold tight and stretch out, wrap my bare arms around this splintery tree trunk. Water floods my shoes, pulls at my legs, swipes at me furious. I feel a sinking fear but I see: I am safe. I cannot be had this time—*this time!* What washes over me is a strange relief. A sudden shame. It is done, and still . . . I survive.

Mose has been answering the phone a lot this morning. Outside there's a ruckus. He says: They found us.

I sit down at the kitchen table, which is piled high with cakes, pies, a glazed ham, a homemade loaf of wheat bread, some kind of noodle casserole. Found 'em on the steps, he says: Folks are kind.

The phone rings. Mose talks briefly and then comes to the table. We sit facing each other. Sipping strong coffee in our nightshirts.

Perfectly quiet. Perfectly removed. There's a sort of comfort and woe I cannot describe. Shut up in this house. Listening to the crunch of tires on gravel. Heavy-handed knocking on the doors. We're sealed tight behind dingy gray windows. So little light in here. I wipe my hand across the kitchen table. Looks to have a thick coat of gray dust, but nothing wipes off on my hand. Should we let people in? I look around. The couch still holds my bedding, the armchair's leg is broken and it leans heavy to the right. What passes for an ottoman is really just a stack of tied magazines with a scarf thrown over it. I won't let anyone in. They wouldn't understand this home . . . home. Mine has Beauty and the Beast and Little Mermaid, Princess Jasmine, a harem of Barbie dolls, hair barrettes and ribbons hidden all over the house like Easter eggs.

He answers the phone. Pitifully thin Mose standing sideways and bent, patting his foot, nervous. He turns to me: You should take this one. It's not the talk-show people. It's Jonah Kind.

He holds the phone up to my ear. I clutch the coffee cup in one hand, rub my neck with the other.

Maggie? Maggie? Jesus—I didn't know where you were. Are you all right? Oh, Maggie . . . Listen, I'm sorry to have to ask this, but I'm gonna have to ask you to come in to the station. We need some kind of formal record of the accident. It's just my job. Maggie, I apologize, Jonah mumbles into the phone.

I move my head away from the receiver. Mose says to Jonah: Fine, but all these news folk are here. How we gonna get out?

I'll come for you then, Jonah tells him, and it booms out of the phone.

I wonder what he does now at night, I say.

Who?

Jonah. He used to come by every night. Walk in and go straight to the refrigerator like he was home. Or go tuck in the girls when Dizzy worked late. Listen to my stories about my day. Mose?

Yeah?

What d'you suppose he does at night now?

Mose blinks fast, then turns away.

• • •

I get dressed to go to the police station. Dressed in the same thin sweater and soiled maternity pants I wore That Day. But my clothes are clean. Mose has washed them by hand, scrubbing them with even strokes on an old washboard. I watched him, though he didn't see me—watched how gingerly he touched the polyester silk of my bra and the cotton of my sweater, how he clutched them to his face a long time. I wear Mose Job's daddy's boxer shorts for underpants and I still drip-drip my water. I am never quite dry. I come into the kitchen. Mose slices ham, shoves thick slabs between wheat bread, heaps collard greens and kale onto paper plates. One by one he passes them out the living-room window. Thanks, they say. Much obliged. The window's open just enough to fit hands and paper platters through it. It brings a slender ribbon of light to cut across the room, a sudden brightness that I can't bear. I rest flat against the wall, which is easy because despite my high, full belly, I grow thinner, my arms and legs and face less fleshy, my back feeling bony. What will this new baby think of me, of this thin, quiet mother, a sort of cutout doll? Flat. And moist: how old will I grow and still leak what has seeped into me? I look behind me for the trail I surely make. I could leave watery figure-eights like graffiti as I grow old and copper-skinned, dancing through Main Street of an evening.

I watch Mose—never saw him move so fast, small beads of sweat on his forehead. Purpose feeding him, pumping into his skinny veins, his hollowed cheeks. Mose Job nearly smiles.

A man's hand pushes back a plate of food. He says: It's Jonah Kind, Mose. Can I come 'round?

Sheriff Jonah Kind pushes his way past reporters and townsfolk—some of them Dizzy's distant kin, I see—and angles his way through the door. He takes stock of the room a long time. Mose stands, hands folded obediently in front of him. Jonah Kind scans the room slow, mesmerized, adjusting to the near-light of my makeshift home. It's clear he doesn't see me. I cough.

Maggie? That you?

Yeah, Jonah. It's me.

Whew, he says, and comes over in big steps like he's wading against tide. He's the biggest-chested man I know. He steps in front of me. I watch his chest rise and fall. He sighs heavy and takes me into his arms. God, Maggie, he says over and over. I loved him. I loved him.

Heah, Jonah, how 'bout a cup of coffee? Folks dropped some off this morning, Mose says.

Jonah releases me. Mose walks toward the kitchen and I hear him mumble, incredulous: Cup of coffee? Sit awhile for some coffee? He repeats it, testing out inflections.

Nah, Jonah says. His skin is about Dizzy's color and texture. I look away from him. Got my deputies outside, to help y'all get to the station. Ready?

Jonah Kind belongs to Ladyslipper. When he was four years old, Felbo Toussand found Jonah in his fields, curled up beside a milking cow, asleep on her teats. He was half-frozen and scrawny. Felbo and his wife wrapped Jonah in warm blankets, took moist towels and liniment to his raw feet, fed him lentil soup and biscuits. They held him in their arms constantly because he shivered so, even after he was warmed. For weeks he shivered and cried, and the Toussands held him. Later, he stammered as though his teeth still chattered. So all winter, on an old loveseat in front of the fireplace, Felbo and Minnie Toussand held Jonah nestled between them until he settled there and took root.

Nobody ever got the straight story on where he came from. They just took him in. Everybody—Felbo for the first two years 'til his wife died, then the Hendrickses, the Norrissons, the Nickelses, the Hoovers, even my family, all took a turn, depending on who could afford an extra mouth that year. Not like shuffling him, more like he was a new baby at a family reunion, passed from warm arms to warm arms, cradled and cooed over. He even stayed with a couple white families in high school so he could get to the demonstration school in Slippery. He lived with Dizzy's family awhile, and he and Dizzy became best friends for life. When he graduated with honors from high school, the town council paid his way to state college.

He's every kid's Uncle Jonah, everybody's brother or son. When he was sworn in as Sheriff and the judge asked his parents to stand, every man and woman over fifty stood up. But the drawback is, he says, every woman in town feels like a relative, so he doesn't date.

I sit between Jonah Kind and Mose Job in the back of the squad car. Jonah takes my hand in his, turns it over and over slowly, like a marble.

Outside the room, people clamor for us. We sit at a long pine table. When I run my hand across it, I remember its story. I get up and walk around it, looking under the sides, feeling my way. Mose frowns at me.

Oh! Jonah gasps and springs up so fast he rocks the table: Here it is.

I walk around to the far right side of the table, near the back corner of the room. Jonah runs his finger along the wood grain, then lifts the table up so I can see it. Scratched there in immature scrawl: First, Butch and Sundance. Now, Jonah and Dizzy.

I've never seen this before, I say, and smile: Skipping school in fifth grade. You two were a couple of rebels. Without a clue. I laugh and I can see Dizzy's silly smirk and hear his reply: Ha ha ha, Miss Honor Roll. Jonah puts the table down. He kneels in front of it and rests his forehead against it. He makes no noise as he cries. I walk back across the room to leave him in peace. I stare through the glass wall. They cannot see me through the blinds, but I count twenty men and women with microphones and notepads and tape recorders.

What for? I ask aloud.

Mose comes to me. For you, he says: For your story.

Jonah rises, sniffing. Jonah Kind is the softest-hearted man I know, Dizzy used to tell me. Jonah sits heavy in front of me, and says: I shouldn't be the one to do this. You and Dizzy are my family. I can't interrogate you.

I laugh and reach for his hand: Hell, Jonah, we're all your family. He smiles and I pull my hand away quick because I feel his sorrow pulling for me.

What d'ya need to know? Mose asks.

What happened that day. Maggie, you remember?

I shrug: Sure. Every day.

So I tell him everything, just as I went over it in my head all that time I was strapped in that damned car, the cold water up to my collarbone and smacking toward my ears. Mose stands stock still while I talk. Jonah holds his chin and shakes his head, his eyes bloody wet.

I say: Nothing was unusual. No premonitions. Nothing. Keisha and Geena did their usual. Geena likes to tattletale that Keisha won't brush her teeth. Every morning she comes downstairs and says to me, Smell her breath, then points to her sister—

My words just stop. Just shut off like a faucet. I stare clear-eyed and silenced.

Well, Jonah stutters: I s-s-s-up-pose I c-can write up a re- re— He pulls a piece of twine from his shirt pocket and works it with both hands, slow and methodical. He clears his throat. Just need some kind of accident report on file, he says slowly.

We'll never find the bodies, will we? I ask.

Jonah stiffens and his fair skin seems to drain more of its color before he turns ruddy. No, he answers: They're saying with that part of flooding emptying into the Atlantic it could be months. Or never. They're gone, Maggie.

No, no, I know, Jonah. I understand.

A deputy at the door says the media wants a statement, they know I'm in here. Jonah pushes him away and closes the door. I sit at the long table, my hands folded in front of me. Mose stands to my left, his corduroy pants baggy in the hips. I can nearly see his pelvic bone protrude. Jonah blocks the door. You don't have to, Maggie, he says, soft but stern: You don't have to talk to them a bit.

I nod: Hadn't planned to.

Okay, he says: Now, tell me what you'd like for me to say. I'll take care of it.

Mose walks to the glass wall, hands shoved hard in his pockets. He peers out, half-blind Mose. I watch him awhile. He turns to me slowly. I'll go, he says.

Jonah looks up at him: Say what?

Well, Mose begins slowly: You're the sheriff. You gotta represent the town. I can speak on behalf of Maggie.

Jonah frowns: I don't see where Maggie and Ladyslipper have competing interests. You forget, maybe nobody else lost like this, but Felbo lost all his milk cows, Miss Ethel and Miss Mae's whole front porch and parlor broke off and washed away. The Yuleses lost everything in that little house, all their belongings just washed out the front door. Everybody lost something even if it was just a house, not a friend or a husband or children.

So you talk on the town. I'll talk on Maggie.

Now, s-s-see here, Jonah raises his voice and taps on the table.

No, I say: Mose is right. He can talk for me. That'll be fine.

Jonah glares at me, that glare at my insubordination just like Dizzy. But I keep focused on Mose, who nods slowly and drinks me in. Mose Job.

Well, so what do you want him to say?

He knows.

Reads minds, does he?

I take Jonah's hand. He remains testy, and when I look at him he seems deeply hurt. It's no offense, I say softly, then I kiss his hand, which is fat with stubby fingers and dark, hairy knuckles. He sighs: All right, Maggie. Immediately I feel guilty. This is how I coaxed Dizzy—was it this generic, that it could've been any man? I look at Mose. He stares with longing outside the room.

I can hear them fine once they go out. Mose recounts the story of the flood, nearly word for word as I hear it in my mind. Mose Job looks at ease at the podium. He talks slow and even and forceful. His shoulders set back and his chin juts forward. It looks like a dance, the reporters alternately scribbling on their pads and popping up their arms for questions, Mose pointing to recognize one or the other, this back and forth that he does with ease and skill and grace. And I swear, each wave of his arm, each gesture to recognize puts a glow on his face. He grows larger in their spotlight. And I see us all as teenagers, lining those high-school hallways watching him return to us: C'mon back, Mose Job.

When he's finished, he comes back to me and takes my hand. He holds it light but sure, as fragile as I hold him.

Jonah watches us, unable to decode our language. I didn't know you two were so close, he says.

I think now of Dizzy—his touch, the sex of his sigh, the anticipation and pleasure of his skin on mine, the steady undertow that swept me to him. I close my eyes and concentrate on Mose's scaly, dry hand. There is something flat and desperate between us.

Jonah looks at me, guarding Dizzy. I go to him. Please don't judge me, I say.

He exhales and his bulky arm wraps around me, pulls me tight to him. He says: Maggie, d'you know what I miss? Watching you put our girls to bed. Hearing you sing to them. He whispers: It's the only thing that reminds me of my mother. It's like, you carry that for me.

I sink into his arms, into what is familiar. Here, in Jonah's arms, he still cradles my babies, he hugs Dizzy, and lifts and twirls me on my wedding day—the scenes of my life spill from his opened arms, his familiar scent of backyard barbecues and spring tulips planted under my windows; this tender place, this home—even now if I close my eyes, he is my high four-poster bed, the basket of sneakers by the back door, all jumbled sizes and colors nestled there—this place . . . this, this is all that is left of me . . . but I fear it. It is not real. I pull away. I reach for Mose's hand quietly, one hand behind my back toward him. I latch on.

THE HERALD TIMES

AS RIVER RECEDES, NORMALCY REMAINS ELUSIVE

Ladyslipper—Sheriff Jonah Kind is ubiquitous. As flood waters recede, he's become a busy man. During the day, he can be found shoveling the brown sludge out of the homes of the town's elderly. Or talking to Felbo Toussand about his plans to replace his drowned livestock. Each day he speaks to schoolchildren about the dangers of playing in flood waters. But by night he ignores his own admonitions. He wades through the flood waters or travels the more treacherous river by boat, with a rope and netting by his side and a spotlight in hand. He drags the river, searching for the body of Dizzy Barnes, the best friend to whom he occasionally refers as his brother. Sheriff Kind figures that while the bodies of Barnes's daughters may have been swept far from town, Barnes may still be found near here.

"He's a big guy like me. Couldn't swim so hot. I figure, maybe he just sank or got stuck on a tree trunk. Maybe it's illogic," he shrugs. "I don't know what else to do."

At home tonight, after we come from our places—his blacktop, my river—I dress for bed. Mose squirrels up in a corner of the living room. He pores over his scrapbook:

Boy Run Over by School Bus, Survives.

Crushed Boy In Critical Condition.

Boy, Flattened by Bus, Returns to School.

He reads each article slowly, runs his hands over the photos of him in traction, of him returning to school with his cane, of Mose and his daddy.

In this deep cottony crater that serves as our bed, Mose crawls to me and embraces my belly. I reach for him, tracing his scars with trembling fingers. I ply my fingers through his moist hair, push aside his penis, and reach for the loose, soft sac. I touch him and it is almost myself I touch. I grow expectant and tender. He lies still. Awkwardly, I move myself down in the bed inching to him on elbows until my face meets his groin. It is warm and musty there as a basement, a locked attic. I kiss him tenderly. I kiss what is empty, loving this forsaken space. His skin is salty and sweet. I hold and caress and kiss him. Mose strokes my hair and sobs: It's been so long.

I know, I say.

I wake up late, after noon. I hear voices coming from the living room. When I emerge, the window is open wide and Mose stands talking with reporters and the neighbors. The kitchen has become practically a restaurant. He takes orders, makes plates heaping with food, tells jokes, asks: Another cup of coffee?

Jonah Kind is sitting at the kitchen table sipping coffee. He flips through Mose's pile of junk mail, and he looks like he's been here every day of his life. He looks up at me and smiles: Mose here makes a mean cup of coffee. Can I pour you some?

The room's normal gray is offset by long streams of sunlight that cut a translucent yellow band around the room. It seems to swirl. The people at the window call to me, pointing cameras in. Their hands reach in and wave, grab at me—*take my hand!*—I rush to the window, snatch it down, nearly crushing hands, leaving long, cleaned-off streaks on the glass. My fingers cake with the sludge of moistened dust. I see their bobbing heads and troubled faces through the cleaned streaks.

What's wrong with you people? I yell. Mose and Jonah are stock-still: What is this? What is this?

Just being hospitable, Maggie, Mose says. He holds two plates piled so high with food that the plate bottoms sag and soak up grease. His biceps bulge and swell as he holds the plates, his chest pumps up.

You're feeding off it! I yell: Look at you! Look at you!

Now, Maggie, Jonah says: Calm down.

Send them away! I don't want them here. The two of you—selling refreshments at my sideshow.

Maggie, Jonah says, and hangs his head.

Mose puts down the plates of food. He glances out the window a long while. He says: Did you ever come see 'bout me? When you was happy? All those years, Maggie, did you come?

Mose looks at me plainly, sharp as a knife. He continues: Even when Papa passed?

I sent a card, I mumble.

He nods: I was obliged. But did you come see 'bout me, Maggie?

Jonah shifts, uncomfortable in his seat. Mose calls to him: Jonah, you ever set to my table before?

Jonah and I look at each other. I know what he thinks about. All those nights sitting on my sofa, drinking beer, me, Dizzy, and Jonah. Them teasing me. About dating corny Mose Job. His flannel shirts. His highwaters. His short, nappy hair always a little too matted to his head and not unknown to hold lint. While I protested some, it was never wholehearted. I never said that Mose used to hold me on a soft blanket in these fields and listen to my problems, tell me my feet weren't too big when I wore a size-eleven shoe at five foot, five inches tall. That we used to meet and maul each other, hungry, like teenagers do, just shy of real sex but still, he was my lover. I didn't say any of that. I just laughed along.

I was something to you once, Mose says so softly and clearly: I thought you'd know. You, of everybody. You'd know how it'd be for me here. Did you ever think of me, Maggie?

Wanna run. But held tight here somehow. Though I struggle to get free.

Now, you see how it is. All that water rushing at you. Maybe it was just me, all dammed up here. Maybe it could've been me let loose. That's what I dreamt last night. That I stole 'em from you. That I swept you back to me.

I run now from the house. Down the field. I know I am followed. I hear the click of cameras; bulbs flash and pop and crackle behind me—I'm a wild giraffe at safari—into the creek, stumbling up on the shore, down the marsh through Felbo's field, double back through the barn, scattering the chickens and the few pigs that survive. Bar the door, panting, holding my belly. They bang outside: Maggie, Maggie, Maggie. I squat and cover my face in my hands.

That's how they find me, how they take my photo over and over again. I never look up, even when they prod me and nudge me, when they put their arms around me to coax me. There is nothing to coax. Nothing to say. Their words are all a drone, a toneless, flat line.

Mose and Jonah come for me. Felbo helps run off the reporters. In the squad car nobody talks. I look up at Mose for the first time and look away quick. When we're far away from everybody I tell Jonah to stop the car. He turns around to me.

I wanna walk from here, I say. Mose, I whisper: I wanna go to our place.

Jonah frowns. Mose says: We'll be all right.

We get out of the car and walk slowly. It's dusk now—I still can't tell how time passes. I reach for Mose's scaly hand. He gives it freely.

Back to the place, my place, past the gooey mud that peels off sections of the Baptist church, peels it perfectly pew by pew like slices of cake. Back to my tree in this place near my salvation. I didn't even think of God when It happened. He never crossed my mind in those terrible moments. I look at Mose behind me on the blacktop. Sitting upright and watching me. I wait for him to take his place. He does not. I see that he won't. So I grab my tree alone. I dangle in water which is nearly still now. Mose stands up, hands in his pockets. He paces slowly, sometimes dragging a foot through small pools of water. When he looks at me, patient and kind, he smiles, then goes back to pacing. But he is different now standing on his blacktop. He's distant. He looks at it not as he did—not as if it were his own skin or nail, not the way he once looked at it, like each rocky crater of the ground was his own, like every scent it expelled bore his own breath. No. It is separate now and he looks away from it and stubs his toe against it and feels nothing. So, I am alone here on my tree, in this river. He sweeps by, sweeps his foot on the blacktop over and over, scraping off whatever residue it holds of him. I dangle here in this river. Unbearably alone. Tired. Tired. And then I let go.

A clean fall down. Does my head go underwater? I cannot tell. I am too filled with relief—this is how it feels. Now I know, taken suddenly, surely. I give over. But the water barely moves now. There is time to see it happen. There is time to touch the shore, to memorize its crags and gaping dark holes, the long tentacles of tree roots exposed. There is time for Mose to catch me. He dives in, and I am furious. He pulls me to him and I think to fight and flail, to push his puny body away. A small core of me rebels. But my body goes limp against him. In front of us, a metal chain looped around a tree hangs long into the water. He drags me to it and grabs on, lacing his knobby fingers through the metal loops, hooking on with tenacity, scraping his knuckles to force his fingers, a tight fit. All the while I am lifeless and heavy, and he whispers to me: Don't go.

We drift here and the chain pulls taut. I watch his finger bend and then break in the loop, popping backward. Still, he clutches me, his eyes shut tight; he whispers: Don't leave me. When the headlights shine on us, I see the blood that gushes from Mose's fingers, three rivers of dark blood from the rusty chain. Jonah Kind brings a rope to the edge of the river: Jesus Christ! he yells. First, I am saved. And then Mose. I sink against the police car, my belly tight and hard, contracting. Mose comes to me and I grab his broken hand. Press hard on the flesh to seal it, to stop the flow of his blood. I press it to my lips and push down hard on his cold flesh.

What the hell you two doing down here? Jonah says, more frightened than mad: I decided to follow you this time—good thing, too! What d'ya wanna do, die out here?

I stare at Mose's jagged skin. He sighs: No.

I wail and this current flows from me, sudden and warm. The water I held, stingy, lets loose from my womb. My baby, I moan: It's coming now.

They stand and look at each other a moment, as if they had not known I was pregnant. As if the risk of being with a pregnant woman wasn't birth. Finally, Jonah coughs: Shit! And they lift me to my feet, help me into the backseat of the car. I cannot sit upright. My pains come fast and hard, my body opens itself. I feel my pelvic bones soften and slide. I feel the head bearing down.

It's coming fast, I say.

Jonah looks at Mose and frowns: What the hell's that mean?

Means drive, Mose says.

I am! Jonah snaps.

Drive faster.

Jonah rubs his forehead and speeds, the tail end of the car sliding out on the mud-slick road. I reach up and slap him on the shoulder: Heah! Watch it, Jonah! I say.

Grass and rotting corn stalks rise like the sea, lapping at the car windows. A big yellow moon hangs low, skimming the grassy waves. We skid. Damn, damn, Jonah says, and cuts his wheel hard. Mose reaches back and puts a hand on my knee, which points in the air while I lie on my back. We skid in a figure eight, zigzagging on the road, Jonah swearing and whipping the wheel back and forth. We veer off the road to the left and land square in the mud. Jonah spins his wheels awhile, then slaps the dashboard: Shit! Shit! Shit!

We are rutted deep. Back where I began.

My baby's head pushes its way out of me. Mose, Mose, I moan. He climbs into the backseat with me.

How the hell can it come so fast? Jonah asks: Doesn't this usually take days?

None of my babies took days, and this is my third.

It's a long time coming anyway, Mose says.

Other than my panting, there is no sound. No wind, and if the river rushes, I cannot hear it. Jonah looks terrified, sweating and swallowing hard.

Pull the front seats all the way up, Mose says to him. He slips off my underpants, yanks them down quickly over my hips. One of my legs he lifts and drapes over the back of the front seat. Jonah gets out and paces. I can run for h-h-help, he says.

Mose shakes his head: Jonah, you are the help.

It's coming fast, I say, and hang my head back: I don't know if I can do this again.

Mose lifts my head: There's never "again." Nothing's ever just the same. You know. Jonah, c'mon now. Hold her head up.

Jonah shakes his head fast and for a moment looks about to weep. I've never done this, he says: I-I-I don't even have a girlfriend.

Cradle her head, Mose says.

Help me push up, I command.

Jonah bends in the mud, his cold hands on my shoulders, his cheek against the back of my head so I feel him tremble.

This baby tears its way from me. When I bear down, half sitting up and supported by Jonah, I see the naked moon, round and bald as a newborn's head. Does this child know how it enters? They sweep by me grabbing, grabbing. I hold on.

I bear down: Mose, I call. And he gives me his hand, his fingers bent and crooked and dried with blood. Beautiful. I moan and out it comes in a sudden bloody rush—it goes so fast, out like a surfer atop a fast wave. It shoots straight for Mose, his face bright in moonlight. He drops my hand and grabs at the baby, which bounces high and slow. Oh, God, Jonah moans in my ear: Oh, Dizzy! Oh, Mother!

Mose fumbles the baby, a cagey, slippery fish wriggling off his line. The three of us are held here—Jonah, Mose, and me, the only three in the world—we pause in the stillness of high grass and mud. This time I am prepared for what I will lose. I am steeled. If this is the last of mine, I will just close this place in me, seal myself as a house, peer out until my view grows too dusty and obscured.

Mose fumbles. My baby fights his grasp. Mose's hands open wide and sure. He leans in and catches the baby in his arms, against his chest. My baby girl rears back, yelping and squirming. He sighs.

The stench that invades Ladyslipper subsides, overwhelmed by fresh blood and tissue. My baby screams her claim to existence. Mose rests her on my belly and cradles her slimy hips. Jonah strokes her perfect round head. In these swollen fields, in this moonlight grace, we are spared.

Dianne King Akers

Small Speaking Parts

My father has one clear word left. It is *no.* We sit side by side on a Friday morning in the new Austin airport, all concrete and glass and sharp edges, while my mother goes to the bathroom for the third time in fifteen minutes. I nudge his arm after she leaves. "What do you think of this place?" I ask.

My father holds out his left hand, moves it back and forth, makes the noise that has made up his conversation since his stroke almost four years ago, a loud jumble of vowels that mostly start with the letters *d* or *l* and do not mean anything in any language. I understand him to say that he has mixed feelings. The airport has its good points. He breathes hard and jabs at his right hand with his left index finger. These must be the bad points.

"It's too industrial?" I ask, because that's what I think.

"No-o-o," he says in three impatient syllables.

"Too bright, too cold?"

My father considers, nods.

"That's what I think, too," I say. I lean my shoulder against his and watch people walk by until my mother returns and sits on my other side. My father reaches over and wags three stubby brown fingers in her face. "Hush," she says.

"What'd he say?" I ask.

"He's giving me a hard time about going to the bathroom."

I am happy in this airport, sitting between my two cheerful parents. But soon my mother's flight is called. She boards the plane to visit my sister in Houston in a flurry of words and travel anxiety, her small mouth drawn tight. "Don't forget to put on his leg brace tomorrow morning, Katie," she tells me. "Don't forget his blood-pressure medication tonight." My sister Beth and I cajoled her into taking some time away from Dad, but I can tell she is afraid he will not be safe in my care, that I will forget something that she would not, that I will leave him alone and he will fall.

Toward her I have all the complicated love-guilt-*oh Mother* feelings I always had. She, after all, is presumably not going to die soon. But toward my father, it occurs to me as I follow his slow lurching pace out into the weighted July heat of the parking lot, that at the bottom of whatever else I might feel about him is a distilled Daddy love, as young as it is fierce.

We pick up my almost four-year-old son Sam from his friend's house on the way back home. I am skittish. Dad and I have not been alone much since his stroke, and I am not sure how to get past the hearty tone I've adopted with him over the last four years. I am also worried about how he will react to prolonged exposure to Sam. He has always believed in well-mannered children, and Sam is not, always.

Our 1942 wood-frame house has four tiny rooms in the original front—two bedrooms, a small kitchen, and an equally small living room—and a big dining room/living room my husband Matt built on to the back with brick-colored tile and lots of windows. I settle my father and Sam at the long dining-room table in the back room. My father's bald head is shiny brown under the overhead light, his face round.

I sing a song that my father used to sing to me while I prepare to cut Sam's hair with my sewing scissors. I've been wondering what he'd look like with really short hair, and I've persuaded him to let me try it. "I'm Popeye the sailor man. I live in a garbage can. I love to go swimmin' with bowlegged women, I'm Popeye the—"

"Huh?" Across the table Dad looks up over the sports page. I know what he's complaining about. He used to sing it *baldheaded* women on Saturday mornings while he'd make us breakfast. "You have your version, I have mine," I say.

"Don't sing," Sam tells me anyway, his head bent to color in a red mouse. "When you sing you make me mess up my picture."

"Watch your lip, kid," I say, amazed and a tiny bit irritated, as always, at Sam's ability to claim his space in the world. *Watch your lip, kid* is another of my father's phrases, but one I never use. Some I do. *Cool it.* But never his *Put up your dukes, creep,* shadowboxing shuffle in the kitchen on Saturday mornings when he was making us breakfast. Not *You're in a world of hurt, kid,* when he was about to whip us at Yahtzee, or Sorry, or Crazy Eights.

"You're getting hair all over my picture," Sam complains, brushing his coloring book with his hand.

"Almost done," I coax. Half of what I say these days to Sam is so automatic that I hear it as an echo, long after it was said. Clumps of his fine pale hair float down over the red lines left behind by his marker. I pick up another tuft of hair and clip it close to his head. My father dismisses us with a laugh and a shake of his head. He loves to laugh at human folly these days, especially mine. He watches me for signs of predictability—the hand snitching the last bite of meat off the serving plate, the dropped spoon wiped carelessly on the hem of my dress—and pounces with an *Ahhhh, ahhh, ahhhh* from across the room when he catches me. I laugh with him, but sometimes I wish that he did not watch so closely.

"Your father is going to kill me for giving you a crew cut," I tell Sam.

Sam pokes his head up. "With a gun?"

"God, no," I say. "That's just a bad expression. I only mean he'll be mad." He may or may not be mad. Matt has known me long enough to know that when I start cutting hair—usually my own, although I'm trying to grow it out—it signals some crisis that is likely to involve him.

My father points at the top of Sam's head. "Da, da, du da," he says.

I stand back and look. Sam is beginning to look like he has mange. "I know," I say. "I'll even it up later."

"We're not supposed to hurt people," Sam says.

My father looks up.

"No," I say.

"In fact," Sam says, "you're not supposed to hit people. Or even to bite people. Or even to push people down."

"Right," I say, wondering if it's Matt or me who says *in fact* so emphatically.

"You can push people *up,*" he says.

"Huh?" my father says.

"On a swing," Sam explains. "You can push people up on a swing."

"True enough," I say, and make a mental note to tell Matt about this conversation, another sign of Sam's cleverness. I put the scissors down, take off Sam's shirt, and brush the hair from his shoulders. His skin is already welting where he has scratched at the hairs. "There," I turn my son toward my father. "What do you think?"

My father draws him closer, and points where the hair is too short, too long, too patchy, too ragged. "Duh, duh duh *duh,*" he says. He shakes his head, returns to his paper.

"All right, all right, all right," I say. "I'll fix it later." I stand Sam in front of me. "You are beautiful," I tell him. It is true. With his hair gone, the blue-gray of his eyes is more vivid, his eyebrows make impressive arches across his forehead, and his skin has the juiciness of a young pear. He looks like a child of the fifties, the son of more conservative parents, parents whose first goal in child rearing is obedience. He looks, I realize, like my father's son would have, if he'd had a son.

It was my mother who brought my father through the rehabilitation after his stroke—the depression, the physical therapy for his paralyzed right side, the doctors' appointments that crisscrossed their calendars—to this day at my house where I almost believe that it is the father I always knew who is reading the sports page, except one who is more genial and wordless, a jolly Santa Claus without a voice. It's as if all the hard biting edges of his disappointments and furies got zapped along with the left side of his brain.

Sam had been my gift to my father, my mute offering, delivered exactly one month after the stroke that may or may not have been spurred by bad genes, but almost certainly was affected by a lifetime of grilled steaks, cigarettes and massive quantities of hard liquor, no matter what he used to claim when he could still make claims.

Look, Daddy. Look, what I made for you.

I am embarrassed to ask him what I want to know now. It is too clichéd, too trite sounding, not enough of what I mean. Did you love me. Do you still. It sits in the back of my throat when I am with him, waiting its chance, crowding all the other, easier words out of my mouth.

While Sam takes his nap, I coax my father into playing Scrabble. My mother says it is good therapy. His ability to write got lost along with his ability to speak, but for some reason, he can sometimes put words together when they play Scrabble.

I do well, better than I do when I play with Matt, and my competitive streak kicks in. I love to win. Whenever Matt and I play games after Sam goes to bed, I end up getting mad. He beats me at Scrabble, at backgammon, at anything that requires concentration. My father spells the word *Ted,* making use of one of my *d*'s. I am quiet. I will not invoke the no proper names rule. I use my *q*'s, my *w*'s, my *y*'s, all the letters that get extra points. My father makes three-letter words; *got, cat, man.* My score is double his. When it triples, I start feeling twitchy, like I'm doing something wrong.

At his next turn, he falters. He turns around his letters and shrugs. All his letters are consonants. "You could put an *s* at the end of this word," I tell him. He does. On his next turn, he turns his letters over to me again. I find him another word.

"Dugh, dugh, dugh," he says. He holds up three fingers.

"I don't understand what you mean," I say.

He holds up the same three fingers. "Dugh, dugh dugh," he says more impatiently.

"You're thinking of a word with three letters?"

"No-o-o," he says.

"You want me to call Mom?" I know this charades routine from watching my parents. It ends most often with two furious people and no answer.

"No-o-o," he says again.

"Where's your communication book?" I ask him. Since his stroke, Mom has bought a computer and two different electronic communication devices. All proved too complicated for him to use. Now he has a simple book divided into sections like *Food* and *Medical Care.* He points to the words he means. At least he's supposed to. He won't use it.

Dad gives me the look that I've seen him give Mom: resignation mixed with reproach. He waves me away and starts plunking down letters on the board. He puts a string of consonants together, looks at it hard, and then shrugs at me.

I watch the board. I cannot watch him. My face tingles with the effort not to cry. "Do you want to keep playing?" I ask him. He shrugs. I hold my face stiff while I make my next word. "Do you want to play cards?" I ask, but he shakes his head. I make the rest of my father's words, and by the time I have gathered up the game and put it back into the hall closet he is back in the living room reading one of my mother's romance novels. The romance novels are a new tic. My sister and I buy him the kind of western novels that he used to favor before the stroke. I bring him mysteries, horror novels, anything without a lurid bodice on the cover, but half the time he comes to visit he sits down and brings a different romance out of his back pocket.

My mother calls to say she has gotten in safely. "How's your father?" she asks, sniffing. She is allergic to Beth's cats.

When I hesitate she panics. "Did he fall? Is he okay—"

"He's fine," I assure her, thinking that I have never given my mother enough credit for what she's been through. I am always defending Dad, telling her not to jump to conclusions about what he's trying to say, getting frustrated over what she imagines. Maybe she needs her anger, maybe she has a lot left over after forty years of marriage to a husband who got drunk every night. "He's fine. Does he read *all* the time at home?"

"He reads a lot," she says.

"He's not the same, is he?" I ask. It is a stupid question, especially four years after the fact. I think I told myself that he was just the same, he was just sober now and couldn't talk. He was in there, intact, whole, complete, complex, good, bad, profane, funny, cruel; only silent.

My mother sighs. "I keep telling you girls that," she says. "He doesn't understand as much as you think he does."

"I know," I say, suddenly anxious to have her off the phone. "Have a good night," I tell her. "We'll see you tomorrow."

Despite the fact that Matt has vetoed any harsh movies or cartoons, Sam is obsessed with violence. In his Walt Disney world, mothers and fathers die at the hands of wicked brothers and uncaring hunters. At the preschool he attends three days a week while I work at the Austin Community College library, children pretend to chop each other's heads off in the playground. When he was six months younger and got mad at us, he would say he was going to tear down the house, pull up trees by the roots.

"Hurry," I say after his nap, steering him toward the car to go grocery shopping. Sam does not want to go. Neither did my father. He waved us away when I asked him to come, and went back to reading.

Sam, balking, hangs his head down and refuses to get into the backseat. He is a prickly-pear child, easily angered, easily wounded, and stubborn. I love him and he drives me batty in equal measures. "He's a *boy,*" my sister reassures me. "They're harder than girls at this age." She has one of each, so I believe her.

"You're hurting my feelings," Sam says to me now. "I want to take Daddy's car."

"Daddy's car is at work with him."

He holds his ground. "You're hurting my feelings."

Today, although I am the one who has taught him to pay excessive attention to his feelings, I do not feel gentle. I know my mother would not approve of my leaving my father alone. "Sam, I am in a hurry. We need to get back to Grandpa. You and your feelings can get in the car seat."

Sam lifts his head and roars. "My feelings are going to knock your head off."

He gets into his car seat. I am silent a moment before I lean over the wheel and laugh. I do not know why it's so funny. Maybe because it's outrageous. Sam is my litmus test for human impulses in their raw form. "It's not funny," he says from the back.

"It's kind of funny," I say.

"Why did Rabbit die?" Sam asks from the backseat, as if he hadn't just figuratively decapitated me. Rabbit was our cranky old cat, who died last week at the age of thirteen. We buried him in a plastic bag in the backyard, and piled rocks on top of his grave. When it came time to say something we liked about him, Sam couldn't think of anything, although he was the only one who had hugged him every day.

"I don't know," I say. "He was old. He got some kind of funny illness."

"I am not going to die," Sam says in the backseat.

"Hmm?" I say, without really hearing. I am trying to figure out what to make for dinner.

"Am I?" Sam asks, all the things he doesn't understand in his voice. *"Am I?"* Then I hear what he has said. I do not know what to say in return. When I told him a month ago that his teeth were going to fall out when he turned six, he got hysterical. "I need to eat," he kept crying, unconsoled by my belated assurance that they would not all fall out at the same time.

But this is life and death, not teeth. "Every creature on earth dies," I say, carefully. "Usually it happens when they are old and they are ready for it."

Sam begins to cry. He cries in the car all the way to the store, so I pick him up and hold him awhile in the parking lot, at a loss and filled with tenderness toward my grieving son. He sniffles as I carry him in. He sits in the grocery cart and leans into my chest when I pick out the apples, his whole face leaking. "It won't happen for a long, long time," I say, stopping the cart and making an uneasy promise. I kiss his forehead and wipe his eyes on my sleeve. "Longer than you can even think of. You will be old. It will be okay."

He snuffles into my neck in the cereal aisle. "You are not going to die now," I say. "Daddy and I are going to take care of you."

In the frozen section, he makes his pronouncement, each word a separate sentence. "I. Do. Not. Want. To. Die. When. I. Get. Old," he says.

"Okay," I say.

"Does that mean I won't?"

"Maybe," I say. I am lost. Perhaps I have made a mistake by answering his question; perhaps he isn't supposed to know about death yet. "Maybe it does."

Sam sniffs.

He helps me put the groceries on the conveyor belt at the checkout line. I cup my hand over his head and smooth his hair back, rest my lips on his forehead again. His skin is salty.

Most of my friends are childless, by choice or otherwise, and nearing forty. "What is it like?" they ask, anxious to know what they might be missing. I try to reassure them that having children doesn't make life miraculously worthwhile. I tell them stories about Sam's aggression, and mine, about the weekend mornings I wake up grumpy before the day even begins with the weight of the day's chores. I tell them how bewildered and lost I feel sometimes, and how guilty. My father fled from his family into alcohol and I retreat from mine into activity, the anticipation of the next thing that needs to be done. Last week when I put Sam to bed I told him a story about a boy named Sam—but not him—and his mother, and how the mother all day would reply to the boy's pleading to play with him, "Just a minute, Sam. First I have to clean the house and wash the windows and wash the car and make dinner and paint all the walls." It was enough of the truth that we both laughed uproariously. I say that if I didn't have Sam, I would find satisfaction by being a doting aunt.

It's not true. Whether it is right or not that Sam fills in the edges of my life, he does.

After I have put all the groceries into the trunk and strapped Sam into his car seat and am backing out, I meet his eyes in the rearview mirror.

"Am I?" Sam asks.

"What?" although I already know.

"Am I going to die?"

"Oh, Sam." I park the car under a tree and roll down the window. No matter what I believe, I cannot leave my son in this place. "Some people," I say, "believe that when a person dies, a part of them stays alive, a part that's inside. So that the body dies, but the part of the person that's most important, the inside part, comes out and goes on living. It's called a spirit."

"Oh," he says. "Do you believe that?"

His eyes are earnest when I turn around to face him. "Yes," I say against my doubts.

"Oh," he says again. His hand reaches out and touches my arm, and strokes it, once. "I'm glad we can still eat in heaven," he says.

"What?" I ask, surprised. "How did you know anything about heaven?"

"You just said."

"Said what?"

"You said parts of us would still be alive. So we can still eat."

"Oh, Sam," I say. "I didn't mean—" I stop. What does it matter about the details?

"I don't want you to die before me," he says.

"I know," I say. I turn around and squeeze his hand a minute before I start the car and head home.

When he was still an infant, we played a game when I changed his diapers. I gave him his foot-shaped teething toy, and when he was not crying too hard he would put it into my mouth. I clamped my teeth on it, hard, shook my head and growled like a dog. It shocked me, the first time, how good it felt to bite. It was a primitive thing. I was a raging carnivore. My teeth ached with pleasure. I bit and growled and roared. Sam's face underneath mine watched, complacent, and then he put out his hand, unafraid, and took the foot back. He did not know what my mouth was capable of.

My father, a career military enlisted man, was taught these things, and these things he passed on to me: Never quit, even when it would be in your best interest. Strike back when wounded. Obey without question. Work hard. Never cheat or steal. Never take handouts, especially from the government. Laugh loudly, eat well, play hard. If you can still do your job the next morning, anything you drink after 5 P.M. doesn't count. If something's worth doing, it's worth doing well. Do your duty at the expense of personal happiness. (This one he did not say so much as he lived it.)

When I was growing up, his refrain to me was *The trouble with you is, the trouble with you is,* and there was sometimes a different ending, but most often it was *You don't think.* All my life those words have resounded. *The trouble with you is.* It came to me only recently that much of what he taught me was not intended to hurt, but to protect; not out of spite, but out of fear; and that it is not his voice that I still hear in my head as an adult, but a meaner-spirited version of it I made up on my very own.

I'm afraid the voice—my voice—that Sam will hear when he is an adult will trouble him as much as my father's does me. *Be nice,* I tell him in a hundred ways every day, even though I know what a dubious lesson it is. *Worry about what other people think more than what you think. Don't take up too much room in the universe.* It's a lesson he doesn't seem to be disposed to learning, which is probably a good thing. When we take long walks at night with Sam asleep in the stroller, Matt drives me crazy by walking with the stroller flat down the middle of the street, as if he is entitled to the whole road, while I keep trying to nudge them to the side, so they won't get run over.

• • •

My father and I were drunks. No nice way to put it. I was a drunk from the time I went off to college until I turned thirty, and he was a drunk much longer: at least from the time he eloped to Las Vegas with my nineteen-year-old mother until his stroke, some forty years later. He never drank before 5 P.M., and during the day he was playful and funny, the cheerful life of our family party. At night, he rapidly turned into a sloppy and often cruel drunk. For years on weekends home I sat with him until late at night, smoking and sloppy drunk myself, and listened to his rambling complaints, until my mother came out and shushed us both to bed.

When I turned thirty, I stopped drinking and smoking, and I stopped sitting with my father at the kitchen table. I could not watch him drink anymore without censure. Wasn't it his life I was running away from?

My father cried at the end of John Wayne movies, always when he heard "The Star Spangled Banner," and once when he watched a young man with a damaged side lurch across the Kmart parking lot in Houston, in much the same way half of his own body pulls the other half along now.

We learned things from my father I wish we hadn't, my sister and I. We hang a curtain between ourselves and those we love, we carry a grief and anger that we cannot get to the bottom of. We put up our dukes. I battle myself, she battles the world, we live in our father's *world of hurt, kid.*

When we come back, Sam runs out of the car as fast as he can. "I have to poop," he says. I unload groceries. My father has fallen asleep with his head back on the couch.

"Mooommmmyyyy," Sam screams in the voice that sends tingles up my spine. It is the voice of a developing drill sergeant. I go to the bathroom door.

"I don't like it when you yell like that for me," I tell him sharply. "Grandpa is sleeping."

"Well, you weren't coming."

"I was coming. Please do not yell."

"Well, I had to because you weren't coming."

I sigh. "I swear to God," I tell him, "you would argue with a doorknob."

"No, I wouldn't," he says. "I needed you to come."

I lean against the doorway. "I'm here. What do you want?"

"I want you to read to me."

"Okay," I say. "Let me put the food in the fridge, and then I'll be back."

"Do you know what?" Sam asks when I come back and sit across from him on the edge of the bathtub.

There is a shuffle down the hall, and then my father appears. Grunting, he sits down on the white bench we keep just inside the bathroom door, sets his cane down on the floor.

"Do you know what, Grandpa?" Sam repeats. "Jonathan eats my lunch."

"He does?" I say, surprised. Jonathan is Sam's classmate at his day care.

He nods his head vigorously. "Yes, he does."

"Are you done?" I ask.

Before he can answer a spray of liquid comes toward me and splashes my dress from the chest down. I put my hands up without thinking. After it stops I realize that Sam has peed on me. I bark out a shocked laugh at the same time I hear a spluttering from my father. He clutches his stomach and points, his face turning pink. At first I am afraid he is having another stroke, and then I realize he is laughing, too.

Sam starts to cry and then to yell. "You forgot to tuck my penis in," he says. When he hears us laughing he yells harder. "You forgot!" he accuses.

"Damn it, Sam." I stop laughing and yell back. "You can pee on me, but you can't blame me for it."

Sam cries, his face all squinched up and pink. "You forgot."

"Sam!" I say, as sharply as my mother used to speak on her worst you-children-have-pushed-me-over-the-edge days. "It's *your* penis!"

The huge rush of my anger surprises me and Sam, who cries harder and then kicks out at me with his foot.

I could count on one hand the number of spankings I've given Sam, but I grab him now by his arm and jerk him off the toilet, conscious of my father watching and judging. Sam yelps.

"Be quiet!" I yell. He screams louder.

I hold him by the shoulders and put my face an inch from his. "You have been complaining all day long," I tell him, my voice white-hot shaky and beyond my control. "I am tired of it. If you do not shut up right now, I am going to bust your bottom." I squeeze his shoulders. The terrible truth is I don't want him to stop screaming. I want a good excuse to spank him with the flat of my hand as hard as I can. "Do you understand me?"

He closes his eyes and whimpers, but I am a long way from being nice, I am miles from pity; I am in the land of a mean and seductive power. *"I said, Do you understand me?"*

He nods his head. I clean him up and push him toward the doorway. "Go get dressed and don't come out until I say you can."

Still crying, he runs into his room and slams the door.

"Huh," my father says, shaking his head and making a face of mild censure, although I am not sure if it is for me, for not being able to control my son or for being too hard, or for Sam, being disobedient.

"Shut up," I say, and even though I mean it to come out teasing, it does not. Standing over him, I put my fists up and do a boxer's dance, my feet scuffling. "Put up your dukes, kid," I tell my father, as he used to tell us. He waves me away with his good hand.

Something in the gesture, the dismissiveness, makes the flash of heat run up from my belly to my head. "Stand up," I challenge. I want to fight my father in the bathroom. I will fight him one-handed, to even the score. I want to punch him in the stomach until he cries uncle.

"Come on," I say, "Come on." I box-dance around him, while he looks up at me.

"Huh?" he says. His puzzled look makes me madder. My throat

is swollen with all the fury that pushes up from my stomach. My head feels like it will explode. There is a black core of rage in my gut that scares me, even as I dance around him, prod his leg with my toe. "Come on," I say in a rough voice I don't recognize. He shakes his head at me and shrugs his shoulders. "Come on," I say, madder still. My toe jabs at his bad leg.

I think of his mean drunk. How he would squeeze our hands, twist our wrists, tell us he could break our arms if he wanted to, squeeze our limbs until *we* cried uncle. I think of the arguments with my mother, the screaming fights that I could never stop, no matter how tightly I held the pillow over my ears. The requirement for absolute obedience. The ever-present, all-encompassing disapproval. The careening drunk rides in the car, the threat around every corner, the mean, thuglike bully of him when he drank.

I want to put my head down and ram it so hard into his belly that he flies through the wall, out of my house, out of my life. I want to clamp my teeth onto his shoulder and bite as hard as I can. I want to tell him what a goddamned rotten person he was when he drank. I want to tell him he wouldn't have to try so hard staying alive now if he had taken any kind of care of himself at all. I want to crush him with my fury. I am so full of a whirl of anger and confusion and grief that I am afraid I might explode—the real kind of explosion, my body bursting apart from the force of all it contains.

"Argghhhhhh," I scream as loudly as I've ever screamed, loud as a sonic boom, loud enough to burst out the walls of this old house, loud enough for my father's eyes to widen, finally, at my impact.

"Hey," he yells back, his face red. It is the first clear word other than "no" that I have heard him say since his stroke. My rage freezes. I look up and see myself in the mirror, the upside down U of my mouth, a shark's mouth, the pink and white of my furious face. I slump inside, slip down and sit next to him.

"Dugh, dugh, dugh," he says vehemently, holding up three fingers. I stare ahead, rigid and stunned, stuck between my still strong desire to bite his shoulder and to cry on it. In a moment, I hear him sigh beside me, and then he picks up my hand and squeezes it in a gesture clearly meant to console. He squeezes my hand again, leans in toward me. He is so close I can smell his Canoe aftershave, see the pores in his nose. He strings some sounds together, gestures emphatically with his hand, knits his brow, gestures some more, laughs ruefully and shakes his head. I do not have any idea of what he is trying to say. He looks at me not understanding and laughs again, pats my hand, tries once more, gibberish and gestures coming together in the nonsensical language of my father.

He might be trying to say what I need to hear. *I did the best that I could* or *I always loved you* or *Please forgive me* or *You're forgetting the good parts.* He might be saying some version of *The trouble with you, kid,* or he might be saying nothing I could think of, nothing I will ever know. But as my father talks I watch his face—brown and round and now gentle, covered with a dry web of wrinkles—until some understanding, wordless and forgiving, flies from him to me and back again. He has lines on his forehead and his Santa Claus eyes are warm and sad on me and I know—don't I know?—that he loves me without telling, as best as he's ever been able to, and maybe the question has never been whether he loves me or not but whether it's ever enough. I stare at my hands, clenched on my knee, and feel myself falling down to a place I do not want to go, a place that has no bottom, the wild young grieving place that says *I love you, I hate you, don't leave me, I'll die.*

Against my will, my mouth stretches back and becomes a clown's mouth, and my face squinches up. I burrow into my father's shoulder and weep as the realization creeps over me four years late that I'm never going to hear the things that I always wanted to hear from him.

I miss my father's voice, I miss laughing with him. I miss riding in the car with him to the liquor store and laughing when he proudly showed me some convoluted route that was twice as far but avoided all stop signs. I miss how meticulously he stockpiled ice in three locations every night so there would always be enough for his drinks: the ice-cube bucket on the kitchen counter, the freezer pail of ice, the pile of ice carefully set on aluminum foil in the bottom shelf, and how we were only allowed to take ice from that pile, until it was gone and we could move up to the next ice step. I even miss his drunken visits to my postcollege apartments on business trips. He would take one look in my empty cupboards and refrigerator, shake his head over my one ice-cube tray, and take me on dizzy shopping sprees for terrible foods like frozen pizza, eggrolls, and taquitos, Diet Cokes, ice, and bourbon. I miss my father, and now he's never going to say something that will make everything all right.

His hand on my head is wry and resigned. It says *Ah, shit, kid, what's the use in crying?* but I do anyway. I cry until my throat hurts, my lips are sore from stretching, my chest burns. I burrow into my father's shoulder and I am five again, and I know what Sam knows: we are not safe at all.

When I stop crying I sit still, raw and somehow better, more clear. I have left a puddle of snot and tears on the front of his shirt.

"Hey," he says when I point it out, a shrug in his voice.

There is a shuffle and then Sam's feet appear in my line of vision. I look up from my father's shoulder. Sam has found dry underwear and a clean red T-shirt and put them on, along with one yellow sock. He is sniffling, and I feel a remorse as sharp as my earlier anger.

I hold out my arms and he hesitates a minute before he crawls into them. I kiss the top of his head, breathe in his sweaty smell, close my eyes. "I'm sorry," I tell him. "I was wrong to yell at you like that."

"You were mean," he says.

"I was very mean. I'm sorry."

"You hurt my feelings," he says.

"Yeah," I say. "Although if you pee on me, you shouldn't yell at me, too. That hurts my feelings."

My father points to the wet front of my dress where Sam is sitting, the damp that is spreading to his red T-shirt, his foot with one sock, the foot without. He begins to laugh the wheezing cartoon laugh that he's laughed since his stroke, the one that ends with him coughing helplessly and wiping his eyes. I picture the three of us sitting against the bathroom wall, the pee-soaked, anger-ravaged woman, the stubborn, feisty boy, the half-working man, all the things that lie between us.

I feel a laugh, fed on punchiness, start deep in my belly. It comes out my mouth in damp hiccups. Mimicking my father's exaggerated gestures, I pull on Sam's arm and point to my dress, his mismatched feet, the growing stain on his clean T-shirt. Sam looks at me with a line between his eyes and then decides to laugh, too, maybe just because we are. We wheeze and cough and snort, the three of us, and every time we slow down my father elbows Sam or points at my dress and gets us started again. We laugh until our stomachs hurt and our noses are running and our eyes are tearing. My father and I hold our hands up to each other like crossing guards; *Stop,* our hands say, *stop, you're killing me,* but we cannot stop. We laugh until we have no more laugh in us, and my father and I are coughing, and Sam is hiccupping into my ear, his arm tight around my neck, and I reach across him to pull some toilet paper off the roll and pass it around.

Monica Wood

Frost: A Love Story

The little girl's mother died coming home one night from the public library where she worked shelving both rare and ordinary books, a job ideal for a woman of her limited education and limitless imagination. It was her job, also, to lock up, which she did that night, certain of the evening ahead of her, her children asleep in their beds, her husband slumbering in a chair, waiting. The keys plinked against her palm in the cool, misty air. Her high heels clicked over the granite steps and across the pavement. Then, the gentle churring of her car engine, a crackle from the radio, the end-of-day sounds to which she had become happily accustomed. Halfway home, the driver of a Volkswagen Beetle jumped the guardrail on Route 4 and hurtled clean across the waxed hood of the little girl's mother's brand-new Pontiac station wagon, which slipped off the glassy road in a long, religious silence, until it crumpled into the trees.

In an era when parents piled kids into the back like a load of Christmas presents, the station wagon held little in the way of safety features. But because the little girl's mother made grand, motherly efforts to be practical in ways that belied her fluttery beauty and love of dancing, the new station wagon did harbor early-edition safety restraints, including a lap belt in the driver's seat, which on the night in question had been buckled and tightened, judging from the pelvic bruising. Upon impact, the belt came apart. Or she unbuckled herself out of shock. Or (this is what the little girl thought) an angel wafted down and removed the restraint from a woman who no longer required restraining. This last was the little girl's regret, for she dearly wanted her mother fastened to the earth.

The new car also featured an excellent radio, which, as the story goes, was still playing the country countdown when they found the library assistant's body lying calmly across the vinyl expanse of the front seat. Her face was smooth as beach stone, her gray dress draped modestly below the knees, her thin calves lying side by side. Her feet were perched together, the toenails painted "Kiss Me" red and pointed precisely downward from her broken ankles as if she might be making ready to present a difficult dance step.

Which is how the little girl, at the age of eight, hearing this whispered version of her mother's death from witnesses she did not know, had to imagine her mother ever after: in heaven with her bare calves showing, standing on tippy toe, teaching something complicated to God.

The little girl's father was a weak man who fell vague and drowsy after the death of his wife. Late that winter, he left a cigarette burning in an armchair. And another on the couch. And another in an ashtray on a windowsill under a polyester curtain. Nothing back then was flameproof, including the one-piece pajamas favored by the little girl's baby brothers. She was sleeping at a friend's that night, her first sleepover, her first entry into a world of women since her mother's abrupt departure. When the friend's mother woke her the next morning she chose her words gently, and the little girl pictured a pinkish curl of smoke carrying the babies' souls straight to the cold, unblinking heavens. Her father, his face as pale as her mother's headstone, spoke of life's unfathomable cycle, then wandered away. The little girl understood, at the age of eight, not only that her loved ones had left her for good, but that anyone who came near her would, sooner or later (more likely sooner, given her unlucky history), fade utterly from the earth's shuddery crust.

This is a truth we all face. Though not at eight.

The little girl grew up to reject a long line of feverish suitors, for she inherited her mother's graceful lines and smooth skin and dancer's legs. She rejected one crimson-faced boy after another—even the ones she liked, even the ones who stirred her toes (which she painted, always, in her mother's honor). She kept no pets, although it occurred to her briefly—on the occasion of her graduation from college, when she left the dais after her valedictory to an empty swatch of grass in which a beaming relative, had she had one, might have stood to congratulate her—that she might consider a notoriously long-lived pet, a horse or parrot or monkey. But the moment passed as she removed her mortar board and skipped the luncheon, and went to clean out her dormitory room, a single.

She went to another school for four more years to study fossils. Turning the dry pages of dry, old books in the light of one library or another, she was reminded again and again of her mother. She imagined that last night, the keys to the library doors jangling against her mother's translucent palm, the tippy-tapping walk out to the brand-new station wagon, the opening of the car door, the useless click of the lap belt, the crackle of the radio, the turning engine. Whether her mother kicked off her shoes right then, grabbing the gas pedal with her pretty toes, or whether her shoes came off during the crash, she did not know, but she liked to think of her mother driving barefoot in autumn, her feet the most heedless part of her, the narrow toes keeping time. She imagined, too, a melodious thrumming emanating from her mother's lips as she hummed along with Charley Pride or Tammy Wynette. This was her one comfort, the thought of her mother's humming and tapping, that simple sign of contentment accompanying her sudden, spectacular, unwanted end.

If the little girl, now a woman, could be said to love anything living, it would be the flower garden she maintained in her tiny front yard. Her house was tiny, too, and covered with blue shingles, a few convenient miles from the lab where she worked sorting bones. The garden was too modest to be a showpiece, but people in the neighborhood noticed it anyway, for she had some interesting plants nestled among the usual coreopsis and Shasta daisies, including an out-of-zone hibiscus with big, red, shameless, trumpet-shaped flowers. Long before first frost in autumn, she would bury her garden in leaves, cutting back even the plants that had not finished blooming, her heart heavy with ritual and a vague sadness and a premature aching for spring.

Her last act every summer was to dig up the hibiscus and bring it inside where it resided in a planter in the foyer of her house. Each spring she unearthed it again and placed it in the same spot at the center of her garden. The plant had been brought over by a young man from the lab who thought a houseplant might please his taciturn, cheerless, beautiful colleague. It might even inspire her to accept his offer of dinner someplace, a cup of coffee, a movie maybe; which—needless to say, since the fellow was exactly her age with the male animal's disadvantage in life span—it did not. Still, the plant pleased her, and the effort. The image of her gift-bearing colleague's thin, hairy arms encircling the plant as he loped up her walk became as fixed in her memory as her mother's painted toes poised for dancing. She liked his gold-red hair, his greenish eyes, his long fingers, and his name: Jarrod. She continued to think of him even after he left the lab and went to work at the main campus; her memory had plenty of room, as she had collected so few experiences since those early, indelible ones. She filled it with thoughts of Jarrod, about whom she knew next to nothing. She considered him a friend.

Then came a spring like no other, a sunny, ripe March, crocuses popping through snowmelt like good news, tulips opening before tax day, a bewildering act of God that had the little girl, now a woman, furtively checking the sky for signs of the people she'd lost. She saw clouds shaped like her mother's ankles, her baby brothers' ears, her father's sloped, unhappy shoulders. One day after another she saw sun, benign white gusts of clouds, then more sun, then a gentle, restorative rain, tuffets of snow vanishing like light, temperatures above sixty. In her one act of faith since the death of her mother, she brought out the hibiscus, by now a heavy, bushy ornament, and dragged it down over her front steps in a struggle so mighty it induced little yips of effort from her throat. As was her custom, she spent the entire afternoon unearthing the thing from its winter grave and returning it to its rightful place in the earth. She laughed. She thought of Jarrod and his thin arms.

But this was April. This was New England. In two days or three, after an inevitable frost turned her ornament of faith into a thicket of broken sticks, she flung open her door at six in the morning, barefoot, barely dressed, thudding down the cold steps, her high, still-girlish voice keening far into the neighbors' windows. She bent her body over the dead thing, its stiff branches pressing at tender spots on her skin. She got up and flailed her arms, turned her throat to the sky, opened her mouth wide, made sounds that lifted birds from the trees.

The woman across the street looked out at the flying hair, the waving arms. She murmured, half-standing, to her husband, "Will you look at that," and to her five-year-old son, "Don't look at that." The husband, who like the other neighbors considered the young woman in the shingled house a cold fish in a lab coat, thought of a scene in a cheap movie where the grips or best boys or what have you keep spraying the heroine's face with a mister between takes. He squinted over his paper at the unbuckled despair in the odd little garden and wondered when in his life, if ever, he would see again a spectacle such as this. He looked away, embarrassed, then looked out again.

She began to whirl, her toes tearing into the damp, half-frozen earth. More neighbors, some of whom did not know each other and none of whom knew the young woman, gaped from their doorways. She danced around the broken thing, cursing the sky, as if her useless cawing might wake the dead plant, restore its waxy leaves, sprout the red, swollen buds that opened every August. When finally she turned her face from the clouds, she raced up the steps for her car keys, hauled a coat over her shoulders, left the door of her house hanging open like a surprised face, and, still barefoot, got into her car to find the man who had given her the plant. Jarrod. It had been four years. She resolved to find him inside the campus research center, a maze of white, conical buildings stacked one upon the other. The entrances were legion, requiring card keys and polite conversations with bored watchmen. She had inherited her mother's practical nature, and also, as it turned out, her swift-moving feet; within an hour she found him. Staring into his startled, marveling face, she told him what had become of the plant, describing in a fountain of words its emerging beauty, its seasonal trips to and from her garden, its final surrender to her foolish impulse. Then she stopped. Her feet were still, her head slightly tilted, her hands clasped in a perfect calm.

It was he who ran out of breath: his color rose, his mouth parted in a stupid, grateful wonderment. She stood before him, her own color blazing, her hair sprawled over her shoulders, bright spots of nail polish glinting through the dirt that covered her feet. She lifted one foot, then the other, visited by a curious thrumming that could be no other thing than her mother's spirit coursing through her. Closing her eyes, she welcomed her mother back, apologized for believing the dead stay dead. Her lips began to move. She spoke his name: Jarrod. Again she said it, liking the sound. It was heavy with consonants, rooted, earthbound. She asked him to replace what he had given her, to appear on her walk one more time, to bestow upon her one more chance, his arms circled around something absolutely alive.

H. G. Carrillo

Leche

Between the sweet distraction of a hangover and the ache of waking, the abuelo who Arnulfo Mendoza has never met—only seen in pictures—towers over him, holding the babies. A great, inky arm wrapped around each—Oné y Tomas o Luis y Carlos—Arnulfo can see the light-brown pingas y rosy huevitos curled and exposed like shelled snails between their thighs. Through the dark sky behind them, he sees the palmas reales near Guantánamo Bay. He remembers their fronds swaying black and white at the end of his own father's finger in the stilled breezes of a photo album where his tío Ernesto, with the fierce, wide grin, stood holding the longest bacalao anyone could remember; and Ernesto's wife, tía Juanita, and their four daughters, all named Ernestina—Ernestina-María, Ernestina-Luisa, Ernestina-Teresa, Ernestina-Gabriela—arranged in order of height in front of the little blue house close to the shore where Arnulfo's father and his father's father and his father's father's father stood with the pride of ownership back for as long as could be recalled.

¡Mira! his abuelo calls as he lets go. And, instinctively, Arnulfo reaches for his shirttails to catch the babies as they spill above the leathery fronds of the palmas calling, Papi, Papi, Papi, in the blackness beyond his reach.

He opens his eyes to the smell of bacon coming from the town house next door. Arnulfo believes the man's name is Magnusson, but he isn't sure. They met once a few months back. Now they wave. Arnulfo watches him when he isn't looking. The man is blond, pink-skinned, a lawyer; his wife kisses him full on the mouth, and his daughter clings to his pant leg each morning at the front door before he leaves for work.

The sheets are soaked through, and, as Arnulfo carries them to the hamper, he sees his wife sitting at the kitchen table waiting for the kettle to boil. Alicia has put away the pillow and blankets she now uses to make the couch her bed. She has picked up the clothes he left in the hallway and the living room last night.

At the bottom of a cup, a teaspoon of freeze-dried coffee holds her attention. Alicia bundles her bathrobe around her. Slumped forward in the chair, her heavy black hair falls over her face and covers her eyes. As the kettle begins to hiss, she decides she'll wait until its whistle screeches bloody murder before she moves. She tries not to think of wind or ice or cold or the thin blanket of midwestern snow covering everything outside the window before her.

Her eyes shut to the sound of the shower, and eventually she homes in on the padding of her husband's feet against the tile, his razor tapping against the sink. He slaps aftershave onto his cheeks, and ruffles his back with a towel that she knows he'll leave on the floor between the toilet and the tub. She is unsure if the wailing she hears comes from inside her head or from deep in her heart, and goes out through her fingertips, her toes, her vagina, her mouth. She has no idea the water is boiling until her husband turns the kettle off.

Without opening her eyes she knows he has wrapped her towel around his waist. The tightly curled black mat of hair on his chest glistens from the shower and there is shaving cream behind his ears. She tracks his presence through the light vibrations he makes as he pours water into her cup, empties more than a teaspoon of coffee into a mug for himself, and leaves the open jar on the counter and the lid on the table in front of him. There is a pause between the scrape of his chair against the black and white tiles and the slurp and grunt of his first sip.

She knows he has stirred the cup with his index finger and wiped it off on her towel. And she scrunches her eyes to suppress a long-ago image of herself using the hem of her nightgown on the backs of his ears. She pushes her tongue back in her mouth, safe from the temptation to taste where he is in need of a haircut at the nape of his neck. She keeps her eyes closed to the empty cupboards that line the kitchen walls and the two eggs that have been in the cardboard crate in the back of the refrigerator since long before she last looked in there. There is no cereal, no rice, no meat, no cheese. No forks, glasses, knives, or plates; no herbs or spices, no sugar. Arnulfo will take the four empty wine bottles that peek from the top of the garbage on his way out. They drink their coffee black.

Alicia avoids his eyes as she gets up from the table. Arnulfo knows she'll wash her cup—caressing it over and over with a kitchen sponge she has soaked in nearly an eighth of a cup of dish soap—rinsing it with the water from the kettle before putting it into the dishwasher. He knows that as she is getting dressed—brushing her hair in the mirror, lipsticking her mouth a light orange—that she'll be listening for him to wash his cup, too. She'll wait until he's dressing before she'll put it on the rack next to hers and turn the machine on. He'll be tying his tie when she'll ask if he'll pick up a chicken or half a pot roast from the delicatessen on his way home, and he won't ask about a salad or vegetable or potatoes. He'll buy more wine.

And as she leaves for work, he imagines her at a time she enjoyed making him breakfast: huevos y frijoles negros; galletas light enough not to be there at all; his arms full of her, warm and fleshy like the girl he met whose mouth tasted hot and insistent; the girl who asked for his help opening and closing the clasp of her bra.

The door clicks and he can hear their two cups clinking in the whorl and slap of the water against the otherwise empty dishwasher. And it's a sound that she'll keep in her head as she turns on her car and as she scrapes the windows and removes the snow from the roof. She'll hold on to it until she can arrange herself behind the wheel and can turn the radio loud enough so that news and the engine might drown out any noises the babies—Carlos y Tomas o Luis y Oné—might make as she turns out onto the boulevard to the freeway.

When she turns onto the exit ramp and merges toward the center lane, she no longer feels the low, heavy swish of them wash through as they had those months they were inside her. Nor did she imagine a groan they might have somehow inherited from Arnulfo: the one he made as he turned over in his sleep or getting up from a chair. The only voice she hears tells her there is more wind, more snow, more freezing rain on the way: When will this end, it chuckles from what Alicia imagines to be a very hairy chest. Just ahead of her, a gray light that seems in no way connected with the sun begins to fill in the sky between the downtown office buildings. Looking at the clock, she thinks of the work piled in her In bin, the phone calls she needs to make, and the letters she'll need to sign as Head of Human Resources. She knows about this time Arnulfo should be turning his truck onto the freeway.

He's headed out of the city to an empty lot in the suburbs.

He knows he's there when the road narrows to a two-lane highway and he reaches what was part of the asphalt leading to a parking lot when a pharmaceuticals distributor stood there. His truck is new and red, and shimmers in places under a thin layer of ice despite the gray overcast light. His head sings a muffled throb and feels raw in the cold air as he wades chest-deep into a sea of dead weeds.

Toward the far end of the lot, where the road curves around and heads back toward the city, a sign tells of the coming of shops, fast food, and conveniences. Under his company's logo, Arnulfo's signature has been painted. Underneath it is the number he was assigned by the American Institute of Architects. The developer, his boss, and the client trust the number he was assigned. We trust Arnie, they say. So, if Arnulfo wants, he can have the cottonwood in the center of the lot removed tomorrow morning; a county surveyor and a refuse collection crew could be summoned to the site at his whim.

He wants to bring his mother-in-law to this place, and have her watch him will a drugstore into being, or create a shop where she can't resist trying on a pair of shoes or sampling a fragrance.

During the weeks she had visited after Alicia had come home from the hospital, his mother-in-law knitted or read or attended to Alicia as her daughter instructed. No matter how cold it was, if Alicia wanted to go for a walk, they walked. And Arnulfo watched from the window as the two women huddled through the snow and rounded the corner. If Alicia wanted lemongrass tea with milk and honey, her mother would make and remake cup after cup until it was the right strength, the right sweetness, the right temperature. Alicia wanted there to be no cooking in the house. She had cried like a little girl catching her breath as she coughed out each sob, and her mother demanded that Arnulfo drive her to places where they made fríturas like she used to make, and a place where the arroz con pollo was seasoned with real saffron and not just dyed yellow like so many places up north liked to do, and somewhere where the yucca was fresh and completely cleared of sand and grit. She instructed him to drive quickly without killing them so that she could get it home to Alicia while it was still steaming, while it could do her some good. As always she had seemed distant to him. Not a coolness, but he was very aware of a ten-year-old polite reserve between them that always made him feel as if he were meeting her for the first time whenever they were alone. Once, while he and his mother-in-law were in the car looking for the mafungo Alicia craved, saying she could eat nothing else, they had passed an apartment complex for which Arnulfo had designed the lobby. He explained how it had taken him nearly a year to come up with the right plan—one that fit the rest of the building, but was still distinctive—and how he had sweated during all the months of construction, not knowing how his vision would turn out. He asked his mother-in-law if she cared to stop and see it. ¿Por qué, the woman asked without turning to look at him, did you build it? Arnulfo, mijo, was there dirt under your fingernails after the earth was opened up and your ideas were poured into it? Besides, the food will get cold, she said.

He paces the steps between where the Midwest's Largest Fabric Emporium will go and a place where pretzels that taste like buttered cinnamon toast will be sold. Down the corridor where security will sit across from a discount beauty-supply store, Arnulfo unbuckles his belt, and pulls his trousers and shorts to the middle of his thighs. As he pushes an arc of urine out onto the exact spot where a firewall will be raised, a station wagon passes on the road just in front of him.

Despite the fact that the car is gone within seconds, he waves as the sound of the tires against the road fades. The car is headed south and Arnulfo is certain a young boy rides in the far backseat; he wants there to have been an entire household of goods and luggage strapped to the carrier on the roof, and imagines the car traveling nonstop out of Chicago, out of Illinois, through Indiana; he imagines it headed south, south, south, until it reaches the Bay of Biscayne, and the back door opens to a white expanse of beach with blue water and air, and the beach ball the boy throws is a bright orange, as a group of gulls picks through the sand, and sun plays on his nose and shoulder blades.

The wind against Arnulfo's buttocks sends a rash of gooseflesh up his back and down to his ankles. His genitals threaten to crawl inside of him, although he holds on to his image of the boy and the bright ball and the sound of the waves and the squeals of gulls until he is blue to the quick.

In his truck with his shirt arranged in his trousers, he rubs his thighs and smacks his shoulders in the blow of the heater as he tries to regain feeling. He's the architect; We trust Arnie, they say. He stomps his feet against the floorboards and presses the speed-dial button that connects him to Alicia's office. He listens to her outgoing message—she's back in the office; it's unfortunate she's unable to take his call right now; she looks forward to talking to him. Instead of leaving a message, he hangs up and dials again. She's back; it's unfortunate; she looks forward, and he hangs up without telling her about the crows that, one by one, streak the sky overhead and grab hold of the bare cottonwood with a screech so clear and distinct it pierces the hum of the truck's engine.

However, it is a baby's screech across the marble lobby of her office building that sets Alicia's body into motion.

She has hung her coat and checked her In bin. Her assistant's desk is empty, and the researchers have yet to make it in. The snow, she thinks. Qué weather, slowing down the trains and buses; the freeways will become full and still in another fifteen minutes.

The phone on her desk blinks. The machine forces her to listen to her outgoing first: She is back (now, for nearly a month after being gone for eleven weeks); unfortunately, she is unable to take your call. But she begins to wonder if she sounds contrite. She knows Arnulfo is the four dial tones in a row. She listens to them as if they are fugitive love songs, boleros of longing and loss; so tender, as if coming from an animal wounded by birth with a vital organ outside its body. When she thinks of him it is no longer of the smell of melon she would search and find in the center of his chest or the sinew of muscle across his back. Nor are the echoes of her girlfriends' whispers—Muy guapo; Y macho; So smart; Tan fuerte; Such a good provider; You're lucky—in her head. Now she thinks of the instant, constant, nervous cant that is his heart.

She would have played them over and over, but the last of them runs into a message thanking her for an interview she had the day before. The woman was pleased that she was able to meet with all the people on staff and looked forward to working there. The next message was from Mike, a researcher, reminding her that he will be late this morning. He has a dentist appointment.

Arnulfo had called at 2 A.M. to leave her his dial tone, and again twenty-three minutes later. Between them her mother said, Escucha, mija, if you want to know what all of downtown Habana smells like during the hottest of August afternoons, take an onion, garlic, the juice of one lime, and olive oil, and fry them in a pan until they become gritty and black as gravel. . . .

Alicia interrupts her mother's message, and as soon as she hangs it up, her phone begins to ring. She lets the call go to voice mail.

The In bin contains applications, résumés, and offers of solicitation from vendors. Her doctor's release to return to work is still there. For any other employee she would have approved it, signed it, and immediately had it filed.

In her mind, her mother is still the thin, tanned woman who raised her, even though she has gained weight and aged quite a bit. The messages, no matter what time of day or night, seem to come from a long-ago noon, poolside in back of the pink house in Miami where she grew up. Her mother's bikini matches the house. Tito, her mother's ancient green parrot whose only word is ¡Coño! marches around the lawn near the gazebo, and the water in the pool is blue, blue. She imagines her mother picking up the white princess phone to begin a story about a cousin in Holguín who ate nothing but wild pineapple for a year while she waited for her lover to come back to her. Alicia knows the story. She knows all of the stories: the tío with the coffee finca who had one arm and more mistresses than socks; or how the recipe that she uses to make picadillo came into the family, and the murder of a diplomat associated with it. She can see her mother check the hard helmet of black hair she kept up for so many years, even though the last time Alicia saw it in the hospital when the babies—Carlos, Oné, Tomas, Luis—seemed so present, so real, her mother's hair was wild and frazzled and streaked with gray.

The phone begins to ring again. Alicia lays the release aside and takes the elevator to the lobby to get a bagel and a cup of coffee.

She is standing in line when she hears the baby screech. The woman in front of her turns in the direction of the baby—she sees a woman negotiating a stroller covered with a pink and yellow blanket through the revolving door into the brightly lit lobby—but Alicia fixes her eyes on the menu above the counter. She notes the prices of scones with currants, scones with blueberries, and scones with raspberries have gone up in the last month, when the woman removes the blanket, and the baby, shocked and red in the sudden light, begins to bawl.

It is an angry, hungry cry, a repeating bleat from quavering lips that resounds in the lobby and stiffens Alicia's spine, causing her to abandon her place in line and make her way to the washroom with her purse over her chest.

In the stall, she checks for spots before unbuttoning her blouse and unclasping her bra. Milk seeps through her fingers as she uses the other hand to fish in her purse for the pump. She watches as it is expressed from her body, and curls down the plastic tube into the container she will rinse and dry before returning it to her purse and taking the elevator back to her office. During a break, she'll find a message from her mother; in the background she'll hear Tito yelling ¡Coño! ¡Coño! ¡Coño! And around lunchtime, Arnulfo will call to hear her voice: she's back; it's unfortunate; she looks forward.

It is after lunch that Arnulfo returns to his office and discovers that he has been entrusted with the design of a closet that is both decorative and functional. The developer, a squat hairy man who appears to be sweating even when he's not, says they are counting on him. We know you'll make it good, Arnie, he says.

Arnulfo stares at the linen paper stretched out on his drafting table waiting for the closet to appear. He balances the point of his mechanical pencil with his index finger in one of the dimples on the clean sheet in front of him. The pocket clip catches his fingernail, sending the pencil flying out of sight. As he is on his hands and knees looking for it, he can hear two women outside his office discussing plans for a coworker's birthday. There will be balloons and a gift certificate; cake from the bakery down the street; they'll begin passing the card around in the morning. He returns to his seat empty-handed. The thin trail the pencil left stops at the end of the page.

There was a time he could place a single line on the center of the page and with confidence whisper, Mira, Alicia, una silla. And he wouldn't stop until she could see it, could name the texture and color of the fabric, the type of wood frame that supported the full cushion that she would sink into as she read by the fire. Mira, Alicia, una ventana, he'd whisper. And she would tell him about the cat—an Abyssinian, she was certain—that she would go after with a bucket of water every afternoon until it stopped lying in wait in the hedgerows to dig up the bulbs she planted. She promised peonies as large as cabbages and cabbages bigger than any cabbage that he'd ever seen.

And when all the floors had been sanded and the dust cleared, they stood in the empty, finished town house and he said, Mira, Alicia, tu casa. And she knew what color the walls would be, and which rugs went where, and what would have to be bought, and what they shouldn't bring with them. She knew she was working against time. Mira, Alicia, Arnulfo had whispered, as her doctor pointed to arms and legs and fingers and scrotums through the shadowy float of an ultrasound.

She is nearly the last person left in the office. Through the windows that line the entire floor, she is too high up and it is too dark to tell if it is still snowing. Cars on the freeway in the distance seem to be moving slowly.

As she files her medical release she notices the light blinking on her phone. She listens to the dial tone blare and fade, and then Tito screeches ¡Coño! Her mother wants to know if Alicia remembers her great tía Adele's hair. Yards and yards of it there was; a strange color of dark red that no one else in the family had or has had since. And when her mother was a girl in La Habana, she and her sisters would have to cover the dining-room table with a cloth and spread it out to be cleaned with arrowroot, anise, and lavender root. Not fond of water she was, your great tía, her mother says. But how you loved her hair, even though you have only seen it through my eyes; you loved it without seeing, smelling it, touching it; you loved it.

In the elevator, Alicia adjusts her scarf and puts on her gloves. She makes a mental note of the things she needs to do the next day. In her In bin are several applications, résumés, and offers of solicitation from vendors; most of her staff will be there; they will have a meeting to plan her day; interviewees will sit outside her office in dry-cleaned clothing and shoes they've tried to preserve from the salt and slush.

She's looking for her car keys when the elevator stops between the third and fourth floors. Waiting in the dim light, she knows that it won't be long before the maintenance people load the Dumpster from the floor above onto the freight elevator. She hums one of Arnulfo's boleros—one of the ones he used to sing upon waking, going to bed, in the shower, in the car, so out of tune she could almost not bear it—over and over to herself, as if she were testing a bad tooth with her tongue. One day, she will be able to hand him a piece of paper and a pencil and say, Una silla, por favor. One day, they'll take their things out of storage and she'll paint one of the garden walls cobalt, and grow yellow clematis over it. She'll keep oranges out on the counter until they are hot with that nearly fermented flavor that is so warm and sweet. She would, one day, look at Arnulfo as he read the newspaper Sunday afternoons at the kitchen table and crumpled peanut shells onto the floor, and think, Tan fuerte, muy guapo. They'd fill the refrigerator with savory and favored tastes; their kitchen would always smell of cooking. And she is as certain as she knows the elevator doors will open, her car will start, she will make her way home through the traffic and the snow, and find Arnulfo there. Certain as she was standing there, she knows that between the two of them, each has kept an island—one neither of them has ever seen, touched, or smelled—poised from the time they were born for just this moment now. Although what frightens, more than anything, is the rocking of the dim elevator car, pendulous on its cable, so reminiscent of the babies—Oné y Tomas o Luis y Carlos—falling out of her over and over again. When will the feeling not leave her chilled and shivering?

She thinks of a blue house just beyond Guantánamo Bay, and plátanos rojos and the summer nights her tíos would burn tarántula nests from the trees, and of palmas reales near a beach so white and water so blue.

Before she gets home, Arnulfo turns the thermostat to seventy-five. He has unwrapped the chicken and is opening a bottle of wine when she comes through the door.

They sit in the dark in their coats at the kitchen table passing the bottle between them. Outside, the moon makes everything in the nearly empty rooms dark purple. If there is wind they do not mention it. If there is more sleet, snow, or frost predicted, neither admits to listening to a weather station on the way home, or to a youth wailing about his angst, or a diva crying about her abandonment, on a rock or from a dungeon. Alicia scratches at nothing on the table with her nail. Arnulfo runs the edge of his shoe on the thin lines made between the black and white tiles.

As they finish the bottle of wine they listen to the child next door confront bedtime. No, no, no, no, no, no, no, the baby says as its mother cajoles with a singsong Night-night. No, no, no, no, no, she says, as she runs away from the wall that divides the houses, until her hard, first shoes can no longer be heard against the bare floorboards.

With his penknife, Arnulfo cuts portions away from the breast of the chicken and lays the ragged slices on the paper bag it came in, and pushes it in front of his wife. No, no, no, no, no, the baby squeals with delight, as the room warms around them. Alicia removes her coat and opens another bottle of wine. No, no, no, no, no, the baby says as the light through the window slowly shifts, and Alicia begins to see Arnulfo as he uses the lid from the macaroni salad container as a utensil. He has taken off his coat along with his tie and shirt. In the shadows, she watches a wash of sweat bead on his forehead and upper lip. His fingers fumble to find the chicken he left in front of her and hand her a piece. No, no, no, the baby says, as he tilts his head toward her, and listens to make sure she is eating. He brings carrot sticks toward her lips, a stalk of broccoli.

Night-night, and again, Night-night. They listen to the baby's feet running across the floors next door. Alicia takes the wine bottle from him and drinks deeply. Close to the wall and then away; little steps, unshod; in socks or pajamas that have feet in them. Alicia has seen them come in pink and blue and yellow and green pastels. Some have duck appliqués, others have bunnies; some come with mobiles to match.

Arnulfo has his shoes off, too. No, no, no, no, no, the baby says, and Alicia watches her husband take the garbage to the wastebasket, and listens as he pads about the kitchen in stocking feet; washing his hands; drying them on the towel in the handle of the refrigerator. On his way to retrieving a fresh bottle of wine, he undoes his belt and allows his trousers to fall to his ankles. He steps out of his socks, and removes his T-shirt. The languidness of his movements is infectious and familiar, like dancing. As she sees his legs and arms moving toward her, her body remembers wanting him to ask her to dance;

she remembers being perched on the end of a wooden folding chair; remembers pretending to admire the decorations in the hall and trying to look deep in conversation with a girlfriend.

He stands in his underwear and offers her the bottle. ¿Qué calor esta noche, no, señora? he asks her. And she responds, Sí, señor. Do you know this beach well? he asks. And she tells him it has been in her family for thousands of years and she knows of a place where the water is so calm that he could be fooled into believing that there are two moons.

You'll show it to me? he asks.

She tells him, Momentito. Asks him to avert his eyes, and removes her clothes. She is standing barefoot in her underwear.

She takes his arm and leads him in front of the couch where the moon shines in the polish of the bare floors. She takes a sip of wine and unfastens her bra.

And for the few minutes he lies curled in her lap, the house where they live is quiet. And she whispers, Mira, this is the cove where afternoons swell with the most dizzying daylight. We'll like it here one day, she says, after all, it is happy.

Susanna Bullock

4149A

It was the summer we lived upstairs and couldn't wear shoes in the house. I couldn't jump rope or do jumping jacks or bounce a ball on the wood floors because of the renters. Momma said, "It's only considerate." Daddy said that the Beatos were good tenants, always paid their hundred dollars the first of the month. He didn't say it covered our groceries most of the months he was out of work and we lived on Mom's substitute teacher's salary. It was something no one talked about unless my brother and I were thought to be asleep. Almost as an afterthought, he added, "Who can say? Mrs. B may let slip her family recipe for lasagne." So we walked softly. No TV after the news, even when there was a good movie on. If one of us went to the bathroom in the middle of the night, no flushing until breakfast. It was how we lived.

The people below us might hear our every step, every cough, but I never heard them unless I was outside on the back steps on a summer evening when everyone was slowing down, settling in, and the alley had no traffic. Davey, the toddler next door, might cry in his sleep. Roni and Ellen might whisper to each other in the bed they shared in the back bedroom. Before Momma called me for my own bath, I thought I'd escape if I stayed out of sight. Mrs. B and Doc would whisper after supper and before the evening quieted everyone into the night.

I could hear each of their voices on opposite sides of what was once my grandmother's kitchen. Mrs. B washing dishes, Doc drinking the last of his wine from a dime-store glass. Once the dishes were done, his voice moved closer and closer to hers. He stayed close until the dishes were dry and put away with a final snap of a cabinet latch. And then their voices softened. Murmurs, then. I'd see fireflies swarming in the mock orange by the alley, and hear the kids out front on the street playing hide-and-seek. Then I could not hear Doc or Mrs. B anymore. Perhaps they, too, didn't want to disturb those of us who lived in the same house.

When I could no longer hear conversation, I could still hear Reva next door practicing scales and hymns before bed. The sour notes on the low end of the piano were not her fault, she always told me later, but I was never sure. Reva and her sister were my age and lived on the far side of the fourplex made of stone blocks with a shadowy, cool porch, only enough backyard for parking, and an overgrown rosebush that produced red roses that smelled like thick cough syrup.

On the other side of our house, Mrs. Manis lived on the lower level and rented the second story of her brick duplex. It had an arched doorway, a tiny yard, and an old wrapped-wire fence edged in violets and purple and yellow iris. I never heard her at night and barely heard her any other time. A small woman with round eyes and nervous hands, she was the only person I ever knew who called my grandmother Annie while she was still alive, and one of the few, it seemed, who mourned her friend and neighbor's passing when she died the summer we moved to St. Louis.

After the funeral she'd brought over a meat loaf and set it next to Mrs. Custer's ham and the fried chicken and slaw from the church ladies. A few days after the funeral, she gave Momma an index card with the meat loaf recipe. It was what we ate, usually Wednesdays or Saturdays, ever after. My brother made it for his Boy Scout cooking merit badge. Dad used it in cold meat loaf sandwiches on Sunday when he mowed the lawn and drank a beer. A budget-stretching food was what Momma said. But it never made Daddy stop and wonder and guess like Mrs. B's lasagne.

On the occasional day Momma was off shopping or visiting family, Mrs. B would give Daddy lasagne for his lunch. The meat loaf would stay in the fridge, and he'd sit on the back steps and eat slowly. When he'd finished, he'd lick his fingers one at a time and say, "Rosemary," or, "Oregano." From inside her kitchen, Mrs. B, with Danny on her hip, would appear at the screen door, smile and nod, and not say a word. Her lasagne was spicier than anything Momma or Gramma cooked. And from all he said and did, Daddy thought it worth walking softly and worth licking his fingers.

I spent that lasagne summer being thirteen and babysitting. At fifty cents an hour, I was building up my money for nylons and a garter belt, which Momma said I wasn't nearly old enough for and would, in any event, have to pay for myself. So when Doc and Mrs. B went to hospital get-togethers for the residents or a wedding, I fed the kids leftovers—my favorite being veal parmigiana—and read bedtime stories. After they were in bed, I read my library books, or books or magazines around their house, and usually fell asleep on the couch.

At the end of one such night, Mrs. B woke me in the midst of a pile of the cookbooks I'd been scanning for lasagne recipes. I'd found a different version in every book. She gathered a stack of books to return to the kitchen and told me, "So you think your daddy really wants to know?" The strap of her black slip slid down her arm. In the kitchen, she sighed and stood in front of the fan with her mouth open and her arms akimbo.

"You might find secrets in books," she said, sweeping her dark, wavy, black hair off her neck, "but I never have."

"Daddy said he thinks your secret is a bit of anise and maybe the kind of sausage Doc gets on the Hill."

Mrs. B laughed. She shook her head.

"Want to stay for ice cream? Doc's gone to Velvet Freeze to bring some home. Peach, I think."

While Mrs. B went to look in on the kids and change into a cool housecoat, I gathered the rest of her cookbooks and put them back on her small bookshelf in the kitchen next to some wine and their old family Bible.

Doc came in whistling and carrying a brown bag. He set the bag on the table and from his wallet pulled a five-dollar bill, three dollars more than I had earned that night. It was crisp, almost new. "Let's pretend you didn't want any ice cream, huh?" And he winked.

I shoved the money into my pocket and headed out the door. I ran up the back stairs faster than usual, faster and louder than I was supposed to. My face was hot. I stopped at the top of the stairs and felt the cool night breeze barely slide over all the houses on our street. I was hot and cold all at once. I shivered. And for a moment, I was sure someday I wanted a man who ate ice cream with me late at night.

That summer I babysat for the Beato kids and a couple of other families in the neighborhood. Toward the end of July, Mrs. Manis's renter Linda asked me to look after her four-month-old little boy so she could go to the movie with Mrs. Landing, who lived across the street. I'd only held my cousin Cyndy as a baby so young. I'd only changed diapers on dolls and in a home-ec class at school, but that didn't dissuade Linda from offering me seventy-five cents an hour since it was Friday night. "Date night," she said. I didn't tell her I'd never had a date. I told her I'd call my momma if I had questions about the baby.

She and Mrs. Landing were going up to the Grand to see whatever was showing and get out of the heat. She held the pins for me and watched me change Leo's diaper. She showed me where she kept his formula and his extra diapers and clothes. All I kept saying was, "They are so tiny," as she held up his little T-shirts.

Linda changed her own clothes twice before she left, and kept telling me what trouble she had finding clothes because she herself was small-boned. Talking to me like I was her friend, she confided that she bought her bras in the girls' department and didn't really need those. She kept asking me if she looked all right.

I didn't know what to say. I thought she looked like a picture in a magazine. Blond hair, blue eyes, like all the dolls I'd thought beautiful, but few people I'd known. Before I needed to say anything, Mrs. Landing came up the stairs saying they'd be late, and with every word puffing on a cigarette and swirling her full skirt covered with jungle leaves and blooms bigger than any flower I'd ever seen. They left telling each other how good they looked and how much fun they were going to have. I envied them.

Holding Leo against my body, I waved the baby's hand to his mommy as she and Mrs. Landing walked down the stairs. I stood wondering how such a tiny person could have a baby who weighed a lot more than a sack of groceries.

I was ready to call my momma for help, but Leo took his bottle and let me change him, and fell asleep in my arms before I could sing to him or tell him a story. He was as good a baby as his momma said he was. I liked holding him. He melted into the curves of my arms and chest, the bend of my lap. He blew a bubble that smelled of milk and burped on my first try. I decided babies were okay. I laid him in his crib and stood there holding his tiny foot, wiggling it to make him smile. He smiled even in his sleep.

After baby Leo was asleep, I wandered around the apartment. It was smaller than our flat, though narrow and high like all the houses on the block. It was wallpapered in a tan print textured like rough paper in every room except the bathroom and kitchen. They were painted a shiny yellow, meant to be cheery but ending up harsh. No pictures were on the walls. No family photographs anywhere. I couldn't find a book or a magazine in any of the rooms. Not even a cookbook. The fridge only contained formula, some beans soaking in water, the Coke Linda'd left for me, some bananas, and what was left of a casserole. I opened the soda and went looking for a place to look out the window. The bit of furniture was all wood and spindly legs, insubstantial and uncomfortable. The modern black couch had been made for sitting up rather straighter than I liked. No pillows or old quilts or afghans to soften the edges.

In Linda's bedroom all the clothes she'd tried on and rejected were spread across the chenille bedspread. I held up a simple blue print dress against me and looked in the mirror, and could see my body sticking out on all sides. I could have worn it when I was ten, maybe. In the mirror, I saw a girl who had hair and eyes the color of brown corduroy, taller than all the boys in her class, who liked kick-rock and tag and keep-away and step-ball, and books with horses and friendship and rivers in them. All I had with me to read was a book of fairy tales I'd brought for Leo. I started with the three bears and fell asleep in the midst of Linda's tiny clothes.

I woke and saw Linda leaning over me. "I see how your momma sees you," she said, handing me two dollars and fifty cents in quarters. I apologized for mussing her clothes, and she waved the notion away and went to look in on Leo. I followed her asking about the movie. But she didn't answer me. She picked him up and changed him in a swift, practiced motion. He slept on, drooling a bit, squirming in a dream. "He's a good baby," we both said at the same time, and we laughed. I lightly pinched her arm above the wrist and she looked shocked.

"If you say the same thing at the same time it's bad luck if you don't pinch the person," I tried to explain the superstition I'd picked up from who knows where.

She pinched me back and smiled. "We are safe now."

It was quiet walking home in the dark. How many steps? Twenty down to the sidewalk, thirty to our steps, another eight to the door. Not a long way home. No traffic on the street. The porch light was on. The hall light was on. The light in my folks' room showed underneath their door, and I poked my head in. Daddy's side of the bed was empty. I assumed he was sleeping again in the room under the eaves he used as his office. Mom was propped up with pillows reading a murder mystery. Her glasses were slipping down her nose. She put her book across her lap to hold her place and pushed her glasses up.

"A good baby," I said.

She nodded as if such a thing was all one needed to say about anything, and went back to her book. On the way to my room, I glanced into the doorless space where my daddy slept. He had curled his tall body to fit on the daybed and still his feet hung over the edge. I could hear him snoring like an engine idling. I pulled the sheet over him, turned out his light, and went into my bedroom.

I didn't sleep for a long while. I wondered how many nights Daddy slept in a knot and how many Momma read until long after midnight. In the dark I couldn't see the yellow roses on the wallpaper Momma picked out and Daddy put up last summer. I lay on top of the sheets and thought about the soft baby next door, his tiny momma and their colorless flat with no books, no comforts, nothing to look at.

I woke the next morning with a headache and a desire to watch cartoons and old movies, but Mom sent me outside after breakfast. So I took my hard rubber ball and threw it against the front porch steps. After twenty minutes I hadn't caught one pop fly worth one hundred points and had missed more than a lot of ten-point no-bounces.

Not many people were coming and going, so I didn't notice anything going on until Jerry Vosky, from three houses down, headed my way. I ignored him and kept on playing step ball. But Jerry and I both stopped when we heard a siren. When a police car pulled up and two policemen walked fast into Mrs. Manis's flat, we moved close together until our arms bumped.

I sat down on the stoop and tossed my ball from one hand to the other. Jerry set his shopping bag filled with books beside me and bent down to tie his shoelaces tighter.

It looked like he was headed to the library. He always won the prize for how many books you read over the summer. On the library wall you wrote your name on a construction-paper shoe and the title of the book you read. He and Barb Knight had feet all over the walls, steps going 'round and 'round. My few shoes were scrunched under the window by the horse stories as if I were keeping time. I didn't like to tell the librarian I'd read the murder mysteries Momma finished or the westerns Pop read and reread until he was calling my brother Pardner and me Little Sis.

"So, do you know what's happening?" Vosky finally asked.

I squeezed the ball. "Something."

An ambulance pulled up and double parked by Daddy's Ford station wagon. Guys in white pulled out a stretcher and looked at house numbers before one of the cops came out and motioned them upstairs.

"Leo?" I asked out loud. I wondered if I'd done anything wrong last night. Fed him wrong. Burped him wrong. Everything seemed okay when I left.

Jerry gave me a funny look and walked across the street to where there was a small huddle of neighbors including his cousin Barb and aunt Zoe. They were all shaking their heads. He walked back to me looking like he'd gotten a bad grade in school. Before he said a word, a policeman came outside with a bundle in his arms and walked across the street to Mrs. Landing's house. I was sure it was Leo. He never made a sound, but the pale blanket was the one from his crib.

"The renter," Jerry began.

"Linda," I said.

"Mrs. Gomez says she heard a shot," he said.

"I didn't hear anything."

"No one else did either," he said. "But she says she knows a gunshot when she hears one. They're all talking about times they heard gunshots. Mrs. Newell says her daddy shot squirrels for Saturday dinner when she was a girl living in Kentucky. But she lives down the block and can't hear me when I say hello, so I don't know."

Mrs. Landing's door opened and the cop with Leo in his arms disappeared inside.

Men wheeled the stretcher out the door and down the steps and lifted it into the ambulance.

"She's not moving," Vosky said.

I walked to the large oak we used as home-free when we played hide-and-seek. I leaned against the trunk, keeping it between me and what I was seeing. They hadn't covered Linda. She was wearing the blue dress I'd admired the night before. Her eyes were closed. Something brown was running out the side of her mouth.

I turned to Jerry, "Medicine?"

"Blood," he said, and when the doors were closed and the ambulance was driving away without the siren, he added, "She took a gun and shot her brains out."

He picked up his books and looked in the opposite direction he was going.

"Is she gonna die?" I asked.

"She ate it all right."

"How could she just die? She went to the movies last night. I stayed with the baby. I didn't see any gun."

Jerry looked at me with his know-it-all eyes and his wet lips and said, "Her heart stopped."

"No," I argued. "You said she died from head wounds."

"I'm telling you," he sounded so sure and leaned toward me as if confiding in me, "it's always the heart."

"Even if someone cuts off your head?" I wanted to prove him wrong.

"The body goes on and on," he said. His cousin Barb had told me he was going to be a doctor. "You are only dead when your heart stops. That is a fact."

His face was close to mine. He had pimples on his forehead and on the side of his nose. I saw his dark eyelashes and the places on his face he shaved. My brother was two or three years older than Jerry and he didn't shave yet. When Jerry got excited, like talking about Linda, spit pooled at the right side of his lower lip. For no reason, he reached out and shook my arm. And I hit him.

He frowned, then laughed. His face was inches from mine. I could hear him breathing. As the thought crossed my mind that he was moving to kiss me, he breathed once hard and said, "Gotta go."

He was halfway down the block when all I knew was I wanted him to keep talking about the heart and what keeps us alive.

"Stand farther back," he yelled. "Aim for the edge. Throw harder." He did not even turn around to deliver these words. He kept walking and sped up almost to a run toward the end of the block.

I don't remember the rest of the day. I only remember when I was called to help with dinner, my throwing arm hurt and Momma told me to mash the potatoes. My brother made a face at me as if he'd lucked out and not been put to work, but Mom slapped his hand away from the olives and told him to set the table. Pop came in from mowing the backyard and washed his sunburned arms in the sink.

"Can't you do that in the bathroom?" Momma asked, but she put a kitchen towel on his shoulder.

He let the cool water run over his arms before he said, "The Beatos found a house and will be moving once Doc's residency is done."

"Oh my," Momma said. "We'll have to advertise for new renters." She wiped her hands on the apron I'd made her in school. Quickly, she lifted the cake from the windowsill where it was cooling and cut several pieces, slid them onto a plate, and covered the plate with a fresh kitchen towel from the drawer.

"Take this to Doc and Dolores," she told me and took the potato masher from my hand.

"They've been such good renters," she said. "Neighbors, really."

"Who knows who will answer the ad," Daddy said, reaching for a beer in the fridge.

I headed out the back door and heard voices in their kitchen as I came down the wooden stairs. I knocked on their screen door. Chewing the last of his own dinner, Dr. B waved me inside. He was still in his white coat with his name on it.

"Mom sent this down," I said putting the cake on the table. "Not an old family recipe, but one we all like." I knew I was sounding stupid. "Lazy Daisy, Momma calls it."

"You heard we're moving before school starts, huh?" Mrs. Beato asked me, drinking the last of her wine.

I nodded and edged to the door.

She stood up and crossed to her bookshelf, scanned the top shelf quickly, and pulled out a thick volume with a red cover. "I want you to have this to remember us all by," she said as she handed me an old, much-used Italian cookbook. I turned to the index before gathering words to thank her.

"Oh, it surely has a recipe for lasagne your poppa will like. More than a couple variations. Just not my momma's secret recipe I tell no one." She winked at me, "Not even my husband."

We all laughed, though I wasn't quite sure at what. Doc grinned at us both and folded back the towel, and took his fork and angled off a bite of the brown sugar and coconut icing and yellow cake. He clowned as if it was the greatest food in the world, and Mrs. B snapped a towel at him. He pulled her onto his lap and began chewing her arm. She freed herself and grabbed the book back and took the pen from Doc's pocket, and scribbled an inscription inside the front cover. She resettled herself on Doc's lap and took his fork and ate a bite of cake. She savored the mouthful and said, "Tell your momma thank you." She fed the next bite to Doc.

I said, "Lasagne," to them both as if it was one of those words that mean hello and good-bye and thank-you and hurried back upstairs. I stopped on the landing and listened to them as they resumed the talk of the day and the future. By the day's softening light, I read the words Mrs. B had written: "Balance makes a dish, a meal, a life."

Upstairs, everyone was in their place and helping themselves to pineapple-carrot salad and potatoes and meat loaf and green beans that had cooked all afternoon with ham hock and onion. My brother had the blue aluminum tumbler I liked, but then he had set the table. Momma had her usual green one; Pop had the red one. I had the silver.

No one said a word about Linda; maybe no one else had heard what happened. Momma had been grocery shopping and running errands. My brother had been in his room gluing together a model plane. Daddy had worked on the lawn-mower blade until it was sharp, then cut the backyard. Or maybe it was not a good topic for dinner conversation. Daddy said no talk of bills or Republicans at the dinner table for digestive reasons. I wouldn't have known what to say about Linda anyway. It was too big. A woman I hardly knew killed herself. A baby I'd held would never again hear his momma's voice except in his dreams.

My brother asked for more potatoes and got up and brought the milk bottle to refill his glass, Daddy's, and mine. He dragged his free hand along the cage of the parakeets and made kissing sounds at them. They had been eating lettuce and scratching their cuttlebone wired to one wall, and now Candy began saying all he knew: *Hello* and *So long.* Rainy Day only chirped and shed feathers the color of the summer sky.

Throughout the talk of baseball, something rattling in Momma's car, and my brother wanting to go outside even if it was after dark, the words *So long* came up more often than *hello. So long* was all I heard. *So long. So long.* I started to count them to see if Candy was working on a record. *So long. So long. So long.* Eleven, then twelve.

My brother said, "Fifteen, not twelve."

Momma nodded and collected each of our plates as we finished eating, scraped the bits of leftovers onto the top plate, and slid the last plate to the bottom of her stack. She carried them to the sink, scraped the top plate into the trash, then submerged them all into the pan of dishwater. Her hands came out red, and although she dried them on a dish towel, they stayed that way while she sliced cake, put it on dessert plates, and passed them to us. Her hands were still red when she picked up her own fork and said, mostly to Daddy, "There's always a gap."

We stayed later than usual at the table. The windows darkened into mirrors giving us back ourselves. I looked at my brother's back and my face peeking around him and beneath my daddy's chin. I didn't look any different than any other glimpse I'd had of myself lately. I took the paper napkin crumpled in my lap and pressed it against my eyes. I couldn't understand why Linda would kill herself and leave Leo. I was not close to understanding. I felt like I would understand sometime, someday. I was not sure, but thought knowing why she chose to die was just a few steps away from me. Like a neighbor I didn't know but would wave at when she passed by.

Underneath the table my bare feet scraped the faded linoleum. On one swing, I touched my daddy's bony foot in his thin cotton socks, then next my momma's own bare feet so close to each other—prim, like good girls—then my brother's feet, stuck in the middle at an angle in his sweat socks, like huge puppies.

Mom finished covering the meat loaf in tinfoil and searched the cabinets for a jar for the leftover green beans. She opened the fridge and moved things around to make room for the leftovers.

My brother kicked my ankle and said, as if he'd won some game between us, "Seventeen—a record, and counting."

I squinted at him and said, "I only wished I'd held the baby longer."

Momma and Daddy nodded to each other. Momma dried her hands and sat back down to be, I suspected, closer to us all, even though all the food on the table was gone and none of us knew what else to say.

A day can't hold more than this one, I thought, but each one will.

Diane Chang

Mother Knows

When the call from the hospital in Nashville came, Ku-ping was enjoying a cup of green tea and taking extra time to read the Sunday *Times.* On that plush blue couch in the living room of her house, she reclined and luxuriously scratched the instep of one foot with the big toe of the other. As she reached for the portable phone, she glimpsed her husband in the backyard through the sliding glass doors. He had his thumb over the end of the garden hose, spraying the young green beans, eggplants, hot peppers, and chives.

Ku-ping's weekend languor vanished as soon as the person on the other end of the phone identified herself as the emergency-room receptionist, even as she watched her husband squat and poke at something in the dirt, and she immediately thought of their son. Wei had always been accident-prone: as a child, he'd fallen out of trees; he'd broken his arm two different ways; he'd shattered his kneecap on a skiing trip with friends in college. By the time he began primary school, he'd been so sickly that the teacher asked if something was wrong at home.

Ku-ping struggled to untangle the meaning behind the receptionist's uninflected voice as the woman explained that Wei had gotten hurt playing Ultimate Frisbee, one of those get-to-know-each-other activities at Orientation before medical-school classes formally started.

Two other guys had gone after the Frisbee, and Wei got caught in the middle, the receptionist was saying. He was out cold for a few minutes, and when he came to, he couldn't say where he lived or identify his roommate. "There is a layer of fluid between the brain and the skull," the receptionist went on. "A concussion happens when the brain is jarred in its fluid bath." The doctors thought Wei would be fine—he was already remembering things—but they were keeping him in the intensive care unit, just in case.

Ku-ping tried to beat back the image of Wei getting crunched between two other guys, each of them blond and a head taller than her son. The anger built up inside her so that she could barely balance the phone in her hand. Why should her son be singled out in this way? Did the other boys think he could not catch a Frisbee? Wei should have been more careful: Was it worth being slammed on the ground to chase after a plastic plate?

And: What a stupid design for the human brain! Why all that liquid in the skull for the brain to rock around in! What good was the human body if it couldn't take a few knocks?

She called her husband in to tell him the news. Li-ping trotted to the sliding glass door and tapped his dirt-edged shoes against the cement steps. He wiped his forehead with the back of his hand, revealing a damp circle at the armpit of his shirt.

His face puckered into a helpless expression as he listened to how their son Wei had suffered a concussion. His eyes floated behind the magnifying lenses of his glasses like dead fishes. He would be no help. He tried to touch her arm, but she pulled back from the dirt on his hands and nails.

Li-ping washed up and changed his shirt, and they both got into the car for the hour-and-a-half drive to Nashville, where Wei was about to start medical-school classes at the private university whose name—Vanderbilt—had resounded of prestige when Ku-ping had first heard her son say it, but was now nothing but an evil portent on their horizons.

Ku-ping drove because Li-ping suffered from high blood pressure, and driving made it worse. Besides, he was such an absentminded driver, he sometimes went ten miles under the speed limit, and old grannies would honk at him. Ku-ping always went fast on major highways, and she'd never gotten a ticket. She watched out for police cars lurking under bridges, at shoulders, and in the oncoming lanes.

The needle on the speedometer of their old Camry edged past eighty. Next to I-40, on the stretch between Knoxville and Nashville, thickets of kudzu clung to the tops of trees. The road wound through the mountains like an unsolvable puzzle. After so many years of careful planning and diligent work, how could some small thing go awry and spoil a brilliant future? She thought of her son's brain reverberating from the blow, and her own head tingled. "How could this happen?" she said aloud, her knuckles white on the steering wheel, "Our son."

Li-ping sat next to her like a stunned child. Another husband might have known just the right thing to say, but he only sat there and sucked the air in through his teeth, little gulps of surprise as if he were reliving the news of their son over and over. When people looked at Wei, they saw that he looked just like his father: thick lips, wider on one side; flat eyelids; a square jaw. But as soon as Wei was old enough to have a personality, Ku-ping only saw herself in him. From the way he played quietly by himself while she studied, the way he neatly lined his toys from smallest to largest, she knew he had something in him that could only have come from her.

When Wei got older, his ambitions for himself coincided so beautifully with her wishes for him that she never had the occasion to doubt he'd inherited the essential part of his personality from her. He received the highest marks in his math and science classes, and even did well in English by high school. He was the valedictorian of his class.

Wei's successes had erased the guilt from a decision they'd made before they came to America. Actually, she was the one who had made the decision in the one-room unfinished apartment back in Changzhou, where all three of them had slept on straw mats on the floor. One night after Wei had fallen asleep, his heavy breathing filling the room, she'd told her husband of her decision, and Li-ping had nodded in the dark. Or rather, she'd assumed that he'd nodded in the ensuing silence, and he did not oppose the decision even when their son stirred in his sleep and the boy called out to his grandmother. In America, it was hard enough relearning everything in the strange, looping script without a child in the house. Chemistry terms that had been only two or three characters, she had to relearn in seven, eight, sometimes ten American letters. During the first two years, she pulled out her hair when she studied, gathered strands until she had a web of them looping between her fingers. Her hair never grew back as beautifully or as thickly, and that was the least of her sacrifices. During those early years in America, she thought of Wei after those fitful dreams in which she fought against herself, from which she woke more tired than ever with the image of guilt ebbing from her brain.

The landscape became flatter as Ku-ping drove west on I-40. On the almost-straight highway, driving was easy; she hardly had to pay attention. The needle of the speedometer teetered past ninety. The late afternoon sun struck the windshield with full force, as if the sun itself were trying to keep her from her son.

Wei hadn't even cried, Ku-ping remembered, when she'd brought him to her mother's apartment in Changzhou and told him they'd be gone for a while. Wei was ten years old, a rational being already, and Ku-ping thought that he'd understood. She'd smoothed down his hair and thrust away the tears at the back of her eyes with a sudden stab of rage. *Zai jian,* she'd said to her son, which meant "see you again." She'd taken his shoulders in her hands and shaken him a little too hard.

When she saw her son again, in America, two years later, he was half a foot taller, and the signs of manliness had already burgeoned all over his body: wide-set shoulders, thick calves, a deepening voice. At the airport, she hardly recognized her own son. For a moment, she thought she saw a hard animal in his eyes, a coldness for what she'd done to him. But then he called her Mother and kissed her. Li-ping had stood there awkwardly, sliding his thumbs through his belt loops and rocking on the balls of his feet, but Wei had kissed him too and called him Father.

When she brought him to their apartment in the university's graduate complex, it was like having a stranger in their home for several days, he'd changed so much, and then, miraculously and all at once, he was their son again, and it was as if they'd never been separated.

By the time they got to Nashville, the last bit of light had faded, and Ku-ping found herself driving under the eerie streetlights of the unfamiliar city. They'd been to Nashville many times before but had never stayed past dark. The city took on an entirely different aspect after sunset. The Southern Bell building—the Batman building, Wei had always called it—looked menacing against the purplish sky, its twin antennas twinkling like a medieval weapon.

She pulled into the parking structure next to the university hospital and parked on the nearly empty first floor. When she opened the car door, a chill brushed the hairs on the back of her neck, and despite everything the receptionist had said about concussions, Ku-ping was struck by the sure knowledge that her son was dying. Or worse: some vital part of his brain had been knocked out, and he would spend the rest of his life as a vegetable, and she would be forever helping him to the bathroom, spooning food into his slack lips, reading to him from illustrated children's books.

At intensive care, she breathlessly gave their names and said that they'd come to see their son.

"Just a sec," the receptionist said through her nose. This must have been a different woman from the one she spoke to over the phone. The woman's hair was pulled back into a high bun. Her lips were painted pink, her eyes lined with thick black circles. Ku-ping recognized the trashy type when she saw it, even in hospital uniform.

The receptionist shuffled through a pile of manila folders, her three-inch maroon nails tripping her fingers. Ku-ping wanted to saw off those nails and slap the girl in the face for taking so long. The girl finally found the right folder. "Shen, Wei," she said, her lips puckered impudently to one side. "If you'll take a seat, his doctor will be with you in just a sec."

Ku-ping sat in one of the uncomfortable plastic chairs and read a news magazine. Li-ping slumped into the seat next to her. She'd watched the slump in his back develop over the years, despite all the times she told him to sit up straighter. He'd become a bent man in middle age because he hadn't listened to her, and now, she didn't bother to point it out anymore.

She opened the magazine to an article on youth violence and read about how high-school gangs locked boys in lockers, how girls got molested behind football bleachers; one girl had her waist-length blond hair chopped off by two black girls, right at school. She studied the photographs of gang members and marveled at how the camera's trick of light and chemistry had managed to capture the rot behind their eyes. Young people just weren't safe in the world anymore.

The middle-aged doctor was thick around the stomach, and his remaining strands of gray hair were combed flat against the side of his head. He didn't bother to hide his baldness. "Mr. and Mrs. Shen," he said with the familiarity of a family doctor, though they'd never met him before. "Wei is only beginning to recover his memory, but you can see him if you'd like." He pronounced their son's name "Y," but Ku-ping didn't correct him. The doctor had had a long day; his eyes looked as if someone had made the imprints of can-bottoms over them.

The air in the back rooms of the hospital seemed sterilized of some of its essential components. Ku-ping found it hard to breathe when the doctor brought her to her son. Wei lay flat on his back in a room all by himself, his head tilted at an unnatural angle, as if he had broken his neck bone. His opened eyes stared out at nothing in particular.

Lying on the hospital bed, Wei was an unbearable combination of helplessness and manliness. He could have been a younger duplicate of her husband, but all she saw was her baby lying on that hospital bed. She wanted to gather up her adult son and take him home so that she could put good food into him and coax him back to health.

She watched her son's chest move up and down and hoped that warm blood pulsed through his body and rushed to the brain to repair it.

"How long has he been this way?" Ku-ping asked. She turned to her son, "Hello, Wei. This is your mother. Are you going to say hello to your ma?"

Her son lifted his head and gave her a demented stare. "Dunno," he said. He shook his head as if she pained him and laid it back down. The image of her son, brainless for life, came back to her again.

"He's been this way since the Frisbee accident at around three this afternoon," the doctor said. "He has gotten better. He knows his own name and recognizes his roommate now."

"Make him say hello to his ma," Ku-ping said and shook her son's shoulders. Li-ping put his hand on her shoulder and squeezed it, but she shook off the weight of his fingers and stepped away from him.

"Dunno," Wei said again, his mouth hanging open a little, his eyes fixed on the ceiling, his body slack.

"You shouldn't worry yourself too much," the doctor said. "The recovery process is unpredictable."

"How can a boy not recognize his mother?" Her hands clenched into fists, and she raised them, "His own mother!"

"We're doing our best for your son," the doctor said. He patted her arm in his unpleasantly familiar way, his face arranged into the expression of concern, though she thought she also detected weariness there.

"Dunno," Wei said one more time, still staring at the ceiling.

They sat with Wei another hour, and then there was nothing to do but to go back home. Ku-ping would drive out to Nashville again in the morning. She would come back every day until her son recovered completely. She would stroke his hand and call him back to the earth.

On the way home to Nashville, she was still thinking of her boy recovering from the blow to his head when red and blue lights flashed in her rearview mirror. She'd been so distracted that she hadn't seen the police car at the road bank, the glinting corner of it visible in her headlights.

She pulled over and cried out her frustration as the lights continued to circle. Her husband flinched in the passenger seat.

The officer who got out must have been seven feet tall. Ku-ping had never seen such an enormous human being, and it was only him in the squad car. He didn't seem to need a partner.

"I need to see your license and registration, ma'am," the officer said. His voice sounded as if it came through twenty feet of lead piping. "You know how fast you were going?"

"I've never gotten a ticket before," Ku-ping said. "I just saw my son, who is in the hospital with a concussion." She heard how small her own voice sounded, carried away by the cars that sped by. To the young yahoos who turned to stare, she must have been nothing more than a pale moth illuminated by police lights.

"You were going over ninety!" Even though it was dark, the officer wore sunglasses so that she couldn't see his overall expression, only a nose like the beak of some predatory bird, and lips pressed into a cynical line, as if he heard a thousand of these stories every day.

"Please, officer, I won't speed again." She'd heard of women who squeezed out tears for the traffic cops and gotten away with a warning, but the officer looked as if he were altogether incapable of kindness.

"The law is the law, ma'am."

The officer wrote her a ticket in the big puffy handwriting of a schoolgirl. When she looked at it, she saw that it was for two hundred and sixty-three dollars. The "6" winked at her in the middle like an evil eye. Even now, after she had enough money to own her own house, this seemed like an incredible sum of money.

"Good evening," the officer said as he tucked the blank book of tickets into his back pocket.

She climbed out of the car, leaving the door open so that its interior looked like the womb of some metallic insect exposed to the night.

"Officer!" she said to his back, waving the ticket in her hand. "Excuse me, officer!"

He turned around. He was even more impressive now that they were both standing, a true tower of a man, his dark glasses glinting in the absence of light. "Please get back in your car, lady," he said in the voice that sounded as if it were being transmitted from another planet.

"There must have been some mistake. You've written me a speeding ticket for two hundred and sixty-three dollars."

"Seventy-three bucks plus five-per-mile up to twenty over, and ten-per-mile after twenty. I clocked you going ninety-four, lady. Two hundred and sixty-three dollars. You're lucky I didn't get you for reckless driving."

She waited for him to shed his disguise and reveal himself as the devil. She wouldn't have been surprised. A breeze stirred, but his hair didn't move. Was there a man inside the tower? His face was the gridiron of unassailable logic, but there had to be a flaw in the computation that had resulted in the speeding ticket for two hundred and sixty-three dollars, because the universe couldn't be that perverse.

"That can't be right," she said weakly, and then Li-ping was out of the car too. She felt a little bigger with her husband standing next to her, their combined forces against the indomitable officer, but not much bigger.

"If you want to dispute the ticket, I'll see you in court. Good evening, ma'am."

The headlights of the police officer's car lit up, casting lights and darks over her and her husband on the side of the road, but it did not pull away. The officer's voice came on over a loudspeaker: "Please move your vehicle." Ku-ping felt as if it pressed against her from all sides, that amplified voice detached from body and soul, the voice of the vengeful universe intent on punishing her.

She could not drive, so Li-ping drove, at a good fifteen miles below the speed limit.

In the passenger seat, Ku-ping found herself doing something she did not commonly do: great heaves began at the back of her throat, and she soon began wailing uncontrollably. The sound of her crying recalled the noises she'd first made when she learned English, when, at the age of thirty-five, she'd learned to speak with parts of her throat and mouth she never knew she had. What must Li-ping think of her? She couldn't help it. The ticket for two hundred and sixty-three dollars in her hand brought on the awful thoughts that chased their own tails and closed in on the fact that her son was lying in the hospital with a concussion. She wondered if Wei would ever come back to himself fully. It was her fault. She could try to protect him from the world's violence, but could a mother shield her child from the injury and brutality that she herself was capable of bringing forth?

Before they'd left for America, during the hours in which she thought up experiments and poured through all the scientific articles she could find in Chinese, and later, when she dissected the logic of the trickiest English sentences, she would lose herself in her work and only remember that she had a son when something happened to him. Wei had put himself in the position to have an accident; he always had. When he came to her with some part of him scraped up or broken, she realized that he was her precious child and that he could be lost. She'd been angry at all his injuries; still, anger was a kind of attention.

Li-ping's hand rested on her shoulder, its dampness spreading through.

"Why did we leave Wei behind in China?" Ku-ping said. Her throat had closed up in the crying so that it was difficult to utter the simplest sentence.

"It would have been too hard otherwise," her husband said.

"That's what we said then, but would it have been too hard, really, to have our son with us?"

"I mean, it would have been too hard for Wei. Do you remember, Ku-ping, how sick he was all the time? His grandmother attended to him night and day. He couldn't have lived without her."

"Why was he so sickly as a child? Why has he always gotten into accidents?"

"I don't know, Ku-ping." Cars honked and cruised by, one whoosh after another that rattled the car doors. For a moment, her husband's face was lit by the headlights of a semitruck, and in the painful bright light, his eyes looked enormous behind his glasses, like wells, or reservoirs. "He's like you, you know. Like how you drive recklessly over curving mountain roads, like how you decided to come to America at thirty-five, when neither of us spoke a word of English. You're always trying foolish, impossible things."

She sniffed and hiccupped in the dark.

His hand slid down her back, and she was surprised at how solid five fingers could feel.

At home, while Ku-ping fixed a late-night supper out of vegetables from the garden, Li-ping watched an infomercial on television. He'd always watched indiscriminately, taking in soaps and sitcoms alike. In the living room, Li-ping's eyelids drooped as if he were studying some sleepy space inside of him she'd never managed to glimpse in all their years of marriage.

Looking at his profile from the kitchen, she didn't think that he was much different than he was twenty-six years ago when she married him, except that the part in his hair had crept farther to the left to hide the spreading baldness. They'd been through everything together, but when she tried to guess what he was thinking at that very moment while he watched television, she couldn't. She shook her head at the mystery of it all. It had always amazed her that their names shared the same Chinese character, but they had nothing in common as people. Li-ping stuck his thumbs into the dirt and knew when the zucchini and eggplant in his garden would be perfect, while she tried to reduce the truths of the universe to columns of numbers in her lab, and there was still so much she didn't understand. But it was reassuring to know that not every mystery was an evil omen. That people lived around it and through it.

"Li-ping, dinner is ready!" Ku-ping said and watched her husband's one eye snap open, the beginning of a grin on his lips. With one leg each in sleep and wakefulness, dangling over that chasm, he must have forgotten about the events of the day, forgotten where he was in the house and what he was watching, forgotten that his wife was in the next room cutting vegetables, and perhaps even that they were in America. Only Ku-ping's voice reminded him they were about to eat, and for this, he smiled.

Richard Bausch

Weather

Carla headed out to White Elks Mall in the late afternoon, accompanied by her mother, who hadn't been very glad of the necessity of going along, and said so. She went on to say what Carla already knew: that she would brave the August humidity and the discomfort of the hot car if it meant she wouldn't be in the house alone when Carla's husband came back from wherever he had gone that morning. "It's bad enough without me asking for more trouble by being underfoot," she said.

"Nobody thinks you're underfoot, Mother. You didn't have to come."

They were quiet after that. Carla had the Saturday traffic to contend with. Her mother stared out at the gathering thunderclouds above the roofs of the houses they passed. The wind was picking up; it would storm. Carla's mother was the sort of person who liked to sit and watch the scenery while someone else drove. It was a form of concentration with her, almost as solemn as prayer. Now and then she would comment on what she saw, and one could answer or not; it made little difference.

"I hope we get there before it starts to rain," she said now.

Carla was looking in her side-view mirror, slowing the car. "Go on, idiot. Go on by."

"We don't have an umbrella," Mother said.

Lightning cut through the dark mass of clouds to the east.

"I have to watch the road," Carla said, and then blew her horn at someone who had veered too close, changing lanes in front of them. "God, how I hate this town."

For a while there was just the sound of the rocker arms tapping in the engine, and the gusts of wind buffeting the sides of the car. The car was low on oil—another expense, another thing to worry about. It kept losing oil. You had to check it every week or so and it always registered a quart low. Something was leaking somewhere.

"Well, this storm might cool us all off."

"Not supposed to," Carla said, ignoring the other woman's tone. "They're calling for muggy heat."

When they pulled into White Elks, Mother said, "You know, I never liked all the stores in one building like this. I used to so love going into the city to do my shopping. Walking along the street looking in all the windows. And seeing people going about their business, too. There's something—I don't know—reassuring about a busy city street in the middle of the day. Of course we would never go when it was like this."

The rain came now—big, heavy drops.

"Where're we going, anyway?"

"I told you," Carla said. "Record World. I have to buy a tape for Beth's birthday." She parked the car and they hurried across to the closest entrance—the Sears appliance store. Inside, they shook the water from their hair and looked at each other.

"It's going to be all right, honey."

"Mother, please. You keep saying that."

"Well?" Mother said. "It's true. Sometimes you have to say the truth, like a prayer or a chant. It needs saying, honey. It makes a pressure to be spoken."

Carla shook her head.

"I won't utter another syllable," said Mother.

At the display-crowded doorway of the record store, a man wearing a blue blazer over a white T-shirt and jeans paused to let the two of them enter before him.

"Thank you," Mother said, smiling. "Such a considerate young man."

But then a clap of thunder startled them all, and they paused, watching the high-domed skylight above them flash with lightning. The tinted glass was streaked with water, and the wind swept the rain across the surface in sheets. It looked as though something was trying to break through the window and get at the dry, lighted, open space below. Other shoppers stopped and looked up. Everybody was wearing the bright colors and sparse clothing of summer—shorts and T-shirts, sleeveless blouses and tank tops, even a bathing suit or two—and the severity of the storm made them seem oddly exposed, oddly vulnerable, as though they could not possibly have come from the outdoors, where the elements raged and the sunlight had died out of the sky. One very heavy woman in a red jumpsuit with a pattern of tiny white sea horses across the waistband said, "Looks like it's going to be a twister," to no one in particular, then strolled on by. This was not an area of Virginia that had ever been known to have a tornado.

"What would a twister do to a place like this, I wonder," Mother said.

"It's just a thunderstorm."

But the wind seemed to gather sudden force, and something banged at the roof in the vicinity of the window.

"Lord," Mother said. "It's violent, whatever it is."

They remained where they were, watching the skylight. Carla lighted a cigarette.

"Excuse me," the man in the blue blazer said. "Could you please let me pass."

She looked at him. Large, round eyes the color of water under beams of sun, dark black hair, and bad skin. A soft, downturning mouth. Perhaps thirty or so. There was unhappiness in the face; she had seen it.

"Can I pass, please," he said impatiently.

"You're in his way," Mother said. They both laughed, moving aside. "We got interested in the storm."

"Maybe you'd both like to have a seat and watch to your hearts' content," the man said. "After all, this only happens to be a doorway."

"All you have to do is say what you want," said Carla.

He went on into the store.

"And a good day to you, too."

"I swear," Mother said. "The rudeness of some people."

They moved to the bench across the way and sat down. The bench was flanked by two fat white columns, each with a small metal ashtray attached to it. Carla smoked her cigarette and stared at the people walking by. Her mother fussed with the small strap of her purse, and then looked through the purse for a napkin, with which she gingerly wiped some rainwater from the side of her face. The water had smeared her makeup, and she attended to that. Above them, the storm went on, and briefly the lights flickered. A leak was coming from somewhere, and water ran in a thin, slow stream down the opposite wall. Carla smoked the cigarette automatically.

"You know, I've always had this perverse wish to actually see a tornado," said Mother.

"I saw one when Daryl and I lived in Illinois—just before Beth was born. No thank you." Carla took a last drag on the cigarette, placed it in the metal ashtray attached to the column, and clicked the mouth shut. Then she opened the mouth and clicked it shut again.

"You're brooding, aren't you?" Mother said.

"I'm not brooding," Carla said. She took another cigarette out of the pack in her purse and lighted it.

"Well, I didn't come with you to watch you smoke."

"We've established why you came with me, Mother."

"I don't see why I have to watch you smoke."

"I didn't ask you to watch me smoke. Leave me alone, will you?"

"I won't say another word."

"And don't get your feelings hurt, either."

"You're the boss. God knows it's none of my business. I'm only a spectator here."

"Oh, please."

They were quiet. Somewhere behind them, a baby fussed. "What were you thinking about?" Mother said. "You were thinking about this morning, right?"

"I was thinking about how unreal everything is."

"You don't mean the storm, though, do you."

"No, Mother—I don't mean the storm."

"Well, but we need the storm. The rain, I mean. I mean I'm glad it's storming."

"I'm not surprised, since a minute ago you were wishing it was a tornado."

"I was doing no such thing. I was merely expressing an element of my personality. A—a curiousness, that's all. And, anyway, that's not what I'm talking about. Let me finish. You never let me finish, Carla. You're always jumping the gun, and you've always done that. You did it to Daryl this morning—went right ahead and finished his sentences for him."

Carla shook her head. "I can't help it if I know what he's going to say before he says it."

They were quiet again. Mother stirred restlessly in her seat and watched the trickle of water run down the wall opposite where they sat. Finally, she leaned toward the younger woman and murmured, "I was going to say it's just weather. This morning, you know. You're both just going through a little spell of bad weather. Daryl's still got some growing up to do, God knows. But all of them do. I never met a man who couldn't use a little growing up. And Daryl's a perfect example of that."

"I think I've figured out how you feel about him, Mother."

"Well, no—I admit sometimes I think you'd be better off if he *did* move out. I promised I wouldn't interfere, though."

"You're not interfering," Carla said in the voice of someone who felt interfered with.

"I *will* say I don't like the way he talks to you."

"Oh, please—let's change the subject."

"Well, I for one am happy to change the subject. You think I'm enjoying talking about it? You think I enjoy seeing you and that boy say those things to each other?"

"Oh, for God's sake. He's not a boy, Mother. He's your son-in-law, and you're stuck with him." Carla blew smoke. "At least for the time being."

"Don't talk like that. And I was just using a figure of speech."

"It happens to make him very mad."

"Well, he's not here right now."

She smoked the cigarette, watching the people walk by. A woman came past pushing a double stroller with twins in it.

"Look," said Mother. "How sweet."

"I see them." Carla had only glanced at them.

"You're so . . . hard-edged sometimes, Carla. You never used to be that way, no matter how unhappy things made you."

"What? I looked. What did you want me to do?"

"I swear, I just don't understand anything anymore."

After a pause, Mother said, "I remember when you were that small. Your father liked to put you on his chest and let you nap there. Seems like weeks—just a matter of days ago."

Carla took a long drag of the cigarette, blew smoke, and watched it. She had heard it said somewhere that blind persons do not generally like cigarettes as much as sighted people, for not being able to watch the smoke.

"But men were more respectful somehow, in our day."

"Look, please—"

"I'll shut up."

"I'm sure it'll be all made up before the day's over."

"Oh, I know—you'll give in, and he'll say he forgives you. Like every other time."

"We'll forgive each other."

"I'm not uttering another word," Mother said. "I know I cause tension by talking. It's no secret he hates me—"

"He doesn't hate you. You drive him crazy—"

"I drive him crazy? He sits in the living room with that guitar of his plunking around, even when the television is on—never finishing—have you ever heard him play a whole song all the way through? It would be one thing if he could play notes. But that constant strumming—"

"He's trying to learn. That's all. It's a project."

"Well, it drives me right up the wall."

A pair of skinny boys came running from one end of the open space, one chasing the other and trying to keep up. Behind them a woman hummed along, carrying a handful of small flags.

"Do I drive *you* crazy?" Mother wanted to know.

"All the time," Carla said. "Of course."

"I'm serious."

"Well, don't be. Let's not be serious, okay?"

"You're the one that's been off in another world all afternoon. I don't blame you, of course."

"Mother," Carla said.

"I'm not going to get into it. I'm not going to make another sound."

"Things are hard for him right now, that's all. He's not used to being home all day—"

"If you ask me, he could've had that job at the shoe store."

"He's not a shoe salesman. He's an engineer. He's trained for something. That was what they all said when we were growing up, wasn't it? Train for something? Wasn't that what they said? Plan for the future and get an education so you'd be ready? Well, what if the future isn't anything like what you planned for, Mother?"

"Well—but listen—it's like I said, honey. You're both in a stormy period, and you just have to sit it out, that's all. But the day your father ever called me stupid—I'd have shown him the door, let me tell you. I'd have slapped his face."

"Daryl didn't call me stupid. He said that something I said was the stupidest thing he ever heard. And what I said *was* stupid."

"Oh, listen to you."

"It was. I said the money he was spending on gas driving back and forth to coach little league was going to cost Beth her college education."

"That's a valid point, if you ask me."

"Oh, come on. I was mad and I said anything. I just wanted to hit at him."

"Well, it's not the stupidest thing he ever heard. I'm certain that over the last month I've said three or four hundred things he thinks are more stupid."

Carla smiled.

"And he still shouldn't talk that way."

"We were having an argument, Mother."

"All right—just like I told you. A little storm. It shouldn't ruin your whole day."

Carla looked down, took the last drag of her cigarette.

"You just have to set the boundaries a little. I mean your father never—"

"I'm going into the record store, Mother."

"I know. I came with you, didn't I? You ought to get something for yourself. I hope you spend your own money on yourself for once. Get whatever Beth wants for her birthday and then get something for yourself."

"Beth wants a rap record, and I can't remember the name of it."

"Oh, God," said Mother. "I don't like that stuff. I don't even like people who *do* like it."

"Beth likes it."

"Beth's thirteen. What does she know?"

"She knows what she wants for her birthday." Carla sighed. "I know what I have to get and how much it's going to cost and how much I'll hate having it blaring in the house all day, too. I just don't remember the name of it."

"Maybe it'll come to you," said Mother.

"It'll have to."

"Of course, you could forget it, couldn't you?"

"It's the only thing she asked for."

"Well, what if the only thing she asked for was a trip to Rome, or—or a big truckload of drugs or something?"

Carla looked at her.

"Well?"

"The two go together so naturally, Mother. I always think of truckloads of drugs when I think of Rome."

"You know what I mean."

"Did you ever do that to me?" Carla asked. "Lie to me that way?"

"Of course not. I wouldn't dream of such a thing."

"How can you suggest that I do it to Beth?"

"It was an idea—it had to do with self-preservation. If she hadn't been playing her music so loud this morning, Daryl and you might not've got into it."

Carla looked at her.

"You have my solemn vow."

"Anyway," Carla said. "You can't put this morning off on Beth."

Mother made a gesture, like turning a key in a lock, at her lips.

"The fact is, we don't need any excuses to have a fight, these days."

"Now don't get down on yourself, honey. You've had enough to deal with. I should never have moved in. I try to mind my own business—"

"You're fine. This has nothing to do with you. It was going on before you moved in. It's been going on a long time."

"Honey, it's nothing you can't solve. The two of you."

"Unreal," Carla said, bringing a handkerchief out of her purse. "It seems everything I do makes him mad."

"We're all getting on each other's nerves," said Mother.

"Let me just have a minute, here." Carla turned slightly, facing the column, wiping her eyes with the handkerchief.

"Don't you worry, sweetie."

"We just have to get on the other side of it," Carla said.

"That's right. Daryl just has to settle down and see how lucky he is. I won't say anything else about it. It's not my place to say anything."

"Mother, will you please stop that? You can say anything you want. I give you my permission."

"I don't have another thing to add."

"Let's just do what we came to do," Carla said. "I don't want to think about anything else right now."

"No, and you shouldn't have to, and you live in a house where you have to think of absolutely everything."

"That isn't true. It's not just Daryl, Mother."

"All right," Mother said. "I'm sorry. I should keep my mouth shut."

Carla hesitated, looked around herself. She ran one hand through her hair, and sighed again. "Sometimes I—I think—we were going to have a big family. We both wanted a lot of children, you know, and maybe it's because I couldn't—God, never mind."

"Oh, no—now that's not it at all. You're imagining that. He's been out of work and that always makes tension. I mean, Daryl's got a lot of things wrong with him, but he'd never blame you for something you can't help."

"But you read about tension over one thing making other tensions worse."

"That doesn't have anything to do with you," Mother said.

"When we had Beth, it—nothing about that pregnancy—you know, it was full-term. Everything went so well."

"Carla, you don't really think he'd hold anything against you."

"I hope not. But Mother, he was so crestfallen the last time."

"Well, and so were you."

"The thing is, we always pulled together before—when there was any trouble at all. We'd cling to each other. You remember when he was just out of college and there wasn't any work and he was doing all those part-time jobs—we were so happy then. Beth was small. We didn't have anything and we didn't want anything, really."

"Well, you're older now. And you've got your mother living with you."

"No, that's what you don't understand. I told you—this was going on before you moved in. That's the truth. In fact, it got better for a little while, those first days after you moved in. It was like—it seemed that having you with us brought something of the old times back, you know?"

"Don't divide it up like that, honey. It's still your time together. There's no old times or new times. That isn't how you should think about it. It's the two of you. And this is weather. Weather comes and changes and you keep on. That's all."

Carla put the handkerchief back into her purse. "Do I look like I've been crying?"

"You look like the wrath of God."

They laughed nervously, not quite returning each other's gaze. The crowd was moving around them, and though the thunder and lightning had mostly ceased, the rain still beat against the skylight.

"Really, honey," Mother said. "Your father and I had these bad spells, too."

"Well," said Carla, "on with the show."

"That's the spirit."

They walked into the store. The man in the blue blazer was standing by a rack of compact discs that were being sold at a clearance price. He'd already chosen several, and had them tucked under his arm. He was rifling through the discs, apparently looking for something specific, that he would recognize on sight; he wasn't pausing long enough to read the titles. Concentrating, he looked almost angry; the skin around his eyes was white. He glanced at the two women as they edged past him, and Mother said, "Excuse us," rather pointedly. He did not answer, but went back to thumbing through the discs.

The store was very crowded, and there wasn't much room to move around. Carla and her mother made their way along the aisle to the audiotape section, where Carla recognized the tape she had come for. It was in a big display on the wall, with a life-size poster of the artist.

"Looks like a mugger, if you ask me," Mother said. She picked up something for herself—an anthology of songs from the sixties. "The Beatles actually wore ties at one point, you know." Somewhere speakers were pounding with percussion, the drone of a toneless, shrill male voice.

"I think that's what I'm about to buy," said Carla. "God help me."

There were two lines waiting at the counter, and the two women stood side by side, each in her own line. The man in the blazer stepped in behind Mother. He had several discs in his hands, and he began reading one of the labels. Carla glanced at him, so dour, and she thought of Daryl, off somewhere angry with her, unhappy—

standing under the gaze of someone else, who would see it in his face. When the man looked up, she sent a smile in his direction, but he was staring at the two girls behind the counter, both of whom were dressed in the bizarre getup of rock stars. The girls chattered back and forth, being witty and funny with each other in that attitude store clerks sometimes have when people are lined up waiting: as though circumstances had provided them with an audience, and as though the audience were entertained by their talk. The clerks took a long time with each purchase, running a scanner over the coded patch on the tapes and discs, and then punching numbers into the computer terminals. The percussion thrummed in the walls, and the lines moved slowly. When Mother's turn came, she reached for Carla. "Here, honey—step in here."

Carla did so.

"Wait a minute," the man said. "You can't do that."

"Do what?" Mother said. "She's waiting with me."

"She was in the other line."

"We were waiting together."

"You were in separate lines." The man addressed the taller of the two girls behind the counter. "They were in separate lines."

"I don't know," the girl said. Her hair was an unnatural shade of orange. She held her hands up as if in surrender, and bracelets clattered on her wrist. Then she moved to take Carla's tape and run the scanner over it.

"Oh, well—all right," the man said. "Let stupidity and selfishness win out."

Mother faced him. "What did you say? Did you call my daughter a name?"

"You heard everything I said," the man told her.

"Yes, I did," Mother said, and swung at his face. He backpedaled, but took the blow above the eye, so that he almost lost his balance. When he had righted himself, he stood straight, wide-eyed, clearly unable to believe what had just happened to him.

"Lady," the man said. "You—"

And Mother struck again, this time swinging her purse so that it hit the man on the crown of the head as he ducked, putting his arms up to ward off the next blow. His discs fell to the floor at his feet.

"Mother—" Carla began, not quite hearing herself. "What in the world—"

"You don't call my daughter names and get away with it," Mother said to the man.

He had straightened again, and assumed the stance of someone in a fight, his fists up to protect his face, chin tucked into his left shoulder.

"You think you can threaten me," Mother said, and poked at his face with her free hand. He blocked this, and stepped back, and she swung the purse again, striking him this time on the forearm.

"Oh, God—please," said Carla, barely breathing the words.

There was a general commotion in the crowd. Someone laughed.

"This isn't right," Carla said. "Let's stop this—"

"Well, look at him. Big tough man—going to hit a woman, big tough guy?"

"I want the police," the man said to the girl with the orange hair. "I absolutely demand to see a policeman. I've been assaulted and I intend to press charges."

"Oh, look," Carla said, "can you just forget about it? Here." She bent down to pick up the discs he had dropped.

"Don't you dare," Mother said.

Carla looked at her.

"All right, I'll shut up. But don't you dare give him those discs."

Carla ignored her.

"I want to see a policeman."

"Here," Carla said, offering the discs.

"If he says another thing—"

The man looked past them. "Officer, I've been assaulted. And there are all these witnesses."

A security guard stepped out of the crowd. He was thin, green-eyed, blond, with boyish skin. Perhaps he had to shave once a week. But clearly he took great care with all aspects of his appearance: his light-blue uniform was creased exactly, the shirt starched and pressed. His shoes shone like twin black mirrors. He brought a writing pad out of his pocket, and a ballpoint pen, the end of which he clicked with his thumb. "Okay, what happened here?"

"He called my daughter a name," said Mother. "I won't have people calling my daughter names."

"I'm pressing charges," said the man.

The security guard addressed him. "Would you just say what happened?"

But everyone began to speak at once. The girl with the orange hair put her hands up again in surrender, and again the bracelets clattered. "None of my business," she said. "I don't believe in violence." She spoke in an almost metaphysical tone, the tone of someone denying a belief in the existence of a thing like violence. Carla was trying to get the officer's attention, and then he was drawing her mother and the man out of the store, into the open area of shops, under the skylight. She followed. Mother and the man protested all the way, accusing each other.

"I've got a welt," the man said. "Right here." He pointed to his left eyebrow.

"I don't see it," said the officer.

"Do you have jurisdiction here?"

"I have that, yes. I have the authority."

"I've been attacked. And I want to file a complaint."

"This man verbally assaulted my daughter."

"All right, all right," said the security guard. "Calm down. We're not going to get anywhere like this. I'll listen to you one at a time."

"This man verbally assaulted my daughter. And I slapped him."

"You didn't slap me. You hit me with your fist, and then you assaulted me with your purse."

"I didn't hit you with my fist. If I'd hit you with my fist, that would be an assault."

"Both of you be quiet for a minute." He stood there writing in the pad. "Let me have your names."

Both Mother and the man spoke at once.

"Wait a minute," the officer said. "For God's sake. One at a time."

"Please," said Carla. "Couldn't we just forget this?"

"I don't want to forget it," said the man. "I was attacked. A person ought to be able to walk into a store without being attacked."

"My sentiments exactly," said Mother. "You started it. You attacked my daughter verbally."

"Both of you be quiet or I'm going to cite you," the security guard said.

They stood there.

"What's your name, sir?"

"Todd Lemke." The officer wrote it down on his pad. "Like it sounds?"

"One *e*."

"All right. You start."

"I was waiting in line, and this woman—" Lemke indicated Carla.

"You be careful how you say that," said Mother.

"Now, ma'am—" the security guard said.

"I won't let people talk about my daughter that way, young man. And I don't care what you or anybody else says about it." Her voice had reached a pitch Carla had never heard before.

"Please, ma'am."

"I won't say another word. But he better watch his tone. That's all I have to say."

"Mother, if you don't shut up," Carla said. There were tears in her voice.

"What did I say? I just indicated that I wouldn't tolerate abuse. This man abused you, didn't you hear it?"

"Ma'am, I'm afraid I'm going to have to insist."

"Pitiful," Lemke was saying, shaking his head. "Just pitiful."

"Who's pitiful?" Carla said. She moved toward him. She could feel her heart beating in her face and neck. "Who's pitiful?"

The security guard stood between them. "Now look—"

"You watch who you call names," Carla said, and something slipped inside her. The next moment anything might happen.

"I rest my case," Lemke was saying.

"There isn't any case," Carla said. "You don't have any case. Nobody's pitiful."

"They're making my case for me, officer."

"—such disrespect—" Mother was saying.

"You're wrong about everything," Carla said. "Pity doesn't enter into it."

"Everybody shut up," the security guard said. "I swear I'm going to run you all in for disturbing the peace."

"Do I have to say anything else?" Lemke said to him. "It's like I said. They make my case for me—ignorant, lowlife—"

"I'm going to hit him again," said Mother. "You're the one who's ignorant."

"See? She admits she hit me."

"I'm going to hit you myself in a minute," the security guard said. "Now shut up."

The man gave him an astonished look.

"Everybody be quiet." He held his hands out and made a slow, up-and-down motion with each word, like a conductor in front of an orchestra. "Let's—all—of—us—just—calm—down." He turned to Mother. "You and your daughter please wait here. I'll come back to you."

"Yes, sir."

"We'll be here," Carla said.

"Now," he said to Lemke, "if you'll just step over here with me, I'll listen to what you have to say."

"You're biased against me," Lemke said.

"I'm what?"

"You heard me. You threatened to hit me."

"For God's sake."

"No. I'm not going to get a fair deal here, I can sense it."

"We're not in a courtroom, sir. This is not a courtroom."

"I know what kind of report you'll file."

"Look, I'm sure if we all give each other the benefit of the doubt a little—"

"This woman assaulted me," Lemke said. "I know my rights."

"Okay," the security guard said. "Why don't you tell me what you want me to do. I mean really—what it is that you think I should do here?"

Lemke stared into his face.

"I think he wants you to shoot me," Mother said.

"Mother, will you please stop it. Please."

"Her own daughter can't control her," Lemke said. "You shouldn't take her out of the house."

"I'm pregnant," Carla said abruptly, and began to cry. The tears came streaming down her cheeks. It was a lie; she had said it simply to cut through everything.

Her mother had taken a step back. "Oh, honey—"

And Carla went on talking, only now she was telling the truth: "I've lost the last four. Do you understand, sir? I've miscarried four times and I need someone with me. Surely, even you can understand that."

Lemke stared at her, and something changed in his face. His whole body seemed to falter slightly, as though he had been supporting some invisible weight, and had now let down under it. But only a little. "Look, hey—" he stammered. "Listen—"

"Why don't you all make friends," said the security guard. "No harm done, really. Right?"

"Right," Mother said. "My daughter had a little—a tiff with her husband this morning, and he said some things. Maybe I overreacted. I overreacted. I'm really sorry, sir."

Lemke was staring at Carla.

"I don't know my own strength sometimes," Mother was saying. "I'm always putting my foot in it."

"A misunderstanding," the security guard said.

Lemke rubbed the side of his face, looking at Carla, who was wiping her eyes with the back of one hand.

"Am I needed here anymore?" the security guard said.

"No," said Lemke, "I guess not."

"There," said Mother. "Now, could anything have worked out better?"

"I have to tell you," Lemke said to Carla, and it seemed to her that his voice shook. "We lost our first last month. My wife was seven months pregnant. She's had a hard time of it since."

"We're sorry that happened to you," Mother said.

"Mother," said Carla, sniffling. "Please."

"I hope things work out for you," Lemke said to her.

"Do you have other children?" Carla asked.

He nodded. "A girl."

"Us, too."

"How old?"

"Thirteen."

"Seven," Lemke said. "Pretty age."

"Yes."

"They're all lovely ages," Mother said.

"Thank you for understanding," Carla said to him.

"No," he said. "It's—I'm sorry for everything." Then he moved off. In a few seconds, he was lost in the crowd.

"I guess he didn't want his discs, after all," Mother said. Then: "Poor man. Isn't it amazing that you'd find out in an argument that you have something like that in common—"

"What're the chances," Carla said, almost to herself. Then she turned to Mother. "Do you think I could've sensed it somehow, or heard it in his voice?"

Mother smiled out of one side of her mouth. "I think it's a coincidence."

"I don't know," Carla said. "I feel like I knew."

"That's how I think I felt about you being pregnant. I just had this feeling."

"I'm not pregnant," Carla told her.

Mother frowned, staring.

"I couldn't stand the arguing anymore, and I just said it."

"Oh, my."

"Poor Daryl," Carla said, after a pause. "Up against me all by himself."

"Stop that," said Mother.

"Up against us."

"I won't listen to you being contrite."

Carla started back into the store, and when her mother started to follow her, she stopped. "I'll buy yours for you," she said. "Let me get in line."

"You know, I can't believe I actually hit that boy." Mother held out one hand, palm down, gazing at it. "Look at me—I'm shaking all over. I'm trembling all over. I've never done anything like that in my life, not ever. Not even close. I mean, I've never even yelled at anyone in public, have I? I mean, think of it. *Me,* in a public brawl. My God. This morning must've set me up or something. I mean, set the tone, you know. Got me primed. I'd never have expected this of me, would you?"

"I don't think anyone expected it," Carla said.

They watched the woman with the twin babies come back by them.

"And I feel sorry for him, now," Mother said. "I almost wish I hadn't hit him. I mean, if I'd known, you know—I could've tried to give him the benefit of the doubt, like the officer said."

Carla said nothing. She had stopped crying. Her mascara was running down her cheeks. Her mother took out a handkerchief, wet it with her tongue, and touched the smeared places.

"Everybody has their own troubles, I guess."

Carla went to the counter, where people moved back to let her buy the tapes. It took only a moment.

Mother stood in the entrance of the store, looking pale and frightened.

"Come on, Sugar Ray," Carla said to her.

"You're mad at me," Mother said, and seemed about to cry herself.

"I'm not mad," Carla said.

"I'm so sorry—I can't imagine what got into me—can't imagine. But, honey, I hear him talk to you that way. It hurts to hear him say those things to you and I know I shouldn't interfere—"

"It's all right," Carla told her. "Really. I understand."

Outside, they waited in the lee of the building for the rain to let up. The air had grown much cooler; there was a breeze blowing out of the north. The treeline on the other side of the parking lot moved, and showed lighter green.

"My God," Carla said. "Isn't it—doesn't it say something about me that I would use the one gravest sadness in Daryl's life with me—the one thing he's always been most sorry about—that I would use that to get through an altercation at the fucking mall?"

"Stop it," Mother said.

"Well, really. And I didn't even have to think about it. I was crying, and I saw the look on his face, and I just said it. It came out so naturally. And imagine—me lying that I'm pregnant again. Imagine Daryl's reaction to that."

"You're human—what do you want from yourself?"

Carla seemed not to have heard this. "I wish I *was* pregnant," she said. "I feel awful, and I really wish I was."

"That wouldn't change anything, would it?"

"It would change how I feel right now."

"I meant with Daryl."

Carla looked at her. "No. You're right," she said. "That wouldn't change anything with Daryl. Not these days."

"Now, honey," Mother said, touching her nose with the handkerchief.

But then Carla stepped out of the protection of the building and was walking away through the rain.

"Hey," Mother said. "Wait for me."

The younger woman turned. "I'm going to bring the car up. Stay there."

"Well, let a person know what you're going to do, for God's sake."

"Wait there," Carla said over her shoulder.

The rain was lessening now. She got into the car and sat thinking about her mother in the moment of striking the man with her purse. She saw the man's startled face in her mind's eye and, to her surprise, she laughed, once, harshly, like a sob. Then she was crying again, thinking of her husband, who would not come home today until he had to. Across the lot, her mother waited, a blur of colors, a shape in the raining distance. Mother put the handkerchief to her face again, and then seemed to falter. Carla started the car and backed out of the space, aware that the other woman could see her now, and trying to master herself, wanting to put the best face on, wanting not to hurt any more feelings and to find some way for everyone to get along, to bear the disappointments and the irritations; and as she pulled toward the small, waiting figure under the wide stone canopy, she caught herself thinking, with a wave of exhaustion, as though it were a prospect she would never have enough energy or strength for, no matter how hard or long she strove to gain it, of what was constantly required—what must be repeated and done and given and listened to and allowed—in all the kinds of love there are.

Her mother stepped to the curb and opened the door. "What were you doing?" she said, struggling into the front seat. "I thought you were getting ready to leave me here."

"No," Carla said. "Never that." Her voice went away.

Her mother shuffled a lot on the seat, getting settled, then pulled the door shut. The rain was picking up again, though it wasn't wind-driven now.

"Can't say I'd blame you if you left me behind," Mother said. "After all, I'm clearly a thug."

They were silent for a time, sitting there in the idling car with the rain pouring down. And then they began to laugh. It was low, almost tentative, as if they were both uneasy about letting go entirely. The traffic paused and moved by them, and shoppers hurried past.

"I really can't believe I did such an awful thing," Mother said.

"I won't listen to you being contrite," Carla said, and smiled.

"All right, sweetie. You scored your point."

"I wasn't trying to score points," Carla told her. "I was setting the boundaries for today." Then she put the car in gear and headed them through the rain, toward home.

Michael Frank

In the Bed of Forgetting

I

In my grandmother's house the spare bed was the bed of forgetting. At least this is how I thought of it. Up until the winter of 1968, it belonged to Grandma's cousin Ellen, a silent, quaking old woman who spent all day crocheting, morning to night. She crocheted covers to pad wooden coat hangers, long fringed scarves, and slippers to keep us children from catching cold. She made the afghan that rose and fell over my bony legs as I lay in the bed, tracing its zigzags of burgundy, beige, and white with my fingers, unable to sleep.

Cousin Ellen joined Grandma Dora's household in the early sixties. She spent several peaceful years with Dora until gradually she began to mistake sugar for salt when she was replenishing the shaker and neglected to fill the Chinese vase with water. She set out for walks and disappeared for hours, so that Dora would have to climb behind the wheel of her navy blue Olds and drive up and down the neighborhood blocks one by one, frantically shining a flashlight out the window as she became her own private search party in the Los Angeles dusk. One day, Ellen walked through the apartment apparently unaware that she was holding her sewing scissors blade-end out and bumping into walls and chairs and the screen door, which was still torn where she sliced it, and eventually into Dora herself, who swatted the scissors out of Ellen's hand and held her stiff, unknowing body, seeing, realizing finally, that she was going to have to give up "the one truly unblemished soul" she had ever known. Ellen was moved into The Home, a long sticky ride from the apartment that took you so deep into the San Fernando Valley that people still kept animals on their land, roosters and cows and goats that ate the weeds that grew between the orange trees. She was visited every second Sunday, brought a tin of butter cookies and half a dozen skeins of new yarn, because while she forgot her life, while she forgot my grandmother and my aunt and her journalist son whose postcards were arranged in a halo around the mirror in her new quarters, Ellen still remembered how to crochet, and an arc of colorful hangers burgeoned in everyone's closets, a continuous woolen rainbow that spanned across our extended family. Pretty though it was, this rainbow could not disguise the fact that, in my grandmother's world, the punishment for forgetting was exile.

In the bed of forgetting, I was especially alert. I was alert to the nubs of yarn that rose out of the afghan, to the pattern of pink and white wallpaper that doubled itself when you stared at it too long, to the busts of Dora's beloved writers, Madame de Sévigné and Madame de Beausergent, that stood on paired pedestals in the corners of the room. I was alert to the pictures on the wall, dark spotted views of a river, an ocean, and a forest. Their subjects were the turbulent Columbia, a lighthouse standing sentinel over the Pacific, and a thick cluster of evergreens titled *The Washington Territory.* I was alert to Grandma Dora's bed next to mine but different from mine, a bed whose head and foot raised and lowered at the touch of a button and whose sides were bordered by rails that looked like fences you might see on a ranch, except that they were hollow and made of aluminum. Swung over this bed was a table that moved on wheels and was piled with stacks of books, tubes of ointment and bottles of pills, a pitcher of water and a drinking glass, a pen and two blunt pencils, and a box of Kleenex in a filigreed brass container, all of which was familiar to me, although there was something that I did not know and was looking at now for the first time. It was a book bound in olive green cloth, its corners trimmed in brown leather but worn, nibbled down to the cardboard underneath, its pages mostly used up and much swollen with writing. Embossed in black on its front cover was a single word that I read not as a noun but as a verb, a command. It said, *Record*.

And Grandma Dora was obeying. Just as I had never seen the book before, I had never before seen the sleeves of my grandmother's satin nightgown pushed back to expose the loose skin above her elbow, white and webbed with faint blue veins and creased in places like a fan, and shivering like whipped cream as she drew her pen across the ruled pages, leaving row upon row of uniformly slanted words, wet words that lightened as they dried, left to right, sentence after sentence. Several strands of my grandmother's silver hair had come loose from her bun, and they floated toward her shoulders, errant stems reaching out of a compact bouquet. Her chin was tucked deep into the cushiony flesh of her neck, and her mouth was folded down at each corner, but otherwise my grandmother's face revealed nothing, only concentration, all other expressions having turned within.

She came to the end. Tapping her pen three times after the last word of the last sentence, she closed the book, pushed aside the over-bed table, and glanced in my direction. Quickly I closed my eyes and simulated the slow, even breath of sleep, but through a grid of lashes I continued to watch as my grandmother lowered the guardrail on the right side of the bed, climbed out, and opened the door to her closet. She reached down a battered dress box, inserted the book, and pushed the box back again before returning to bed. Then she pulled down her sleeves and turned off the light.

Her eyes, though, stayed open, stayed level with the prints that hung over her dresser and looked even murkier, smokier now in the dark. She lingered over each one, cocking her head as she moved across the row. When she reached the last print, she continued to rotate her head until she faced me. "I saw you, Matthew," she said. "I saw you watching me write."

My heart began to bang around in my chest. I squeezed my eyes closed, but this only made the lids flutter, then twitch. "It's all right," she added.

I looked at her. "That was my journal," she said. "I've been keeping it since the late twenties, which means, golly, over forty years. I intend for you to read it one day."

"Me?" I whispered.

"You. Your brothers and your cousins. All my grandchildren. It's not quite as important for my children, because they've lived through so many of these events with me, and they won't forget me the way you will. But I'd like each of them to read it alone, and quietly. There are still parts of my life that they don't know about."

"Do you mean Annie Rozzie too?" Annie Rozzie was my nickname for my father's sister, my aunt—thus auntie, thus "Annie"—Rosalind. She and my grandmother were uncommonly close. My aunt maintained that they weren't like most mothers and daughters; they were "beyond that"—they were best friends.

"Rozzie knows, but she'll want the journal for other reasons. She'll want to hear me talking again." This she said more to herself, it seemed, than to me.

"What do you put in it?"

"Oh, all kinds of things. I began it in Portland, as an account book. Your grandfather and I had money once, and then, all of a sudden, we were very poor, and I had to manage the household on almost nothing. This was in 1929, after the Crash, when many people lost fortunes. I kept track of every penny I spent, every head of lettuce and streetcar ride. In October of 1930 I started adding words to the figures. 'This has been the worst year of my life'—that was the first sentence I ever wrote. It wasn't the only period I would see fit to describe with that phrase," she added, emitting a small, faraway laugh, "although it felt like it at the time. My world had crumbled, you see, and my life, well, my life felt . . . better once I wrote it down."

"Am I in it?"

She nodded. "I described the day you were born. That very happy day."

"And Dad?"

"Walt too, yes. Not the day he was born, because that was before I began keeping the journal, but his childhood and Rozzie's too, Rozzie's too." Grandma was quiet for a moment. She lifted her right arm and rested it on the pillow above her head, a position Annie Rozzie often said she'd seen me assume. I knew that, now and then, I would awaken in the middle of the night with a stiff right arm that I would have to bring down from over my head and flex several times to wake up again. "Your aunt was rather like you when she was young. She was shy. She preferred the company of adults. I used to have to coax her to attend parties when she was a girl. I taught her how to dance myself. I rolled up the rug in our living room in Portland and turned on the Victrola. I led and she followed. I wrote about it afterward. I remember thinking it would help draw Rozzie out, but she said, 'Mamma, I can dance with you, why do I need to dance with anybody else?'"

Again Dora fell quiet. Again her eyes lingered over the river and the ocean and the forest. Then, groping for the controls, she elevated the head of her bed, lowered the guardrails, and swung herself off the mattress. Barefoot, she crossed the room and knelt in front of the bureau. Her bones cracked up and down her spine as she bent down, making a sound like the one our house made when it settled in the night. Her nightgown spread out around her, pooling in a perfect white circle, a small frozen pond. She opened the deepest drawer, the bottom drawer, and pushed aside sweaters in plastic envelopes, felt hats with veils sewn to their brims, and linen blouses so long unworn that they had turned brown along the folds. Finally she withdrew a green cloth ledger that was almost an exact duplicate of the one she had been writing in, only fresh—not new, since it was as old as the hats and blouses it kept company with, but unused. She hoisted herself erect, closed the drawer with her foot, and approached my bed. "I want you to have this, Matthew," she said, placing the journal on my pillow. "I want you to begin recording your life the way I have recorded mine. You don't have to write every day or even every month if you don't want to, but when you are moved, when you are troubled, when you are confused or struck or illuminated by something, take a few minutes to describe it. Time is very slippery. The mind is very slippery. It has a rhythm of its own, and it conceals the past in unexpected ways. One day, you will flip back through these pages and be grateful to find pieces of your experience captured on them. You will return to the moment I gave you this book and told you to write in it, and you will thank me. Thank me then—not now."

Dora pivoted and walked toward her bed. "What about you, Grandma?" I asked. "What happens when you run out of room in your book?"

"I don't believe that will be a problem, sweetheart."

"But you don't have many pages left."

"Oh, I have enough to last me."

The curtains on the window had blown open, split down the middle in a thin bar that glowed with the cold white light of the moon. Dora reached up to yank the wooden rings closer together, and the moon shined through her nightgown, making it as translucent as tissue paper. I studied her and I studied the window and the place where the moon was now covered up. Something was not right. Only after my grandmother had returned to bed and pulled the sheet up to her neck and closed her eyes did I realize that her chest was missing its plush fleshy shelf and was as flat as a man's.

I woke to the music of a kitchen appliance, the swish-scrape-swish of an electric mixer beating batter. My right cheek was numb. I opened my eyes. Instead of an expanse of smooth white pillow, a coarse green field spread before me: in my sleep I had rolled onto the journal, and my cheek had stuck to its textured cloth cover. I peeled my face off the book and ran my fingers over my skin, which was imprinted with hundreds of tiny indentations and, along a ridge just beneath my eye, a line of larger shapes. I got out of bed and went into the bathroom to look in the mirror. There the shapes organized themselves into letters, and I saw that word stamped into my cheek, that *Record*.

I brushed my teeth and splashed water on my face, blending hot and cold in joined palms. Then I sat down to the bowl of cereal my grandmother had set out for me on her dining-room table.

While I ate, Dora hovered over the oven, beaming a flashlight through its tinted-glass door. After a few minutes, she slipped her hand into a pot mitt and removed a shallow pan. Sizzling on the aluminum and glistening with butter, the peaks in their dough a golden hue, were two narrow blueberry strudels. Dora set the pan on the counter to cool just as the screen door behind me swung open.

At home I would have heard the car minutes earlier, but there was heavier traffic near the apartment, and there were clanging pipes and neighbors' footsteps and the general foreignness of my grandmother's environment, so I was forced to identify our visitor from more immediate evidence—the specific pitch of her bracelets jingling on her arm and the sweet prickly whiff of Caswell-Massey's men's aftershave, which was her perfume, and by the hour: it was nine o'clock, and every single day at nine o'clock, or as close to it as possible, my aunt Rosalind arrived at her mother's apartment to perform the immutable morning rituals that had launched both of their days for as long as I had been conscious of the two women and long before.

"Matty!" she said as she came through the door, her eyes sparkling and her shoulder bag sliding into the crook of her arm. "I didn't know you were here. What a nice surprise." She lowered her cheek for me to kiss, and the Caswell-Massey came toward me more strongly. "You spent the night? Mamma must have enjoyed that."

"I did," Dora said, joining us in the dining room.

"Mamma, what are you doing up?"

"Baking strudel."

"But you baked strudel yesterday."

"Well, today I made two more. I thought I'd send some home with Matthew."

Annie Rozzie set her hands on Dora's shoulders and turned her toward the bedroom. "Back to bed, naughty girl. You'll tire yourself out with all this work."

"Your mamma's a *shtarker*. You know that."

"What I know is that Dr. Markoff said you're not supposed to be on your feet."

"Ach." This was part protest and part relief, because Dora was easing herself onto the mattress, which Rozzie had tidied, rolling the blankets back and slapping the pillows into shape in a single fluid gesture.

My aunt pulled the blankets up around my grandmother's chest. "Breakfast or hair?"

"Breakfast," Dora answered. Rozzie nodded and left the room.

My grandmother's head bisected the pillow, which inflated on either side of her, two swollen clouds nesting her colorless, lined face. I sat Indian style on the bed of forgetting and opened the journal Dora had given me. I decided to try out the lesson in perspective I had recently learned in my art class and draw my grandmother's bedroom. I began at the wall with the closets and the door to the hall. This was going to be my background.

Annie Rozzie returned with a tray. *Make beauty whenever possible* was a rule of hers that she consistently obeyed: the tray was covered with a gingham cloth and had a small glass vase with a bright red geranium in one corner and a cup of steaming tea in the other. In the middle was a bowl of wheat germ combined with yogurt and slices of banana, and next to it a slice of rye toast. Rozzie believed that a healthy breakfast supplied a "real zest for living," in the phrase of Adelle Davis, her nutrition advisor, whose *Let's Eat Right to Keep Fit,* much tattered, was among the books stacked on my grandmother's over-bed table.

Dora opened her eyes. "Who would have thought it?" she said foggily.

"Thought what, Mamma?" Rozzie asked as she set the tray onto the table.

"That little Dora Isvansky would have such a daughter as my Rozzie."

"Oh, Mamma," Rozzie said, taking Dora's hand and pressing it. "What makes you say this all of a sudden?"

"Seeing you . . . and thinking, drifting. That's who I was just now, little Dora Isvansky of Spokane, stretched out on her mother's horsehair sofa, holding a book on her chest but not looking at it, looking beyond it, into her future. I spent so many rainy afternoons lying there, years of afternoons imagining the pages beyond the book, but I don't believe I got any of it right. Not one bit."

The liquid in Annie Rozzie's eyes thickened. "Are you tired? Is that why you're talking like this?"

"The *shtarker* is a little tired, I guess."

"You need to eat. You need fuel." Dora dipped her spoon into her bowl. "I've been reading about Colette, Mamma. She had rheumatoid arthritis too. She had to stay in bed *all* the time."

Dora gazed at Rozzie over her wheat germ. "I wonder how she found the energy to write. All I want to do these days is sleep."

Annie Rozzie didn't seem to have an answer. She began rearranging the objects on top of my grandmother's bureau. "How long are you staying, Matty?" she asked.

"Till tonight. Isn't that right, Grandma?"

She nodded and explained that my father was coming by for me around four. Then she pushed the table aside.

"That's all I can manage. I'll have the rest for lunch."

"You will not. I'm making you a proper lunch, tuna sandwiches and fruit salad. They'll be in the fridge."

My aunt proceeded to the second part of her ritual. She disappeared into the bathroom and returned with a shower bench and a hairbrush. She angled her mother so that Dora's back was facing her. Then she sat down on the bench and removed the combs and pins from my grandmother's hair, freeing the long silver locks. I had seen Dora's hair loose before, but I was always surprised by its length and its luxuriance and by the way, particularly when you were sitting at a distance, as I was at that moment, and squinted and imagined a little, it made her look like a young girl, the little Dora Isvansky she had just spoken of, whose appearance I knew from the photograph in the ornate silver frame on her living-room bookshelf. In this picture, Dora was thirteen or so, but her posture or her clothes, or maybe her expression, made her seem older. She pulled her shoulders back and thrust her arms forward. Her dress was made of white eyelet with a black ribbon threaded down the front and a thicker black ribbon cinching her waist. One long yank of hair, so tightly wound it might have just been taken off a spool, inched over her left shoulder; the rest of her head was covered with a large hat, its brim wide and round. Her face was in shadows, but her eyes looked straight out at you, through the shadows and across time. This girl was not at all dreamy. I didn't see her lying on a horsehair sofa—I saw her winning essay contests and running for class office and triumphing as the lead in her school play, all of which I knew Dora had done. "She stood out, your grandmother did," Annie Rozzie liked to say. "She was a star from the beginning."

Rozzie began to brush Dora's hair in slow, tender strokes that started at the crown of her head and finished at the tip of the longest strands, which she patted into place to counter the static that was causing them to dance about like unruly daddy longlegs. Crown-center-tip she brushed, gathering loose strands, following every other stroke with a stroke of her palm. Dora lowered her head and closed her eyes and breathed in a rhythm that matched the brushing, spreading her shoulders and inhaling between strokes, retracting them and exhaling gradually as the bristles parted and straightened and smoothed. When the stripes of differently shaded gray and silver and white were all in line, Rozzie brushed Dora's hair to the right and wound it back toward the center, twisting it into a meticulous bun. She took gray bobby pins from between her teeth and buried them out of sight. Then she inserted the silver combs and once again anchored the familiar conch to the top of my grandmother's head.

"This sleepiness," Dora said, as Rozzie lowered her back onto the pillows. "It reminds me of that other sleepiness, in Portland, after I was married. Only it's different now. It's in my body as well as my mind."

"You've done too much this morning."

"I've baked two strudels. There was a time when I'd prepare half a dinner party in the morning, work all day at the studio, finish the other half when I came home, converse with some intelligence across the table, and read two-thirds of a book before going to sleep. *That* you might call doing too much, though it never felt like it then."

"Mamma, you're older."

"No, I've lost my way. I recognize the feeling. I lost it once before, for a long, long time, and I only found it again the spring I went out to find work and you turned thirteen and seemed suddenly to be my friend as well as my daughter. That's when I woke up. I realized I didn't have to let life happen to me. I can't imagine what will come along to rouse me now."

"It's the arthritis. The pain is debilitating. Dr. Markoff said it would be."

A silence opened up between my aunt and my grandmother. It wasn't a casual or accidental pause, but a still quiet, a deep quiet. At first I thought it might be one of those silences engineered by adults to elude "little pitchers," but soon I understood that it had nothing to do with me, that my aunt and my grandmother weren't particularly aware of me sitting hunched over my drawing. I had completed the closets and the door and had gone on to the dresser, the prints, the windows, the busts of Madame de Sévigné and Madame de Beausergent (which I only roughed in, as they were difficult to reproduce accurately), the over-bed table, Dora's bed, and a piece of my bed in the foreground. Now that Dora was sitting back again I was prepared to begin drawing her in bed, but the silence had broken my concentration. I looked up. My grandmother was studying my aunt expectantly, almost inquisitively, but my aunt was focused on her rings, turning them around so that all the stones faced front.

"Well, Rozzie," my grandmother said finally, "I guess the body works in mysterious ways."

"Yes, Mamma," my aunt said into her lap. "I guess it does."

• • •

Pausing at the screen door, Annie Rozzie told me to take care of Grandma. She had closed Dora's bedroom curtains, turned off her reading light, and insisted that she rest until lunchtime. "I'll look in later this afternoon," she said as she put on her dark glasses, reset her bag high on her shoulder, and walked into her morning. As it was Saturday, she would be making the rounds of the antique shops, most likely in Pasadena, with either Mamie Glantz, her best friend, or her sister-in-law, Aunt Hillary.

And so I was on my own for a few hours. I was tempted by the sunlight in the courtyard beyond the apartment and by the narrow, sloping brick wall, low at one end and high at the other, that tested the dexterity of a boy's feet, but Annie Rozzie's *Look after your grandmother, Matty,* was still reverberating, and I decided I had better stay inside. I went to listen at the bedroom door. My grandmother was breathing regularly; she was asleep. I turned the knob slowly, until I opened a crack between the door and the jamb, a sliver of bedroom but enough to reveal Dora's wan face, highly foreshortened, more chin and nostril than anything else. This was what I tried to draw, to capture, all morning, practicing on a second page in my new book, until the sheet was covered with images of my grandmother at rest.

When Annie Rozzie returned at the end of the day, Dora was sitting up in bed, reading and finishing the last of her fruit salad, and I was stretched out on the bed of forgetting, once again working on my drawing. My aunt bustled in with two bags of groceries that she put away in the kitchen before joining us. She had found each of us a present: a Chinese brush pot for my grandmother, "Eighteenth century but late, I'm sorry to say," that depicted a calligrapher sitting at his desk and writing, and for me a lacquered pencil box. "You shouldn't spoil me," Dora said, but she seemed pleased with her gift, since she put it to use at once, collecting the loose pens and pencils on her over-bed table, the thermometer, and the tubes of salve and tossing them all inside.

She continued to admire the brush pot, spreading out and

adjusting the pens and pencils. "The pickings were good, Rozzie?" she asked.

"And how. It was just like the old days, Mamma," my aunt said, sitting in a chair at the foot of Dora's bed. "I found all kinds of things. I could have antiqued for twelve hours straight if Mamie hadn't conked out on me."

Antiquing was my aunt's lifelong hobby, "The only way," she said, "I know how to relax, really and truly." My aunt was really and truly in need of relaxation because she worked so hard. Annie Rozzie was a screenwriter, and she put in long days at her typewriter or at one of the studios, where she had several scripts in various stages of production. My grandmother used to work at a movie studio herself, MGM, where she had been Louis B. Mayer's story editor. "You've been spending a lot of time antiquing lately," my grandmother observed.

"Why shouldn't I? It's my recreation."

"That's true."

"And my money. I earn half of every dollar that goes into our bank account, sometimes more."

"That's also true. It's just that now and then I wonder whether, in order to sustain your hobby, your way of life, you choose to . . . take work that's beneath your talent, that's all."

My aunt sat back in her chair and crossed her arms. "If you're talking about the last job," she said, "I took it to help pay for the new house."

I had finally succeeded in drawing my grandmother in bed, but there was an awkward white space in the foreground of my picture. I decided to add my aunt to it. I began with her feet.

"And what about the job before?" Dora inquired.

"It was a respectable meller. I thought I could do something with that marriage. The studio liked the material. I thought I pulled off the script. You did too, if I remember correctly."

"The script was skillful, Rozzie." Dora smoothed out her blanket. "That's not really what I'm saying, though, or what I'm asking." She paused. "You were forty-five years old a few months ago. You've proven that you can have a career in Hollywood. You have so much talent, my darling, my Mutsky," she added, using her most intimate nickname for Annie Rozzie. "What I wonder is, why don't you take a break from the movies and the money for a while? There'll always be work if you choose to go back, but I really think you ought to try your hand at a novel."

Annie Rozzie continued to sit stiffly in her chair. With my pencil I was tracing the outlines of her back, her shoulder, her neck and her ear, the scarf tied to her head, then her ear and neck again and her other shoulder. When I came to her right arm, the arm closest to me, it shot into the air. Her hand tightened into a fist, and it began to make a pumping motion, a gesticulation that matched her voice. "But Mamma, I've done good work! I've won awards! And I haven't done real *schlock* for money since I was starting out."

"All I'm saying is that you might consider—"

"I'm no genius. Believe me, I know that. I'm a professional writer, and there's no shame in that. Besides, Hollywood was good enough for you, and what's good enough for my Mamma—"

"Darling, sweetheart, it's impossible to hold a conversation when you're so highly strung. It's simply too tiring." Rozzie's arm floated toward her lap, a kite cut off from its current. "The comparison is irrelevant. I don't have one-tenth your talent."

"Of course you do."

"Not your kind." Dora took a pencil out of her new brush pot and tapped its eraser against the over-bed table. "When you were born I knew you were going to be a writer. I just knew it. I named you Rosalind because that sounded like a writer's name to me and because of Shakespeare's Rosalind, who was so clever. But maybe that was a mistake. I feel ambivalent about cleverness now." Dora paused. "Don't you want the challenge of rendering a world all by yourself?"

"Mamma, I tried."

"You were twenty-three. You were inexperienced. You didn't trust your imagination, you wanted to earn your way—I understand that, of course, I respect that. But isn't now maybe the time to be daring? You must never settle, Mutsky, never."

The drawing had been coming up out of me all by itself, an electricity of contouring and crosshatching and shading that made the two figures, Grandma Dora in bed and Annie Rozzie in the chair across from her, seem to vibrate on the page. I was particularly pleased with my aunt's arm, which I had depicted at three different heights to suggest that it was moving up and down as she spoke. Now my listening caught up with me, and my pencil slowed, then stopped. I studied my grandmother. The sentence *You must never settle, Mutsky, never* was still humming in the air. Clearly she had been the one to say them, yet didn't the words belong to Annie Rozzie? Hadn't she spoken them to me, these same words, this same admonition, this incantation, many times? Wasn't *Never settle* one of Rozzie's Rules? I regarded my aunt. Once again, she was adjusting the rings on her hands, but she had trouble getting all of the stones to face the same direction.

"I suppose this means that if I continue to write screenplays you'll be disappointed in me," she said.

"Rozzie, darling, there are times when I worry about you. Seriously worry. It's because I believe so strongly in you that I can even bring this up. Don't you understand that?" Annie Rozzie shook her head. "Then I've failed you somehow. I've not helped you find your core. My job should have been to send you farther into your own life."

"But I don't want to go anywhere. I want to stay right here with you."

"You can't, not forever." When Dora spoke again, her voice modulated, burning the shadow off what she'd just said. "Not even for the rest of the day, because the *shtarker* needs her rest. She is suddenly very tired again."

My drawing was finished. Across the top of the page I wrote, *Get well soon, Grandma,* and at the bottom, in smaller letters, *Love, Matty.* I carefully removed the page from the journal and gave it to my grandmother. She looked at it closely, then smiled and said, "That's a very accurate likeness of this room, Matthew. A very good drawing indeed." Annie Rozzie was looking at it too, but upside down, since she was tidying the over-bed table. This was probably why, I told myself, she didn't say anything to me about my picture.

II

I saw the cars as soon as we reached the eucalyptus tree at the foot of the hill. They were wedged into our driveway and spilling into the street. The rear door of one was hanging ajar. The mood in our car shifted as six pairs of eyes were drawn in the same direction. My mother's friend Bea Gold had taken all of us—her girls Mona and Audrey, my brothers Jeff and Noah, and me—to the beach for the day. She didn't appear to know anything, although I had noticed that she'd been smoking more cigarettes than usual. I knew. As soon as I saw the cars, I knew. I knew, yet I skirted the knowledge. I didn't say anything. I didn't think—let myself think—anything. Bea parked. We got out of the car. Bea told Mona and Audrey to wait for her. She put out her cigarette. Then she walked us across the street, stopping at our driveway. She said we had better go inside.

Time slowed. I listened to my beach thongs click against the cement. I watched Jeff and Noah walk ignorantly forward, then not so ignorantly: as soon as we reached the lawn Jeff's shoulders dropped, and Noah bit his lip. The sun was sliding behind the acacia, glittering faintly through hundreds of oblong leaves. I followed a ray of waning light from the horizon to a branch of the acacia to the dining-room window. The back of my mother's head was folding into a sea of faces. I recognized a number of my outlying aunts and uncles, a few cousins, several of my parents' friends. Jeff and Noah and I were on the walkway now. Another few steps and we would be told. The door opened. My mother came outside and closed it behind her. This gesture, this precaution, made my heart twist. She'd been waiting for us; she was heading us off; the breaking of this news was laid out, prepared for, planned. It was very bad. "Come," she said.

We were crossing the grass now, Shirley and her children. We were going into the backyard. In the next window, the guest room window, my other grandmother, Grandma Becky, stood watching us, her hands folded together, holding each other, her face worried and still.

Planned. Down to the kitchen chairs my mother had painted yellow only a few weeks before, a yellow so strong it seemed to have inhaled the sun. Someone had carried three of them outside, one for each of us boys, and arranged them in a semicircle. Standing in the garden, my mother's yellow chairs possessed the illogic, the incongruity, of a dream, and yet she kept leading us toward them. But we were intercepted by my father, who emerged from the door to the guest room.

"Boys," he said.

He came down the two narrow steps and joined us in the garden. "Boys," he repeated. He looked away, at the hillside, and then back at us. "I have something to tell you." He took hold of the frame of our swing set, fusing himself to something solid. "Your grandmother," he said. "My mother—Dora—she died this morning. Dora is dead."

It was the equivalent of a great, noble, thriving tree suddenly shedding all of its leaves: my father cried.

He cried physically, shuddering because he was fighting the tears, swallowing them, trying to insulate us but failing, because the moment his voice cracked it was already too late, we were crying too, in unison, Jeff and Noah and I, not drifting toward the chairs that had been so painstakingly set out for us but, like our father, reaching for the frame of the swing set, supporting ourselves with it, clinging to this scaffolding as if it had been erected earlier in our childhood just for this day and just for this purpose, to keep us from dropping onto the grass, which suddenly seemed so far away that to drop onto it would have meant to fall from a great height, to crash.

And then, in time, my tears stopped and my eyes were caulked dry; the watching caulked them, watching Annie Rozzie through the window as she sat on the bed in the guest room, keening, rocking her torso back and forth wildly. I went inside to be with her, to try to help her, although I didn't know how to or even if I could.

She swept me into her arms and rocked me with her and said, "Dora wouldn't want us to cry," and cried as she said this, and pulled her hair out of its scarf, and then stopped to catch her breath, to correct her breath because she was choking on her sobs, the way she choked when she ate her salad too quickly and Uncle Abe took away her fork, only this was different, there was no fork for Abe to take away, there was no Abe, not then, just Annie Rozzie and me on the bed, Annie Rozzie shaking and rocking and me following. And watching. There was nothing else to do but absorb. I could not keep up; I didn't have any tears left, certainly not Annie Rozzie-sized tears. I could only hold on. If I didn't hold on, I thought, surely I would drown, and surely Annie Rozzie would drown too.

People arrived, people left. Platters of food, deli and baked goods mostly, swelled and diminished. A turkey was carved down to the bone, the gravy boat scraped dry.

My cousin Agatha, who was older than me and wore earrings in the shape of peace signs, told me that she thought death was only a phase, a sort of holding pattern until people could come back in another form. She had had a dream once in which she saw herself as a bird, so she knew that it was her fate to be airborne. Dora, she believed, was a leopard or maybe a lion, a creature of power and beauty. She asked me what animal I thought I'd come back as. I said I didn't know.

Friends of my parents, and of my aunt and uncle, began arriving in couples, or pairs of couples; they made formal, almost choreographed rounds of the house, speaking in turn to my father and my aunt, then spending the bulk of their visit with the sibling they knew best. My parents' contingent was larger, although there were friends the siblings shared, like Dr. Markoff and his wife Elaine, who arrived just after eight o'clock. Dr. Markoff spoke to my father in a corner of the kitchen, where he kept his hand on my father's shoulder, as if he were holding up a precariously balanced piece of wood. Elaine held Annie Rozzie in her arms for a long time.

After a while, Elaine took my aunt's hand and stroked it and said, "Rozzie, you were a terrific daughter to your mother. You have to let that be a comfort to you. It may not seem like much now, but in time . . ."

"Yes," my aunt said, wiping her eyes, "maybe in time."

"To have spared her the way you did, you and Walt, to have kept her from knowing she was dying, that was—quite something."

"It gave Mamma more peace at the end," said my aunt. "At least I hope it did."

"I'm sure it did," confirmed Elaine.

I listened to this conversation from across the room. I was standing next to Grandma Becky, who was sitting in our wing chair. I didn't think very hard about what I was going to say. The sentences just came out of me, rising up out of my puzzlement and confusion. "But Grandma did know she was dying," I said. "She told me she did."

My aunt turned away from Elaine and toward me. A disturbance was working itself into her face, though of what kind I couldn't tell, because Annie Rozzie tamped it down, for my benefit I assumed, before she said, "Matty, that can't be."

I suddenly felt very small. I wished I hadn't spoken.

"You must be mistaken," she continued, unable to keep the quiver out of her voice. "Where did you get such an idea?"

I didn't want to let go of any more words, but Annie Rozzie insisted. "Matty, answer me, please."

"She told me she had enough pages in her book to last her."

"Her book?"

"Her journal. She gave me one just like it. She told me to write about my life. She said she didn't need much more room to write about hers."

"You're remembering incorrectly," she said emotionally.

"But I—"

"You're confused." Annie Rozzie stood up. "You're wrong. What can you know?"

"Rozzie, please," my mother interjected.

"He's a child." She took me by the shoulders and began shaking me. "He can't be right. He can't know anything."

"I'm just saying what Grandma—"

Becky stood up and whispered into my ear, "Sha, Mattalah. Sha."

Observing this, observing us, Annie Rozzie released me, froze for a moment, then burst into tears, great hiccupping sobs that blended together and augmented each other. "She didn't know, she didn't know," she said, first to Elaine, then to my uncle, who came to comfort her. The rest of the people in the room were willing themselves to look away from this rawness.

"It doesn't matter, Rozzie," my father said to my aunt. "Dora's gone now. What does it matter?"

But this only made her cry harder. Uncle Abe said, "She didn't know, my love. She never knew."

Suffused with guilt, I fled down the hall to the guest room. It was like escaping from an avalanche. My aunt's sorrow was too strong and too large, and I was afraid that if I remained in its way any longer, it would crush me. What's more, I felt I deserved to be crushed.

My mother followed me into the guest room, and my grandmother followed her.

"It's all right, Mattalah," Becky said. "You only said what you thought was true."

"But is it true?" I asked anxiously. "Did Grandma Dora know, the way I said she did?"

My mother and my grandmother looked at each other. "Yes," my mother said. "Dora knew she was dying."

"But Annie Rozzie—"

"Your aunt didn't know that she knew. It was your grandmother's wish."

I didn't understand—I couldn't understand.

I turned to Becky. "Are you going to die soon, Grandma?"

She drew me into her arms. "No, darling. Not soon."

"You promise?"

"I promise."

I buried my head in her chest and left it there for a while, a long while. When I looked up again, my mother was standing by the window and staring at the swing set. It was dark outside. Beyond the swing set and the lawn and the acacias that enclosed our garden I could see a piece of the night sky. It looked as if it had been packed with lumps of coal—clouds, I realized, as they began to ripple, animated by a faraway wind. In one place the clouds separated, opening in the shape of an eye, and like an eye, the opening began to glow, purple at first, then violet, then white. The eye widened. The clouds broke away from each other, and the moon swung into the night sky, as if someone had tossed it just there, just then.

This is the image I see now, this round white moon. The more I study, though, the more it seems to me to have the texture of a piece of cloth, a napkin maybe, one of Grandma Dora's linen napkins with their fragile lace trim. In my mind, I reach for this object, I grasp it. It takes me back to my grandmother's apartment. Yet when I look down at my hand I see that I am not holding a napkin after all. The material is not soft, like cloth, but brittle. It is paper. I flatten it. The circle spreads into a square. In front of me suddenly is the drawing I made all those years ago, of my grandmother and my aunt talking—arguing. The picture I remember and the moment it was made too, but memory delivers something new. A piece of stilled film is activated as my aunt tidies my grandmother's over-bed table, gathers up the drawing, and throws it away. She did not want me to have seen; she wanted only her version to last. But I find that I did see, and memory did make its record, and it is before me now, more and more of it, unspooling.

Ayşe Papatya Bucak

Hitch

My grandmother was obsessed with money, so while I drove she guessed the salaries of the people in the cars around us. She had never been in a pickup truck before and I think she liked looking down into other people's cars, seeing what they had on the floors of their backseats. She faced the window with one hand resting on Genghis Khan, her Pekinese, who lay between us in the cab. Occasionally she stroked his back and tufts of his long, white hair floated up into my vision.

For hours I had been offered a view of the back of Grandma's twisted head, as if she were showing me how clean she was behind the ears. She was mad. A month ago she had called to lecture me on my lack of career plans—specifically for not calling some friend of hers she insisted could help me—and I had hung up on her. In the truck, at first, she had slept—her head tilted so firmly against the glass that I reached around and locked her door to ensure she wouldn't topple out. After waking, she stared out the window. Then the catalog of incomes began.

"Eighteen thousand," she said of an orange Nova that had a door-size dent in the driver-side door. A man in a baseball cap was behind the wheel. His arm was out of the car and his hand drummed on the roof.

I refused to confirm or deny her estimate. She read the cars literally, but I imagined people who spent more than they could afford, tycoons who owned fleets of Volkswagen Beetles. Grandma tapped her finger on the glass so that I would look, but I pretended to concentrate on the road, going so far as to turn my head and check traffic in the opposite lane. When Grandma tapped again, Genghis Khan climbed onto her lap to see what she was pointing at, and I said, "Yeah, I saw it."

Maybe Grandma wasn't mad at me, but rather I was mad at her.

It was in Grandma's nature to save time, so we had left her Delaware home at dawn. I hadn't eaten and by the time we hit stop-and-go traffic in Connecticut I was both sick and hungry. I put my right blinker on and flexed my fingers, which were cold from the air conditioning. It was August. "Grandma," I said, "can we eat somewhere?"

It was the same question I asked on similar trips twenty years ago, and it didn't matter that I was now the driver and she the passenger, she still got to decide. Mine was no shrunken, hunched, and tiny grandmother. She stood five-foot-nine without her heels, though the only time she was without them was when she was sick, and that wasn't often. Her sight was going, which was why she wasn't allowed to drive, but in all other ways she was fully operational. Her strength amazed me, made me wonder if I was found on a doorstep.

"Betsy, there's a good restaurant not too far ahead," she said without turning from the window. "Let's wait until we see it. It has good hollandaise sauce." Hollandaise sauce was her restaurant gauge.

I turned the blinker off. It would have been impossible to change lanes anyway. We were pulling a boat and any nonlinear movements required a lot of forethought.

Traffic stopped and Grandma and I sat not talking, as if we were dolls that needed to be in motion in order to speak. When we moved again, I could not tell how long we had been still. I was as good at losing time as my grandmother was at saving it.

My stomach growled and I turned the blinker back on. "Grandma, we have to pull over."

"I remember it perfectly," she said. "We're close. Just a few more exits."

I turned the blinker off again. Traffic slowed and I hit the brakes harder than I needed to, afraid that the boat would stop me from stopping. Genghis Khan slid to the floor without a sound.

Normally I liked to travel alone, to put my name on things, to take a seat on a plane and turn it into a shrunken version of my living room, to inhabit a small space with everything I could need, water, a book, a pen, paper, but when my parents asked me to drive Grandma and her boat to Maine for the wedding, I couldn't refuse. Never mind that I had never hitched anything to my truck before. Never mind that Grandma had been criticizing my life. Never mind that it was my wedding.

Besides, the boat was for me, a present. It had been my grandfather's.

My to-be husband and I were moving from New Mexico to Maine. His parents owned a summer house, which they had winterized a few years ago thinking they might like to retire there. But they were addicted to work, and to New York, and to living well in a city that most people lived poorly in. When they heard of Paul's proposal, they offered their own: we could have the house as long as we maintained it, and, in summer, gave it back. Paul was writing his dissertation on Emily Dickinson and it would be a good place to work. He'd started a different dissertation on Robert Frost, but he'd changed his mind. It seemed to me he was more interested in Emily than her poems, which he hadn't finished reading. He was obsessed with her.

The house had a circular drive and a porch that went all the way around. I would have loved to have lived there, if it had been mine. The wedding would be held at the house in a week.

By the time we found my grandmother's restaurant, the Lafayette Inn, I felt less hungry. My head ached and a bad taste was in my throat, but I held out hope that food would help. If my mother had been with us, she would have asked if I was pregnant; she asked that all the time, but I knew I wasn't. My period had been scientifically engineered to come the week before. While Grandma and Genghis paraded the grounds, I hung my head out the window to negotiate parking and tried to stem the nervous sweat trickling down my arm. Getting engaged had made me want to be a better person. When I shopped for this trip, the wedding, the honeymoon, I bought a natural deodorant that was billed as smelling like woodlands. It did smell like woodlands, in the store, but up close I smelled like a football player who'd slept in his practice uniform. All morning I'd leaned away from Grandma.

The Lafayette Inn was no truck stop. Each parking space was no bigger than an Oldsmobile. After one pass through the lot, just missing the rear bumpers of a row of cars, I drove around back and pulled up in front of the Dumpster. When I stepped out of the cab, I had to steady myself against the smell of garbage combined with my woodland scent and the warm air. With one hand on the prow of the boat and one to my nose, I closed my eyes and tried to stop the earth from moving. I wasn't going to make much of a sailor.

The boat was my grandparents' old-age boat, their second boat. Their first, the one my mom remembered, had been a sailboat, forty-five feet long. The boat that had been behind me all morning, a twenty-one-foot power yacht, was the one my grandparents bought when they were too old to sail, and too poor to afford a boat at all. When I was a kid, my parents and I sometimes drove down from New Jersey and my grandparents motored us around the bay. Mostly, though, I remember eating picnic lunches on the deck while still docked. I liked to go below and lie on the narrow bunks and marvel at the boat's interior, miniaturized world in which everything had two purposes. Beds were couches, cabinets were tables, nothing had only one function.

"Nice boat," a voice called out, and I opened my eyes. A kid with sunburnt arms, who clutched a beat-up knapsack, stood by the restaurant Dumpster. I stepped closer to my boat.

"Sorry, didn't mean to scare you," he said, staying where he was. His beard was barely filled out. "Are you all right?"

I nodded my head.

"Well, it's a nice boat," he said and turned away.

Grandma found me still leaning there. She rubbed my back. "Come wash your face. It will help."

"Let's put Genghis in the cab," I said reaching for the leash. He lay down on the blacktop. Sometimes he would lie down during walks.

Grandma bent over and lifted him. "Why don't we leave him in the back of the truck? He'd be cooler," she said stroking his ears. Fur drifted off his body and through the air. He sneezed.

"What if somebody steals him?" I said. My grandmother was notorious for leaving things unlocked.

"I think we can chance it." She held him pointed downward over the truck bed as if it were a pool and he was supposed to dive in. I climbed onto the bed and took him from her. The truck's surface was warm from the sun and felt good after the air conditioning in the cab. We were carrying only a few boxes—stuff I had left at my parents' house and they had threatened to throw away—certificates for high school achievements, my diploma, books from college, my prom dress, things without a purpose. Paul had driven our mutual belongings to Maine already. He was waiting for me there.

As I tied Genghis down he circled me, licking my bare legs, and Grandma walked around the boat checking it. It had been in dry dock in Maryland since my grandfather died two years ago. It was named Elizabeth, after her. The first boat, the sailboat, had been Beth, the name of her youth.

I enjoyed the feeling of standing on the truck bed, clambering down over the side, landing on the ground. It made me feel tough, like I could still climb trees, like I was the kind of girl who owned a truck, not the kind of girl who had rich in-laws and no real plan for the future, except to unite that future with a partner who also had no real plans. Grandma watched me, and then, as we walked toward the restaurant, took my hand. As we walked that way, hand in hand, to the front, I felt calmer.

• • •

Each of my childhood summers had been marked by a drive from Delaware to Massachusetts. For all of August I was entrusted to my grandparents and their rented house along Buzzard's Bay. My grandmother and I had been close and I loved her now mostly for how she had been then. We had a hundred rituals that we repeated each summer: swimming from the private pier, buying sweet corn at the farmer's market, welcoming guests and then bidding them good-bye.

The house had been a miracle to me, and I loved returning to it and its claw-footed bathtubs, its garden with actual paths, its bookcases stuffed with books, each summer. I think that was part of what attracted me to Paul, that he had a house like mine in his childhood. His contained a dollhouse stocked with miniature antiques that he rearranged each summer only to find them returned to their original places when he came back the next summer. Before they bought their house in Maine, his parents, too, had rented.

When I looked back on it, it was like that whole period of my childhood had been rented, like I had borrowed it from someone else.

Over brunch, we discussed the wedding.

"Are you nervous?" Grandma asked. She poked at her eggs Benedict.

"I just don't want anyone to be disappointed," I said, leaning back, and sipping at my soda. "It's not going to be very fancy." We sat in a booth in the nearly empty restaurant. A couple of older men sat at the counter drinking coffee. One of them wore a fishing hat. We could hear the waitresses at the busing station talking about their boyfriends.

"I don't mean are you nervous about the ceremony," Grandma said. "I mean about being married."

I shrugged. "Should I be?"

Grandma laughed and ate a mouthful of eggs. "Yes."

Paul and I had lived together since he started graduate school in New Mexico. I taught English classes at the Hilton hotel, for Hilton employees who spoke English as a second language. It didn't pay much and I'm not sure it did much good. I had trouble teaching verbs.

"I really love him," I said. "We have a good thing."

Grandma nodded. "You know Mrs. Dubois's son? Marcus?" she said lifting her coffee. It took her ages to drink a cup since she put it down after every sip. "He's clerking for a Supreme Court justice."

"I don't remember him," I said.

"Do you remember Bennett Dusen?"

I nodded. "He's a history professor."

"He was supposed to be a history professor. He sells donuts." Grandma sipped her coffee, put the cup down. "His fellowship ran out and he never finished his dissertation. And he never will."

"Maybe he likes selling donuts."

"Maybe he likes living alone because his wife and kids left him."

"Paul is going to finish," I said. "Besides, I would never leave him over donuts."

"You should," Grandma said.

I plucked the toothpick out of my sandwich and stuck it between my teeth. She hated that.

Grandma had told my mother that Paul didn't seem ambitious enough. For years, my mother had been trying to convince me Grandma was a snob and she used this as evidence. She said Grandma was a terrible mother, that for years all she cared about was what her children wore and that they were polite to dinner guests. She said Grandma couldn't love anybody who didn't love her. Why would she want to, I said. My mother said I was missing the point. She used to try to convince Grandma that I was selfish, that being a good student didn't make me a good kid—it was like she didn't want either of us to love the other too much, like we were lovers she wanted kept apart.

My mother was raised on formal dinners and long vacations that all disappeared when she graduated from college and married. Meanwhile, after my grandfather retired, he and Grandma lived their way through their savings until eventually my uncles, both lawyers, ended up financing the lifestyle my grandparents, at their age, couldn't bear to give up. They did sacrifice some things—the maid, the cook, the summer house they used to rent. I felt sad for them even though I knew they were spoiled, privileged, ridiculous.

"What happens when Paul starts looking for a job?" Grandma asked, putting her coffee down.

"I don't know, Grandma. We work it out. That's how we do things."

My grandmother never worked, but I think she wished she could have. She'd only met Paul once, when we cleaned out her attic. She came up the stairs right when Paul was trying on her wedding dress. When Grandma told my mother Paul wasn't ambitious enough, she meant me, that I wasn't.

I was a serial careerist. After college, I rethought my major and decided to become a zoologist. After one biology class, I decided to be an editor for a small press. I couldn't live on the salary so I taught English on the side. Soon I was only teaching. In Maine, I would teach; at least I thought I would.

After eating half of my club sandwich I decided it was making me feel worse. Slumping back against the cushioned booth, I watched my grandmother sip at her iced coffee. The waitress had dumped ice into the boiling cup and it was melting fast. I wondered if this place had been nicer years ago, or if we were in the right restaurant at all.

The thing was, I was ambitious. I wanted everybody I knew to like me best.

With Genghis Khan returned to his seat and my grandmother again staring out the window, this time at the Dumpster she had to brush up against in order to climb in the passenger-side door, I managed to twist and turn our caravan out of the parking lot and onto the parkway. I felt guilty for fighting with Grandma, my stomach hurt, and my heart beat rapid fire from fear of crash landing her and her namesake boat. I checked the rearview mirror compulsively to make sure the boat was still there and safe. I suspected my mom didn't approve of Paul either. She always talked to him about television shows, as if he couldn't handle a more serious conversation.

As I picked up speed, I checked the mirror again. When I saw a figure at the boat wheel, I had to look twice. "Grandma," I said calmly.

She followed my eyes to the mirror and tilted her head back in surprise. To her credit, she recovered quickly. "Stowaway," she said, as if it were a word she used all of the time.

After I pulled to the side of the road, Grandma and I sat silently in the cab. If we waited long enough surely our stranger would leap from the boat and run away. Trees lined the parkway. The guy's escape route was clear. I left one hand on the ignition and watched in the mirror as he climbed out of the boat and out of my sight. Sweat dripped down my arm.

"What's he doing?" I asked.

Grandma twisted in her seat, then rolled down the window and stuck her head out. "Can't tell," she said. She opened the door and stepped out. I barely had time to grab Genghis Khan before he followed, trailing his leash behind. As it was, his front feet were in the air, and he dangled for a moment, before I dragged him back into the cab. He turned on me and snapped at my hand. I smacked him on the nose, but when he whimpered I hugged him to me and patted his head. "She'll be right back," I said, and tried to see what was happening through the rear window. I couldn't see anything, and Grandma didn't come back, so finally I climbed with Genghis out of my grandmother's open door. She stood talking to the kid I had seen earlier, the one who'd spoken to me behind the restaurant.

"What are you doing?" I said, standing five feet from the both of them. Genghis Khan pulled on his leash, wanting to go to Grandma. It was hot outside and bright. I felt muddled. I took a step forward and the kid—even with the beard he looked about eighteen—took a step back.

"You're the kid from the restaurant, aren't you?" I said.

"Yeah," he said. "You feeling better?"

I straightened my shoulders. "I feel fine. What's your name?"

"Stewart," he said turning back to Grandma.

"What are you doing here, Stewart?" I asked.

"I thought maybe I could catch a ride."

On the parkway, cars drove by, nobody seeming to wonder if we were in trouble.

"That's crazy," I said, jerking back on Genghis's leash. He was trying to pull me closer to Grandma. "Maybe if you'd asked, we would have given you a ride."

"You would have given me a ride?"

"Maybe if you'd asked," I said.

He turned to Grandma again. He asked her, "Would she have given me a ride?"

"No," she said. My head throbbed. I would have said no.

"That's what I thought," Stewart said, and backed away from us.

"I'll give you a ride right now," I said. "Where are you going?"

Stewart paused.

Sweat ran down the backs of my knees. It occurred to me that this kid might be in trouble. "Get in the truck, I'm giving you a ride," I said.

Stewart backed away. "I don't think so."

"Fine," I said tugging again on Genghis's leash. "Let's go, Grandma."

I had my hand on the door when I heard a sharp *Oh* of surprise.

I turned back and saw Stewart headed for the woods. "It was nothing," Grandma said. "He kissed me. It was nothing."

My face flushed. Already I could hear Grandma telling the story to the rest of the family, making it cute. "Wait a minute," I called to him, handing Grandma Genghis's leash and walking after Stewart, following him into the shade of the trees. "Wait a minute," I yelled. I was queasy from eating and not eating, I was tired from driving, and I was sick of everybody and everything and how nothing could be a good thing and left at that. I was mad I had let this kid have the last word. I was mad I had offered him a ride and he had refused it. I was mad he was probably judging me because I had a boat and a grandmother and somewhere I had to be. I was mad he liked my grandmother more than me.

"Wait a minute. What's your problem?" I said.

Stewart kept walking, but I followed farther into the trees. Behind me Genghis Khan was barking, and I was grateful for his protest. "You're just some spoiled college kid, aren't you?" I said. "A rich kid with dirt on his face, playing hobo for a year. That's it, isn't it?"

In my experience life was measured by other people's questions: where are you going to college, when are you getting married, when are you having kids, where are they going to college, when are they getting married, when are they having kids. Even if I pretended they didn't, the answers mattered to me, and I couldn't understand people who didn't plan for the future, people who weren't afraid of what could happen next.

As cars rushed past, the smell of exhaust in the air, nobody noticing us, Stewart turned and looked at me. I stopped, fifteen feet from him. "So that is it," I said. "You think you can hide out in someone's boat and call that living. You think that's living, don't you? You don't know what living is! You could have gotten hurt." I stopped when Stewart started back toward me.

He walked slowly, his eyes on the ground, but he didn't stop until his body was an inch from mine, and his lips by mine. This close he looked older, the corners of his eyes held creases and his skin was toughened by the sun. His fingers loosely encircled my arm. "Don't fuck with me," he said. And then he was gone.

Grandma came up behind me. At her feet, Genghis was still barking. "Did he kiss you, too?" she said with a laugh. She looked happier than she had all day.

"He's just a stupid kid," I said and turned away from her. I bent over with my hands on my knees to give my breathing a chance to slow. I faked a cough, but then I kept coughing, unable to clear my throat, and Grandma put one hand on my back and cupped the other over my forehead in a way I had always wished for as a child. In my family, everyone got sick alone, as if it were a sacred act meant to be kept private.

"It's going to be okay," she said.

I glanced at the woods, then the truck and boat. "Why did you let him kiss you?"

"I didn't," she said. "He just did it. He was harmless."

"You don't know that."

"He was harmless."

"You *don't* know that." I turned from her, back to the boat. "I'll check the boat. Maybe he did something to the boat."

My grandmother didn't follow me below deck. I knew there was nothing Stewart could have taken, everything on the boat was latched down so it wouldn't hit you on the head if the boat rolled. I stood in the cabin, by the beds, and my stomach swayed as if we were actually at sea. I could smell myself, my sweat. I walked into the galley and checked that the cabinets were latched shut. We would stock the boat in Maine. Throughout the interior, on the sides of tables and on walls, were built-in wooden handholds, to grab when the boat rocked. What a good idea, I thought. Something to hold on to in a storm.

I watched for Stewart the rest of the ride, but we didn't see him again. That seemed even creepier, like he might pop out at us from anywhere, at any second. When we arrived at the house, I didn't want to pull the boat into the circular drive, so I parked on the front lawn. It was going to be used for parking during the wedding anyway. Paul came out of the house and stood on the porch.

"Thank God," I said, as I ran up the steps to hug him. Grandma was out on the lawn with Genghis.

"Tough trip?"

"Just weird," I said as Grandma walked toward us. "Go help her," I said, and nudged him.

"My parents are gone for the night," he said. "But they bought us lobster."

"That's nice," I said. "Go help her."

"I'm scared of her."

"Go."

It was easy to be with Paul. I felt a sense of ease with him.

"We could put the boat in the water," he said.

"Now?"

"It'll look good in the water. Better than on the lawn."

"Tomorrow," I said, "Now . . ."

"I know," he said and walked down the steps to take Genghis's leash and offer my grandmother his arm.

We ate the lobsters on the porch with candles for light, and Grandma let Paul crack hers. It was the kind of behavior I wasn't used to from her, and I thought maybe it was a sign she was giving Paul a break. She and I hadn't spoken much the rest of the ride up, after Stewart. Mostly she looked out the window, with Genghis on her lap, and I fiddled with the radio trying to find some talk. As we ate, Grandma kept asking Paul about the house and what kind of things he had done as a child. I was so sure she would bring up Stewart that every time she started a new sentence I tensed up. I wanted to tell Paul about him, but not until we were alone, and I could tell the whole story.

"Do you sail often?" Grandma asked as she wiped her fingers on a paper napkin.

"Sometimes," Paul said.

"Grandma and I had a stowaway," I said, and if I could have, I would have turned to myself in surprise and given myself the look I had planned to give Grandma. I suppose I wanted to take control of the situation.

"A what?" Paul said.

"This kid hid on the boat when we stopped for brunch. We saw his head pop up while we were on the road," I said.

"What happened?" Paul asked.

"I pulled over and the kid ran away." I looked down at the lobster carnage on my plate. I couldn't bring myself to tell the rest of it, and Grandma didn't say anything except, "It was very strange."

"That is strange," Paul said.

I looked up from my lobster plate and at Grandma, who was

regarding me steadily. I asked her, "So do you two like each other now, is that the deal?"

It was a horrible thing to say. I'd never done that before, said something horrible.

"Betsy!" Paul said. "Of course, we like each other. We love each other. We're family now."

"I don't know why you'd say such a thing," Grandma said. She tried to stand up, but we were sitting on a bench, and she and I were on the same side and she couldn't push it back. She stood partway, teetered a little, and sat back down as I put my hand out behind her.

"Let me help you," Paul said. He came around the table and helped Grandma slide out. The two of them left me sitting at the table with lobster and dirty napkins all around. Maybe that was what I wanted, to unite them somehow. I half-expected to spend the night out there on the porch, alone, but Paul came back a few minutes later.

"I showed her to her room," he said. "She wanted to take a bath." He sat back down at his place and started to eat again.

"Would you marry me if I didn't want children?" I asked.

"Yes," he said.

"And if I wanted ten children?"

"Yes."

"So you'd marry me no matter what?"

"Yes."

When he had proposed, he had said, "I have an idea. Let's spend our lives together." "Get married?" I had said. "Okay," he had replied, as if it had been my idea all along.

I covered my lobster shells with a clean napkin from the pile on the table. "That can't be right, can it?" I said. "Shouldn't you have some ground rules? I mean that makes it seem awfully arbitrary. You'd marry me no matter what?"

"Not no matter what. Based on past evidence."

"I don't know, Paul. I feel really scared."

He stood up and came round to my side of the table and slid in beside me. I hated couples that sat like that in restaurants, next to each other rather than across from each other. That seemed so strong then, to actually hate them.

"I'm such a snob," I said.

"I don't care. I'm going to marry you anyway."

"I'm going to turn into a bitch. Maybe I already have."

"Why would you even say that?"

"Because," I said, but I couldn't finish. "I was mean to that kid on the boat," I said.

"I thought you didn't talk to him."

"Yeah, we did. He kissed Grandma and I yelled at him and then he said something rude to me." I started to laugh. "Actually he said something kind of scary."

Paul laughed, too, and he put his arm around me. His chin was shiny from butter and his hands smelled like lobster.

"I feel like I need some kind of guidebook," I said. "Like the world is so weird, and I don't have the survival handbook."

Paul laughed again, and I felt the vibration in my chest and my throat. Across the yard, the hull of the boat was a white light in the dark. I couldn't see the truck it was hitched to or the wheels it was on. It was a floating white light, either a beacon or a warning, or just a light.

The next day I woke late and when I stood and looked out the window, I saw that the boat was gone from the front lawn and my truck was parked in the driveway. In the distance, I could see the bay and I knew that Paul had gotten up early and put the boat in the water. I could almost remember it, feeling him leave the bed and then my drifting back into sleep.

When I went downstairs, I found Paul and Grandma in the kitchen. Paul was making sandwiches at the large center table and Grandma was dropping pieces of cold cuts onto the floor where Genghis Khan lapped them up.

"Grandma!" I said and she dropped a piece of ham onto Genghis's back. He spun around trying to get at it. "You spoil that dog," I said.

"Ah, the drunken sailor," Paul said. "Just in time for lunch at sea."

"I'm not drunk," I said, though I knew he was kidding.

"You're still in time for lunch at sea," he said.

In the water, the boat was a different beast than it had been on the road. Paul let me steer for a while, but then he accused me of being drunk again, and I decided to go down below to check on Grandma, who wanted to stay out of the sun. I was feeling cheerful because of the grace of the boat and the way Paul was taking charge, and because we had yet to talk about the wedding plans, which had dominated our lives for the past six months.

Down below, Grandma was lying on the pulled-out couch at the back of the hold. She was reading a fat book and the bedside lamp cast a circle of light on her hands, which looked worn and thin. Genghis was snoring at her feet. "I'm sorry if I was cranky yesterday," I said as I stood beside her. "The drive made me tired."

"It's okay," she said in a voice that suggested it wasn't.

"Stewart didn't kiss me," I said. "He told me not to fuck with him."

"You shouldn't use that word," she said, but she was trying not to look surprised. I don't think the world ever seemed dangerous to her. I could feel myself getting mad again.

"I don't think he was a good kid," I said. The boat rocked and I had to put one hand against the wall. Of course, there was no handhold where I needed one.

"Your mother wants to know if you're pregnant," Grandma said.

I looked around as if expecting to find my mother tucked in one of the boat's efficient spaces. "You talked to her?"

"I called last night, to tell her we made it."

"Oh. Well, I'm not," I said.

"Good," Grandma said still looking at her book. "One thing at a time."

"Yeah, probably not for a while," I said. "We're not in any hurry. Besides, this world. I don't know."

"You should have a daughter."

I laughed. I glanced around the hold again, saw a cabinet ajar. I was distracted by the memory of Stewart's having been down there. "I'll see what I can do," I said. "While I'm at it, I'll make a lot of money. And have a great job. And Stewart will have a great job. And we'll—"

"Stewart will have a great job?"

I could feel myself blush. "Paul. Paul will have a great job."

"Have a daughter," she said, and looked straight at me.

"Grandma," I said, but I stopped because I felt about to cry. She put her book down, then slid over on the bed. She patted the mattress where she had been and I lay down, in tight next to her, and put my head on her chest. She was so thin and narrow. She felt like the bird skeletons we had studied in eighth-grade science. I shifted my head to the pillow next to hers and closed my eyes. "Have a daughter," she said in a voice just like my mother's. She patted my head, gently, a little awkwardly, but enough so that I could feel it. The boat rocked again and I could hear Paul, up above, shout, "Sorry." "Grandma," I said again, but I still didn't know what I was trying to say.

"Don't fuck with me," she said, and I laughed.

My mother, my grandmother, and I, we were three lines that overlapped. They knew more of the past; I would know more of the future, but only after it happened. I took one of Grandma's thin hands in mine and held it tight. The boat rocked again, and I knew where I was.

George Makana Clark

Backmilk

My Mother

I was born facing the heavens and my nose caught on my mother's cervix, arresting my progress into a larger world and turning what had promised to be an easy labor into thirteen hours of unmedicated suffering for the woman. She moaned with each contraction, low at first, and rising in an excruciating glissando.

Mrs. Gordon's husband stood over her, and her coloured servant gently coached her between contractions, and the gardener stood outside the window pruning his bougainvilleas. But at the height of her pain, it seemed to Mrs. Gordon that she was alone in Africa, and she stared without recognition at the faces surrounding her.

Mrs. Gordon, a dour woman during the best of times, would carry traces of the protracted agony in her every expression until she died, eleven years later. Her gloom would have only deepened had she known she'd ruined her health birthing a coloured child. *If I'd been capable of focusing my filmy eyes and appreciating nuance, I might have noticed the melancholy in my mother's tight-lipped smile as I, still slick with serous fluid, latched on to our servant's nipple.*

• • •

Mahulda Jane Braxton

Mahulda Jane Braxton, who passed a sleepless night attending the home birth, would spend much of the following day scrubbing her mistress' blood from the sheets, walls, and ceiling of the parlor.

Mahulda Jane Braxton was a Capetown coloured who immigrated to Rhodesia twenty years earlier to keep the house and cook for its inhabitants. Mr. and Mrs. Gordon engaged her services when they acquired the bungalow through an estate sale. Mr. Gordon liked to say the woman came with the house.

I was delivered beneath the corrugated-iron roof of the wooden bungalow outside Umtali, on the eastern frontier of Rhodesia, on a Saturday morning. Although the bungalow was large, Mahulda Jane Braxton did all the housekeeping, except for the setting and winding of the clocks. She never thought to look at them, and the duty was given over to Timmy, the gardener.

Mahulda Jane Braxton worked without complaint, even when called on to sacrifice her free Sunday afternoons. The only requirement she placed upon her employers was that they address her by her full name. *It was she who sank both her hands to the wrists between my mother's legs and turned me in the womb, enabling me to be born alive.*

When Mahulda Jane Braxton, hair matted with her employer's blood, finally succeeded in extracting the baby, she began lactating spontaneously at the sound of its cry. This greatly surprised her, for she was approaching her fiftieth year.

"It is a boy," she told her employers, absently.

Mahulda Jane Braxton clamped one clothespin on the base of the umbilical cord next to the baby's belly and another clothespin an inch farther. *Using a pair of the gardener's pruning shears that had been boiled for three minutes, she cut the cord between the two clothespins, severing me from my mother. Seven days after my birth, when the nub of my umbilical cord withered and dropped off, Mahulda Jane Braxton would give it to the gardener along with a lock of my hair to bury beneath one of his jacaranda trees for good luck.*

"Push, Madam," she told the panting woman. "You must still expel the afterbirth." This, Mahulda Jane Braxton placed in a shallow pan.

Mrs. Gordon reached into her open blouse and drew out her breast, but the baby refused.

"Babies do not know how to nurse, Madam. The child must be taught." Mahulda Jane Braxton gently squeezed the baby's cheeks until its lips curved outward around Mrs. Gordon's nipple. But still the child refused to nurse.

Mrs. Gordon buttoned her blouse and handed the baby to the housekeeper.

Mahulda Jane Braxton had been pregnant long ago, in Capetown, but she had lost the baby in its eighth month, scarring her uterus during parturition and leaving her barren. Mahulda Jane Braxton had asked to hold her stillborn child, and she rocked it in the dark labor room until she fell asleep and awoke alone. Thereafter, she carried a wisp of the child's reddish hair in a sealed, heart-shaped locket.

After losing her child, time held no meaning for Mahulda Jane Braxton. She was unable to distinguish any moment of her life from the one which preceded it, and clock winding became a neglected duty.

Mahulda Jane Braxton immediately assumed the duty of nursing Mrs. Gordon's newborn baby. The infant's eyes were almond-shaped and they slanted downward at the corners, as did Mahulda Jane Braxton's, and they shared the same broad, flat nose. She broke the seal on her locket and matched the wisp of hair to that of the baby. It was identical in color. She smiled down on the infant as it nursed. *Mahulda Jane Braxton's milk was sweetish and tasted faintly like nutmeg, thin and tepid at first. But the backmilk was rich and hot, and I drank greedily.*

My Father

Mr. Gordon was a successful merchant who, for nine months previous the birth, spent much of his time in his study counting receipts from his stores, keeping his accounts, and avoiding his gravid wife.

As Mrs. Gordon bore down on her final contraction, Mr. Gordon turned his back to the spectacle of his child's birth. Proximity to nature discomfited him.

Following the child's refusal of its mother's milk, Mr. Gordon carried his wife into her darkened bedroom. Mrs. Gordon would later direct the gardener to paint the walls of the room a hunter green, deep almost to the point of blackness. There she would remain until her death eleven years later, emerging only for holidays and occasions such as the anniversaries of her child's birth and her wedding. Life had become altogether too much for her. *Mahulda Jane Braxton showed me how to nurse, squeezing my cheeks until I opened my lips wide enough to form a seal around her aureole, then chucking me under my chin so I would begin sucking. It was the first of many life lessons she would teach me.*

My father stood over us, impatiently waiting for his child to complete its suckle so that he could remove it to his study for a careful inspection and, if necessary, smother it with a leather arm pillow from his reading chair.

The child seemed pink enough to him, and its eyes were navy. But that proved nothing, as all humans are born with blue eyes. He craned his neck to see if the baby had negroid features. Its nose was wide and flat above his servant's nipple.

His sharp intake of breath was audible.

"All babies have such noses," the servant woman told him. "It is so they can breathe while they nurse."

The woman unnerved Mr. Gordon with her ability to read his thoughts. Though he considered public nursing unseemly, he could not resist angling for a better view of the child's face to determine if it possessed any atavistic traits.

Mahulda Jane Braxton modestly covered breast and child with a receiving blanket and gave her employer a reproachful look. She was not embarrassed, but there was something menacing in his stare.

She knew Mr. Gordon was coloured, passing for white. Each Wednesday he would disappear into town to have the kink removed from his brownish-red hair. But at the base of his neck, Mahulda Jane Braxton discerned the telltale curl that no chemical could straighten.

When the baby finished nursing, Mr. Gordon bent over Mahulda Jane Braxton to take up the child. She was uneasy with the way he grasped for the infant, and there was an unnatural glint in his eyes. She instinctively drew the baby closer to her chest.

Mr. Gordon pulled at the child. "I'll take it now," he told her.

But the servant held fast.

"Leave off, woman!" Mr. Gordon said, taking the child away. He examined it. Although the infant carried no outward traces of its African ancestry, Mr. Gordon saw his Xhosa grandmother staring back at him through slit eyes, and he decided that his son would be a chrisom child.

Two generations of Gordons had enjoyed the rewards of passing for white, guarding their lineage even against their own wives, until their fear overshadowed the secret itself. Mr. Gordon's eyes narrowed, and he tried to look upon his nascent son as he would a bushpig that was raiding his garden.

"That will be all, Mahulda Jane Braxton," he told his servant when she tried to follow him into the study.

Mahulda Jane Braxton nodded doubtfully at her employer. She was expressly forbidden to enter the study, except on Wednesdays when her employer went into Umtali. Then Mahulda would dust the shelves of books—*Specimens of American Poetry with Critical and Biographical Notices.* Readings for the Railways. Historae Romanae Breviarium—books chosen more for their crushed-morocco gilt edges, three-quarter polished-calf bindings, unbroken spines, and engraved frontispiece portraits than for their content. After tidying the study, Mahulda Jane Braxton would open the books at random and read until she heard footsteps or voices.

Mahulda Jane Braxton could guess why her employer had insisted on a home birth. *She paced the hallway for almost a full minute before entering my father's study, thereby saving my life twice in as many hours.*

Timothy the Gardener

Upon her arrival in Umtali two decades earlier, Mahulda Jane Braxton had ignored the young Shona men who waited for her at the market on Mondays and Thursdays when it was her habit to buy groceries for the house. She refused to respond if addressed by anything other than her full name, and so kept herself at a distance.

Timmy, the humpbacked Shona who kept the garden and set the clocks, thought her haughty and intimidating and beautiful. On the rare moments when she wasn't bustling around the house, Timmy observed her staring into another time, fingering the pewter locket that hung on a chain around her neck. He spoke to her only on Fridays, when he asked permission to clean his cages in her laundry sink.

Timmy supplemented his income by stealing bush babies away from their mothers during the day when they slept in the trees. Despite his hump, Timmy could scale a baobab tree swiftly and silently. The yard behind the servant's quarters was piled with cages filled with young bush babies waiting to be smuggled to England to grace country gardens. At that time, the creatures were popular among the rich because of their enormous eyes and their cry, which resembled a human baby weeping.

"There, there," he'd say when he comforted the youngest ones, staring into their wet eyes while they wrapped their tails around his wrist and nursed from a bottle of goat's milk. Timmy fed half his bush babies ground glass before shipping them to England, to maintain a keen demand for the little monkeys and to keep their prices high.

Timmy often watched Mahulda Jane Braxton when he thought she wasn't looking. Something had halted the flow of life inside the woman.

"Why you so hard, Mahulda Jane Braxton?" Timmy asked one Friday as he scrubbed his cages.

Mahulda Jane Braxton stiffened. She did not look at Timmy while she lighted the paraffin stove. "It is not my intention to be so, Timothy."

Timmy nodded. He said nothing more, but on the following Tuesday, Timmy began washing his cages in her laundry sink twice weekly, watching the beautiful Capetown coloured with sidelong looks.

On the day of my birth, Timmy busied himself in his garden, glancing nervously at the drawn curtains of the parlor, behind which my mother, on all fours, stared inward, isolated in her pain, pushing with all her strength to be rid of me.

Each time Mrs. Gordon screamed, Timmy's head retreated deeper into the hump of his back, and he began pruning the bougainvillea even more energetically. The humpbacked Shona had arranged the garden in such a way that at no time of the year would a stroller be out of sight or scent of a newly unfolded blossom. Canopies of jacarandas and flame trees, copper and burgundy msasa leaves, shocks of orange honeysuckle and golden shower, and the loud keening of insects assaulted visitors in violent waves of color and smell and sound. Mr. and Mrs. Gordon found Timmy's garden unbearable. Mahulda Jane Braxton stared at the vibrant efflorescence from her kitchen window.

Timmy heard loud voices coming from the study. He began rapidly trimming along the hedge toward the window where the imbroglio was taking place.

Mr. Gordon's cross voice floated out to Timmy between the slats of the closed blinds. "Calumny! I was only arranging the cushion beneath the child's head." Timmy detected fear in the voice.

"I know what I saw," Mahulda Jane Braxton stated flatly.

The voices moved out of the study, and Mahulda Jane Braxton appeared on the veranda, followed closely by Mr. Gordon. Timmy tried to concentrate on his bougainvilleas.

"Don't get your head up, woman. I'll not have you slandering me, d'you hear?"

Timmy could see Mahulda Jane Braxton in his peripheral vision, cradling a bundle as she settled into the rocking chair. Mr. Gordon stood over her, opening and closing his fists. Timmy pruned furiously.

Mahulda Jane Braxton was thankful for the presence of Timothy.

"I have no interest in speaking of this matter further," she told her employer. "The baby needs milk and quiet now, Mr. Gordon. I'll care for it until Mrs. Gordon is herself again, no worries." Mahulda Jane Braxton began unbuttoning her blouse, fully aware of the discomfort it caused her employer. She reached behind her back and unfastened her brassiere, exposing both breasts.

Mr. Gordon turned away, embarrassed as his servant nursed his child. A stick bug crawled up his trouser leg, and he slapped at it. The gardener stopped shearing the ruined bougainvilleas and stared openly at him. Mr. Gordon's gaze traveled over the pulsing aberrance of Timmy's garden. A Christmas beetle's high-pitched sawing whined in his ears. He didn't know where to look, and so he retreated into his study to rework his accounts.

Timmy bustled in the flower beds closest to the veranda and the kitchen, while Mahulda Jane Braxton cleaned the blood from the parlor and made a soup from the placenta to help with her milk. *Between the two of them, I was never left alone.*

And thus the matter of my upbringing was settled. On the following day, Mahulda Jane Braxton would brew whip beer and Timmy would slaughter a goat, and the Shona would come to Timmy's strange garden to sing, weaving everchanging patterns around a simple chant in spontaneous six-part harmony, welcoming me into the world.

Creche

On the evening of my birth, Mahulda Jane Braxton stared at the curve of my cheek against the larger curve of her breast as she rocked on the veranda, stripped naked to the waist.

Outside, a mother bush baby wailed for her stolen child locked away in one of Timmy's cages. Milk leaked from Mahulda's free breast at the sound of it.

Mahulda gently nudged the child beneath its chin with her knuckle each time it fell asleep at the nipple.

Her breasts had begun forming early, even before she menstruated, and yet it wasn't until that moment, nearly forty years later, that Mahulda fully appreciated their function. *These memories flowed into my blood with my mother's milk, or perhaps it is only me, storytelling. Africans are a storytelling people.*

Mahulda remembered a nonsense song from her childhood and she sang it softly to the child:

What would you do if the kettle boiled over?
What would I do but to fill it again?
And what would you do if the cows ate the clover?
What would I do but to set it again?

Mahulda listened to the tick of the grandmother clock in the parlor.

Her finger traced one of the fine veins in the baby's pale skin.

A rout the da doubt the da diddly da dum

A cat ambled onto the veranda and curled around Mahulda's ankle.

She watched a cloud of moths make shifting patterns in the aura of the veranda light.

A rout the da doubt the da diddly da dum

Mahulda lightly touched the locket that hung on her neck.

The baby's face fell away from her breast, glassy-eyed and sated.

Da diddly da dee da dee da dum

Milk dripped from Mahulda's breast as she stood and paced the veranda and burped the child.

Each drop struck the floorboards with the regularity of a timepiece.

Da diddly da dee da diddly da dum

The cat followed in her steps, lapping.

Mahulda tread slowly, savoring each moment.

She returned to her chair and resumed her rocking.

Mahulda looked deep into the blue eyes of the child *and I stared back into the warmth of my mother's eyes, and we remained that way until sleep came upon us.*

Ronald F. Currie Jr.

Visiting Your Grave

For r.m.c., 1930–1992

My mother said to me, I'm sorry, Laurel, when she shit on the kitchen floor.

She was sick, of course. Grown women do not shit on the kitchen floor unless they are very sick.

Maman, I said. I was wiping the ridged and bumpy linoleum of her kitchen floor with a washcloth and depositing the mess in a plastic grocery bag. I was near tears, from the smell, and from the absurdity of her apologizing to me for being so sick she couldn't hold it until she reached the bathroom and instead shit on the kitchen floor. Don't, I said.

Fred! My mother called out in her sleep. I'm on my way! I love you, you bastard!

She said these things in French. Canadian, not Parisian. When she talked in her sleep she always spoke French.

Fred was my father's name. He did a better job of drinking and smoking himself to death than my mother, and died in 1979 when he was forty-eight years old. He learned to drink and smoke in Korea, and then he came home and taught my mother. When he died he was completely bald and his mouth sagged tiredly at one corner, and his eyes bulged with a rheumy, yellow wetness.

There is a picture of him looking like this. In the picture he is wearing a light blue tuxedo for my brother's wedding. The shirt of the tuxedo, a lighter blue than the jacket and pants, has ruffles down the front. He is dancing with my mother. She has on a pink dress. His right hand and her left are clasped together gently. My mother is smiling. Fred looks like he's given up, more or less.

My mother woke from her dream and saw me sitting in the chair by her bed.

You shouldn't get married, she said to me in English. You're much too pretty.

I told her I most likely wouldn't.

My mother said to me, I miss my job.

My mother worked for a hospice, caring for terminally ill people in their homes, for fourteen years. The irony of this was not lost on her.

Hospice was her calling. She found it after a lifetime spent working as a waitress and secretary and school lunchlady. She loved it so much that, when she was forced by her boss to choose, she gave up drinking rather than give up her job.

There were things, when my mother got really sick, that my brother and sisters and I couldn't handle. So the people she used to work with came to her home and cared for her, because she was the terminally ill person. She accepted their help, smiled weakly, and said kind things, but when they left she puffed up with indignation at having girls she used to tell what to do wipe her backside. She loved them dearly, but she still had her pride, after all.

And when she died, the girls at the hospice placed a paid notice in the newspaper near her obituary, commending my brother and sisters and me for being so strong and dutiful. It didn't change anything, but it was nice.

My mother lit a Kool and drew on it and coughed and coughed and vomited a thin stringy brown fluid into the basin on her nightstand and said to me, Don't ever smoke.

I told her I wouldn't, even though I'd been smoking for seventeen years and had left twice that day, under the pretense of running errands, in order to have a cigarette.

My mother said to me, No more solids. I hardly have any stomach left.

So I fed her broths and Gatorade, and this was a reason why her stool was so loose and she ran to the bathroom but didn't make it and shit on the kitchen floor.

My mother said to me, I was a good mother, Laurel.

This was not a question. I nodded.

Remember when your brother sent us those pictures from Vietnam? my mother asked me. And there was that shot of him standing in front of his boat without a shirt on, and he was so skinny we could count his ribs? Remember?

I said, Yes, I remember.

My brother was serving with the Navy in Vietnam and I wrote him and said, "Eat more. Or at least put a shirt on. *Maman* is worried sick." And he wrote back in a letter addressed to me only, "If I sent pictures of what this place is really like, *Maman* wouldn't worry about how well I'm eating."

That boy was nearly the death of me, my mother said, there in her bedroom.

You are a good mother, I told her.

My mother said to me, I don't know how your father smoked so much. I don't know where he found the time.

My father smoked four packs of Chesterfields a day for thirty years. He would light his first cigarette with a match in the morning, then light each new cigarette with the smoldering butt of the old one. He went through eighty nonfilters in a day, but it took him a month to use up a book of matches.

The sagging corner of his mouth was where he tucked each cigarette after he lit it.

He used to keep me up at night, my mother said to me. Not by snoring. He didn't snore. But when he breathed his lungs sounded like they had gravel in them. I couldn't sleep with that racket.

He was very bad to himself, I told her.

My mother said to me, I don't understand their fancy words. All I know is—the pain, it gets worse.

The fancy word was *metastasis*. I'd taken her to an appointment with her oncologist, and he'd used this word. He was trying to explain that the cancer had spread from her lungs to her throat to her stomach, and was now chewing away at her intestines, and this was another reason why her stool was so loose and she ran to the bathroom but didn't make it and shit on the kitchen floor.

She told the oncologist that the oral painkillers were no good anymore. So he arranged for her to receive a morphine drip at home, administered by a nurse from the hospice. He told her that, in addition to relieving her pain, high doses of morphine might also help solidify her stool, so she wouldn't run to the bathroom but not make it and shit on the kitchen floor anymore, if she was lucky. Maybe, maybe not, he said, then excused himself to go to lunch.

My mother said to me, We didn't have much, but boy we laughed a lot, didn't we?

Yes, *Maman*, I said, and this was the truth. My strongest memories of childhood were ones of laughter.

What about that damn dog, she said. The one we had before your baby sister was born.

I said, Rascal. The black-and-tan mutt.

Rascal! she said, and smiled. That little *batard* ate a chicken and a whole loaf of bread off the counter while we were at church. Then pissed in your father's work shoes. Rascal did not last very long, did he? Your father wanted to kill him dead right there. He was so angry he didn't care if he messed up his church clothes.

And we couldn't stop laughing, I said.

Yes, and your father got mad at us because he thought we were laughing at him, my mother said.

We were, I said, and smiled.

My mother said to me, Ask Father Thibodeau to come.

She was too weak to leave the house Sunday mornings anymore. Plus she had the morphine IV stuck in her around the clock. I went to St. Francis Church and asked Father Thibodeau to come and give her communion.

He came the next Sunday. I met him at the door and thanked him for taking time to see my mother.

Where have you been, Laurel? he asked me. We haven't seen you for a long time. Did you move out of state?

She's this way, I told him, heading down the hallway. Come in, please.

I led him in and closed the door, and waited outside the bedroom. I could hear Father Thibodeau's voice through the wall, a deep comforting baritone, giving my mother absolution and communion in French. He'd been the priest at St. Francis since I was a little girl. He still sounded like God Himself to me.

When he finished he opened the bedroom door and said goodbye and that he would see himself out. I went in to my mother.

She said, Father Thibodeau is worried about you. He wonders where you spend your Sundays.

The next time he comes, I said, you can tell him I spend my Sundays right here with you.

My mother said to me, Laurel, I'm scared.

For a while the morphine helped with her pain, but it did nothing to firm up her stool. Of course now she wasn't even getting out of bed, so she didn't have to worry anymore about running to the bathroom but not making it and shitting on the kitchen floor. When she shit in her bed I screamed at the hospice girl to let me take care of it. Then I took care of it.

• • •

My mother said to me, Laurel, don't be scared.

I can't help it, I said, crying.

My mother said, Laurel, I'm sorry if I didn't understand you sometimes, and the things you did. Now I see none of that matters. Little differences, arguing and all that. There are deeper, more important things. I see that now. I understand. I understand you.

None of that matters, *Maman,* I said. You're right, none of it matters. Now shhhh . . .

My mother said, No, don't cry, Laurel, it's okay.

. . . shhhhhhh, I said, Please, *Maman,* shhhhhh . . .

My mother said, Don't cry, baby.

Then I realized I had plenty of time to feel sorry for myself after she was gone, so I gathered myself and stopped weeping and said with a sniffle, No, *Maman,* I won't cry anymore.

My mother said to me, Laurel, will you please sleep next to me tonight? Don't sleep in that chair. Sleep here, with me.

I got out of the chair and pulled the blankets back and got into my mother's bed. I moved in behind my mother and put my arm around her, but there wasn't much left under her nightgown except bones and intense, baking heat. She was breathing in quick little gasps, like a mouse caught in someone's hand.

Don't turn away from God, my mother said in the dark. Don't lose your faith over this.

I didn't tell her that I had no faith to lose. I wrapped my arm tighter around her waist, and I could smell that she needed to be changed, but I thought, Well, it's not on the goddamn kitchen floor, and let it alone.

Sleep, *Maman,* I said. Sleep.

Jennifer Seoyuen Oh

JANUARY

Dedicated to my grandmother

The child was dead. Myung knew because the mouth pressed against her neck had stopped releasing air. So slight had been the little girl's breath that it was a wonder anyone could have noticed its cessation. But the mother had been listening, day in and day out, through the rain and the noise of the sea and the cold, to the hopeful sound of her child breathing. Feeling the air pulse against her skin, in a wordless whisper that pleaded: Um-ma, I am still here. Stay alive for me.

But the mother's neck was cold now. It was winter and even the child's feverish heat would no longer keep her warm. Smallpox and weariness and war were killing the Koreans by the thousands, but the mother, alone with the body of her little girl, thought not about the war, but about how the child used to play in the courtyard of her home, singing wordless songs, her small hands smeared with mud. Days otherwise chore-filled and dreary could be brightened by a smile in a face streaked with dirt: Um-ma, this mud is sweet. Like red bean paste.

She cradled the child in her arms, crowded with others under a makeshift tent. They, too, had buried their own children. It was nothing new to them. Neither was the cold wind that battered the tent, the sour smell of unwashed bodies, the island ground covered with sharp rocks. And so she slept, in the darkness that offered the steady comfort of sightlessness.

How does one bury one's own child? How does one dig a grave and watch the dirt cover a daughter's delicate cheeks, her closed eyes, the soft mouth?

She wanted her husband to take their dead baby from her arms, to relieve her of her burden.

Eight days and nights she had been separated by the war from her husband.

And it was without him that Myung wrapped the child in a blanket and found an open grave. She threw in the body. She ran, covering her mouth, from the smell of the dead. She fell into the muddy weeds. On her hands and knees she cried. "Ah-gi-ya, ah-gi-ya." *Baby, my baby.*

She hit the ground, pounded it until her sleeves were soaked with mud. Her fists were a blur of sorrow and fury, disturbing the steadiness of the early morning.

Myung had known that the war was coming, but she did not believe in its reality. She was always busy; there were the meals to cook, the clothes and diapers to wash, the house to be swept clean. Happy with her baby and in love with her husband, she was surrounded by the comfort of her kin and friends.

She mended clothes with her niece every Thursday. They were close in age, twenty and seventeen; they were like sisters. Both had married young, and Sunia was seven months pregnant.

Sunia picked at a loose stitch, resting her arms on her blue dress, which had a patch covering her growing belly. They often joked that it was the baby's door, and that the baby would knock when ready to be born. But today, they sewed grave and silent at a low table, lacquered black and inlaid with stone, a wedding present to Myung from Sunia's mother. Bowls of steaming tea sat near their elbows, still waiting to be tasted.

"Will your husband join the army?" Myung asked.

"It is expected of him. He will go away to the army camps to train." Sunia's young face was stalwart in its sad acceptance.

Myung reached across the table to rub her niece's hand, their gold wedding rings clinking against each other. "If we need to leave the village, you and your family can come with me."

Sunia pulled back, spreading the fingers of her other hand. They watched as a bead of blood slowly appeared on her palm, caused by the prick of a needle.

Myung took a cloth and dabbed the blood away. Sunia clutched at the carved side of the table, unable to look up from the patterns of milky lavender stone, but her eyes and tears were grateful. Myung brought out pressed rice cakes, filled with sugar and crushed red beans, her niece's favorite. Soon they were laughing over Sunia's latest mishap with the fish-seller, who was in love with the married young woman. Myung's daughter heard the chatter and came to sit in her mother's lap, her fists and cheeks becoming messy with bean paste.

Sunia was killed on the first day. The day after Myung's husband left, to escape the North Korean forces.

"Myung. We will see each other again." Ji-yoon stood before his young wife on the steps of the courtyard, his short, thin body unflinching and straight.

Her head lowered, Myung was kneeling on the ground, her hands leaving damp spots on her thick cotton robe. She had been washing rice for her husband's supper. Beside her, the pot sat brimming with water; some grains of rice floated on the surface as if they were boats lost in the ocean. Dipping her hand into the pot, she skimmed away the errant grains, clutching them. The water ran down her arm, bathing her elbow with coldness.

"Yau-bo." *Dearest.*

She did not lift her head. The rice began to feel sticky in her warm hand. She opened it, tilted her palm, letting the grains scatter into a white pattern in the dirt. They reminded her of maggots, sodden and dead.

"The North Koreans are not likely to attack the village. It is just a precautionary measure, to have the men sent away. The UN army will keep you warned of developments, and you can join me in Pusan."

"Can't we go with you?" She knew they couldn't. The women and children would only hinder their South Korean men.

"We'll see each other in a few weeks. It won't be long."

"What if we never see each other again?" she whispered.

"We will. I believe in Heaven."

He went down the steps to where Myung sat. She felt the touch of his hand on her forehead. Rising on her knees she clutched her husband's legs, pressing her face into his trousers, smelling the heavy odor of canvas, cigarette smoke, and grass stains.

"Um-ma." Myung pulled away from her husband, turning to look. Her two-year-old daughter stood half-hidden by the door, eyes wide and unknowing. She held the hem of her yellow dress to her mouth, revealing sweet white legs, bare little feet.

"Um-ma, why sad?"

Ji-yoon took two large steps and snatched the child into his arms, swinging her around. "My beautiful daughter, my beautiful child," he sang as he tossed her up and down. Myung watched, wiping her eyes and smiling.

Her twelve-year-old nephew, whom she had raised from infancy, came to her house that evening to return a borrowed spade. He had been preparing a garden for his sister, Sunia, overturning the dead, mushy plants, leaving them to decompose until the coming of spring. This nephew loved Myung better than he did his own mother. He often followed her around the house, offering to wash rice or carry kindling. Se-jun was already taller than his aunt, but she adored his double-creased eyes, his curly lashes, so winsome in his round, smooth face. His left-hand thumb was shorter than the other one and Myung told him it meant good fortune and future riches. Neither of them knew if the saying was true, but she always had a special caress for the deformed thumb—not quite a handshake, not quite a kiss.

"Little Aunt, is it true that we have to leave home soon?"

"We might be able to stay. Perhaps the North Koreans will take another route into the South." She wiped her plates, the gray-blue dishwater reflecting the lamplight. The soapsuds were lukewarm; soon the water would be as cold as the stone steps upon which she sat.

"I want to go with you."

"Of course I will go with you and your family, but you must take care of your mother and sisters."

"I can protect you, too," Se-jun insisted. He held the dirty spade like a sword, chopping at imaginary soldiers, gnashing his teeth and growling in his high-pitched voice. He flung his narrow body about the courtyard, hopping and flailing as if the house were filled with imaginary enemies.

Myung could only smile at his bravery.

The first day, the day after Ji-yoon left, the terror began.

Ji-yoon and his older brother were village leaders, easy targets of persecution for enemy armies. When news came during the night that the Chinese army was close to the thirty-eighth parallel, they were the first to escape, leaving their wives and children behind. They departed in the early morning, heading on foot for Pusan, far south of their village. Still tousled from making love to her husband, Myung stood in the doorway, until the outline of Ji-yoon's body faded into the gray of the cloudy dawn. She thought of how he had kissed her breasts and held her that night, the straw mats that lined their floor pressing into their backs. Warmth from the black stove had made their skin glow like hot ashes.

It was midmorning the next day when the soldiers poured into the village, their faces painted into darkened anonymous masks. She heard the rifle shots filling the air, sounding as if fireworks were being set off for New Year celebrations. Dropping her kindling, she ran to her sleeping child and wrapped her in a blanket. I must hide, she thought. But where could she hide? The closet? The outhouse? The door crashed open. She saw a soldier, his eyebrows covered by a muddy helmet. The soldier was young. He seemed her age, barely twenty, but he looked like Death, holding a gun, grim in his search of living targets. And yet he reminded her of Se-jun, who loved her better than his own mother. The soldier had double-lidded eyes.

"Where is your husband?"

"I don't know," she said. She covered the baby's head with the blanket. The child's grandmother had sewn it for her first birthday, gold silk, with embroidered white cranes. Its tassels trembled as she held the sleeping toddler close.

"Don't kill me. I have a child."

"Shut up!" He seized her sleeve and shoved her out the door.

It was a sunny day. Walking, her child wailing in her arms, she thought she was going to die. When they reached an open field, yards from the well where she drew her daily water for chores, he ordered her to turn around.

She obeyed. Waited for the sharp crack of the gun that would signal the end of her life.

But she heard sobbing instead.

The young soldier told her to cover her face and run. "I cannot bear to see your face," he said. "Go. Go home."

Home she went, to find her nephew waiting for her.

"There is a boat that the government sent. We must go," Se-jun told her.

"But your mother, your sisters."

"They are dead. They were shot."

"How did you manage to escape?"

"I wasn't there. I was collecting berries on the creek bank."

The three of them left together. Their footsteps were steady and sober, leaving behind their village. In the distance they heard soldiers bellowing, running back and forth like tormented bulls. There was no time for tears.

They journeyed to the seashore, to board the ship that would take them to Pusan.

• • •

The tide was starting to come in when they reached the shore the next day. The boat seemed to be stranded on the slushy ground, a great beached whale besieged by clambering hands and feet, seeking to avoid the swift incoming tide.

Those who escaped the waves waited fearful and crowded on the ship, as if they were geese in a pen, waiting to be slaughtered. The rough ocean noise muffled the screams of the drowning, until they sounded like seagulls, keening, flying farther and farther away. Some of the people were crying; most were quiet, stunned by the indifference of the sea. Myung stood by the rail, her eyes fixed on the clouds.

Dearest, I believe in Heaven.

She felt her nephew shudder beside her, and she gripped his head with a soft clenched hand, letting him sob into her neck. Her child held her other hand. The daughter had not spoken a word since they had left the village. Still silent, she listened to Se-jun weep.

His tears were warm and thick.

The smallpox fever came on the fourth day. It afflicted half the people on the boat. The child's skin was as pale as moonlight, but hotter than a porcelain bowl filled with boiling tea. And still she did not speak. The noisy hiss of the waves rocking the boat troubled Myung's thoughts, and she wrapped her arms towel-fashion around her child. At night she sang lullabies under her breath, hoping to ease the darkness.

On the fifth day, the ship was anchored midmorning at a small island. As Myung and Se-jun walked down the ramp their ears rang with the moans of the sick. The soldiers set up black tarps to shelter the refugees from the rain, but the smell of the dying drove the healthier ones out, into the gray drizzle. Myung tried to cool the fever raging in her daughter's body with rags wetted with seawater so salty it made her chapped hands sting. When the sun went down everyone huddled under the tarps, praying or cursing or sleeping. Even the stench of disease could not persuade anyone to pass the night unsheltered, vulnerable to the cold and the creatures that came to peck at human flesh, rotting or half-alive.

On the sixth day, the rash and the redness came. The rash made the child's face look like a rough pink seashell. In the evening the blisters burst and ran with yellow fluid. Myung bound the girl's hands with strips of cloth to keep her from scratching her sores. She prayed that her daughter would not go blind.

There was little fresh water. Se-jun fought the morning lines to ask for more, but the soldier in charge said there was none. Se-jun insisted, just one cup. The South Korean soldier hit him on the head and called him a smelly dog child for his trouble.

Crouching outside their tent, Myung held her daughter, shivering. Their black hair was damp and matted, from the seawater and the rain. The girl's feet were unwrapped, her dull toenails matching the grayness of the sky.

On the seventh day, the child finally spoke.

"Um-ma, where are you? It's dark."

The child died on the eighth day.

Weak arms encircled Myung, picking her up from where she lay.

Her eyes were too swollen to see. A gourd was laid against her lips; a miracle of water trickled down her chin, dribbling onto her breasts, like the spit of a newborn eager to suckle its mother. It was the nephew's share of water.

"Little Aunt, get up. It's muddy. The ship is leaving again soon." Her nephew nudged her, a gentle but urgent shove. They walked past the grave, filled in with dirt by the stronger of the refugees. The anchored ship was waiting to take them to Pusan.

Myung was seasick, vomiting nothing into the waves, as the ocean tossed the crowded ship. But there were no tears. No tears left, she would later tell her family. Not a tear left. Not after these eight nights and days.

When they arrived at Pusan, they were swept onto the port along with hundreds of other dirty, stinking bodies, hollow-eyed by what they had left behind: laughter, rice filling their stomachs, family homes.

Few had money. Myung had none, for she had left with nothing but a silver spoon and the child that she had carried. Her child was gone, but the spoon would buy food, enough for a few days.

When money from selling the spoon was gone, she and her nephew found work. Work clearing roots from swampy rice fields, skirt or pants tied around their knees, cold and barefoot amid the muddy paddies. The midday wind froze their fine pale skin but they earned food enough to feed themselves.

Those first few days, they lived in a tent, fashioned out of plastic left by the South Korean army. At night the two of them crouched under rough blankets garnered from the refugee stores, listening to the rustling of their shelter's loose corners. When she fell asleep Myung dreamed of her husband. Dreaming, she cried aloud, tossing as if caught in the heat of lovers coupling.

Her nephew lay awake, listening; he was too tired and haunted to dream.

She started to smoke cigarettes. She smoked Lucky Strikes when she had the extra money. Smoking would later kill her, at the age of sixty-eight. But nothing else could ease the memories of her daughter's face, so like the backside of a seashell.

Once Myung caught her nephew sneaking a cigarette from her pack. She smacked his face until he cried, crawling away into the corner of the tent. She followed Se-jun and wept, smoothing his greasy head with her cold pink hands.

At night she and Se-jun sang sad folk songs of lovers lost and fate unkind. Her nephew's voice was still high and childlike, and whenever he sang "Arirang" she reached for her cigarettes. *Walking over the peak at Arirang you left me behind. You will be tired before you reach one mile. Walking over the peak at Arirang the sorrows in my heart are as many as the stars in the sky.*

It was at the bathhouse that Myung finally heard news of her husband.

Myung learned of the bathhouse when buying radishes at the market for the evening's soup. The vegetable seller was a frank old woman with more wrinkles and sags than a badly laundered shirt.

"You need a good scrubbing, none of those sponge-bath affairs out of buckets. What would your mother say if she saw you?"

Myung was embarrassed, and she rubbed the back of her neck, her palm coming away covered with sweat and dead skin, the consistency of damp ashes. She saw that the woman's brown face was weathered but kind, and she asked for directions to the nearest bathhouse.

The old woman studied her appearance, noting the ragged but well-made clothes, the protruding cheekbones, the large shadows under her eyes. "You a refugee?"

She nodded, yes.

When she got home she found that she had an extra radish tucked into her basket.

The next day after work she took her nephew to the public bath. It was a large stone building with two massive doors; one section was for women and the other for men. Se-jun clutched a ragged towel to his chest and opened one of the doors. A great burst of steam stopped him momentarily, but he eventually made his way into the arena of wet, naked bodies.

Myung watched him enter, then she pushed open the other door. She removed her cloth shoes and walked across the damp floor, searching the huge bathing pool for an empty corner. At the other end of the room was a long wooden bench piled high with clothes and shoes. Taking her washcloth and soap out of a pocket, she removed her own clothing and bundled it neatly under her towel. The noisy women and children splashing about in the water seemed to ignore the newcomer.

Facing the wall, she stepped gingerly into the hot water, then she submerged herself all at once, numbing her limbs until almost all sensation vanished, allowing the water to touch her neck with gentle slaps. She briskly attacked her body with the rough washcloth, sloughing off lint-colored crumbs of skin and dirt. She scrubbed her neck, washed her armpits; more gently she soaped her breasts and between her legs. Only once did she turn around at the sound of a child laughing, but she quickly looked at the wall again, staring at the yellowing tiles.

As Myung stood drying her hair, clothes clinging to moist skin, a woman approached her end of the bench. She was thin and care-worn, wrapped in a faded robe, but her freckled skin had the texture of finely sanded silk.

"You are new?" It was less a question than a confirmation. The stranger bowed. "I am Kim Soo-Chun."

"Lee Myung Hwa." She averted her gaze; a naked young girl clung to the woman's legs, her black eyes peeping around her mother's waist.

The woman was silent, then she bowed again, deeply.

"Your husband gave me your picture and a forwarding address. He stayed with our family for two days, then he left to sign up for the army. He had feared that you were dead."

Myung fell at the woman's feet.

She wrote a letter that evening after supper, planning to post it the following morning. It would tell her husband that she and Se-jun had arrived together, that the child had died on the way, and that they waited for him in Pusan, staying at Kim Soo-Chun's house. "We have even," she wrote, "been to a bathhouse. Exactly like the ones back home."

That night while Soo-Chun spread out her guest blankets, Myung and her nephew sat outside to breathe in the night air. She thought she could hear her child's laughter, twinkling down on her like starlight, but this time she did not reach for a cigarette.

She held her nephew's clean left hand, and they listened to a man's distant voice calling his daughter home.

Junot Díaz

Invierno

From the top of Westminister, our main strip, you could see the thinnest sliver of ocean cresting the horizon to the east. My father had been shown that sight—the management showed everyone—but as he drove us in from JFK he didn't stop to point it out. The ocean might have made us feel better, considering what else there was to see. London Terrace itself was a mess; half the buildings still needed their wiring and in the evening light these structures sprawled about the landscape like ships of brick that had run aground. Mud followed gravel everywhere and the grass, planted late in fall, poked out of the snow in dead tufts.

Each building has its own laundry room, Papi said. Mami looked vaguely out of the snout of her parka and nodded. That's wonderful, she said. I was watching the snow sift over itself and my brother was cracking his knuckles. This was our first day in the States. The world was frozen solid.

Our apartment seemed huge to us. Rafa and I had a room to ourselves and the kitchen, with its refrigerator and stove, was about the size of our house on Sumner Welles. We didn't stop shivering until Papi set the apartment temperature to about eighty. Beads of water gathered on the windows like bees and we had to wipe the glass to see outside. Rafa and I were stylish in our new clothes and we wanted out, but Papi told us to take off our boots and our parkas. He sat us down in front of the television, his arms lean and surprisingly hairy right up to the short-cut sleeves. He had just shown us how to flush the toilets, run the sinks, and start the shower.

This isn't a slum, Papi began. I want you to treat everything around you with respect. I don't want you throwing any of your garbage on the floor or on the street. I don't want you going to the bathroom in the bushes.

Rafa nudged me. In Santo Domingo I'd pissed everywhere, and the first time Papi had seen me in action, whizzing on a street corner, on the night of his triumphant return, he had said, What are you doing?

Decent people live around here and that's how we're going to live. You're Americans now. He had his Chivas Regal bottle on his knee.

After waiting a few seconds to show that yes, I'd digested everything he'd said, I asked, Can we go out now?

Why don't you help me unpack? Mami suggested. Her hands were very still; usually they were fussing with a piece of paper, a sleeve, or each other.

We'll just be out for a little while, I said. I got up and pulled on my boots. Had I known my father even a little I might not have turned my back on him. But I didn't know him; he'd spent the last five years in the States working, and we'd spent the last five years in Santo Domingo waiting. He grabbed my ear and wrenched me back onto the couch. He did not look happy.

You'll go out when I tell you you're ready. I don't want either of you getting lost or getting hurt out there. You don't know this place.

I looked over at Rafa, who sat quietly in front of the TV. Back on the island, the two of us had taken guaguas clear across the capital by ourselves. I looked up at Papi, his narrow face still unfamiliar. Don't you eye me, he said.

Mami stood up. You kids might as well give me a hand.

I didn't move. On the TV the newscasters were making small, flat noises at each other.

• • •

Since we weren't allowed out of the house—it's too cold, Papi said—we mostly sat in front of the TV or stared out at the snow those first days. Mami cleaned everything about ten times and made us some damn elaborate lunches.

Pretty early on Mami decided that watching TV was beneficial; you could learn English from it. She saw our young minds as bright, spiky sunflowers in need of light, and arranged us as close to the TV as possible to maximize our exposure. We watched the news, sitcoms, cartoons, *Tarzan, Flash Gordon, Jonny Quest, Herculoids, Sesame Street*—eight, nine hours of TV a day, but it was *Sesame Street* that gave us our best lessons. Each word my brother and I learned we passed between ourselves, repeating over and over, and when Mami asked us to show her how to say it, we shook our heads and said, Don't worry about it.

Just tell me, she said, and when we pronounced the words slowly, forming huge, lazy soap-bubbles of sound, she never could duplicate them. Her lips seemed to tug apart even the simplest constructions. That sounds horrible, I said.

What do you know about English? she asked.

At dinner she'd try her English out on Papi, but he just poked at his pernil, which was not my mother's best dish.

I can't understand a word you're saying, he said one night. Mami had cooked rice with squid. It's best if I take care of the English.

How do you expect me to learn?

You don't have to learn, he said. Besides, the average woman can't learn English.

Oh?

It's a difficult language to master, he said, first in Spanish and then in English.

Mami didn't say another word. In the morning, as soon as Papi was out of the apartment, Mami turned on the TV and put us in front of it. The apartment was always cold in the morning and leaving our beds was a serious torment.

It's too early, we said.

It's like school, she suggested.

No, it's not, we said. We were used to going to school at noon.

You two complain too much. She would stand behind us and when I turned around she would be mouthing the words we were learning, trying to make sense of them.

Even Papi's early-morning noises were strange to me. I lay in bed, listening to him stumbling around in the bathroom, like he was drunk or something. I didn't know what he did for Reynolds Aluminum, but he had a lot of uniforms in his closet, all filthy with machine oil.

I had expected a different father, one about seven feet tall with enough money to buy our entire barrio, but this one was average height, with an average face. He'd come to our house in Santo Domingo in a busted-up taxi and the gifts he had brought us were small things—toy guns and tops—that we were too old for, that we broke right away. Even though he hugged us and took us out to dinner on the Malecón—our first meat in years—I didn't know what to make of him. A father is a hard thing to get to know.

Those first weeks in the States, Papi spent a great deal of his home-time downstairs with his books or in front of the TV. He said little to us that wasn't disciplinary, which didn't surprise us. We'd seen other dads in action, understood that part of the drill.

What he got on me about the most was my shoelaces. Papi had a thing with shoelaces. I didn't know how to tie them properly, and when I put together a rather formidable knot, Papi would bend down and pull it apart with one tug. At least you have a future as a magician, Rafa said, but this was serious. Rafa showed me how, and I said, Fine, and had no problems in front of him, but when Papi was breathing down my neck, his hand on a belt, I couldn't perform; I looked at my father like my laces were live wires he wanted me to touch together.

I met some dumb men in the Guardia, Papi said, but every single one of them could tie his motherfucking shoes. He looked over at Mami. Why can't he?

These were not the sort of questions that had answers. She

looked down, studied the veins that threaded the backs of her hands. For a second Papi's watery turtle-eyes met mine. Don't you look at me, he said.

Even on days I managed a halfway decent retard knot, as Rafa called them, Papi still had my hair to go on about. While Rafa's hair was straight and dark and glided through a comb like a Caribbean grandparent's dream, my hair still had enough of the African to condemn me to endless combings and out-of-this-world haircuts. My mother cut our hair every month, but this time when she put me in the chair my father told her not to bother.

Only one thing will take care of that, he said. Yunior, go get dressed.

Rafa followed me into my bedroom and watched while I buttoned my shirt. His mouth was tight. I started to feel anxious. What's your problem? I said.

Nothing.

Then stop watching me. When I got to my shoes, he tied them for me. At the door my father looked down and said, You're getting better.

I knew where the van was parked but I went the other way just to catch a glimpse of the neighborhood. Papi didn't notice my defection until I had rounded the corner, and when he growled my name I hurried back, but I had already seen the fields and the children on the snow.

I sat in the front seat. He popped a tape of Jonny Ventura into the player and took us out smoothly to Route 9. The snow lay in dirty piles on the side of the road. There can't be anything worse than old snow, he said. It's nice while it falls but once it gets to the ground it just causes trouble.

Are there accidents?

Not with me driving.

The cattails on the banks of the Raritan were stiff and the color of sand, and when we crossed the river, Papi said, I work in the next town.

We were in Perth Amboy for the services of a real talent, a

Puerto Rican barber named Rubio who knew just what to do with the pelo malo. He put two or three creams on my head and had me sit with the foam awhile; after his wife rinsed me off he studied my head in the mirror, tugged at my hair, rubbed an oil into it, and finally sighed.

It's better to shave it all off, Papi said.

I have some other things that might work.

Papi looked at his watch. Shave it.

All right, Rubio said. I watched the clippers plow through my hair, watched my scalp appear, tender and defenseless. One of the old men in the waiting area snorted and held his paper higher. When he was finished Rubio massaged talcum powder on my neck. Now you look guapo, he said. He handed me a stick of gum, which would go right to my brother.

Well? Papi asked. I nodded. As soon as we were outside the cold clamped down on my head like a slab of wet dirt.

We drove back in silence. An oil tanker was pulling into port on the Raritan and I wondered how easy it would be for me to slip aboard and disappear.

Do you like negras? my father asked.

I turned my head to look at the women we had just passed. I turned back and realized that he was waiting for an answer, that he wanted to know, and while I wanted to blurt that I didn't like girls in any denomination, I said instead, Oh yes, and he smiled.

They're beautiful, he said, and lit a cigarette. They'll take care of you better than anyone.

Rafa laughed when he saw me. You look like a big thumb.

Dios mío, Mami said, turning me around.

It looks good, Papi said.

And the cold's going to make him sick.

Papi put his cold palm on my head. He likes it fine, he said.

Papi worked a long fifty-hour week and on his days off he expected quiet, but my brother and I had too much energy to be quiet; we didn't think anything of using our sofas for trampolines at nine in the morning, while Papi was asleep. In our old barrio we were accustomed to folks shocking the streets with merengue twenty-four hours a day. Our upstairs neighbors, who themselves fought like trolls over everything, would stomp down on us. Will you two please shut up? and then Papi would come out of his room, his shorts unbuttoned and say, What did I tell you? How many times have I told you to keep it quiet? He was free with his smacks and we spent whole afternoons on Punishment Row—our bedroom—where we had to lie on our beds and not get off, because if he burst in and caught us at the window, staring out at the beautiful snow, he would pull our ears and smack us, and then we would have to kneel in the corner for a few hours. If we messed that up, joking around or cheating, he would force us to kneel down on the cutting side of a coconut grater, and only when we were bleeding and whimpering would he let us up.

Now you'll be quiet, he'd say, satisfied, and we'd lie in bed, our knees burning with iodine, and wait for him to go to work so we could put our hands against the cold glass.

We watched the neighborhood children building snowmen and igloos, having snowball fights. I told my brother about the field I'd seen, vast in my memory, but he just shrugged. A brother and sister lived across in apartment four, and when they were out we would wave to them. They waved to us and motioned for us to come out but we shook our heads, We can't.

The brother shrugged, and tugged his sister out to where the other children were, with their shovels and their long, snow-encrusted scarves. She seemed to like Rafa, and waved to him as she walked off. He didn't wave back.

North American girls are supposed to be beautiful, he said.

Have you seen any?

What do you call her? He reached down for a tissue and sneezed out a double-barrel of snot. All of us had headaches and colds and coughs; even with the heat cranked up, winter was kicking our asses. I had to wear a Christmas hat around the apartment to keep my shaven head warm; I looked like an unhappy tropical elf.

I wiped my nose. If this is the United States, mail me home.

Don't worry, Mami says. We're probably going home.

How does she know?

Her and Papi have been talking about it. She thinks it would be better if we went back. Rafa ran a finger glumly over our window; he didn't want to go; he liked the TV and the toilet and already saw himself with the girl in apartment four.

I don't know about that, I said. Papi doesn't look like he's going anywhere.

What do you know? You're just a little mojón.

I know more than you, I said. Papi had never once mentioned going back to the Island. I waited to get him in a good mood, after he had watched *Abbott and Costello,* and asked him if he thought we would be going back soon.

For what?

A visit.

Maybe, he grunted. Maybe not. Don't plan on it.

By the third week I was worried we weren't going to make it. Mami, who had been our authority on the Island, was dwindling. She cooked our food and then sat there, waiting to wash the dishes. She had no friends, no neighbors to visit. You should talk to me, she said, but we told her to wait for Papi to get home. He'll talk to you, I guaranteed. Rafa's temper, which was sometimes a problem, got worse. I would tug at his hair, an old game of ours, and he would explode. We fought and fought and fought and after my mother pried us apart, instead of making up like the old days, we sat scowling on opposite sides of our room and planned each other's demise. I'm going to burn you alive, he promised. You should number your limbs, cabrón, I told him, so they'll know how to put you back together for the funeral. We squirted acid at each other with our eyes, like reptiles. Our boredom made everything worse.

One day I saw the brother and sister from apartment four gearing up to go play, and instead of waving I pulled on my parka. Rafa was sitting on the couch, flipping between a Chinese cooking show and an all-star Little League game. I'm going out, I told him.

Sure you are, he said, but when I pushed open the front door, he said, Hey!

The air outside was very cold and I nearly fell down our steps. No one in the neighborhood was the shoveling type. Throwing my scarf over my mouth, I stumbled across the uneven crust of snow. I caught up to the brother and sister on the side of our building.

Wait up! I yelled. I want to play with you.

The brother watched me with a half grin, not understanding a word I'd said, his arms scrunched nervously at his side. His hair was a frightening no-color. His sister had the greenest eyes and her freckled face was cowled in a hood of pink fur. We had on the same brand of mittens, bought cheap from Two Guys. I stopped and we faced each other, our white breath nearly reaching across the distance between us. The world was ice and the ice burned with sunlight. This was my first real encounter with North Americans and I felt loose and capable on that plain of ice. I motioned with my mittens and smiled. The sister turned to her brother and laughed. He said something to her and then she ran to where the other children were, the peals of her laughter trailing over her shoulder like the spumes of her hot breath.

I've been meaning to come out, I said. But my father won't let us right now. He thinks we're too young, but look, I'm older than your sister, and my brother looks older than you.

The brother pointed at himself. Eric, he said.

My name's Joaquín, I said.

Juan, he said.

No, Joaquín, I repeated. Don't they teach you guys how to speak?

His grin never faded. Turning, he walked over to the approaching group of children. I knew that Rafa was watching me from the window and fought the urge to turn around and wave. The gringo children watched me from a distance and then walked away. Wait, I said, but then an Oldsmobile pulled into the next lot, its tires muddy and thick with snow. I couldn't follow them. The sister looked back once, a lick of her hair peeking out of her hood. After they had gone, I stood in the snow until my feet were cold. I was too afraid of getting my ass beat to go any farther.

Was it fun? Rafa was sprawled in front of the TV.

Hijo de la gran puta, I said, sitting down.

You look frozen.

I didn't answer him. We watched TV until a snowball struck the glass patio door and both of us jumped.

What was that? Mami wanted to know from her room.

Two more snowballs exploded on the glass. I peeked behind the curtain and saw the brother and the sister hiding behind a snow-buried Dodge.

Nothing, Señora, Rafa said. It's just the snow.

What, is it learning how to dance out there?

It's just falling, Rafa said.

We both stood behind the curtain, and watched the brother throw fast and hard, like a pitcher.

Each day the trucks would roll into our neighborhood with the garbage. The landfill stood two miles out, but the mechanics of the winter air conducted its sound and smells to us undiluted. When we opened a window we could hear the bulldozers spreading the garbage out in thick, putrid layers across the top of the landfill. We could see the gulls attending the mound, thousands of them, wheeling.

Do you think kids play out there? I asked Rafa. We were standing on the porch, brave; at any moment Papi could pull into the parking lot and see us.

Of course they do. Wouldn't you?

I licked my lips. They must find a lot of crap out there.

Plenty, Rafa said.

That night I dreamed of home, that we'd never left. I woke up, my throat aching, hot with fever. I washed my face in the sink, then sat next to our window, my brother snoring, and watched the pebbles of ice falling and freezing into a shell over the cars and the snow and the pavement. Learning to sleep in new places was an ability you were supposed to lose as you grew older, but I never had it. The building was only now settling into itself; the tight magic of the just-hammered-in nail was finally relaxing. I heard someone walking around in the living room and when I went out I found my mother standing in front of the patio door.

You can't sleep? she asked, her face smooth and perfect in the glare of the halogens.

I shook my head.

We've always been alike that way, she said. That won't make your life any easier.

I put my arms around her waist. That morning alone we'd seen three moving trucks from our patio door. I'm going to pray for Dominicans, she had said, her face against the glass, but what we would end up getting were Puerto Ricans.

She must have put me to bed because the next day I woke up next to Rafa. He was snoring. Papi was in the next room snoring as well, and something inside of me told me that I wasn't a quiet sleeper.

At the end of the month the bulldozers capped the landfill with a head of soft, blond dirt, and the evicted gulls flocked over the development, shitting and fussing, until the first of the new garbage was brought in.

My brother was bucking to be Number One Son; in all other things he was generally unchanged, but when it came to my father he listened with a scrupulousness he had never afforded our mother. Papi said he wanted us inside, Rafa stayed inside. I was less attentive; I played in the snow for short stretches, though never out of sight of the apartment. You're going to get caught, Rafa forecasted. I could tell that my boldness made him miserable; from our windows he watched me packing snow and throwing myself into drifts. I stayed away from the gringos. When I saw the brother and sister from apartment four, I stopped farting around and watched for a sneak attack. Eric waved and his sister waved; I didn't wave back. Once he came over and showed me the baseball he must have just gotten. Roberto Clemente, he said, but I went on with building my fort. His sister grew flushed and said something loud and rude and then Eric sighed. Neither of them were handsome children.

One day the sister was out by herself and I followed her to the field. Huge concrete pipes sprawled here and there on the snow. She ducked into one of these and I followed her, crawling on my knees.

She sat in the pipe, crosslegged and grinning. She took her hands out of her mittens and rubbed them together. We were out of the wind and I followed her example. She poked a finger at me.

Joaquín, I said. All my friends call me Yunior.

Joaquín Yunior, she said. Elaine. Elaine Pitt.

Elaine.

Joaquín.

It's really cold, I said, my teeth chattering.

She said something and then felt the ends of my fingers. Cold, she said.

I knew that word already. I nodded. Frío. She showed me how to put my fingers in my armpits.

Warm, she said.

Yes, I said. Very warm.

At night, Mami and Papi talked. He sat on his side of the table and she leaned close, asking him, Do you ever plan on taking these children out? You can't keep them sealed up like this; they aren't dead yet.

They'll be going to school soon, he said, sucking on his pipe. And as soon as winter lets up I want to show you the ocean. You can see it around here, you know, but it's better to see it up close.

How much longer does winter last?

Not long, he promised. You'll see. In a few months none of you will remember this and by then I won't have to work too much. We'll be able to travel in spring and see everything.

I hope so, Mami said.

My mother was not a woman easily cowed, but in the States she let my father roll over her. If he said he had to be at work for two days straight, she said okay and cooked enough moro to last him. She was depressed and sad and missed her father and her friends. Everyone had warned her that the Unied States was a difficult place where even the devil got his ass beat, but no one had told her that she would have to spend the rest of her natural life snowbound with her children. She wrote letter after letter home, begging her sisters to come as soon as possible. I need the company, she explained. This neighborhood is empty and friendless. And she begged Papi to bring his friends over. She wanted to talk about unimportant matters, and see a brown face who didn't call her mother or wife.

None of you are ready for guests, Papi said. Look at this house. Look at your children. Me dan vergüenza to see them slouching around like that.

You can't complain about this apartment. All I do is clean it.

What about your sons?

My mother looked over at me and then at Rafa. I put one shoe over the other. After that, she had Rafa keep after me about my shoelaces. When we heard the van arriving in the parking lot, Mami called us over for a quick inspection. Hair, teeth, hands, feet. If anything was wrong she'd hide us in the bathroom until it was fixed. Her dinners grew elaborate. She even changed the TV for Papi without calling him a zángano.

Okay, he said finally. Maybe it can work.

It doesn't have to be that big a production, Mami said.

Two Fridays in a row he brought a friend over for dinner and Mami put on her best polyester jumpsuit and got us spiffy in our red pants, thick white belts, and amaranth-blue Chams shirts. Seeing her asthmatic with excitement made us hopeful that our world was about to be transformed, but these were awkward dinners. The men were bachelors and divided their time between talking to Papi and eyeing Mami's ass. Papi seemed to enjoy their company but Mami spent her time on her feet, hustling food to the table, opening beers, and changing the channel. She started out each night natural and unreserved, with a face that scowled as easily as it grinned, but as the men loosened their belts and aired out their toes and talked their talk, she withdrew; her expressions narrowed until all that remained was a tight, guarded smile that seemed to drift across the room the way a splash of sunlight glides across a wall. We kids were ignored for the most part, except once, when the first man, Miguel, asked, Can you two box as well as your father?

They're fine fighters, Papi said.

Your father is very fast. Has good hand speed. Miguel shook his head, laughing. I saw him finish this one tipo. He put fulano on his ass.

That *was* funny, Papi agreed. Miguel had brought a bottle of Bermúdez rum; he and Papi were drunk.

It's time you go to your room, Mami said, touching my shoulder.

Why? I asked. All we do is sit there.

That's how I feel about my home, Miguel said.

Mami's glare cut me in half. Such a fresh mouth, she said, shoving us toward our room. We sat, as predicted, and listened. On both visits, the men ate their fill, congratulated Mami on her cooking, Papi on his sons, and then stayed about an hour for propriety's sake. Cigarettes, dominos, gossip, and then the inevitable, Well, I have to get going. We have work tomorrow. You know how that is.

Of course I do. What else do we Dominicans know?

Afterward, Mami cleaned the pans quietly in the kitchen, scraping at the roasted pig flesh, while Papi sat out on our front porch in his short sleeves; he seemed to have grown impervious to the cold these last five years. When he came inside, he showered and pulled on his overalls. I have to work tonight, he said.

Mami stopped scratching at the pans with a spoon. You should find yourself a more regular job.

Papi smiled. Maybe I will.

As soon as he left, Mami ripped the needle from the album and interrupted Felix de Rosario. We heard her in the closet, pulling on her coat and her boots.

Do you think she's leaving us? I asked.

Rafa wrinkled his brow. It's a possibility, he said. What would you do if you were her?

I'd already be in Santo Domingo.

When we heard the front door open, we let ourselves out of our room and found the apartment empty.

We better go after her, I said.

Rafa stopped at the door. Let's give her a minute, he said.

What's wrong with you? She's probably facedown in the snow.

We'll wait two minutes, he said.

Shall I count?

Don't be a wiseguy.

One, I said loudly. He pressed his face against the glass patio door. We were about to hit the door when she returned, panting, an envelope of cold around her.

Where did you get to? I asked.

I went for a walk. She dropped her coat at the door; her face was red from the cold and she was breathing deeply, as if she'd sprinted the last thirty steps.

Where?

Just around the corner.

Why the hell did you do that?

She started to cry, and when Rafa put his hand on her waist, she slapped it away. We went back to our room.

I think she's losing it, I said.

She's just lonely, Rafa said.

The night before the snowstorm I heard the wind at our window. I woke up the next morning, freezing. Mami was fiddling with the thermostat; we could hear the gurgle of water in the pipes but the apartment didn't get much warmer.

Just go play, Mami said. That will keep your mind off it.

Is it broken?

I don't know. She looked at the knob dubiously. Maybe it's slow this morning.

None of the gringos were outside playing. We sat by the window and waited for them. In the afternoon my father called from work; I could hear the forklifts when I answered.

Rafa?

No, it's me.

Get your mother.

How are you doing?

Get your mother.

We got a big storm on the way, he explained to her—even from where I was standing I could hear his voice. There's no way I can get out to see you. It's gonna be bad. Maybe I'll get there tomorrow.

What should I do?

Just keep indoors. And fill the tub with water.

Where are you sleeping? Mami asked.

At a friend's.

She turned her face from us. Okay, she said. When she got off the phone she sat in front of the TV. She could see I was going to pester her about Papi; she told me, Just watch the TV.

Radio WADO recommended spare blankets, water, flashlights, and food. We had none of these things. What happens if we get buried? I asked. Will we die? Will they have to save us in boats?

I don't know, Rafa said. I don't know anything about snow. I was spooking him. He went over to the window and peeked out.

We'll be fine, Mami said. As long as we're warm. She went over and raised the heat again.

But what if we get buried?

You can't have that much snow.

How do you know?

Because twelve inches isn't going to bury anybody, even a pain-in-the-ass like you.

I went out on the porch and watched the first snow begin to fall like finely sifted ash. If we die, Papi's going to feel bad, I said.

Don't talk about it like that, Rafa said.

Mami turned away and laughed.

Four inches fell in an hour and the snow kept falling.

Mami waited until we were in bed, but I heard the door and woke Rafa. She's at it again, I said.

Outside?

You know it.

He put on his boots grimly. He paused at the door and then looked back at the empty apartment. Let's go, he said.

She was standing on the edge of the parking lot, ready to cross Westminister. The apartment lamps glared on the frozen ground and our breath was white in the night air. The snow was gusting.

Go home, she said.

We didn't move.

Did you at least lock the front door? she asked.

Rafa shook his head.

It's too cold for thieves anyway, I said.

Mami smiled and nearly slipped on the sidewalk. I'm not good at walking on this vaina.

I'm real good, I said. Just hold on to me.

We crossed Westminister. The cars were moving very slowly and the wind was loud and full of snow.

This isn't too bad, I said. These people should see a hurricane.

Where should we go? Rafa asked. He was blinking a lot to keep the snow out of his eyes.

Go straight, Mami said. That way we don't get lost.

We should mark the ice.

She put her hands around us both. It's easier if we go straight.

We went down to the edge of the apartments and looked out over the landfill, a misshapen, shadowy mound that abutted the Raritan. Rubbish fires burned all over it like sores and the dump trucks and bulldozers slept quietly and reverently at its base. It smelled like something the river had tossed out from its floor, something moist and heaving. We found the basketball courts next and the pool, empty of water, and Parkridge, the next neighborhood over, which was full and had many, many children. We even saw the ocean, up there at the top of Westminister, like the blade of a long, curved knife. Mami was crying but we pretended not to notice. We threw snowballs at the sliding cars and once I removed my cap just to feel the snowflakes scatter across my cold, hard scalp.

Nancy Reisman

The Good Life

My mother Sadie—giddy matriarch, geriatric sweetheart—is not as many women as she used to be. Former selves wink like satellites from the far side of her cerebrum: in Chanel suits and tiny high heels, in pastel housecoats and backless slippers, in flowered aprons, in one-piece swimsuits, in pink negligees. I see her fingering mah-jong tiles, flirting with waiters, sneaking butter into the mashed potatoes despite my father's kosher mandate. She applies lipstick without ever checking a mirror. At the piano she coaxes out the Hit Parade. In the kitchen she'll gossip: *Rhoda Dobkins, sour from the day she was born. You watch, she'll mark cards, crimp the corners.* I'm in my thirties, forties, turning fifty, and she asks, *Elaine, honey, did you get enough for lunch?* She pops a chocolate into her mouth and tells me, *It's a good life if you don't weaken.*

At the nursing home, I shore Sadie up to keep her from vanishing. I kiss her white cheeks and feed her low-fat cookies. "Coffee?" she says. A word this winter's stroke has left her with. I wheel her out to the main floor, past the TV lounge where Regis and Kathy Lee shout from the big screen and her postwar nemesis, Rhoda Dobkins, stacks and restacks playing cards. Today my mother notices Rhoda and narrows her eyes.

"That's right, Mom," I say. "Sour old Rhoda." I kiss her again for remembering the grudge.

You're in the good life a short forever, and then it twists. Last Thanksgiving, my mother could still make the trip to my house; she was still talking in full sentences, playing the piano, flirting with her baby brother, Uncle Irv, a lecher and scam artist I invited for her sake. When my sister Margo and I were growing up, Uncle Irv would pinch our behinds and make low mooing noises: my mother adored him in spite of his obvious sleaziness. She adored him in spite of the loans he never repaid. She gave him her shares of the family house on Lancaster and their father's store downtown. Irving was the spitting image of their father, and he courted Sadie with carnations, steady compliments, lunches at the Howard Johnson's on Delaware. In other words, he made her laugh.

At the piano, my mother played her medley of song fragments and Margo sat beside her singing *Ma, he's making eyes at me,* and "Dark Town Strutter's Ball." Sadie was still managing to hit most of the notes—her fingers curved from arthritis, the nails polished salmon, still wearing her diamond engagement ring, still wearing her wedding ring. Hands of a queen, always, even as those fingers stiffened and rebelled. Queen of Hearts, my mother.

So there we were, Uncle Irv already into the hard liquor, my youngest, Emily, singing along with Margo and my mother, "I'm going to dance off both my shoes/when they play the jelly-roll blues," my husband Daniel carving the turkey, our London-bound son Adam parked in front of the football game, and Jessie, my oldest and most confounding child, taking the coats of our cousins the Goldbaums and plying the rest of us with wine. Jessie had arrived in from Boston with the look of a sated cat. Twice she'd hugged me for no apparent reason. She'd lifted a gerbera daisy from the centerpiece and stuck it in her hair, and for once she was wearing aqua instead of black. I thought maybe Daniel wrote her a check; I thought she was going too fast with the Merlot. We were on the third bottle by the time we sat down to eat. Jessie bided her time, waited until we were past the appetizers, grinning from the wine, until Daniel was done with his speech-making and our mouths were stuffed with food.

"A toast," Jessie said, "to true love." She glanced in the direction of the Goldbaums, a still-young couple.

My younger daughter Emily choked.

"That's what it is," my sister Margo said. "Jessie's in love."

Jessie smiled at her father, batted her eyes at Margo, and gazed at me. "I have a girlfriend," she said. She wasn't even blushing.

Silverware clattered. Daniel covered his mouth with his napkin. The light in the dining room grew oddly sharp and I took a long swallow of water. Adam elbowed Emily. "Told you," Adam said.

My palms began to sweat and I clutched my napkin. "What do you mean?" I said to Jessie.

"Just what you think I mean," Jessie said.

"Let's talk about this later," Daniel said. He was a little green. He nodded at the turkey carcass. "There's still a lot more food."

"And wine," Margo said. "Let's try the Pinot Noir." She stood and yanked the cork from a new bottle, then circled the table, leaning over our shoulders, her rainy scent wafting counterclockwise as she filled the glasses.

"A girlfriend?" Irv said. "Like the way a man has a girlfriend?"

"Sort of," Jessie said.

His eyes glazed over. "I've seen that," he said.

"What?"

"I've seen that. A little place downtown. Girls Girls Girls."

"Uncle Irv," I said.

"Is she a looker?" Irv said.

"She's beautiful," Jessie said.

"Who's beautiful?" my mother said.

"You are," Irving said. He blew Sadie a kiss across the table. He slurped at his wine, spilling it onto his checked sport jacket. "So long as we're making confessions," he told Jessie, "let me say that I also have a girlfriend."

"Who has a girlfriend?" my mother said.

"Irving," I said.

"Such a flirt," my mother said. "Flirts with all the girls. Never serious."

"Is," Irv said. "Nothing but serious."

"What's her name?" Jessie said.

"Gertrude," he said.

"I don't know a Gertrude," my mother said.

"No," Irv said. "She isn't someone you know."

"You actually date someone named Gertrude?" Emily said.

My mother scanned her plate, a little lost. "Did I have some coffee?" she said.

"I call her Gertie," Irv said. He went misty eyed at the chandelier, then turned to Jessie. "What about your girl?" he said.

"Emily, would you get your grandmother a cup of coffee?" I said.

"Stephanie," Jessie said. For a moment, she stared off at the beige drapes behind Daniel. I pictured her disappearing into a crowd of women with shaved heads.

"Honey," I told Jessie, "we should talk about this later."

"You don't approve," Jessie said.

"Approve, not approve, they haven't even met her," Irv said.

"Met who?" my mother said.

I sighed. "Emily, make sure it's the decaf."

"Stephanie," Jessie said.

"Didn't you say Gertrude?" my mother said.

"That's Uncle Irv's girlfriend," Adam said.

"Irving," my mother said. "You have a girlfriend?"

"No one who can hold a candle to you," Irv said, and blew another kiss.

Adam wrinkled his nose at Jessie. "It isn't Stephanie Jamison?" he said.

"Not that Stephanie," Jessie said.

"Stephanie Jamison? That cheerleader Adam followed around?" Emily said. She set a cup of coffee in front of my mother.

"Shut up," Adam said.

"Who you telling to shut up?" my mother said.

"Emily. Gram, don't you think she has a big mouth?" Adam said.

"A fine mouth. You might try a little lipstick," my mother said. "What a doll. Isn't she?"

"She's a beautiful girl," I said. "Jessie too."

"Oh yes," my mother said, "real dolls."

"I'm lucky to have daughters like them," I said.

"Oh, Mom," Emily said.

"They're your daughters?" my mother said.

"Sure," I said. "And you know what? I'm your daughter. So's Margo."

My mother gazed into her lap. "Imagine that," she said.

Late that night I showered, soaped around and around my navel, little cavern, little whirlpool of tucks and creases. Sadie still knew my name. *Elaine,* she'd say, *don't you look stunning. Elaine, give me a kiss.* But "daughter"? I had already merged with Sadie's sisters and cousins and girlfriends, a cast of familiar women, all drenched in fuzzy-edged love. *I never thought Papa would let us study art,* she'd say, *did you?*

Such fickle things, our bodies and brains. Such mysteries. How does a woman forget babies? For that matter, how did I make a daughter who wants other girls? All those peptides scrambling up and spelling out *lesbian.*

"A phase?" I said to Daniel, "Could it be a phase?" He was propped up in bed with a colleague's article entitled "Cancer Risks in California Agricultural Migrant Labor Populations" and a spy novel.

"Maybe," he said.

"Like Birkenstocks," I said. "Like marijuana?"

He shrugged. "No chance of pregnancy," he said. "Low risk for STDs."

"Public-health talk," I said. "That's not what you said at dinner."

"She's fine." He turned to his Le Carré. "Jessie's just fine."

The Friday after Thanksgiving I began to clean a house I'd cleaned the Wednesday before. I vacuumed unsoiled carpets, wiped down counters, dusted yet again. While I was mopping the kitchen floor, Jessie decided it was time for a heart-to-heart. "We need to talk," she said, and landed in the chair closest to me. "Okay," I said. I dipped my mop into the bucket and ran it in front of the refrigerator.

"About Stephanie," she said. "About my life."

"Sure," I said. She tapped a pencil on the table, then held it like a cigarette, tilted her head and talked to the ceiling above me. "I was really nervous at first. You know, when things started."

"Uh huh," I said. I rubbed the mop over a speck of yam.

"Mom." Jessie said. "Would you stop?"

"I'm listening," I said.

"No you're not." A sliver of hurt stuck in her voice.

I put down the mop. I sat. "Yes," I said. "I am."

"Forget it," Jessie said. She chewed on the pencil end and closed her eyes. Sitting in Daniel's bathrobe, her hair still sleep-wild, Jessie looked like a kindergartner.

"Don't forget it," I said.

She scrutinized my face, wound a loose strand of hair around a finger. "Stephanie was in my women's group," she said.

Since when are twenty-four year olds "women"? I thought, and then remembered. "Umm hmm," I said.

"Oh God," Jessie said. "I knew you'd be weird about this."

"Honey, I want you to be happy."

"I am," Jessie said. "Very."

"Well that's good," I said. "That's important."

"You're right," she said, and softened. "You'd really like her, Mom."

"Sweetie, I like all your friends," I said.

"Yeah. But you know what I mean."

"I think so," I said. "Did you want to go shopping today?"

The next week Daniel and I received a five-page letter from Boston in which Jessie discussed the failures of past relationships and raved about Stephanie. In closing she wrote, "I know you didn't expect this, but you should be relieved. Stephanie's Jewish." She had enclosed two bumper stickers: *I (heart) My Gay Child*, and *Straight But Not Narrow.* "P.S.," she wrote, "Uncle Irv's not so bad. He has a big heart."

Irv has a big heart? And I'm the Pope's daughter, I thought. I refolded the letter and sifted through Irv's catalog of sins, the worst of which was disappearing for three months after my father's funeral, while Sadie crumbled. Jessie was too young to remember, and why should I bring it up? She'd only defend Irv as misunderstood. I left the letter on Daniel's dresser and visited the nursing home.

After a few days, though, I began to waver about Uncle Irv. Jessie's love life gave me hives, but maybe, just maybe, she could see a whole different Irv than I could. Maybe this Irv was better than the Irvs of my girlhood, the prodigal uncle, the sleazy spendthrift my father always had to bail out. True, I was impressed by the kisses Irv blew across the table at Sadie, the Fanny Farmer chocolates he'd brought to dinner; I was impressed by his weekly visits with my mother, all those Howard Johnson's lunches when she again became a woman men attended to. I relented, and for the next couple of months my tolerance and gratitude surged. Then in January, my mother had her stroke, and Uncle Irv once again dropped out of sight.

"What did you expect?" Margo said. "He's a leech. Mom can't write checks anymore."

"He could be sick," I said.

"Just warped," Margo said. "Elaine, don't waste your time."

I tried without luck to reach him by phone. I dropped short notes in the mail. No response. But eventually, in late March, Uncle Irv called me at home. "Elaine," he said. "I'm having an emergency. Come to my store."

"You need an ambulance?" I said. "Police?"

"No, no," he said. "When will you be here?" and hung up before I answered.

Emmy was lying on the family-room sofa, knees up, a Walkman strapped over her head, bare feet flexed on a pillow: she'd stuck cotton balls between her toes and painted her toenails crimson. Her trig textbook was propped against her thighs, and the TV, sound off, flashed an ice-dancing competition. "Listen," I told her. "Something's up with Uncle Irv. I'm going to the jewelry store."

She pulled off the headphones. "Alone?" she said, and sat up to blow on her toes. She hit the TV remote and told me she was coming too. "It's not safe to be around Uncle Irv alone."

"For Pete's sake, he's eighty years old."

"He's a creep. Besides, maybe he's got some little pearl studs."

I wasn't sure if Irv even sold pearl studs; he sold yellow diamonds, old watches, pawned rings in a dingy storefront in the red-light district, the remains of my grandfather's once respectable business. The place was poorly lit, heavy metal grates blocking the windows; the cases were cracked and thick with dust. When we arrived, talk-show voices buzzed through a black-and-white TV. The store smelled of mildew and old cigars. Uncle Irv stared out the filmy, gated window, fingering watch parts. Sagging.

"Good of you to come," he said. "It's my girlfriend."

"Gertrude?" Emmy said.

Irv sighed and rubbed the casing of a silver pocket watch, his eyes moony and distant.

"Uncle Irv?" I said. I waited. Emmy waited. Across the street, a woman in a tight minidress and stiletto heels rummaged in her purse and pulled out a paperback and a cigarette.

"Uncle Irv, you got any pearls?" Emmy said. "Little earrings?"

He dropped the watch and suddenly returned to us. "I'm heartsick and she wants to talk pearls," Irv said.

"What about your girlfriend?" I said.

"She's dying." His jaw tightened, his pupils darkened, and he brought a hand up over his face.

"I'm sorry," I said.

"She wants to meet you," Irv said. He straightened up and picked a piece of lint off his trousers. "I told her I have a niece and she wants to meet you."

"That's fine," I said.

"Today," he said. "Now." He gave me the address of his girlfriend's apartment and reached for his coat.

"You come too," he said to Emily. "Only don't mention about having a girlfriend."

"That's not me," Emmy said. "That's Jessie."

"Well, don't say anything," Irv said.

"Duh," Emmy said.

"Another thing," he said. "She knows me as Don."

"Don?" Emmy said.

"Yeah," Irv said. "Don Jones."

"Is that your middle name?" Emmy said.

"You ask too many questions," Irv said.

"Well, what should I call you?" Emmy said.

"Uncle Irv. I told her yesterday. I said you all call me Uncle Irv." For months, he said, he'd been living with Gertrude, taking care of her. I asked if she had any family. "Me," he said, "I'm her family." He shook his head, pressed his lips together and swallowed hard. "So many years."

"Years?"

"Twenty-four." He pulled a handkerchief out of his pocket. "Elaine, don't mention this to Sadie."

We followed Irv down the long fifth-floor corridor of Gertrude's apartment building, a place full of elderly. All the sound had been sucked out of it. He opened the door to her apartment and called, "Honey, it's me," his voice tender. We stepped into the dim living room, where Gertrude lay on the sofa, propped up with pillows: a tiny paper kite of a woman, her blue eyes pearled by cataracts. She was wrapped in a pink robe, her fuzzy halo of white hair rising above the bedclothes. She was the exact size and shape and colors of my mother—only here was a smaller nose, a sharper chin. I was dizzy with familiarity, and the dizziness increased as I glanced around her apartment. The coffee table. The reading lamp. The sofa Gertrude was lying on. All from my parents' old house. The quilt I recognized from my parents' bedroom. I circled the love seat: the royal-blue fabric was shiny from wear, threadbare in spots, the frame chipped. New, it had floated among trouser legs and long hemlines, cocktail parties in my parents' living room: my father slapping the other men on the back and threatening to light his pipe, my mother smoothing her black sleeveless dress, her hair done at Louie's that afternoon. She was shy and beautiful in these gatherings, my mother; the shyness surprised all of us. She'd sip at her sherry, smile at the men, compliment the women on their accessories, then fade into the background while the waitress she'd hired passed hors d'oeuvres, smoked salmon and capers and vegetable tarts.

"Good of you to come," Gertrude said. She waved in Irv's direction. "Don worries too much. It isn't my time yet."

Then she started to cough: her rickety body shook and her eyes began to water. Uncle Irv stood paralyzed in the corner. I sat her up and sent Emmy to the kitchen for a glass of water. Gertrude sipped and coughed, sipped and coughed, and finally regained her composure.

"Bless you," she said, and nodded at Emmy, who was hovering behind me. "This is your daughter?"

"This is Emily," I said. "My youngest."

Gertrude extended a bony hand to Emmy and motioned for her to sit at the edge of the sofa. She studied Emmy's face and grinned. "I bet you have a boyfriend," she said.

Emmy blushed. Uncle Irv cleared his throat. "You're right," Emmy said. "I'm in love with Leonardo," someone I'd never heard of.

"An Italian boy," Gertrude said.

Emmy smiled and smiled. "He's handsome," she said.

"And he treats you nice?" Gertrude said.

"Like a gentleman."

"You make sure," Gertrude said.

Uncle Irv, leerer and pincher, nodded along. Earnestly. But he said almost nothing. I told Gertrude I'd grown up in Buffalo and he looked at me in alarm. I mentioned my mother and he began to pace. I said we'd always been a close family and Irv wrung his hands, then interrupted to ask Gertrude if she'd had her medicine. When I offered to get Gertrude something to eat, Irv asked me to make him a cup of coffee.

Emmy raised one eyebrow. "You live here, right?"

But I put on the coffee and washed a sinkload of my mother's old dishes, while Emmy and Gertrude played solitaire together, Gertrude pointing and Emmy moving the cards.

"So good of you," Gertrude said.

As we readied to leave, Uncle Irv's hands were trembling. He stroked his beard stubble and stared at the floor.

"You need something, Irv?" I said. "Don."

He nodded. "Oh, Elaine," he said. "Such a good woman you are. I've always said, That Elaine, she's got a heart."

"What is it?"

"If you wouldn't mind, if it isn't too much trouble," he said.

"What?" Emmy said.

"If you could bring some clothes from my house, my mail." And then he drew me aside and waved at the bottles of pills. "This medicine," he said, "so expensive. Could you lend me a little, until my next check?"

"Of course," I said. "How much?"

"A few hundred," he said. "Maybe four."

I glanced at Gertrude under my mother's quilt, the collection of pills. Four hundred, I wrote.

"Leonardo?" I said. Emmy and I were in the car on the way to Irv's house, Sadie's childhood home, and Emmy was punching buttons on the radio. "Who's Leonardo?"

"Brian," Emmy said, meaning her boyfriend-of-the-month. "Better than Don Jones, isn't it? Better than naming yourself after Wall Street."

I turned up Lancaster and began to watch for Irving's block. What I remembered most about the family house was its wood: the waxed parquet floors, the polished banisters, the sliding parlor door, the heavy-grained piano. But I hadn't been inside for over fifteen years, not since my mother signed over her share of the house to Irving and he banned the rest of us from visiting. From the street, driving by, I'd witnessed the neglect. Paint peeled in long strips. Dead leaves and stray litter cluttered the lawn, and dead stalks of old shrubs shrank against the house. The roof sagged; the rain gutters hung loose. But to either side spread a neighborhood of renovation and fresh paint.

We parked and made our way up the pitted front walk.

"It's not like this on purpose, is it?" Emmy said.

"Emmy."

"Well, how should I know?"

The mailbox was stuffed with envelopes and the postman had taken to leaving them on the porch floor. Emmy scooped them into a paper bag while I fiddled with the front lock. She followed me into the front hall, which was barely navigable, lined with four-foot stacks of old newspapers, a little city of them that expanded into the living room. There the sizes of the stacks were varied, yellow and more musty yellow paper, the tabletops and piano black with soot and dust. The dining room stank of urine and wood rot; brown stains spread across the ceiling. But the heavy oak table was empty, and a package of laundry from Quik-Kleen was propped on one of the chairs. Along the far wall, away from the ceiling stains, Irving had set up an army cot, which was surrounded by rumpled clothes and back issues of *Penthouse.*

Emmy held her nose. "Ew," she said.

It was worse in the kitchen, where plastic bags of garbage were piled into a small pyramid, and a slimy liquid seeped from the upper kitchen cabinets. I opened one. Prehistoric canned goods had corroded through the metal seams. I didn't dare open the refrigerator.

"Disgusting," Emmy said. "I'm getting out of here."

I felt like I was in prep for oral surgery: light-headed, my own voice remote. "Meet you outside," I said. I took the back stairs to the second floor, which was as silty as the living room, but emptier. It was clear the roof had leaked for some time: in room after room the bureaus and bed frames, the mattresses and night tables were water stained and mildewed, the floorboards damaged. But the closets held ordered rows of women's clothes on metal hangers: calico dresses, nylon dresses, moth-eaten sweaters. On the floor, fallen belts, stray gloves. The clothes of middle-aged women, my mother's sisters, who lived with Irv until their deaths fourteen and twenty years ago. In what had been my grandfather's room, I opened the drawers of the bureau to find a stack of men's shirts, wrapped in cellophane from a dry cleaner that went out of business in 1963.

I made my way to the end of the hall and the bedroom my mother had shared with her youngest sister. Bare walls, twin beds with cherubs carved into the frames, two small, wooden rockers, armless, the caning in need of repair. A heavy bureau, empty, a dressing table with a large, oval mirror, its silver marred by ink-black spots. Nothing in the closet. Nothing in the dressing table. I checked and rechecked the drawers, bending over, sniffing at them. No scraps of paper. No old lipsticks, no ancient face cream. The smell of nothing, a whiff of mildew and dust. I circled the room and sniffed at more: the walls, the bed frame, a rocker, which I sat in. Hard wood, slow motion, creaking. I closed my eyes and rocked and for a moment I drifted away from myself, as I do when I'm awake too early in the morning. My face and neck flushed, and when I opened my eyes the room seemed even more foreign. I felt hollow and unmoored. Then I heard Emmy's footsteps on the front stairs, and she was a blob in the doorway.

"Mom," she said. "What are you doing?"

I blinked at her. "This was Gram's room," I said.

She walked over to the dressing table and traced a squiggle in the dust, then pulled her hand back suddenly. "This doesn't feel like her," Emmy said. She wrinkled her nose. "Can we go?"

When I dropped Irv's clothes and mail at Gertrude's apartment, I wrote him another check and gave him the name of a cleaning service.

"I thank you," he said, and narrowed his eyes a little. "Elaine, you don't mind me saying, you've put on a little heft."

"Heft?"

"*Zaftig*," he said. And, after a moment, "A fine thing in a woman."

"I'll call you soon," I said, "to check on Gertrude."

When I got back into the car, Emmy, my underage schemer, patted me on the shoulder. "We need a drink," she said.

I turned the key in the ignition. "Good try," I said.

"Okay then, milkshakes." She squeezed my hand. "Cheer up, Mom," she said. "We'll get mocha."

The following week I called Uncle Irv and asked him how Gertrude was doing. "A miracle," he said. "I think she's going to recover."

When Sadie moved to the nursing home, Margo and I hung a bulletin board in her room and covered it with family photos. *Sadie in Florida, 1955. Sadie and Bill's wedding, 1927. Sadie at Jessie's third birthday.* We left a stack of photo albums on the closet shelf and covered the dresser with framed pictures. Every few months I'd update snapshots of the kids. In late April, Jessie sent me three copies of a photo of herself holding hands with Stephanie: one print for Sadie's room, one for Daniel's office, and one for the house. Jessie and Stephanie stood in front of a pier—windblown hair, toothy smiles, big eyes—cobalt ocean in the background. Stephanie's head tilted toward Jessie, a walnut-brown swath of hair flying into Jessie's shoulder. She was more olive-toned than Jessie and even more petite. They looked like girls at summer camp. I handed Daniel his copy.

"That's her?" he said. "She's cute." But he didn't look at the snapshot for very long.

"So you don't have a problem with this," I said.

"No more bumper stickers, right? She didn't send more bumper stickers, did she?"

"Just earrings for Emmy. Pink triangles."

Daniel took off his glasses and rubbed his eyes. "We don't have to wear triangles too, do we?"

"Maybe armbands," I said. "Maybe funny hats."

"She used to like boys," he said, wistful.

"It isn't you," I said. "You know that."

"Maybe I wasn't around enough," he said.

"Honey, this isn't about you," I said. "Jessie is who she is."

"I suppose."

This was not where I'd expected to end up, switching places

with Daniel, something we often do. "Jessie is who she is"? Of course, I believed Daniel had nothing to do with her choice. But I wondered about myself. Too overbearing? I thought. Too gratified by her toddler shyness, her attachment to me? Too affectionate?

At first, I didn't take Jessie's new photo to the nursing home; instead I took one of her and Emmy from Thanksgiving. I sat with my mother and turned the pages of a photo album, going over and over the family snapshots. She touched the pages, but randomly, distractedly, her expression flat and unchanging. I picked up a larger, framed photo of my father and held it out for her to see. She wrinkled her brow and frowned. Then she wouldn't look at me, or the photos. I kissed her. I praised her blue dress. I started to sing to her, but she frowned for several more minutes and tugged at the fringe on her blanket.

At home, Emmy propped one of the prints of Jessie and Stephanie on the mantel, next to her own photo from the Junior Holiday Dance. I ignored it. That Saturday, I took Emmy out for lunch at the grill by the marina downtown, on the shore of Lake Erie. We sat in the wind at the picnic tables eating French fries and chicken sandwiches. Emmy was wearing her pink-triangle earrings and Brian's varsity jacket. She told me lesbianism was in. "You know about Jodie Foster, don't you?" she said.

"Let's not talk about this," I said.

"Wouldn't it be great if Jessie dated Jodie Foster?"

"Okay, Emmy."

"I'd go out with Jodie Foster."

I wanted to slap her. I set down my drink and walked off in the direction of the skyscrapers. "Mom," Emmy called. "I'm kidding. Remember kidding?"

She followed me and I walked faster. "Mom," she said, starting to worry now, starting to be afraid. I stopped walking. Whitecaps dotted the water and smacked against the promenade's concrete wall. "You know I'm in love with Brian," she said. "We're practically engaged."

"What?"

"Figuratively speaking," she said.

"You're not even eighteen."

"Oh, right," Emmy said, "I forgot."

In the distance, freighters moved south along the shoreline, and above us jagged bits of blue opened up between cloud banks. I started to cry. Emmy's remaining bravado collapsed. She put her arm around me, awkwardly hugging me. But I didn't hug her back. My nose was running and I choked when I tried to talk. I gave up. Then Emmy started to cry too, red blotches spreading over her cheeks. "I didn't mean to upset you," she said. "Really, Mom."

I pulled Kleenexes out of my pocketbook for both of us and we sat on a bench. "Sweetie, it isn't you," I said.

"Are you sure?"

I nodded. We dried our faces and blew our noses and stared out at the freighters.

"It's these earrings, isn't it?" she said. "You don't like them."

"They're fine," I said. "Really, Emmy. You look very chic today."

In May, when Jessie called to tell me she wanted to bring Stephanie for a visit, I clammed up. I said I'd have to call her back. I knew Jessie would get off the phone and write poems on injustice and death, but I couldn't help myself.

Daniel gave me a long look and turned off the sound on the baseball game. "She's a grown-up," he said. "It isn't our place to interfere."

"Okay," I said, "but visiting? You want Jessie walking around the neighborhood with her girlfriend? Kissing? You know there's going to be kissing."

"That's what people in love do, Elaine." He hesitated. Another Yankees batter struck out. "You really think they'd kiss on the street?"

"I don't know."

Daniel shook the idea away. "Kisses," he said. "What's the big deal?"

"It's an example."

"Well, I'm sure they've already kissed," he said.

"That's a fine thought."

"You know what I mean." He sneaked another glance at the game.

I stepped in front of the TV set. "And," I said. "Where are they going to sleep?"

"I thought so," he said. "Jessie's room?"

"Both of them?"

"Jessie wouldn't put up with the study," he said. Mr. Nonchalance. Mr. Modern Dad.

"Okay, Daniel. Fine. You call Jessie. You make the arrangements."

"What?"

"Call Jessie."

He shook his head. "You're the one she always talks to."

"Time for a change," I said.

"Look, I'm not crazy about this either," Daniel said. "I'm just being practical. You know, live and let live. Isn't that what you say?"

"If my mother knew about this," I said.

"Here we go," Daniel said.

"What do you mean, 'Here we go'?"

"This has nothing to do with your mother. And who knows, maybe she'd be fine about it."

"My mother?"

"Maybe not," Daniel admitted.

"She'd have a heart attack," I said.

"She's already had one," Daniel said. "And a stroke."

"And just think what another one would do," I said.

"Enough with your mother," Daniel said.

"She's a wonderful woman, my mother."

"Honey, of course she is."

"I can't talk about this anymore," I said.

"Okay," Daniel said.

"Just tell Jessie it's a bad time for company."

"Uh uh," Daniel said. "If that's what you think, you tell her yourself."

"Fine." I said, "That's just fine." I stormed upstairs and spent the night in the study.

Daniel is braver than he lets on. He called Jessie from work and explained that I was struggling with personal issues. He told her that we'd love for her to visit, but it wasn't a good time to bring guests.

Jessie immediately called me at home. "You don't approve of me," she said. Didn't she used to be shy?

"What do you mean?" I said.

"Dad said you were having a hard time. Personal issues."

"That's right, I am."

"I think you're homophobic," Jessie said.

"Excuse me?"

"You feel threatened."

"So telling me I'm homophobic makes me less threatened?" I said.

"You need to face your feelings," she said.

"That's my business," I said. "Not everything's about you."

"I want to come in for a visit. I want to bring Stephanie."

"It's a bad time to bring Stephanie."

"Why? Because of Gram? I want her to meet Gram."

"Wonderful."

"I can't believe you're being like this," Jessie said.

"Like what?"

"Gram loves me," Jessie said. "If she could still talk, she'd say so."

"That's not the point," I said.

"That is the point. Gram wouldn't think I'm a mutant."

"And I do?"

"I am *not* a mutant," Jessie said, "no matter what you think." Her voice broke and then she hung up the phone.

I started to write her a note. *Of course you're not a mutant.* I took a long bath. I wrote in my datebook, *There isn't enough of me.* Then I made a tunafish sandwich with extra celery and onion.

Irony was not lost on me. This Stephanie, this wily lesbian who had seduced my daughter into a strange life, and, God help me, into her bed, couldn't wait to visit my beloved mother, but Uncle Irv wouldn't go near Sadie. He'd called me again to say Gertrude had taken a turn for the worse. "And all those medicines," he said.

"How much?" I said.

"How much medicine?" he said.

"No, Irv. How much do you need? You know, I saw Sadie yesterday."

"To be honest, a few hundred. You can mail it to the store."

"What about your sister, Irv? Remember your sister?"

"I think about her every day," Irv said. "I pray for her."

"Maybe you can visit," I said.

"Sure, sure," he said. "You'll send the check?"

"When will you visit?" I said.

"Soon. I would take more time to talk, Elaine. Too bad I have business. Give Sadie my love."

Before my daily visits to the nursing home, I started to take long walks. Spring had progressed without my noticing. The pale green coronas on our maples had deepened and spread. The dogwoods had bloomed; tulips filled the border garden. Every few days I brought bouquets to the nursing home. Sometimes my mother would light up when she saw them, but often she'd ignore them. More and more she'd act the same way with me. The aides from the home coaxed smiles out of her. But when I said hello, her look became blanker and blanker.

The problem was that we'd all gotten older too fast. The problem was that there weren't enough moms to go around. Jessie left a message on the answering machine saying she'd be coming in with Stephanie and they'd be staying at a motel. I walked a three-mile loop through the neighborhood and pledged to behave like a grown-up. Later, I called Jessie back.

"You'd really stay at a motel?" I said.

"Sure," she said, faking bravery.

"But this is your home," I said.

"I don't know," Jessie said.

"I'd like it if you stayed here."

She didn't answer.

"Of course if you're happier at a motel, I understand," I said.

"It's not a question of happy," Jessie said. "It's a question of Stephanie."

I paused. "Stephanie can stay here too."

"What?"

"Stephanie is welcome to stay here too," I said. "Only please don't neck on the front lawn."

"Mom," Jessie said, "have I ever made out with anyone on the front lawn?"

"Backyard," I said. "You and the boy with the goatee. Kenneth."

"That was five years ago," Jessie said.

"It's precedent," I said.

"But I'm an adult now," Jessie said. "I just want to see Gram. You know?"

When my mother first moved to the nursing home she met up with Frieda Kaplan, an eighty-five-year-old widow who read the daily paper and could still use a walker. The two of them took breakfast at the same table and spent sleepy afternoons holding hands in the TV lounge. When my mother fell asleep in her wheelchair, Frieda would stroke her forehead and call an aide to bring Sadie's extra blanket or prop her head at a more comfortable angle. Every day when I visited, Frieda would report to me on the situation in Israel and on my mother's sleep patterns. Even after Sadie's stroke, Frieda would watch over her. I'd relax a little. Someone lucid, I thought. An almost-mother. But one afternoon in May, Frieda told me that the previous night she and Sadie had gone bar hopping and gotten wildly drunk.

"What?" I said. In spite of myself, I felt sparks of happiness. My mother, cutting her eyes at some bartender. My mother silly on Bristol Cream.

"Oh yes," Frieda said. "We had trouble getting back. We had to call a cab."

Sadie napped on in her wheelchair, her tiny feet poking out from her rose afghan, her skin translucent in the late-afternoon light.

"Your mother," Frieda said. "She's a real pistol."

Out the window, a thin streak of red ran along the horizon, bounded by woolly clouds and the pink-tinted field behind the nursing home. Frieda patted my hand, her smile gummy and wide.

"Glad you had a good time," I told her. "Glad you made it back."

In late June, Stephanie arrived in a turquoise sundress, all pleases and thank-yous, a gold Star of David around her neck. There wasn't a single pink triangle on her. She brought us snapdragons and wine. She made conversation about the house and I made conversation back. I offered her a glass of iced tea. I offered her fruit salad. I offered to give her a tour of the garden. Jessie and Emmy exchanged looks.

"What?" I said.

"Nothing," Jessie said. "Maybe we'll wash up before we go to the nursing home." She picked up a suitcase and led Stephanie upstairs.

"What?" I said to Emmy.

"Nothing," she said. "But when did you get so polite?"

At the nursing home we found Sadie spiffed up and alert: hair washed and set, lipstick on, teeth in, her blue-and-white suit neatly buttoned and zipped. She was having a good day. I wheeled her into her bedroom, away from the TV-lounge distractions, and we took turns visiting her there. When Jessie came in, she started paging through a photo album with Sadie. "Here's you," Jessie said. "Here's Irv." My mother gave no sign of recognition. "Here, this is Elaine." Sadie blinked, touched the slick pages, then turned her attention to her polished fingernails. Did that mean anything? Jessie closed the album, then started clowning around: she ran my lipstick over her mouth and left kiss marks on Sadie's hands. Sadie cracked a smile. Jessie sang Hit Parade songs and swung Sadie's arms, jitterbugging with the wheelchair. Then Sadie laughed, a small laugh, but a real one, and she waved at Jessie as if to say, *Oh, you're too much.* Jessie kissed her on the cheek and said to me, "Did you see that? That was such a Sadie thing to do."

And then Jessie's smile fell; she began tearing up, because what had happened to the rest of Sadie? And Sadie, my mute, distracted mother, reached up and took Jessie's face in her hands, pressed those arthritic fingers against Jessie's cheeks, and looked Jessie in the eye, steadily, as if they were both very much younger.

I gave them their time together. Emmy and Stephanie were in the Common Room, pretending to play gin with Rhoda Dobkins. I walked on and said hello to Frieda. I said hello to the other residents, the bald men, the dandelion-haired women, some of them talking thickly, some of them shouting, some of them blinking from their chairs. I returned to the Common Room just in time to see Rhoda throw a couple of cards down, to hear Stephanie say, "Look at that!" as if it were a royal flush.

A few minutes later, Jessie emerged from my mother's room, red-eyed and sniffling. Stephanie set down her cards, pushed a strand of hair out of Jessie's eyes, and let her hand linger against Jessie's cheek. Something in me began to loosen. It was the gesture I would have made. The gesture Sadie made. The one you can't stop craving. The one that catches you on the brink of your deepest despair, and carries you back, safe, into the good life.

Karenmary Penn

Rift

Matthew had been the only one to see the thick branch break loose from the oak tree and drift onto the frozen gravel. Somehow, not a single, spiny twig had touched the Volvo, even though it was parked directly beneath the tree.

"The thing floated," Matthew told his family. "Like invisible hands were carrying it."

His younger brothers and his sister stood in a semicircle before the fallen limb, stomping to keep their feet warm, fogging the air with their breath. Flannel pajama pants were stuffed into their snow boots. Matthew stood behind his father, who stared up at the pale spot where the branch had torn loose from the trunk.

Sean finally said, "Maybe a gust of wind carried it."

Matthew licked a finger and held it up. "What wind?"

"It probably bounced off another branch," Luke said.

His father removed his gloves to prod the exposed end of the branch. Watching him, Matthew felt anxiety squeezing his temples and then the faintest breath blowing in his right ear. He brushed the tickle away.

"Let's drag this thing out of the driveway and finish breakfast," his father said.

Matthew stooped to wrap his mittens around the thickest part of the branch just as the tickling in his ear returned: a remote sizzling sound that quickly distilled itself into a piercing *S*. He shook his head violently, as if ridding his inner ear of a drop of water, until the noise disappeared.

"Did anyone else hear that?"

Everyone stood. Somebody groaned softly.

"Hear what?" His father gave Matthew a sharp look.

"That hissing sound." Matthew tried to approximate the noise.

"It was probably a bug," his father said. His glare gave way to an expression of weary concern. Looks were exchanged up and down the heavy branch: eye-rolling and irritation. Matthew had seen similar looks six months earlier, when he'd been unable to sit with his mother, listening to the rasping from her fluid-filled lungs, watching her succumb like a cut flower that shrivels in its vase. He'd participated in all efforts to make her more comfortable, though, as long as his role removed him from her presence. He didn't know how the others all took turns changing the washcloth over her spiritless gray eyes or feeding her ice chips when he could barely look at her. They still resented him for it.

On the count of three, they lifted the fallen limb and trudged into the woods with Matthew at the thick end, bringing up the rear. Brittle twigs and leaves snapped underfoot. The wobbling bough kept digging its branches into the ground, as if resisting separation from the rest of the tree.

That afternoon, Matthew climbed to the top of an aluminum ladder to dab creosote on the bald patch of tree trunk where the bough had torn loose. The exposed wood felt soft and pulpy. Although the gray bark looked the same as that of any other oak, it was brittle and bits rained onto the ground when Matthew dragged his fingers across it. He wondered why disease had singled out this tree, or if any of these others that looked so tall and sure were also rotting from the inside out. The sharp odor of the black gum burned his nostrils and he slapped it on hastily to escape the stench.

Matthew spent the afternoon kneeling on the floor of his room, assembling a model B-52 bomber. He could still smell the creosote because it had burrowed into the fine lines of his fingertips. Model gluing was an activity his mother would never have allowed for certainty that he'd ruin the carpet. Out of habit, he listened for the low hum of the garage door opening and the familiar knocking the station wagon made after she cut the ignition, prepared to slide the model pieces under his bed and sprint downstairs to settle into an armchair with a book.

As he clamped the landing gear into place, scraping away a teardrop of oozing glue with his fingernail, Matthew detected a swell of motion in the air beside him. It felt the way a TV screen does just before the spark of a shock bites an approaching hand. His body shuddered. A feathery brush—an invisible, silky spiderweb—drifted down his cheek, neck, and bare right arm. When he struck out at emptiness, the barrel of the plane sailed from his hand and bounced off the wall, leaving a slash of yellowed glue and a tiny rip in the wallpaper.

As soon as Matthew yanked the door open, the room became hushed and inert; the electricity evaporated. Every arm hair stood on end. It was his mother, he knew, as he gently laid the fragmented wing inside the model box. He blamed himself for her unrest.

One bleak Tuesday—after twelve months of gut-twisting chemotherapy—the doctors announced that she had a week to live, and Father Dugan from St. Andrews came to call. He sat beside her, sandwiching her bony, colorless hands between his meaty fingers, and murmured prayers. All the while, she stared at nothing, and tears spilled from her murky eyes.

Afterward, Matthew shadowed his father and Father Dugan into the garage. "There might be a miracle," the priest said. "You never know."

"There isn't going to be any miracle," Matthew's father said. With his foot he nudged a wet leaf on the floor. Skin hung on his cheekbones in loose, ashen folds. For the first time, Matthew noticed that his father had become an old man.

"I've had some experience with this sort of thing." Father Dugan paused to blow his nose. "It's important that you tell her it's okay to go."

"Go where?" Matthew said.

The priest patted Matthew's face with a cold hand. "Where she'll be more comfortable."

The following day, Matthew awakened feeling as if his organs had turned to stone and were crushing him into the mattress. He wasn't sick, just sad, but he faked the flu with an electric blanket and a scant drizzling of cream of mushroom soup in and around the upstairs toilet.

Minutes after his father herded his brothers and sister out the back door with their lunch boxes and book bags in hand, Matthew languished in front of the television, savoring the decadence of wasting hours. He watched show after show without changing the channel or his position on the old couch, which still smelled like his mother—like curry and salt and faintly of flowers, or maybe brown sugar. He lay on his stomach with both arms wrapped around a rectangular seat cushion, smashing his knuckles into the frame. He half-expected to see his mother walk around the corner with a basket of loose socks for him to match up. This anticipation of seeing her, so quickly overshadowed by reality, filled his body with a blunt, unyielding ache.

He had just dozed off when the television shut itself off. He sat up. Sneakers, the Labrador, lay sprawled on the kitchen floor with all four legs twitching. Outside the sky had faded to the cheerless shade of burned charcoal. The bare limbs of trees swayed slightly and a breeze shuttled curled gray leaves across the patio. Matthew relaxed and pulled the warm wool afghan up to his chin.

The television sprang to life with a crackle of static electricity. First a hollow pop, then canned laughter blared. Sneakers scrambled to her feet in the kitchen. Matthew pulled his knees to his chin. Onscreen, a man hauled a limp woman out of the surf and deposited her on the wet sand. A second staticky thump and country music bellowed from the stereo speakers. In the kitchen, the microwave whirred to life, the oven timer began beeping insistently, and the disposal started grinding air. Matthew's heart hammered crazily against his rib cage. The man onscreen lowered his mouth to the woman's and blew. Her cheeks puffed out.

"Hello?" Matthew eased off the couch onto unsteady legs. "Mom?" He crawled toward the television, dragging the afghan. He ripped cords from the wall until the screen snapped black and still. He yanked every cord he saw in the kitchen until the only sound he heard was the wind spraying bits of dirt against the glass patio door.

"The power went out. That's all." His father touched the back of his hand to Matthew's forehead. "Every clock in the house was blinking." Sean, Luke, Josh, and Maggie watched from the doorway of the family room, as if waiting for their father to rid the area of a snake or a rat. "The wind uprooted that oak you patched. We're lucky it fell the way it did or it might have—"

"It was probably the fever. I'm not thinking straight," Matthew said. He wished the gap between the seat cushions would swallow him whole.

"Maybe we should look into getting you a counselor," his father said softly.

"I don't think so, Dad."

When his father left to feed the baby, Luke was the first one to approach, although he walked right past Matthew to fiddle with the stereo receiver. Sean and Maggie hung back in the doorway. Josh eased onto the couch by Matthew's feet and said, "Is it Mom?"

Luke stopped fiddling with the stereo but kept his back turned.

"No. It was just a power failure," Matthew said, embarrassed.

"Does she talk to you?" Sean said.

"No."

"Can you see her?" Maggie said.

"No."

"Is she here now?" Josh said. He swept his arms back and forth through the air as if he were treading water, stopping when he realized everyone was looking at him.

"How should I know?" Matthew wished they'd go away. He swore a silent oath to no one in particular that he would never again glue models on his carpet or fake the flu to miss school, if his mother's ghost, or whatever it was, would stop making its presence known. He wished he'd told his mother it was okay to die the way the others had. Josh had composed a long poem about Heaven, which he memorized and recited in a barely audible voice. Luke had asked what type of flowers she preferred at her headstone, then promised to plant and water them himself.

When he was alone with her for the last time, Matthew had stood by the cold bay window, wiping imaginary smudges with his sleeve, watching her silvery reflection gaping on the couch. Frigid air seeped in along the window edges. Muffled voices floated in from the kitchen.

She called him over. Purplish half moons of skin sagged beneath her eyes. Morphine slurred her words. "You'll have to help your father more." When he knelt beside her, she squeezed his clammy hand with her own, which felt as warm and frail as a hatching bird.

"Does it hurt?" Matthew tilted his head toward her swollen abdomen.

She nodded her hairless head.

"Are you scared?" Matthew said. "Are you mad?"

"No."

He wanted to say that he was sorry and that he didn't know how to be without her, but instead he cleared his throat and mumbled, "You should rest, Mom."

"I always knew that you weren't the one who broke my porcelain music box." She stared at him with eyes devoid of color or light. "But I've always admired you for saying you did."

He felt a quaver in his throat, so he kissed her hairless head and withdrew.

At the wake, he'd granted the gleaming casket a wide, wary berth, then delayed the funeral by retreating to the playground across from the church when the hearse rolled up. He'd thought that if he didn't consent to her death, he'd win her a tiny reprieve, and him a chance to voice the many things he needed to say.

"Have any of you seen her?" Matthew asked his siblings. They stood at various distances from the couch, as though he might be contagious.

After a long moment, Josh said, "Every night I have this dream about her where she's skinny and bald and living in her coffin." He curled his hands into fists and stared into their faces, daring anyone to say anything. "Every night, I dig her up."

"That's it?" Matthew kneaded a seat cushion with his feet, enjoying the rough texture between his toes. "She doesn't say anything?"

"One time she said, 'I'll never get to see your wedding.'" He pressed his chin to his chest and muttered, "But I told her I don't even like girls."

Luke said, "Did you tell her you like boys?"

"Shut your pie hole," Josh said.

Sean touched Matthew's shoulder and said, "We should have a séance." Matthew perked at the thought, though he lacked even the sketchiest notion of the mechanics of a séance.

"That's the dumbest idea I've ever heard," Luke said.

Josh tried to look up séance in the *S* volume of *Encyclopaedia Britannica,* but there wasn't anything listed. He slammed the encyclopedia shut when their father shuffled in carrying a bowl of quivering lime Jell-O.

"What are you kids doing in here?"

"Nothing," Matthew said, after Josh nudged him with his foot.

Two days passed. They gathered in the basement at midnight. While Luke, Josh, and Maggie skidded past on roller skates, windmilling their arms and grabbing on to one another for balance, Matthew arranged folding chairs around a card table, draped filmy scarves over the lamp shades, and placed a votive candle on a coaster at the table's center. He'd checked out a book from the public library called *Nineteenth-Century Spiritualists.* The cover depicted a disembodied hand, bluish white, floating in blackness.

Sean tore the cellophane off a cassette and thrust it into a portable tape recorder. He'd placed himself in charge of taping the whole thing, although Matthew wasn't sure he wanted an enduring account of the event.

When Matthew called them over to start, Luke picked up the book and said, "Couldn't you find anything more recent? Hasn't anyone done this in the twentieth century?"

"You can leave," Matthew said.

"I'm just saying—"

"Do you have any better ideas, genius?" Matthew said.

"Maybe I will leave." Luke searched the others' faces for a confederate. Sean, who was struggling to duct tape batteries into the recorder, ignored him. Josh and Maggie picked at smudges of blue chalk on the pool-table felt.

"In or out?" Matthew said.

Luke slid into the chair opposite Matthew. The others settled into their seats and looked at Matthew expectantly. "We have to hold hands," Matthew said, tapping the book to bolster his authority.

"What for?" Josh said, but he laid both hands, palms up, on the table.

Once everyone had grabbed hold of two hands, Matthew glanced down at a note card in his lap and said, "Okay. Don't ask the spirit any questions and don't ask it to do anything specific. It'll show us what it wants to."

Sean groaned and said, "Do you have to do the *spooky* voice, Matthew?"

Matthew pretended not to hear him, but he read the remaining instructions in a monotone. They frequently interrupted him regarding the particulars: Do we look it in the eye? Can we touch it? Is this a sin? What do we do if Dad comes downstairs? Does one person do all the talking? What if we call the wrong ghost and make it mad? How would we make that one go away? What if more than one spirit showed up? How long will this take? Matthew made up what answers he didn't know from reading the book; he thought it best to preserve his authority.

Sean punched the *Record* button and pressed his mouth to the silver mesh of the tape deck. "Hello, Mom. We hope you stop on by." He set the recorder on the floor beside him.

For nearly a minute, no one said anything. They unyoked their hands to lay their palms flat on the table. Then the table lifted, ever so slightly, off the floor. The flickering candle dribbled clear liquid down one side. A stream of wax wandered in a hardening white line toward Sean, who lifted his hands off the table and held them aloft. Maggie covered her mouth with both hands. The table began to bob and tilt, pitch and plunge, rapping the cement floor with its legs. Watching the others inch their chairs away from the table, Matthew felt a validating mingling of elation and fear. He wasn't cracking. His excitement evaporated, though, the second he spotted the tiniest hint of a smile tickling the corners of Luke's mouth.

Matthew slammed both fists down on the table as hard as he could. Luke howled in pain and jumped up. He flipped the table onto its side at Matthew's feet. The candle bounced across the floor. Luke hopped around on one foot, clutching the opposite knee with both hands.

"Real funny, Luke," Matthew said.

"You didn't have to break my leg," Luke said.

"You should've broken both of them," Maggie said.

"Can we just do this and get it over with?" Josh said.

They righted the table and sat quietly with their palms flat on the table while Matthew read the spirit call off the card and felt foolish. Ten minutes later, the only sound they'd heard was a pinging in a pipe somewhere, and the clicking of the dog's nails as she trotted along the floor overhead. As the minutes dragged by, Matthew's feelings kaleidoscoped. Initially, he felt shame for divulging the ghost idea to anyone, followed by aggravation with Luke for continually serving as the thorn in his side, which dissolved into a gnawing dread that he might, in fact, be unraveling mentally. In the end he experienced an undivided longing—of such intensity that it became a physical cavity expanding in his chest—to see his mother again, even to hear her scold them for lurking around the basement when they should be in bed.

Sean began drumming his fingers on the tabletop. Maggie tilted her chair back on two legs and whispered, "I don't think it's working."

"Maybe I need to read up on this more," Matthew said, reaching down to click off the tape.

Everyone but Matthew plodded upstairs to go to sleep. He folded up the table and chairs and stowed them in the crawl space. On his way upstairs, he remembered the tape recorder. He sat on the cement floor, listening to the machine rattle and screech as it rewound. He pressed *Play* and listened to his own tinny voice, the table bouncing around, muffled conversation, then a prolonged, hissing hum. He had just reached for the *Stop* button when he heard it, harbored in a burst of static:

"Hello, all."

The skin on his arms, legs, and neck prickled. It was her voice. He pressed his ear to the speaker to hear the rest of the tape, but all he heard was the empty hum of dead air until the clack at the recording's finish. Awe and fear bloomed inside him as he rewound the tape to listen again.

Upstairs, Matthew felt his way through the bedroom to his brother's bunk. The darkness made him feel unhinged. He prodded the sleeping form with the tape recorder until Sean swung a slack arm at him. "Leave me alone. I'm asleep."

Matthew yanked his blanket off. "Did you put that voice on the tape?"

A rustle, then Sean turned on his reading light. "It was a brand new tape." He squinted at Matthew, then pushed his body against the wall, folding his thin arms over his chest. While the tape played, Sean looked from the recorder to Matthew to the shadowy air surrounding them. Matthew could tell from his brother's wide-eyed look that he hadn't tinkered with it. Josh and Luke crept over from their bunks to listen.

"It's like hearing someone talking when you're under water." Josh pulled his knees up under his pajama top. "That's creepy."

Sean said, "Sounds more like a radio that's not tuned in all the way."

"The tape is probably warped," Luke said.

"It's her. Can't you hear that it's her?" Matthew said.

"That's not her." Luke pressed the tape recorder to his ear and paced from the door to the cold windows. He rewound and listened again before dropping the tape recorder into Matthew's lap.

Luke readily swayed the other boys with a long, corrosive diatribe. Matthew watched their expressions change and their support leak away like water seeping through cupped hands. They folded their arms and kept their eyes downcast. That strip of speckled carpet that lay between Matthew and his brothers became a dark and yawning abyss that widened by the minute. Luke concluded his rant with a disdainful wave. "Matthew can't handle that she's gone so he's trying to pretend she's not. It's not a ghost. It's *sad.*"

The therapist's office was brightly lit and smelled of lilacs, though the only plant in sight was a tall, spindly cactus. Painted Disney characters tumbled across the walls. The desk was bare except for a plastic brain and a clock that she'd covered with a small, white handkerchief.

Dr. Levine slipped her pumps off to kneel on the floor across from Matthew. Two chopsticks held her hair back in a loose bun. Her face was beige though her neck looked as arrestingly white as the soft belly of a bullhead. The right lens of her glasses framed a smudged, oval fingerprint. She jotted notes on a legal pad. Matthew answered every question with a grim smile, lest she report him to his father as uncooperative.

"Do you hear other voices?" Dr. Levine said.

"No."

"But you do hear voices."

"No."

"Do you hear her now?"

"No."

Matthew pictured his father sitting in the waiting room with his overcoat on, reading a magazine, or maybe pressing his ear against the door to listen. That's what Matthew had done earlier while his father played the tape for Dr. Levine. He had lain on the dusty wood floor of the reception area and pressed his ear to the crack beneath the door to hear Dr. Levine explain how his colorful imagination somehow managed to read his mother's voice into dead air and static. Though Matthew had yearned to hear his father defend him or offer an alternative explanation, all he heard were bland murmurs which could only be interpreted as assent.

Dr. Levine asked if he thought his mother had abandoned him. Before Matthew could respond, he noticed a brilliant circle of white light on the floor beside him. He searched the walls and ceiling to identify the source of the light. Dr. Levine looked at him expectantly, exhibiting no signs of alarm or even awareness of the quarter-size spot, so he said no, and she returned to questions about voices. Matthew slid his hand along the coarse cables of the rug toward the light. The air surrounding his fingers pulsated, warm and alive. The sensation reminded him of touching wet fingers to a disposal switch.

"Do you ever feel angry with her?" Dr. Levine said. "It's perfectly normal if you do."

One second he was shaking his head for Dr. Levine, and the next, he was watching his mother lift up, a silvery form unfurling from the circle in the floor. She wore the silky green pantsuit they'd buried her in, with a scarf wound around her head, and the leather sandals she wore every day in summer. Her clothing and skin had a translucent, ivory sheen that Matthew could see through, as if she were made of thick, rippling ice. She pointed at Dr. Levine, scrawling something on her pad, and gestured for Matthew to keep quiet. He reached his hand out, expecting her to shrink back or vanish, but she stood still while he passed his fingers through her smoky feet. It felt slightly humid and comforting, like steam from cider on a wintry day. He took a deep breath and closed his eyes to better feel her in the air against him.

Dr. Levine jarred him out of his reverie. "Do you think she's here now?"

Matthew peeked at the bare place on the floor that the luminous spot had occupied.

"Do you see her now?" Dr. Levine said.

He closed his eyes again and shook his head, anticipating the ripple in the air created by someone passing by without touching, like a warm breeze against his skin. He enjoyed the idea of his silent but ever-present mother, drifting in the shadows, keeping him out of harm's way. He imagined astounding a packed school auditorium by shuttling inanimate objects about the stage by no visible means.

Dr. Levine snapped her fingers, then pushed her glasses against her face with her thumb. "You were just stroking the air as if it were a cat. What did you think you were touching?"

Matthew dropped his eyes to the floor in front of him, already aware that the form had evaporated, the energy collapsed. "I was just trying to get a rise out of you," he said.

"Interesting choice of words," Dr. Levine said, scratching notes onto her yellow pad.

For over two weeks following his visit with Dr. Levine, Matthew had longed to feel another vaporous trace of his mother settle like mist on his skin. He'd engaged in one prohibited household activity after another, undertaken one-man séances, and vigilantly recorded dozens of hours of blank, lifeless air, trying to draw her out. Though he remained watchful, his expectation of further encounters withered. Doubts badgered him. The possibility that none of it had happened, that the explanation lay in a fracture in his psyche rather than some innate gift that allowed him to hold on to her spirit, made him deeply uneasy.

Matthew perched on the couch, watching his father's eyes flick from the ceiling to his face to the ceiling again. Outside, the wind bowed bare tree branches and buffeted the house. Matthew heard the muffled shouts of the others cavorting in the mountain of leaves heaped in the front yard and wished he were out there, instead of sequestered with his father, bracing for questions. His neck and back felt so taut he began to worry that cords of muscle might snap loose from his bones.

"So, you never told me. Was your talk with Dr. Levine illuminating?"

"In a way."

"Would you like to see her again?"

"Who?" Matthew said, startled by the question.

His father slumped into his favorite armchair. "Dr. Levine."

"I'm not crazy."

"I didn't say you were."

To divert attention, Matthew said, "Sean wet his bed last week. And Luke gets nosebleeds almost every day." He understood by the sag of his father's shoulders that it was not the ideal time to suggest that those two might benefit greatly from a visit with Dr. Levine.

His father sighed. "Should I make another appointment for you?"

"No." Matthew pulled his legs to his chest and wrapped his arms tightly around them. He noticed an indentation on the seat cushion next to him, an impression created by a person sitting there. Matthew's heart galloped in his chest. He snuck a look at his father, who had removed his glasses to rub the red marks they left on his nose.

Matthew wondered why he hadn't felt the hum of current rocketing through his muscles. He placed his hand flat on the couch and eased it along the coarse fabric of the adjoining seat cushion, expecting, at any moment, the tingling just below the surface of his skin. His hand reached the dent, which was cold, and glided around its entirety without sensing a single pinprick of life. Even with his eyes closed, Matthew felt only the fine ridges and imperfections of the cushion's surface. He thought he could feel the cushion's faded stains: popcorn grease wiped by small fingers, blood from scraped knees, and sooty grime transferred from sites unknown.

He didn't want to open his eyes, even after his father had moved to the couch. Matthew could smell his tangy aftershave. He squeezed Matthew's shoulder hard enough that Matthew could feel the bones in his fingers. The touch was reassuring in its solidity, but then it was gone.

Matthew went outside and leaned against the upended oak to

watch the others play. They entombed themselves in leaf mounds to burst free moments later, squealing and laughing. Next door, the smoke from Mr. McAlister's burning leaves rose and dissolved into the overcast sky.

Matthew walked the length of the fallen oak. He had difficulty picturing it as it had once stood: leafy and strong. He stopped to trace a thumb along the concentric ridges inside a football-size canker just below the creosote poultice.

An unfortunate sapling had been bent nearly in half by the fallen tree. In time it would either be crushed or grow crooked by necessity, forced to shoulder this inanimate weight, twisting and stretching to find sunlight or water. Matthew tried to yank the sapling free, but his hands were numb with cold and he couldn't get a decent grip on it. The big oak had sheared branches off nearby trees and ground a dozen shrubs into the dirt, but it felt no regret. It was totally, blissfully oblivious to the wreckage in its wake.

Matthew poked the snapped roots of the oak with a stick. They were speckled with fuzzy, white patches of fungus. Even frozen, they felt spongy and rotten, disintegrating within the earth they once held in place. He wondered how long it would take before the massive trunk began to cave in on itself. Eventually, other trees would crowd into this space until it would seem that—except for its presence in the backgrounds of old photographs—this oak had never existed.

He tore off a piece of bark, stuffed it into his pocket, and walked toward the house. Fog was billowing from the dryer vent. He paused before it to savor the saturated warmth. Even though the smell was all wrong, it mimicked the texture he coveted: steamy and vital. Matthew squatted before the vent, steadying himself by pressing his fingertips to the frozen ground, and waited for the soapy cloud to engulf him.

J. Patrice Whetsell

The Coconut Lady

My mother taught me to cook the summer before I went to college because she believed I would starve to death if left to rely on the services of the campus dining hall. "What you will eat? They nuh know how fe make rice and peas there," she would say. "You must learn to cook your*self*."

I am not surprised my mother worried so much about my diet. She has always believed in the power of food, a necessity that, with a little ingenuity, can be made into a luxury, and is indispensable in the art of seduction. In her estimation, food is power to a woman, even more so than beauty. "You will never find love until you learn to cook," she has often said. "True love is made in the mouth."

My mother holds three basic ideas about food: that it should be pleasing to the eye as well as to the palate, that it should be enjoyed, and that it should not be restricted to what is good for you, although those things good for you should be included when possible. She is a wonderful cook, her meals being inspired by whimsy rather than recipe, desire rather than diet. She never reads nutrition statistics and has never counted a calorie in her life.

We began with coconuts because they are the most difficult fruit and my mother's favorite, a secret weapon in almost all of her dishes. The first thing to do is to look at the "eyes" of the coconut, three small craters, distinguishable but partially concealed by hair.

"Naked eyes, like eyes without lashes, no good," Mother warned. "Ignore them." She called them having poor sight. An experienced shopper will never shake a *poor-sight fruit.* A good ear is also necessary for choosing a coconut because you must shake it. A good coconut will be *full up* of water.

Every week we bought two coconuts, one to use in rice and peas and one to snack on. My mother inspected each coconut on the shelf, shaking her head and sucking her teeth as she picked the bad ones up and put them back. "So many gone bad by the time they get here, all dry up," she would say. But she always succeeded in finding some that looked decent.

Opinions differ as to the best way to crack open a coconut, but my mother believes in the virtue of simplicity. She cracks coconuts by throwing them against the ground. Maybe that practice wastes the milk, but some of my fondest memories are of me and my mother on the back patio, the sound of a hard shell smashing against concrete. If it was good, she would hold the coconut high above our heads, milk spilling everywhere, and the two of us dancing underneath, sticking out our tongues and lapping it up. Very often these coconuts were not good, though, and we would have to return them.

The first time my mother tried to return a coconut, the cashier stared open-mouthed at the woman pushing a sticky plastic bag of broken coconut, leaking milk and covered with hairs, toward him on the counter. "We can't take this back. It's open," he stammered. My mother said, "It's no good. I don't want it." The boy looked back and forth between my mother and the puddle of coconut milk now dripping slowly onto the floor. "Won't take it," my mother said. He called his manager and then maintenance for a cleanup.

That day my mother discovered it was easier to let the men in the grocery store open the coconuts. She took her 99 cents and went back to the produce aisle, chose another coconut and stopped an employee. "Open this for me, please?"

The man laughed while he talked. "Lady, I can't do that. You have to *buy* it first."

"I won't buy it first. It's bad, I just return it anyway, so you can just open it now." My mother handed him the coconut and he walked away.

The men at the grocery store make a hole in one eye to save the milk and let my mother taste it. She pauses and either shakes her head vehemently or nods languorously with pleasure, and we know instantly whether the fruit is worthy or not. That day the coconut was bad. My mother demanded that the man open another coconut, and another. I stood at her side, holding her hand and squirming in my shoes, whispering, "Let's go, Mama." She ignored me until finally all the coconuts in the store were sitting in the stockroom, broken and useless. My mother refused to pay for any of them. She thanked the man for his trouble and said simply, "Let's go home now." The next week when we went shopping, the man called out, "Hey, it's the Coconut Lady!" when he saw us. My ears burned red, but my mother only laughed.

My mother says that back home people would laugh to see us eating the dry coconut, only good for cooking with. In Jamaica coconuts grow large and hard and green. And when you cut one down and chop off the top there is a cream-colored fibrous layer inside, and then a layer of clear jelly you can eat with a spoon, and the coconut water you can drink with a straw. The brown, hairy coconuts we see in the grocery stores here are only the dried remains of those fresh green glories. But she would take a bite out of the dry coconut and laugh, and throw the rest into the blender to grind for her rice.

My second lesson was in selecting all other produce. This is easier because it only requires sight, smell, and touch. I had gone to the grocery store with her every Saturday since childhood, and in the spring and summer also to various farms. We spent hours on the weekend driving around to different markets so that she could buy fruits and vegetables at her favorite places.

My mother's words still echo in my ear. She has lost most of her Jamaican accent from twenty years in America, but I love the unique sounds she makes, how she sucks her teeth when she is unsatisfied, the way she enunciates all the letters of certain words like vegetables and Connecticut. Ve-ge-*te*-bels.

Fresh vegetables always when possible. Frozen, second choice. Canned only for certain recipes or emergencies. Tomatoes from Ann's farm, over on 22. Cucumbers, peppers, and squash from the Abbots on the east side. They grow plenty things, but they have the sense not to make them grow big and tasteless. Peaches from Glengarry Orchards. Ed Burns's plums are the best. Strawberries and blueberries you can get in May, but raspberry season's not till July. Apples in the fall from Dell's. Gala sweet for snacking, Granny Smith, sour, and McIntosh, baking. Never buy anything that ends in Delicious. It's usually not. Use your thumb to buy pears—you should be able to press them in slightly near the stem. Apples should stay firm. Sniff melons.

Lettuces and all produce not grown in our area we bought at the local grocery store. Potatoes and onions individually, never bagged because too often they're sweaty, cabbages, mushrooms, bananas, avocados, mangoes. These can be red or green, bi- or tri-toned, even speckled when ripe. They're all still common mangoes, imported en masse to consumers who have never heard of guinea hens and don't know what they're missing—Julies and Bombays, East Indians and Saint Julians and Robins. I've often marveled at my mother's trading a dozen varieties of mangoes and a papaya tree in the backyard for three kinds of berries, hard-to-peel oranges, and pineapples that burn the roof of your mouth.

Presentation was the third lesson, color being the major principle. Salads are a good starting point for contrasts, and they're usually the first thing a guest will see.

Start with a dark green lettuce; the other vegetables show up better against it. Bright red tomatoes make a beautiful contrast; so do carrots. Red cabbage is good. There are few things that purple. Red onions for the same reason, and they're sweet too. But white or yellow ones for cooking. Always use fresh Vidalia when you can get them. Red peppers are good too, although yellow are more distinctive. A little fruit can go a long way in traditional salads. Like spinach salad with orange slices and mushrooms. Cantaloupe on Romaine.

You can make salads more interesting by mixing and matching flavors, textures, and shapes. Sweet and sour, crisp and soft, cubes and circles and shredded things.

And never underestimate the importance of table setting: flowers and tablecloths should complement the colors of the food as well as of the room it's being served in. White tablecloths are basic, and you can never really go wrong with them, especially on dark wood, but sometimes you want something more original. They're also good if you're serving dark dishes, like stews and chilis, or anything with a lot of different colors, although you have to be careful because these things stain. Gardenias are good for the same reason, but never against a white tablecloth unless you're trying to make some kind of statement. Gladiolas are always nice; any tall flower really, to add height. Yellow and purple go well together. Hyacinth is a lovely shade for curries. You can also go the other way and use daffodils with eggplant. Stuffed eggplant is best because it retains its royal color. Almost anything will liven up pale whites like stroganoffs and chicken. I like red flowers, but sometimes plain green plants are better. Never skimp and never buy store-made arrangements. Cheapness shows.

During the next few weeks, my mother taught me what size pots were best for making which dishes, how to use spices, and how to prepare the dishes I had been raised on—rice and peas, hominy, curried goat and chicken, jerked pork, ackee and saltfish, pepper-dash stew, fried plantains, gazottas.

On my last night home, my mother and I made dinner together. I started washing handfuls of gungu peas for rice and peas while she searched for the pressure cooker.

"You can soak the peas and cook them on the stove, but the pressure cooker's faster and it always make them soft. They never come out so soft on the stove," she said.

I nodded. I took out the other ingredients—white rice, coconut, onion, garlic, parsley, fresh thyme, and little rainbow-colored hot Scotch Bonnet peppers. My mother found the pressure cooker and started to boil water. Then she came over to see what I was doing.

"How do you do the coconut, Mom?"

"Here, it's easy after you already have it broken up. Just take off the shell and grind it up."

Her arms moved quickly as she dug the coconut out of its shell with a knife and threw large pieces into the blender. We fell silent as the blender whizzed, turning the coconut into gray mush. I started to peel the onion and garlic on the table.

"Remember to mince it up. And chop those peppers tiny, too. You don't want to burn him when he eats."

I grinned. "Who says there's going to be a him?"

She smiled knowingly. "You'll find a nice man at school."

"I'm not going to school to meet a man, Mom."

"I know. But lots of girls meet a man in college. And now you'll know how to cook well, you'll find a nice man. There's no secret to love. Just remember: live with the little things. No man is perfect. And neither are you."

"Is that how it is with you and Dad?"

"Put the rice on to boil while you finish that chopping. Use a sharper knife for the garlic—it will go faster. Here, let me do it."

Her wrist bobbed up and down rapidly as she chopped. Tiny pieces of garlic jumped in the air before landing in golden piles. I stopped chopping spices.

"He's never around anymore."

"You are."

"He doesn't eat your food anymore."

"You do."

"Who will eat it when I'm not here?"

She laughed. "Don't worry about me and your father. Besides, I'm tired of cooking every day. It will be nice to order out and eat TV dinners instead. I can just cook when I want to.

"We need something to go with this. You want to make ackee? Make sure you get all the bones out of the saltfish. They're tiny, and I don't want anybody to choke."

She put the peas and spices into the pot with the rice. "Parsley last," she said. Then she joined me at the kitchen table, and we pulled bones out of the saltfish until the rice was cooked.

That night, as I was packing the last of my things, I noticed a small wrapped box in the corner of my suitcase. Inside was a bottle of Jamaican white rum and an apron with the words Coconut Lady embroidered in script across the top. There was also a small piece of white paper, folded several times. It read: *Always use pressure cooker for beans. The tall black pots for rice or stews. The red heavy one is good for chicken. Use the round green ones for cooking vegetables—that way they don't stick.*

There are certain things a kitchen must have—curry powder, onion and garlic, turmeric—for color and taste. Parsley, ginger because it goes well with coconut, basil, condensed milk, and honey. And a bottle of rum. It's nice to drink at night, plus it's good if you're getting sick. Never buy curry powder in a grocery store. Get a real Jamaican one. Cumin is nice too, and a dash of oregano goes a long way.

Curries are simple; you just need to make sure you have enough water in the pot to make a sauce. And curry will cover almost any mistake, unless you add too much; then you just make a new one. Buy good jerked seasoning same way you get curry powder. Stuff it in the pork. Remember to spread it evenly; you don't want to burn someone. Hominy is just corn and condensed milk, ginger, nutmeg. Do the corn in the pressure cooker. Fried plantains are easy, green and turning black is ripe. Better to use shortening than oil. Gazottas—just grind the coconut and boil it with sugar, a little ginger too if you want. Make your dough and fill it. Watch the oven because they burn fast, but they're best when they've browned. Sorrel we always make at Christmas, but it's good for any party. Bright red, very festive. Boil the sorrel leaves, strain the juice, and mix it with white rum. Everything else you must learn yourself.

Nathan Long

Tracking

The train full of wedding guests struggled up into the mountains. What had appeared to the bride to be powdered sugar over a heap of cocoa in the distance was now distinct chunks of snow: dirty, gray, and hardened. Still, she beamed, listening to the murmurs, then bursts of laughter throughout the train compartments. In the front car, three women, each holding a small bowl of rice, sat on the train in a cluster. They took turns folding and refolding the lengths of their dresses, without thought, like cats rearranging their tails, while several men stood with glasses in hand inventing progressively obscure toasts to celebrate the occasion.

The night before, an upright piano had been wheeled onboard and a young man in a rented tux played voiceless renditions of songs everyone recognized but no one could name. It gave them all a great sense of familiarity and peace.

Everyone circulated through the train back to the end car reserved for food as their palm-size plates emptied. There, a man in white served meatballs, crab soufflé, and a cold vegetable stew. He was a student of biology taking on a summer job. Across from him a bar was set up, with champagne and ginger ale—*Only things bubbly,* the bride had said—with real glass glasses. Under the table a tiny broom and dustpan sat ready, in case a glass broke.

The women with the bowls of rice were all friends of the bride.

One of them was pregnant and laughed at the whole affair. Another looked a little sad. The third seemed to have no expression at all. They were waiting for the photo session, with the Rockies as backdrop, to throw the contents of their bowls into the air. In the meantime, the expressionless one sifted the grains through a tiny hole where the tips of her fingers pressed together. The men saw an elk in the distance, mistook it for a caribou, and talked of hunting, though none of them had ever held a rifle in their lives.

The wedding had been in Boulder; this was only the reception train. Still, the men gathered with other men, the women with women, as though they were all in second grade, out on the playground. It was 1999, when divorces outnumbered weddings, and so weddings were really about the past, not the future, and those who came to them fell into old habits, as these men and women did, there on the train.

All but one: an older woman who had nothing to do with either the groom or the bride. She had come to meet her daughter Judy at the end of the line, to bring her back to Boulder. Judy had been camping for a month, far in the mountains.

One of the wedding mothers—they seemed the same to those who weren't related, the same calm, idiosyncratic politeness—went up to talk to Judy's mother.

"You're with the one they're picking up?" the wedding mother said. She was rubbing her fingers together in a circle, but beneath this anxiety rested a deep pool of calmness (her child was finally married, after all), which lay on an even deeper bed of anxiety (for how would it all turn out?).

"My daughter, yes," said Judy's mother. She thought of the wedding mother as a distraction; the wedding mother thought the same of her.

"Oh, heavens. How lovely," the wedding mother said, sipping from her glass. "Is she alone? Has it been long?"

Judy's mother hardly knew where to start. "Well, she does go out alone, quite often. She's a real outdoors type. But this time she's gone with Peter. They've been out there a month." She held back a smile of pride.

"A month! My!" the wedding mother said. She glanced at the casual clothes Judy's mother wore and felt both sad and pleased by the formality of her own dress. She recovered from this thought and said, "At least she's with her husband."

"Oh no, just a boyfriend."

"But they're engaged?"

"No," said Judy's mother. There was a tiny silence between them. Then Judy's mother, against her will, said, "Not yet."

The mother of the bride—or groom—stood up, smiled. The train had been going quite slowly for a while, pushing its way uphill. The trip had been smooth. The wedding mother said, "I'm so glad you could join us. I hope you help yourself to champagne and to the buffet. There's so much food. We can't possibly eat it all, even with the whole trip back."

Judy's mother smiled, in lieu of thank you, and the universal bond between mothers was resealed, like an envelope no one was ever to know had been broken.

A moment later, a piano string broke as it was struck, a loud slap of sound, which startled everyone. The best man took a red cocktail napkin—bunched and wet—and held it to his chest, pretending to be a caribou, shot.

"The altitude," the assistant engineer said, his jacket off, a heavy hand around one of the thin glasses. No one was certain if his comment was about the string or the man. He held his glass high to prevent it from spilling, though it looked as though he were making a toast. "The altitude," he repeated and laughed.

The trip went on like this for an hour, until the horn sounded, which meant they were approaching the end of the track. Those who stuck their heads out the windows could see the end of the line: two round metal signs painted red, with a tiny supply shed off to the side, on the near edge of a snow-covered field.

Religiously, the train came to that spot every week. This afternoon the shed door would be unlocked and the engineers would send a signal of their arrival. They would check supplies and replace the battery that powered the two-way radio. They would pick up Judy and her boyfriend. During all this, the wedding guests would walk around the snow field, which had once been a mining site, and take their wedding pictures against the sublimity of the mountains. Then the engineers would fire up the engine on the other end of the train—there was no track for them to turn around—and return.

Except, of course, that Judy and her boyfriend were not there. Her mother and half a dozen wedding guests called out for them. They looked for messages posted on the outside of the shed. A couple of the wedding men who had brought jackets and boots traced the perimeter of the field, looking for footprints and calling out the names again and again into the side of the mountain. "Judy! Peter! Judy!"

Judy's mother listened in terror, afraid that the sound of these strangers, men in tuxedos calling her daughter's name, would be the one memory she would carry from this day. *Let them appear,* she said, over and over, like a mantra. *Let them appear.* Twice she lost track of the men circling the field and when they reappeared, she momentarily mistook them for her daughter and Peter.

The engineers talked to her between tasks. "There's not been any major storm or nothing," the old one said.

It was August.

"They could have just gotten the days messed up," said the assistant. "It happens a lot with folks in the woods." The engineers were familiar with hikers who did not appear on schedule. In the past, such situations had ended in either way.

The bride and groom huddled close to each other and didn't leave the train. The man in white, the one who served the food, stayed at his post. He felt it was his duty. The piano player, however, took his break, eating quickly from a slightly chipped plate while he peered out the train window. Not all the wedding guests seemed to understand what was going on, and a few of them took several bottles of champagne and pitched them into the snow, like the world was their ice bucket. One held an ice pick he'd taken from the emergency box on the train, and with a bottle in the other hand, posed for the photographer.

It was late in the day, but the snow made flashes superfluous. The photographer was glad the gentle brush of his aperture as it shut was nearly silent. The sound, invisible to the mother missing her daughter, was a comfort to him, the register of a moment of time that he was living and recording. He believed he was an invisible figure in all his prints and reveled knowing his photographs would find themselves in strangers' houses, as though his very eyes would be there, even long after he and the people he photographed were gone.

They all waited until the last fabric of dusk slipped between the mountains.

"We're not supposed to, but we left the shed unlocked," the main engineer said to Judy's mother.

"There's food enough there for a week, but we'll get someone up here tomorrow, for sure," said the other. They were older men and knew what to say—but had little to say. They could not lie beyond the possibility of hope.

"Just five more minutes," Judy's mother begged.

But they had to return. The bride and groom had reservations at a ski lodge that night and many of the guests had to work the next day, though none of them mentioned these things—they simply offered silence as they boarded. The photographer closed his camera into its case as he passed Judy's mother.

The engine began to churn, like waves rapidly breaking on the shore. Everyone was in and the door was closed.

"Just five more minutes," Judy's mother said again to herself, but the train was already in motion. The mothers of the bride and groom then each took a turn comforting her, though it was impossible to know if they should be consoling or optimistic. And soon they realized that between them and Judy's mother lay the unspoken truth that she was missing a child and they were not, so they left for their own compartments.

The piano lid remained closed; its shiny surface reflected the first stars of night. The rice bowls were stacked, the three women still. The pregnant one held her stomach in both hands, as though it were a porcelain bowl she might drop.

Judy's mother gazed out the window at the blue snow piled high against the tracks, and at the wet slate color of the forest beyond. The man in white, the one who served food, came up to her then and stroked her hand as the train rocked from the pressure of the brakes.

And over the train, high above, an eagle flew, following close for a few miles, as though tracking a snake in the night.

Margo Rabb

How to Find Love

How do you fall in love?

This was what I awoke wondering the morning I turned sixteen. It was August, during one of New York's record heat waves; even my bedroom windows seemed to sweat. When I opened my eyes all I could think was that it wouldn't be so bad to wake up sweating, if, as in movies and romance novels and dramas on TV, you awoke beside somebody else.

But there wasn't anyone else. In our quiet, empty house, my single bed was filled only with pancake-flat, fur-mangled stuffed animals, steamrolled from years of being slept on. For ages my father had been trying to get me to throw them out; he'd only given up recently, after my mother's death in January, when I stood before my bears, rabbits, gorillas, kangaroos, and, with all the passion of Scarlett O'Hara, vowed in a fierce, husky voice, *"Never."*

But now all I could think was, I was a sixteen-year-old girl still sleeping with gorillas. Not like *Sixteen Candles,* or any of those coming-of-age movies; there were no boyfriends, no hopes of boyfriends waiting outside my door. Just my father, one room away, snoring on his side of my parents' double bed.

Birthdays had been a big deal when my mother was alive: parties with tons of kids pinning the tail on the donkey, batting piñatas, gorging on Duncan Hines SuperMoist cake with Fudge Frosting. We didn't have a lot of money but she always bought some surprise—a three-tiered set of Ultima II makeup, silver-plated hair clips—despite the groans of my father that we were killing him with the bills.

This year I knew what my father had gotten me—he'd left it in a bag in the hall closet—Teen Lady shampoo, body wash, and scented powder from the supermarket. He must've asked the store clerk, "What do you get for a *girl?*" and been told this. I often wished there were some guidebook I could give him, *How to Raise a Daughter* or something; he seemed near cardiac arrest when I asked for money for tampons, had no comprehension of the magic word "shopping," and thought reupholstering the couch made for a fun Saturday night. In fact, the couch was now his whole existence; he'd retired on my mother's life-insurance money, and spent each day there reading the complete *New York Times.*

Every afternoon when I came home from school he'd narrate his day: "This morning I had myself a bagel with the no-fat cream cheese; lunch, a Wendy's grilled chicken. In Topeka they had a scandal with the honey-mustard sauce; people got sick I read on page six of the Living Section. I saved the article for you—" And I'd gaze longingly at the television, as if I could jump into a family on the set.

Aside from the Wendy's cashiers, I was often the only person he talked to during the day. "Why don't you bring your friends over, I'll bake a chicken?" he'd ask me. Or, "Invite Sarah, we'll play Scrabble," "Isabel can help us fix the bird feeder," or, "I bet Rebecca would like this Sherlock Holmes movie, too." It didn't matter that I hadn't seen Sarah, Isabel, or Rebecca since sixth grade, or that if I asked them over now, they'd surely run off. Our house had become Spooky House, one of those run-down, weedy, crumbling places, which is the nightmare of every kid on the block. Each room was a tomb, a vault, a mausoleum of lost love and unrelieved grief: the freezer of casseroles left over from the funeral, the untouched closets of my mother's clothes, bags of supplies from her office, her magazines, her used-up shampoos; we hadn't moved the tiniest thing, as if we feared even the dust would shift.

It was like the scrapbook I kept of her, which I'd put together after the funeral, pasting in the memorial-service announcement, the obituary, photographs. I'd been staring at it every night, as if I could conjure her love out of the sticky cardboard, and I only stopped when I finally realized I was pouring all my love into a book.

It was still two hours before I had to be at summer school, but I got dressed and left the house. I lingered at the newsstand by the subway, and there I saw it, gleaming at me from the cover of *Cosmopolitan:* "How to Find Love." I devoured it during my hour-long subway ride to school:

HOW TO FIND LOVE

> Love may *happen* to some women—goddesses, movie stars, models—knights descend on them, scooping them onto white horses, hunks of the month call and ask them for dates. But the rest of us have to go out and *find our true loves.*
>
> It isn't as hard as you think. He's out there, you just have to look for him. If you seem friendly and receptive, somebody attractive will get the message and start a conversation with you. So here's the secret to finding love: get out there, make yourself available, be open to love! Here are some places to start your search.
>
> Libraries. Law, medical, university. Bring something to look up. Ask questions of male researchers: "How do I use this microfiche?"
>
> In the supermarket. Look into his basket and ask where he got the fresh pesto. (Stay away from men with tampons in their carts—they have other interests.)
>
> Be a hospital volunteer. A wealth of opportunities here: doctors, staff, patients—they do recover!
>
> Car shows. Men flock to them . . .

"What the hell kind of guy are you gonna meet at a car show, someone from *Grease*? Danny Zucco? Kenickie?" a voice said over my shoulder. It was Kelsey Chun, my Spanish Level Two deskmate. I hadn't noticed when she'd gotten on the train, I'd been so engrossed in the article, and it was strange seeing her on the subway; I'd never seen her outside of school before. We were packed like sardines on the #7 train—mornings were always the worst, commuters scowling, grumbling in ten different languages, reaching desperately for the silver poles as the train squealed and tilted like it was about to topple off the tracks.

I smiled at her and stuffed the magazine into my book bag, embarrassed to have been caught reading it. What if she thought I was desperate?

But I was desperate. I was always daydreaming, getting a crush on some guy—Luigi Bamboni, the cook at the Queens Burger, where I waitressed part-time; Richard Bridgewald, a doctor I met while my father was in the hospital; the list went on. During even the most awful day a crush could change everything, like a good-luck charm you took out and polished and revered, a jumping-off point for dreams and fantasies. Every new person I met, every crush I had, opened up reams of possibilities: people who could remove the world, who could fill in all of life's gaping holes.

And it wasn't so different with friendships: at Grand Central several passengers got up and we took their seats, and I loved the thought of it, riding the subway with Kelsey, walking the long blocks to school beside her. I stared at our reflections in the darkened window. My visions of friendship seemed no different from my crush fantasies—I wanted a best girlfriend as much as a boyfriend. In the first months after my mother died, my friends had seemed afraid to be with me, as if losing your mother was catching. Conversations hushed when I approached, eyes averted or else searched me with a horrified fascination, as if my mother's death showed physically, like a huge wart or missing limb.

Those friendships had been hung on so little, I realized now, unlike the kind of best-friendship I imagined—someone who I could unburden my heart to wholly, in the dark, to sit beside at night and tell everything to. But was it a myth, that kind of friend? A myth like having a mother was a myth, or a father like the ones on TV?

Kelsey glanced at her watch. "How come you're going to school now? I've never seen you here before."

I shrugged. "I woke up early." I didn't want to say that it was my birthday, that I hadn't wanted to be home alone with my father. "What about you?"

"I usually get to school early to do homework—I never have time after school. I work at my parents' store or I make dinner for my stupid brothers or something. I'm a nerd now," she added with a resigned sigh, though with her sleek black hair and high-heeled boots she clearly wasn't. "I'm turning over a new leaf. You really just woke up early?" She looked at me oddly, as if she couldn't imagine a stranger thing to do.

"Well—it's actually . . ." Why not just say it? "It's my birthday."

Her eyes lit up. "Happy birthday! How old are you?"

"Sixteen."

"How are you celebrating? Are you having a sweet sixteen?"

"I don't think so." My father and I hadn't made any plans except for eating the Sara Lee cake in the freezer. "It's not such a big deal."

"It is," Kelsey said. "The last place you should be on your birthday is in school."

"That's true." High school was misery. Aside from the boring classes, the building itself was unbearable—desks bolted down, barred windows (did they think we'd steal the desks and jump out?), the soiled bathrooms, the cafeteria that smelled like cold oatmeal and cottage cheese. Then there were the people, guards who wouldn't let you in without your ID card, teachers taking attendance by ID number, the whole prisonlike, nameless, faceless state of being in public school.

At the Fifth Avenue station, we walked down the corridor to switch to the D train. "I know what we should do today," Kelsey said. "We should hang out in a supermarket and ask some guy where he got the pesto."

"Or we could saunter around a hospital, looking for cute patients," I said.

"I always wanted to be a candy striper."

"We should do it. We should stay out until we fall in love." I said it jokingly, but Kelsey raised her eyebrows in earnest.

"It is Friday," she said. "Neither of us has missed a day yet.

Although not showing up is what got us into summer school in the first place."

I remembered the first day of class: Mrs. Torres had asked why we'd failed Spanish during the regular year. I'd said, vaguely, because of an illness—not mentioning it had been my mother's—and Kelsey had answered that it was her appetite; she was always hungry. She was stick-thin, but she had a penchant for skipping class to find something good to eat.

I imagined it, the two of us off on our own, eating delicious things, roaming about the city, and it seemed more important than class or anything. "Have you ever been to Manhattan Bakery?" I said. "It's right near here. They have the best croissants in the city."

Before we could change our minds we were out on the street.

Businessmen marched up Fifth like a gray-tweed parade; we strode to the bakery and gazed at the pastries rising up like a hundred half-moons in the window. We bought two croissants and shared them in the park, digging our fingers into the soft buttery insides, puffs of cotton. How good they tasted, how good everything tastes when you're not supposed to be eating it, when right then we should've been saying *hola* to Mrs. Torres.

We wandered through Central Park and bought a romance novel at the Strand carts; at Sheep Meadow we lay reading in the grass, skipping to the good parts, watching Frisbees slice up the sun. Kelsey read aloud:

> Tristan reached his hand down to Anastasia's furry domain. He let it rest there, as the sensations swelled and swarmed through her tawny thighs and womanly petals . . .

"It's worse than *Cosmo,*" I groaned.

She smiled. "My sister and I own more at home. Three shelves."

We saw a movie at the Paris theater, with subtitles and a plot neither of us understood, and we walked across all of Manhattan, through uptown, midtown, and downtown, to the Village, where we could shop.

Shopping: a girl's true cure for any ailment of the soul. It had begun to rain lightly, and we sauntered through the dampened Village streets, pausing in stores, admiring shop windows, buying earrings and barrettes from the umbrella-covered street vendors, sharing honey-roasted peanuts beneath an awning, the sweetness whirling out from the cart like a cloud. Years after I would still remember the sweet smell and softness of those peanuts in my mouth, almost melting, the warmth and satisfaction and escape from the damp.

We bought sleek black barrettes, the same kind, and silver rings with imitation rubies; we huddled under an umbrella and laughed at the crazy people walking by, muttering; we dipped our fingers into the peanut bag and clutched our packages by our sides.

And I realized, then, how with a new girl, just like with a boy, it's another kind of falling in love: I was enamored with her elegant stance, her effortless beauty, which she didn't even seem aware of; her easy laughter; her craziness, trying on a leopard-print bikini and three-foot-wide sombrero; the way her eyes darkened and widened as she spoke, and the circles underneath her eyes, like a sadness. And I think it was this sadness beneath, more than anything else, that made me know that I could love her.

We shared bits of ourselves in passing:

"My father sold gum on the streets of Seoul to put himself through college, and what was the fucking point of it, to own a goddamn store?"

"I wish my father'd reopen his shoe-repair shop and get off the fucking couch. I almost even miss the stories of everyone's smelly feet and bunions and corns. . . ."

"This old Jewish man steals from us. Bread, stuffed in his shirt. My mother lets him, she feels sorry. . . ."

"Oh my God, what if he's my father?"

Clutching our packages, we stopped in Roy Rogers for dinner. We loaded our buns up high and took them to the top section, all to ourselves. "We still haven't met our true loves," she said.

I glanced at my watch. "I think the libraries are closed." It was already five o'clock; my father was probably home on the couch, ready to tell me how his grilled chicken was.

"Do you have to be home a certain time?"

"No," I said, thinking of the Sara Lee cake in the freezer. We hadn't made any specific plans for when we'd eat it; it was surely still frozen rock-hard in its foil pan. My father never made any rules for what time I had to come home, unlike my mother, who always stayed awake worrying, waiting for me to return. I'd hardly gone out since she died, and the few times I had he hadn't waited up, but I didn't want him to start now. "Maybe I should call him," I said.

I fished out a quarter and used the pay phone by the entrance. "Daddy? It's Mia. I'm out with my friend Kelsey. I think I'm going to be home a little late, okay?"

I half-expected him, like my mother had, to launch into a barrage of questions—wanting the full itinerary, with phone numbers, addresses, exact longitudes of where I'd be—but he didn't. He told me happy birthday, and then said, "You're missing *Picket Fences.*"

"Yeah, well. You can tell me what happened."

"I don't know if I'll remember," he yawned, and told me to have a good time, and we hung up.

Back at the table I asked Kelsey, "What about you? Do you have to call your parents?"

She shook her head. "They keep the store open till midnight; usually they don't get home till one. I never even see them. I could stay out all night and they wouldn't notice—it's fine as long as I don't wake them up, barging in at three." She smiled. "Let's do that—let's stay out all night."

I nodded. "Until our womanly petals bloom."

We didn't have to enter a hospital, a supermarket, or a car show; we only had to sit in 10th Street Bar for fifteen minutes before two men sat down. Miraculous, I thought.

"You must be a wonderful Spanish teacher," Perry was saying to Kelsey. Perry and Corky: Corky was mine. They sounded like the names of goldfish, but they were handsome, gorgeous—they were men. They were from London, soccer players, coaching at a camp in Connecticut, in the city for the night.

Kelsey laughed delightedly. She'd clearly done this before; she'd said we'd have no problem sneaking in, they never carded. And she was right, and the two men were swallowing her stories as eagerly as their drinks: she was a Spanish teacher at a high school, she'd told them, and, staring into her Black Bunny beer, explained that I was studying to be a vet.

I'd sipped half my gin and tonic but already I could feel it. "Ready for another?" Corky asked.

I shook my head. "Work tomorrow," I said gravely.

"Veterinary medicine—I imagine that must be a rewarding profession."

"Oh, it is. You get that sick bunny on the examining table and—oh, it's rewarding."

What the hell were we doing? It was thrilling, exciting (Were these men really taking us seriously? Could they really be interested in us?) but it also made me feel a little ill, and frightened, as if we were crossing over into territory I wanted to enter, but wasn't sure how. Earlier, in Central Park, Kelsey and I'd mutually confessed our virginities, and agreed we'd wait until we fell in love. This wasn't love, with these men, that much was clear, but it was intimidating just the same. It was one thing to read romance novels, and another to have the physical fact of a man right there, itching to get into your furry domain.

"Have you been in class all day?" Perry asked.

"No," Kelsey said. "We've been celebrating Mia's twenty-second birthday. *Feliz Cumpleaños!*"

She and Perry raised their glasses, and Corky bought me another drink. The clock ticked away, midnight, one. Kelsey told them about lying in Sheep Meadow, and the movie, and shopping, as if we'd been friends for years.

"Do you do this on your birthday every year? Make it a full holiday?" Corky asked me.

"Kind of," I said, and for the first time I thought of my previous birthday, before my mother got sick. She'd bought me half a cake from a gourmet shop in Manhattan, because she didn't have time to make one, and she figured we never ate the whole thing anyway. She'd placed it on the table and I'd peered around it, looking for the other half. "What happened? Did you get hungry?" I'd asked her, and she'd shaken her head and blushed, saying it was expensive, she'd thought half seemed like a better idea. I'd sulked, feeling sorry for my measly half-cake, and, oh, I could kill myself now for not appreciating it then. Now I'd jump into her lap and hug her and savor every single bite, and why had it seemed so imperfect then?

And why, in the morning when I'd awoken, had my memories of past birthdays been so sugar-coated, why had I not thought of the less-than-perfect ones too? And even more frightening was the way these memories still haunted me, dredging themselves up, unwarranted, constantly poking through—remember me, remember me—when I didn't want to remember any of them; I didn't.

I stared at the floor. Tears brimmed in my eyes and I blinked them back, but they poured out anyway; I cried into my drink. This always happened. It was pathetic, I was a professional weeper; if they had a course in it at school I'd excel for once. I cried on every holiday, on Mother's Day, her birthday, and the twenty-sixth of every month, the anniversary of her death.

Corky looked horrified; he stood back. "What's wrong?"

I shook my head.

"What's up with her?" Perry asked Kelsey, as if I were some kind of freak. Kelsey didn't answer; she put her hand on my shoulder and waited for me to stop crying, which I didn't. We went to the bathroom for tissue, and when we came out the two men had left.

We sat on the wooden bench in the subway station, waiting for the #7 train to take us home. "Why did you do that?" Kelsey asked. "Why did you start crying?"

I shrugged. We hadn't spoken since we'd left the bar. I looked around the station. It was surprisingly packed, but only with men. A big, toothless man paced by us back and forth, leering like he was hungry and we were lunch. Perhaps we're just going to die, I thought, and at two A.M. this began to sound good: then I'd see my mother.

I stared at the tracks. "I don't know."

After a few moments she said, "Where's your mother? You've never talked about her."

My heart jumped, as it did whenever anybody asked; each time it was still a surprise. I shrugged. I looked down at the floor. Scuff on my black shoes. Snickers wrapper. Discarded gum. She's in the cemetery. Decomposing, I once thought to say. But I said the usual, "She died in January," as if giving the month made it real. It didn't. Seven months had passed and here I was, the words still crumbled into me, hollow breaking lumps, screws in the chest, never-ending.

"I'm sorry."

She didn't say anything else, she just looked at me, but not in the odd, surprised way—she looked at me plainly, like she was taking me in. Like she was waiting for me to say something more. And that plainness surprised me, that open vast simplicity of her face, and I stared back at my shoes, the dirty floor. What purpose was it, all the crying, the heartbreak? I ruined our chances with those guys, I ruined our perfect day, I ruined love.

"I'm sorry I made those guys run off," I sniffed.

"They were creeps—I'm glad you did."

I wiped my nose on my sleeve; a few latent sobs were still working their way out.

"I've cried in the worst places, too," she said quietly, as the train finally pulled into the station. "When my parents first opened the store, I cried nearly every day. I couldn't understand why they were working such long hours; I thought each morning when they left that they were never coming back."

"But you were like six, or seven."

She shrugged. "It doesn't matter."

I sniffed again. "I'm still sorry. It's been seven months. I should be over it by now."

"No you shouldn't," she said.

• • •

At Queensboro Plaza, three stops before my house and six before hers, Kelsey checked her watch. "It's almost two. My parents'll kill me if I come home now and wake them up. Do you mind—can I stay at your house?"

"Oh, sure," I croaked, horror rising up in my throat at the idea. How could I bring her to Spooky House? But I didn't have a choice; I couldn't say no. I braced myself during the rest of the ride, and cringed as we walked the three long blocks from the subway to my house, past the weeds, the slanting trees, the overgrown roots cracking up the sidewalk, the peeling paint on our red stoop. That stoop I'd played on, hiked up jauntily so many years, and now dreaded, loathed, winced to even look at.

I drew in my breath as we entered our dark living room. Pillows and newspapers were strewn on the floor; dirty mugs, plates, and the partly eaten Sara Lee cake cluttered the coffee table. My father was asleep on the couch in his sweatpants and undershirt; he woke up and blinked at us when I shut the door. For a moment he seemed alarmed, and then confused, and then he just looked awkward, and I wondered if he was thinking, oh, now she brings a friend over, at last, at two-thirty in the morning.

He pulled his button-down shirt off the chair and buttoned it off-kilter, so it hung about him loosely, like a tablecloth. He hadn't shaved in days. There was dried ketchup on the pocket of his shirt. The hair he usually brushed over his bald spot hung down one side of his face, like a new-wave haircut. I told him we were at a party that ended late, and introduced them to each other.

"You'd like some coffee, Leslie?" my father said.

"Kelsey," I said.

"Kell-see. Kell-see. A slice of cake? Skim milk?"

I shook my head. "Maybe in the morning. I'm sorry. We're really tired."

But Kelsey was eyeing the chocolate cake. "I'd love a slice," she said.

So the three of us sat there, on our living-room couch, drinking skim milk, and eating birthday cake (it was still partly frozen in the middle) off yellow napkins imprinted with *Wendy's.* My father pulled my birthday presents out of a grocery bag beneath the table; they were wrapped in newspaper and tied with a bow of string.

"Oh, wow," I said, tearing off the paper, "Teen Lady. I love them." My father seemed pleased; we said good night and I led Kelsey upstairs to my room, all the time waiting for her to revolt, to refuse to be with me any longer in my crazy, decrepit house.

I opened the door to my room—the old single bed, the felt giraffe on the wall. I hated it, our frozen house, my stupid childhood room, which I'd never changed, redecorated; I was never able to part with a fucking thing. I thought we'd go to bed quickly: I gave her a toothbrush, nightgown, towel, and turned down the sheets, but she didn't seem ready to sleep.

The scrapbook, the one of my mother, the one I'd resolved to stop looking at, lay on the shelf beside my bed; she picked it up. Quilted cover, photos pasted in. My heart flinched to watch her open it: there were my insides, spilling out—this naked love on the page. I was embarrassed to show it, this raw, doting, unharnessed outpouring. My mother, in every period of her life, and every year of mine. Ridiculous things, I'd pasted in there: not just the birthday cards and postcards, volumes of them—that might be all right, but I'd included doodles on a telephone pad, a price tag from a dress we'd bought together, her signature on a credit-card receipt, a grocery list I'd found in her pocketbook with just three words: *bread, milk, chocolate.*

Kelsey fingered the plastic sheets, touching it all.

"You're lucky," she said. "You're lucky to have had her."

I stared at her. It was the first time anyone had ever said that to me.

She lay back in bed, and we stared up at the shapes in the peeled-off plaster of the ceiling. There was something between us in the air; something tangible, real. I had cried, the men had left, my father had served us cake which was still frozen in the middle—but at the end of the day, we were lying here together, in the quiet, the edge of her warm nightgown touching mine, and I thought that this was what she meant by lucky: simply this.

Joyce Carol Oates

The Missing Person

His name was Robert, and he was not the sort of man you'd feel comfortable calling Bob, still less Bobbie, or Rob. He was tall, not large-boned but densely, solidly built, an athlete in school, now years ago, but retaining his athlete's sense of himself as a distinct physical presence; the kind of man who, shaking your hand, looks you directly in the eye as if he's already your friend—or hopes to be. In his own mind, he moved through the world now easily, now combatively—as if he had no name, no definition, at all.

He'd fallen in love with the woman before he learned her name, and even after he learned her name, and they'd become in fact lovers, he couldn't deceive himself that he knew her, really. And sometimes this made him very angry, and sometimes it did not.

He was thirty-six years old, which is not young. He'd been married, and a father, and divorced, by the time he was twenty-nine.

He told himself, I can't wait.

One April evening, when Ursula had been away for nearly two weeks, without having told Robert where she was going, or even that she was going away, he turned onto her street, driving aimlessly, and he saw, passing the small wood-frame house she rented, that she was back: lights were burning upstairs and down, her car was in the drive. It had been raining lightly most of the day, and there was a gauzy, dreamy, scrimlike texture to the air. Robert told himself, It's all right, of course it's all right, behave like any friend since you *are* the woman's friend, and not an adversary. He was shaky, but he wasn't upset, and he didn't believe he was angry. That phase of his life—being possessive of a woman, intruding where, for all his manly attractiveness, he wasn't always welcome—was forever ended.

So she was home, and she hadn't so much as told him she was going to be away, but he was in love with her, so it was all right, what she did had to be all right since he loved her—wasn't there logic here? And, if not logic, simple common sense?

The important thing was, she *was* back, in that house. And, so far as Robert could judge—he could see her moving about, through the carelessly drawn venetian blinds at her front windows—she was alone.

So he parked his car, walked unhesitatingly up to the door, rang the doorbell, smiling, seemingly at ease, rehearsing a few words to take the edge off his anxiety (just happened to be driving by, saw your lights), and, when Ursula opened the door, throwing it back in that characteristic way of hers in which she did most things, with an air of welcome, of curiosity, of abandon, of recklessness, yet also of resignation, and he saw her face, he saw her eyes, what shone startled and unfeigned in her eyes, he thought, she *is* the one.

Not long afterward, upstairs, in her bedroom, in her bed, Ursula said accusingly, though also teasingly, "Hey. I know you."

"Yes?"

"You're the one who wants me to love you. So that you won't have to love *me*."

Robert laughed uneasily. "What's that—a riddle?"

It was the first time the word, that word, *love,* had passed between them.

Ursula laughed too. "You heard me, darling."

She slipped her arm across his chest, his midriff, and pressed her heated face into his neck, as if into forgetfulness, or oblivion.

Robert marveled how with such seeming ease the woman could elude him even as she was pressed, naked, the full length of her lovely naked body, against him.

He had sighted Ursula at least twice before he'd been introduced to her, once at a jazz evening, very sparsely attended, at a local Hyatt Regency, another time at a large cocktail reception at Squibb headquarters, where, striking, self-composed, she'd been in the company of a Squibb executive whom Robert knew slightly, and did not like. That woman, that's the one, Robert thought, brooding, yet half seriously, for, though his appearance suggested otherwise, he had a romantic, even wayward heart; his habit of irony, and occasional sarcasm, didn't, he was certain, express *him*—as he expected women to sense, and was hurt, disappointed, and annoyed when they did not.

Eventually, they met. He was struck by her name, Ursula, an unusual name, not exotic so much as brusquely melodic, even masculine. It suited her, he thought—her large green-almond eyes, her ashy-blond-brown hair in thick wings framing her oval, fine-boned face. She had presence; she had a distinct style; not a tall woman, but, moving as she did, with a dancer's measured precision, she looked tall. Her habit of staring openly and calculatingly wasn't defiant, nor meant to be rude, but had to do, Robert eventually saw, with her interest in others, her hope of extracting information from them. She was a medical-science journalist and a writer associated, on what seemed to be a freelance basis, with such prominent area companies as Squibb, Bell Labs, Johnson & Johnson. She said of this work-for-hire that it was "impersonal—neutral—what I do, and I usually do it well, while I'm doing it."

So Robert understood, and was touched by the thought that, like him, or like him as he'd been in his early thirties, Ursula was in readiness for her truer life to begin.

And what truer life that might be, what ideal employment of the woman's obvious intelligence, imagination, energy, and wit that might be, Robert did not know, and had too much tact to ask. Ursula was only a few years younger than he, maybe she'd catch up.

• • •

It wasn't the bedroom upstairs, which he'd rarely glimpsed by daylight, nor even the living room with its crowded bookshelves and spare furniture, but the kitchen of Ursula's rented house with which Robert was most familiar. Ursula liked preparing meals, and she liked company while she prepared them; several times they'd eaten together in the kitchen, at a mahogany dining-room table, oddly incongruous in this setting, set in a rectangular alcove at the rear, in what had been a porch, now closed in, with a bay window. By day, there was a view, green, snarled, somehow foreshortened by steepness, of an untended rear yard sloping up to a weedy railroad embankment; there were tall, elegantly skeletal poplars scattered amid more common trees; there was vestigial evidence of farming, and a badly rotted tar-paper-roofed shanty that had been a chicken coop years ago. The neighborhood in which Ursula lived was semirural but the houses, one- and two-story bungalows, were owned by working-class people; Ursula liked her neighbors very much, but scarcely knew their names. She'd rented the house because it was so reasonably priced, she'd said. And because she hadn't meant to stay long—just to catch her breath, to see what was coming next.

That was five years ago. Ursula hadn't gotten around to buying curtains for the windows, nor had she taped over the name of the previous tenant, which was on her mailbox. Each spring she meant to have a plot in the backyard plowed, so that she could plant a vegetable garden; but the seasons plunged by, and she hadn't had a garden yet. Just as there'd been no specific reason for moving into the house, so there was no reason to move out.

Robert, who'd been living for the past several years in a condominium village, so-called, backing onto the New Jersey Turnpike, thought of Ursula's house, for all its air of being only temporarily inhabited, as a home. He liked it, he felt comfortable in it, he told Ursula, though he couldn't envision her remaining there forever.

Ursula's eyelids flickered, so very subtly, as if to express distaste. She said, "Forever is a long time."

Robert laughed, and said, unexpected, "Yes, but doesn't it sometimes seem to you, we've already been living forever?—but forgetting, almost at once, as we live?"

Ursula had stared at him, her eyes resembling cracked marbles, a tawny light-fractured sheen, unnervingly beautiful, as in a moment of extreme intimacy. Though she'd made no reply, Robert had sensed her surprise, her compliance; yet in that very instant, her denial.

As if, so unexpectedly, she'd been forced to reassess him.

In the kitchen, a can of cold beer in hand, Robert looked about as if curious whether things had changed in his absence. The tips of leaves on the hanging plants in the bay window were curled and browning; the soil, beneath his fingertips, was dry. On a counter, carried in from Ursula's car and set down untidily, were issues of the *New England Journal of Medicine* and *Scientific American* and several large sheets of construction paper with a child's primitive yet fussy drawings on them, in crayon. Robert glanced at the top two or three drawings, then turned quickly away.

He said to Ursula, who was at the sink, her back to him, "Why not let me take you out, Ursula?—it's been a while."

Ursula said, "God, Robert, I couldn't get into a car again today. I was nine hours in my own."

"Nine hours! Coming from where?"

Vaguely Ursula said, "Upstate New York."

Robert said, smiling at her back, "Yes, but you like being alone, don't you. You like to drive your car, don't you, alone."

Ursula, picking up the edge in Robert's voice, did not reply.

Robert was feeling good, yes, feeling very good, after love a man feels good, the burden of physicality eased for the time being; no problem to him, or to others.

He was feeling good, and he was feeling happy, as, he had to acknowledge, he hadn't felt happy, in some time.

And how close he'd come to driving away from Ursula's house—seeing the lights, the car in the drive, seeing, yes, she was back, she was home, it would be up to her to call him, since he'd called so many times in her absence.

A few years ago, he'd have driven away. Now, he was shrewd with patience.

Thinking, I can wait.

For love, for revenge?—for love, surely.

In any case Robert had risked embarrassment, he'd walked briskly up to the door and rung the doorbell, and Ursula had thrown open the door, a lack of guardedness in the gesture that would trouble him, later, when he thought of it, but she'd been happy to see him, genuinely happy, crying, "Oh God, Robert—*you.*" And she'd stepped into his arms, and hugged him, hard. As if he had come by her invitation. As if she hadn't disappeared for two weeks without telling him where she'd gone, or why. As if this embrace, and the feeling with which they kissed, signaled the end of a story of which, until that moment, Robert had scarcely been aware.

Ursula was breaking eggs for an omelet; her can of beer was set on a narrow counter beside the stove. Robert came to slide his arms around her, tight around her rib cage, beneath her breasts, and said, "Don't you want help with anything?" and Ursula laughed, and said, "My mother used to say, when I was a girl, and I'd wander into the kitchen and ask, 'Do you want me to help you with anything,' that, if I meant it seriously, I wouldn't ask 'anything,' I'd be specific." She paused, methodically breaking eggs, scooping out the liquidy, spermy whites with the tip of a forefinger. Robert wasn't sure how to interpret her words.

He said, exerting a subtle pressure with his arm, feeling her rapid heartbeat, "Well, I did mean it seriously."

Ursula said, "Oh, I know you did, Robert."

He said, "I'm not the kind of person to play games."

Ursula said, laughing, "Oh, I know *that.*"

He'd forgotten how Ursula's laughter sometimes grated at his nerves, like sand between his teeth.

In fact, there wasn't much for him to do: he set out plates and cutlery on the table, and floral-printed paper napkins; he opened a bottle of California red wine he'd brought Ursula upon another occasion, months before; he switched on the radio, to a station playing jazz, old-time mainstream jazz, the kind of music he'd cultivated in his thirties as a reaction against the popular rock music with which, like all of his generation, he'd grown up . . . that heavy hypnotic brain-numbing beat, narcotic as a drug in the bloodstream. While Ursula prepared the omelet, Robert rummaged through the refrigerator, and laid out butter, bread, several wedges of cheese, dill pickles. He was reminded, not unhappily, of the slapdash companionable meals he and his former wife had thrown together, those evenings they'd returned home exhausted from work.

In such cooperative domestic actions, as in action generally, Robert believed himself most himself. It was in repose, in brooding, and willful aloneness, that another less hospitable self emerged.

As she was about to sit down at the table, Ursula replaced the paper napkins with cloth napkins; napkins her mother had given her. Robert said, "A needless luxury, but very nice," and Ursula said, smiling, "That's the point of luxury, it's needless."

They ate, they were both very hungry, and grateful, it suddenly seemed, for the activity of eating; like lovemaking, it was so physical, and as necessary, momentum buoyed them forward. But Robert asked, "Your mother—where exactly does she live?" and Ursula hesitated, her look going inward, and he felt a stab of his old irritation, that, in the midst of their ease with each other, that very ease was revealed as merely surface, superficial. He added, in a tone not at all ironic, "You don't have to tell me if you'd rather not."

Ursula said, slowly, "My mother and I are estranged. I mean, we've been estranged. Much of my life."

Robert said, "That's too bad."

"Yes, it's too bad." Then, after a pause, "It was too bad."

"Things are better now?"

"Things are—" Ursula hesitated, frowning, "—better now."

Robert laid a hand over Ursula's; both to comfort her, and to still her nervous mannerism—she'd begun crumbling a piece of bread. Her hand went immediately dead. She said, with a harsh sort of flirtatiousness, "*Was* it too bad? What does 'too bad' mean? We're the people we are because we've turned out as we are; if things had been otherwise in our lives, we wouldn't be the people we are. So what kind of a judgment is that on me—'too bad'?"

Robert said, joking, but squeezing her hand rather hard, "Since you've turned out to be perfect, Ursula, obviously it's an ignorant judgment."

Ursula laughed, and withdrew her hand, and poured the remainder of the wine into their glasses. She said, "You've turned out to be perfect, too. But you know that."

Seen from an aerial perspective the desert landscape is an arid, desolate, yet extraordinarily beautiful terrain in which narrow trails lead off tentatively into the wilderness, continue for some miles, then end abruptly. Whoever travels these roads comes to a dead end and has to turn back; if he proceeds into the wilderness, he will be entering uncharted territory.

Their relationship is such a landscape, seen from above, Robert was thinking wryly. The wine had gone to his head, he was feeling close to understanding something crucial. In such a terrain you followed a trail for a while, it came to an end, you had to retreat, you tried another.

In such a way, years might pass.

Yes. Well. They were the children of their time, weren't they, this was how, as adults, they lived, so it's to be assumed that this is how they wanted to live. Isn't it?

Half past midnight, and Robert supposed he should be going home, or did Ursula expect him to stay? The matter seemed undecided. Ursula, grown quiet and preoccupied, was drinking more than usual; her face had taken on a heated, winey flush, its contours softened. Before coming downstairs she'd carelessly pulled on a cotton-knit sweater with a low neckline that stretching had loosened, and Robert could see the tops of her breasts, waxy pale, conical-shaped, with dark nipples, and he could smell that sleepy-perfumy smell lifting from her, and he was thinking, yes, why not stay, he loved her and he didn't want to leave her and it didn't matter that he was angry with her too; that (this was a truth the wine and the late hour allowed him) he'd have liked, just once, to see the woman cry.

He said, "What did you mean, before—I want you to love me so that I won't have to love you?"

Ursula smiled, and creased her forehead, and shook her head, as if she'd never heard of such a thing. "Is that a riddle?"

"*Is* it?"

"I don't remember saying it, if I did."

"You said it upstairs. You know—when I first got here."

Still, Ursula shook her head. With seeming sincerity, innocence. Forcing her eyes open wide.

They'd opened another bottle of wine, a good rich dark French wine Robert had located at the rear of Ursula's cupboard. He had not asked if this bottle too had been a gift.

Ursula rubbed the palms of her hands against her eyes and said, with a shy dip in her voice, "I'm drunk, how can I remember what I said." She giggled. "Or didn't say."

"Do you want me to go home? Or do you want me to stay?"

There was a brief pause. Ursula continued rubbing her eyes, she was hiding from him that way, as a child might. Robert let the moment pass.

He said, softly, "Tell me about your mother? And you."

Ursula said quickly, "I can't."

"Can't? Why not?"

"I *can't.*"

She was trembling. Robert felt both sympathy and impatience for her. Thinking, why didn't she trust *him.* Why, sitting close beside him, wouldn't she look at *him.*

Robert's former wife, whom, for years, he'd loved very much, had too often and too carelessly opened herself up to him. Like a sea creature whose tight, clenched shell, once pried open, can never be shut again.

He said, "That's all right, then, Ursula. Never mind."

"If I thought that it was important, that it mattered to . . . us," Ursula said, choosing her words with care, "I would."

"I'd better go home. Yes?"

"You'll never meet her, probably."

"Probably, no."

"My father's dead."

"I'm sorry to hear that."

"So, you won't meet *him.*"

Ursula laughed, and hid her face. A crimson flush, as if she'd been slapped, rose from her throat into her face.

Robert was stroking the inside of her arm, the faint delicate bluish tracery of veins. Her skin was heated, he could feel the pulse, he was feeling aroused, excited. Yet subtly resentful, too.

He said, a little louder than he'd intended, "So. It's late. I'd better go home and call you tomorrow."

"All right," Ursula said, then, without a pause, "—wait."

"Yes?"

"I didn't say 'love,' before. I'm sure I didn't. You must have misunderstood."

"I'm sure I did."

"I was very tired from driving. I hadn't expected you."

"I could see that."

"You don't have to call me tomorrow, if you don't want to."

When Robert, stiffening, didn't reply, Ursula said, "Unless you want to."

Robert got to his feet, draining the last of his wine as he rose. His face felt like a tomato, heated, close to bursting.

He laughed, and said, "How'm I going to tell the difference?"

Robert's present job was a good job, busy, distracting, kept his mind off himself and what he considered "negative" thoughts, the kind of job that propels you into motion and keeps you there, Monday mornings until Friday afternoons, a roller coaster. He liked even his title: Manager, Computer Disaster Division, AT&T, what a flair it had, what style, a bit of glamour. When he explained his work—his clients were primarily area banks which, when their computer equipment was down, hooked onto an emergency unit at AT&T, to continue business as best they could—he saw that people were interested, and they listened. Most of the people he met in this phase of his life were associated with businesses that used computers extensively, or worked with computers themselves, and the subject of computer disaster riveted their attention.

You lived in dread of computer disaster but you wanted it, too. Something so very satisfying in the idea.

Ursula told Robert, medical technology has developed to such an extent, there are now entire communities of men, women, and children, electronically linked, oblivious of one another, whose lives depend upon systems continuing as programmed, without error; one day, the earth's total population might be so linked. Yet people persist in imagining they are independent and autonomous; they boast of shunning computers, despising technology. "As if," Ursula said, "there is a kind of virtue in that."

Robert said, thoughtfully, "Well. People need these stories about themselves, I guess. Believing that, when things were different, years ago, they were different. Life was different."

Ursula laughed. "It had a more human meaning."

"It had *meaning.*"

"Not like now."

"God, no. Not like *now.*"

And they'd laughed, as if to declare themselves otherwise.

A final number before the jazz program, the very radio station itself, signed off for the night: Art Tatum, Lionel Hampton, Buddy Rich, "Love for Sale," recorded 1955.

Robert listened reverently. He was holding Ursula's cool hand, fingers gripping fingers. Listening to such music, you felt that, at any moment, you were about to turn a corner; about to see things with absolute clarity; on the tremulous brink of changing your life.

What happens of course is that the music ends, and other sounds intervene.

Ursula said suddenly to Robert, "I saw you looking at them, before. Those drawings."

At first Robert had no idea what she meant. "Drawings?"

"These." Ursula brought the child's cartoon drawings to show him. Her hands were trembling, there was a sort of impassioned dread in her voice. Guardedly, Robert said, "They're very—interesting," and Ursula laughed, embarrassed, and said, "No, they're just what they are. A young child's attempts at 'art.'"

The sheets of construction paper, measuring about twelve inches by ten, were dog-eared and torn. There were strands of cobweb on them, dust. Robert, smiling uneasily, knew he was expected to inquire whose child it was who had done the drawings; what the child was to Ursula; no doubt they'd end up talking about the father. But he couldn't bring himself to speak.

Of course these stick figures in red crayon, these impossibly sky-skimming trees, clumsy floating clouds, reminded Robert of his own child, his son Barry, now ten years old and very distant from him; reminded him most painfully; for how could they not. He'd been drinking for hours but he was hardly anesthetized. It had been years since Barry had done such drawings, kneeling on the living room floor, and years since Robert had thought of them. (Did he have any stored away for safekeeping—mementos of his son's early childhood? He doubted it, closet space in his condominium was so limited.) Barry lived in Berkeley with Robert's ex-wife, who was now remarried, very happily she claimed; coincidentally, her husband was a computer specialist at IBM. Robert had last seen Barry at Christmas, five months ago; before that, he hadn't seen the boy since April. Nor did they speak very often on the phone—with the passage of time, as Robert figured less and less in his son's life, these conversations had become increasingly strained.

Robert was looking at the first of the child's drawings. In what was meant to be a grassy space, amid tall pencil-thin trees, a sharply steepled house in the background, there were two stick figures: a stick man, wearing trousers; a stick woman, with hair lifting in snakelike tufts, wearing a skirt. In the lower right-hand corner, as if sliding off the paper, was what appeared to be a baby, in a rectangular container that was presumably a buggy or a crib, yet, awkwardly drawn as it was, it could as easily have been a shoebox, or a mailbox, or a miniature coffin. The adult figures had round blank faces with neutral slit-mouths and *O's* for eyes; the baby had no face at all.

After a moment Ursula said, with the breathy embarrassed laugh, "They're mine. I mean—my own. I drew them when I was two or three years old, my mother says."

Robert glanced up at Ursula, genuinely surprised. He'd expected her to say that the drawings belonged to a child of her own, unknown to Robert until now. "*You* did these—?"

"I don't remember. My mother says I did."

Robert could see now, obviously, the drawings were very old, the stiff construction paper discolored with age.

Now Ursula began explaining, speaking rapidly, in the mildly bemused yet insistent tone she used when recounting complex anecdotes that for some reason needed to be told, however disagreeable or boring. "My mother has finally sold the house, she's moving into a 'retirement' home, and I was up there helping her, she'd called me, asked me . . . it's unusual for my mother to ask anything of me and I suppose I've been the kind of daughter who may have been difficult, growing up, to ask favors of. So there's been a certain distance between us, for years. And a number of misunderstandings. I won't go into details," Ursula said, quickly, as if anticipating a lack of interest on Robert's part (in fact, Robert was listening to her attentively), "—you can imagine. But now Mother is aging, and not well, and frightened of what's to come . . . and I drove up to Schuylersville, where I vowed, after the last visit a few years ago, I'd never go again, and I helped her with the housecleaning, helped her pack . . . and up in the attic there were trunks and boxes of things, old clothes mainly, the accumulation of decades, and when I was going through them, I came upon these drawings, and old report cards of mine, old schoolwork. I was going to throw everything away without so much as glancing at it but Mother was upset, she said, No! Wait, she'd come up into the attic with me. She hardly let me out of her sight the entire time I was in the house . . . this woman from whom I've been estranged for more than fifteen years. I asked her why on earth she'd kept such silly things, and she looked at me as if I'd slapped her, and said, 'But you're my only daughter, Ursula!' This is the woman, Robert, who failed to show up at my college graduation, where I'd waited and waited for her, claiming, afterward, that I hadn't invited her; this is the woman who complained bitterly to everyone who would listen that I neglected her, never called or visited, when I was in my twenties and living in New York, and, once, when I drove up to visit, having made arrangements with her, she simply wasn't home when I got there—wasn't *there.* Nor had she left any message for me." Ursula began to laugh, more harshly now. Robert could hear an undercurrent of hysteria.

"So we were looking at these drawings, this one on top first, and Mother told me approximately when I'd done it, and I said, 'My God, that long ago—of course *I* don't remember it. I don't remember drawing at all, and I was pretty bad at it, wasn't I,' and Mother protested, 'No, you were talented for such a small child, you can see you were talented,' and I laughed and said, 'Mother, I can see I was *not* talented, here's evidence, my God.' Then I asked her what is this down in the corner"—Ursula pointed at the baby in the box—"and Mother said, 'I guess that must be your baby sister Alice, who died,' and I stared at her, I couldn't believe what she'd said. I said, 'Baby sister? Alice? What are you talking about?' and Mother said, her voice shaking, 'You had a little baby sister; she died when she was eight months old, her heart was defective,' and I just stared at her, 'A baby sister: I had a baby sister: What are you saying?' and Mother said, 'Don't you remember, you must remember, you were two years old, we never talked about it much when you were growing up but you must remember,' and she started to cry, so I had to hold her, she's frail, she's so much shorter than she used to be, I felt as if I'd been kicked in the head. I was thinking, is this possible? how can this be possible? is she losing her mind? is she lying? but would she lie about such a thing?—it was so unreal, Robert, but not as a dream is unreal, no dream of mine, it was no dream I would ever have had, I swear."

Ursula paused, and ran the back of her hand roughly across her eyes, and said, "You know, darling, I think I need a drink, something good and strong, will you join me—just one?" and she brought down a bottle of expensive scotch from the rear of the cupboard, and poured them both drinks, straight, no ice, no ceremony, in fruit-juice glasses; and she resumed her story, telling it in the same bemused ironic tone.

"So, Mother and I, we were looking through these drawings, and I asked her if that was supposed to be my baby sister Alice, there, in that box, or whatever it is, and Mother said yes she supposed so, and I said, 'And here's you, Mother, obviously, and here's Father, but where am I?'—because, in all the drawings, there is just the baby, and no other child. And Mother said in this plaintive mewing voice, defensively, as if she thought I might be blaming her, 'Well I don't know, Ursula, I just don't know where you are,' and I was laughing, God knows why I was laughing, I said, '*I* don't know where I am either, and I don't remember a thing about this.' And later, before I left, Mother showed me the dead baby's birth certificate, she'd found it in a strongbox, but she couldn't find the death certificate, and I said, 'Thank you, Mother, that isn't necessary.'" Ursula was laughing, rocking back on her heels, the glass of scotch raised to her grinning mouth. "'Thank you, Mother,' I said, 'that isn't necessary.'"

Then she put her glass down abruptly, and walked out of the kitchen.

Robert followed her into the living room, where a single lamp was burning. She was laughing softly, fists in her eyes, turned from him at the waist, or was she crying?—he went quickly to her, and put his arms around her, and comforted her, and though, initially, unthinking as if it were a child's reflex, she pushed against him, he was able to grip her tight; to prevent hysteria from taking over her; he knew the symptoms of hysteria; he was an expert.

They stood like that for a while, and Ursula wept, and tried to talk, and then Robert drew her down onto the sofa and they sat there, on the sofa, for some time in the shadowy room with the carelessly drawn venetian blinds. Robert was deeply moved but in control, he was saying, stroking the woman's hair, feeling her warm desperate breath on his face, "Ursula, darling, Ursula, no, it's all right, you're going to be all right, I'm here, aren't I? *I'm* here, aren't I? Darling?"

Doug Crandell

Colored Glass

She holds a shard of ocher up to the fluttering leaves; tinged light flashes from above, as if the sun has changed colors. Is it a piece from an old milk bottle, yellowed from the soil's rich phosphates? Next to the dump is a hog pasture; a whiff of manure is carried by the wind to the edge of the woods. Harper says, "Pew-ee!" as she fans the air below her nose, overacting, more like a child than a middle-aged woman. She places the glass over her right eye and giggles, a sound Leslie has begun to associate with a certain type of crazy.

"Oh, my," says Harper, plucking something from inside a rusty and nearly squashed saucepan. "Look, Leslie, this one is from a milk of magnesia bottle."

His mother's been full of contradictions since the operation, a trait that the boy thinks is repeated in her hair: some streaks of reddish brown, loose strands of gray and white, and jet black spots along the crown, none of it following any pattern. She is just as inconsistent as her hair, he decides. At times she cries so hard she laughs, and at others she chuckles until she tears up and runs from the house, descends into a deep depression for twenty minutes only to reappear from outdoors, clutching a bundle of dead phlox tied tightly with jute rope and carrying the desiccated weeds, scurf falling onto her coat, to the sink for water.

The boy doesn't look at his mother. He is too busy with his own glass. Leslie peers through his slice of amber at the hogs inside the fence. They look like they've already been butchered and cooked: the four white shoats appear reddish. Stick an apple in their mouths, the boy thinks, and they're goners. Leslie hates his name and that it sounds like a girl's; he wishes he and his mother could trade. Harper, he says over and over in his head, that's a man's name. Lately, as he's tried to grow up and accept it, the thought has occurred to him that his mother may have been cruel, naming him as a girl because she'd suffered a life with a man's.

Harper Royal, only months after her hysterectomy at age forty-five, has dragged him to the old dump on the farm to search for colored glass. She'd met Leslie at the end of the lane as he got off a Friday bus ride home from school. Also in tow is her father, Basil, a man who can't remember his last name, let alone why the three of them are digging with hand spades through piles of garbage from the late forties.

The old man has left the trash pile and is now standing near the hogs, whispering something to them; the sound of it drifts over the stinging winds of a Central Indiana March. He kneels down to feed them grass through the fence. Even though they have a pasture full of it, the pigs gobble down the fescue, root ball and all, from the old man's fingers as if it were candied blades of truffles. He suddenly stops whispering and stands up as straight as his slumped back will permit. He is looking out across the steep incline of the hill: a swarm of sparrows dips down in a rush, then upward again, flying sideways out of view.

"Good morning, colonel!" he shouts, saluting the pigs, the crisp bend of his elbow slicing the air as he weakly claps his feet together. Leslie tosses his glass to the mucky heap and walks to his grandfather's side.

"Grandpa, come on. Come look at this piece Mom found." He takes the old man by the arm and escorts him back to the pile. Leslie makes sure his grandfather doesn't stumble over the loose clods and metal limbs sticking up from the heap of dark loam. Once the two are next to Harper, the old man quickly reaches out and snatches the glass from his daughter's hand.

"Give me that," he demands, a big grin framing his stubbed teeth. Leslie wonders if the old man's face has always looked so womanly, with its soft rosy cheeks and full lips, the brow delicate and smooth. Maybe that's why he was given a girly name? Because sooner or later he'd look like his grandfather? He'd gladly compare his teenage face to his father's, but that would require a shovel and one of those computer-generated-face experts, someone who could use technology to remake the features of a dead man, to portray him as he once was, Leslie thinks.

He watches to make certain that a squabble doesn't start between his mother and grandfather over the glass. Since Harper's hospital stay, many moments have required him to intervene, pulling father off daughter over everything from the last Pop-Tart to joint sobbing sessions started from one or the other's memory of a farm near Fort Wayne. When they talk about it, it's referred to romantically as the Duffey Place, a name they used before it was their own, when they cash-rented the farm and the woman they loved was still alive. Rebecca was Leslie's grandmother's name, a name he finds doesn't fit an old woman, because he's not yet able to conceive that we are not always young and can sometimes grow to be eternally old.

Harper doesn't even blink when the glass has been filched from her. She smiles and winks at Leslie, an inside joke about how nutty family can be, how we must trust our love for them and not doubt, or cause waves, or think of the remedies for such behavior.

The pigs behind them get spooked when Basil cheers wildly after placing the colored glass over his ear. He shouts, "I can hear the ocean in this blue shell. I can. I know I can, I know I can!"

Leslie turns to watch the hogs sprint up the hummock in the pasture. The four pigs stand together at the crest, puffing and grunting, the warm air from inside them visible as it streams from their frightened lungs. The boy thinks what their pulmonary arteries must look like now. In his seventh-grade biology book with a blue amoeba on the cover, he is required to memorize lungs, their maroon filigree and subtle weaknesses. The old man laughs and tosses the glass over the head of his daughter; it pings off a metal bed frame behind her. They all three watch as the shoats disappear over the green swell.

The dump pile is quiet now. Harper walks to the edge and picks up a wicker basket she's brought along. She begins to sniffle and pout. She gathers up shards of colored glass: saffron, purple, clear, milky, sienna, and others, all of it from the medicine cabinets of Basil and the dead wife of forty years ago. Leslie has a picture of Rebecca in his bedroom. She looks out at him from a black frame, her face like his mother's, sad and drawn tightly around the lips, a look of disbelief in her eyes. Sometimes he thinks the woman's face is on the verge of laughing. When he notices this, after staring at the picture for a long while, he puts it down on his nightstand. He thinks, how can a woman the age of my mother be my grandmother?

Harper piles colored glass into the basket until the handle bows from the weight. She has stopped crying and is now singing a song. Her father joins in as Leslie takes the brimming basket from her dirty hands. They creep back to the house. Leslie walks behind them, pieces of color falling over the edges of the basket and onto the cold green ground. He watches as ahead of him his mother and grandfather, arm in arm, sing songs that are wholly made up. He reaches down to the basket, finds a piece of amber like the one he'd fingered earlier, and puts it to his eye. The glass is cold around his socket, and smells of damp earth. Through the middle of the glass they look like thin, red lines, vertical and swaying. At the outer edges of the lens, muted landscape flicks past. As he views the morning through the glass, Leslie thinks of a new name for himself. Butch sounds good, a bully. So does Randall: it has the sound of importance. Finally, he settles for the time being on Scott, a nice, regular name, like an older boy he knows at school.

The old man stops abruptly in the grassy lane, pulling his arm free of his daughter's as if about to escape. Harper turns to speak over her shoulder. "Honey, don't drop so much of the glass." She points to the basket in Leslie's hand. He thinks she sounds almost like her old self.

His grandfather is now standing stock-still. He stares straight ahead, not peering back from where they've come, but rather pointing toward the house. He says to Harper and Leslie, "I think I left my seashell back there." Leslie hands the old man a blunt triangle of blue from the basket.

"Ahh," he sighs, putting the glass to his long ear as if it were a warm compress. "There she is. There she is."

Months ago, during an ice storm in November, Harper had knocked on her son's bedroom door, crying. She wore a cream-colored nightgown, a tail of crimson in the middle, wet with some blood. She gasped, "I'm sorry, baby. You shouldn't have to see this at your age. I'm sick. I need to go to the hospital. Your grandfather can't drive."

Leslie drove the best he could into the city limits and parked the station wagon under the port to the emergency room, neon red flashing above the automatic doors as he brought his mother to the nurses' station. Later, a woman doctor would tell him something had burst inside his mother, that she needed a quick operation, but that she'd be fine, which he assumed meant normal—which he now understands to be wrong. Since then, his mother has been weird in any number of ways: sometimes up so high she wants to dance with Leslie in the living room to his indie music on the stereo, and other times so low all she wants to do is stay in bed and call the help lines the hospital gave her at discharge. For a couple of weeks she took some pills that made her the way she used to be, but after they ran out, she wouldn't get them refilled, even though Leslie tried and tried to get her to go back to the doctor.

On Saturday morning, Harper sits at the kitchen table with the basket of glass in front of her. She is sorting it into piles based on size, shape, and color. All the glass is safe, thick and rounded at the edges, made dull from the many years in the dump. Basil is next to her, lightly chewing on a piece of toast, a steaming cup of tea between them. Leslie walks into the kitchen, dressed already in jeans and a thick sweatshirt. His hair is combed back, wet from a hot shower the boy has snatched before his mother and grandfather were awake and up.

He goes to the cupboard and pulls out two packets of instant oatmeal, brown sugar, and cinnamon. At the sink he uses hot tap water to mix the dry cereal into a paste. He turns from the sink and speaks.

"Good morning."

Harper looks shocked that he can talk, or that someone else is in the room.

"Well, hello to you, young man," she says, her eyes brimming with energy from the sorting task. She turns quickly back to arranging the piles of glass. The old man smiles as he nibbles on the crust hanging off the toast.

Leslie gulps down the oatmeal off a large spoon. He puts the bowl in the sink and floods it with water and several pumps of dish soap. He watches the bits of food floating in the bubbles, not liking how they seem to be moving on their own, like bugs trying to survive, floundering and swirling about. He must remind himself that it's just food, not poor creatures in danger. Leslie turns and goes to the front door, and unhooks a jean jacket from a nail next to the jamb. He talks loudly so they know he's leaving.

"I'm going to walk into town. See the lights at the courthouse." His grandfather stands up as if to come along, then slowly slides back down into the chair, a perfect gesture denoting: *On second thought.*

Harper smiles broadly. "Wait." She gets up from the table and paces to the center of the room. "Take this," she says, tossing him a piece of reddish glass. "See what that big lightbulb looks like through it." In an instant, she is back at the table, flicking through other pieces. As Leslie puts the glass in his pocket and opens the door, he hears his mother's work: clink, clink, clink.

His grandfather says, "That kid looked familiar. What's his name?"

The farm Leslie lives on is just outside the city limits of Wabash, the first electrically lighted city in the world. It sits on top of a hill, so close to the town that from anywhere on its intricate plats the city lights are easily visible, like living in both worlds, Harper used to tell Leslie when he was a child. Every spring, to commemorate the day Charles Brush first lit the city with a carbon-arc lightbulb, the town holds a festival. Leslie's elementary-school teachers all recited the same speech: "When the crude electrical switch was thrown in March of 1880, the Miami Indians watched from the banks of the river in lit dismay. It has been said that when our forebears were first introduced to electric light, they had the tendency to stare at them and then report with disdain that the lights had caused them not to be able to see *anything at all.*" The teacher would continue, a broad smile beaming warmly, "You guys are lucky—you're from the same town where electric light and Crystal Gayle were born."

People come from all over the state to eat funnel cakes, drink cider, and don caps with glowing bulbs on the bill, little stuffed things perched there like a Tweety Bird, yellow and round, plush. Every year, the same hats, thousands of them, made up again and again, Leslie thinks, always just alike, as if they'd all been created way before time ever began, before light was on the surface of the earth. On Sunday there's the grand finale: a staged blackout to remind the town what couldn't be seen before the discovery.

Leslie walks briskly along a ditch beside the road. He can see the cupola of the courthouse, its many strings of light tee-peed from a weather vane down to the ring of black metal circling just under the oval windows. In his pants pocket he lets his fingers tickle the glass. For a moment he thinks of fishing it out and hurling it toward a passing car, but the thought fades away, like his grandpa did earlier in the chair: raring to move, then thinking better of it and accepting his limitations, sitting down to let it all go.

The streets running off the town square are lined with all varieties of booths and stands. There is one for the credit union, circled by three competing grocery-store chains handing out toothpicks heavy with cheese and meat; next to those are booth upon booth of farm-machinery dealers and seed-corn distributors. There is the high-school band and Spanish club, along with an assortment of computer dealers and cell phone companies. People milling about, nearly all chewing on something, carry plastic tote bags to lug all their loot home. The bags have a mascot lightbulb on them named Sparky. On a dialogue balloon floating from his electric smile it reads: *Energy Is a Bright Idea!*

Leslie walks among the booths, looking at how happy all the people appear. They sit behind the skirted two-by-fours and plywood structures and smile and wave at the crowd passing by. Leslie thinks a man with a cowboy hat selling riding equipment, his counter lined with rope and saddles, the smell of leather pungent, is waving at him. Leslie pulls his hand from his pocket and holds it up just as a man behind him, out of his sight, yells, "Dan Frazier? Is that you over there? Well, I'll be damned!" Leslie puts his hand down quickly, as if the answer he thought he knew had gotten away from him. The man behind him rushes by, charges the cowboy man's booth, shaking his head and repeating, "Well, I'll be damned!"

The boy walks on, now careful not to assume anyone is making an effort to connect with him. He keeps his head down and follows the broken sidewalks to the center of town. The courthouse is surrounded by hordes of people, all waiting to count down, like at New Year's, the sixty seconds before a switch is thrown on the lawn and a giant replica of Charles Brush's lightbulb surges with electricity, the same light that on the next day, at dusk, will be ceremoniously extinguished for the blackout. A whole night, the brochure from the tourist office states, of how the Miami Indians must've seen this area before the dawn of electrical energy.

Leslie begins to lift his head some, looking around for kids from school. Next to a salt-water-taffy wagon he spots Scott, the kid three years ahead of him, his namesake. Leslie watches him as he flirts with two girls in droopy letter jackets popping bubble gum, their jeans unlike Leslie's snug ones, the butt of theirs so saggy they must hold the waist with a clenched fist. Automatically he feels out of place, wishing he'd just stayed home and gone to the dump with his mother and grandfather. More people start to encircle the courthouse. In colorful throngs that remind Leslie of his mother's basket of glass, more and more festival-goers crowd in around him, one older woman accidentally goosing him with a John Deere yardstick. Leslie allows himself to laugh some over the incident as the lady creeps on by, clearing her throat, expecting people to let her get closer because of her age. From somewhere behind him a marching band plays and then stops, plays again, horns and tubas hacking through a snippet of a John Philip Sousa piece, then abruptly ending, a snare drum now rolling, readying the crowd for the big event.

Leslie clamps his elbows in closer to his side as a family with three small children riding in one long baby carriage squashes in beside him, the father smiling, mouthing, *Sorry,* a look of genuine apology under his wide-set eyes. The enormous lightbulb is hoisted off a wooden platform, lifted by several strands of steel cable into the air so that everyone can see it. Leslie turns his head to find out if Scott is still where he'd been, but the spot is vacant; only a man with a washrag wiping down a veneered table is visible. Leslie spots the two girls near a trash barrel, spitting their gum out and quickly unwrapping more, pushing the pink hunks into their mouths, fixing their hair at the same time. Leslie realizes he is staring, so he pretends to look past them, surveying the crowd, he hopes, like a man looking for some complex indication that he's not the only one who finds the event shoddily pulled together. Once the heat of a slight embarrassment has subsided from his cheeks, he turns his attention back to the lightbulb twisting in the breeze, the official countdown beginning. The crowd is already on fifty-one before Leslie joins in softly.

The girls and their bubble gum edge closer to him. He allows himself to catch the upturned whites of their eyes, lashes batting, the two of them whispering, oddly pointing at Leslie as they approach, not caring if they step on toes or knock over packages. He turns away, trying to appear uninterested. The crowd is on forty seconds now and counting. One of the girls taps him on the shoulder. Leslie turns, giddy in his limbs, a sense of nascent power flooding his brain, all of it rare for him, brand-new to his body and mind. The girl speaks but Leslie cannot hear what she's said. Her mouth, lovely and red, lips so glossy they appear greased, is moving, but the crowd is ultrasonic now; it's down to ten seconds before the bulb will come alive, pop into an achy glow, and cause those in the front rows to shield their eyes from light they can't see.

The girl gives up, gives in, and puts her mouth to his ear; standing on the tips of her toes she forgets and whispers, still not giving Leslie any clue about what she is proposing, stating, wishing, telling, demanding. The crowd cheers; a communal *oooh!* is chanted. Leslie can't decide on how to behave. He tries to clap along with the multitude; his hands form a jagged wedge, and cannot come together evenly. The girl falls away from him, her face receding as she and her friend smile and retreat, walking backward, looking past Leslie, their faces unsure, as if they've interrupted something.

Leslie feels stupid, like he's again assumed more than he can accept. He detects someone at his side, standing too close, almost on his feet. It is a shock to see his grandfather next to him, a look of childish delight in his red eyes. Next to the old man is Harper, the basket of glass dangling at her knee. She hands out pieces to the crowd, shouting over the drone of celebration, "Look at it through this!" She is happy one second, handing a fat little boy a hunk of green, and crying the next, never looking at her son, as she kisses her father on his smiling cheek. The basket dumps at her feet; other people's children rummage through it and are scolded for doing so by parents who disapprove of Harper's actions. Leslie waits until the children withdraw, then bends to the ground to sort it out. He inspects the feet of his family, untied work boots gaping at the tongue, as he plucks the ugly glass from the ground. Leslie hopes the girls think he's helping a couple of strangers; he prays his hot face is not noticeable. When he's finished picking up the mess, he spots a piece of clear glass inside his mother's boot, stuck between her ankle and the leather upper. Leslie keeps his head down as he takes it out, the warmth from her body on his fingertips. He stands, leaving the full basket at her feet, and walks away, hoping they won't follow him closely home.

• • •

Sunday afternoon, almost evening, the weather outside harsh and erratic: bright sunshine in temps just over forty. Leslie watches through the kitchen window as the sunlight bears down from out of nowhere for a few seconds, and is sucked back up into the sky in an instant. Over and over it happens, as he sips soda from a paper cup, leaning on the sink, waiting for his mother and grandfather to finish putting on their coats. The plan is to hit the dump, then head into Wabash for the end of the festival.

In the brisk weather they walk slowly to the rear of the farm. Instead of spades, Harper has asked cheerfully if Leslie would mind getting a wheelbarrow with several long-handled shovels in it from the shed. Leslie pushes it behind Harper and the old man until he must slow to a crawl, which makes his back hurt. He waits for them to get ahead some before resuming. The pigs have gotten a whiff of the human bodies; they've come to the fence, sniffing along the row and oinking as Harper and Leslie and the old man make their way down the lane to the dump. The pigs expect to be hand fed again, desiring something from outside their world that also exists in it. The sun from earlier has completely vanished; it's now gray and solemn, the sky heavy with dark clouds, moisture that will become snow.

At the edge of the dump, Leslie peers through the dimness, over the drop of the hill toward the town as more lights are switched on, an act from the business owners that is supposed to make the fake blackout more striking. He wonders if the girls will be back, if they'd laugh at him if he tried to be polite and approach them to find out what they wanted yesterday.

The old man is tired. He ignores the pigs grunting at the fence. He sits down on a stump near the trash and watches as Leslie and Harper pull the shovels from the wheelbarrow and drag them to the pile. Without asking why they've brought heftier tools this time, Leslie uses his foot to plant the tip of the shovel into the ground; he jumps onto the metal lip with both feet, jamming it into the earth with some force. When he bends the shovel back, soft dirt flowers outward, spills onto the old ground, displaying rusty bolts and the brittle sheaves of corroded cans. He takes another dig and another, moving quickly around the pile, until it appears that the entire heap has been loosened at the edges and could be peeled from the woods like a sticker. He focuses and works hard.

When Leslie looks up, sweaty and unaware from throwing himself into the thrust of the shovel, he sees that his grandfather and mother have disappeared. They are gone. He pulls his sleeve from his watch; time has passed him by. It is getting dark. He looks to the fence where the pigs should be, thinking the two of them might be feeding the shoats grass again: nothing, only the soft swish of friable weeds, the faint clicking of their heavy seed heads against one another, tapping, pecking out a coded song Leslie thinks he should know. He begins to holler for them; twisting around in circles, he calls their names again and again. He stops and listens to the wind blowing past his ears, the trees creaking, the town just over the ridge talking to him, saying the festivities are getting closer, that darkness is real and will be forever, that it cannot be changed, and that age and blood and family make up the darkest parts of our lives. The sound is Leslie's first understanding of his obligations, of how he must watch over this family until he has his own, until the light from these years makes all the difference, and he can use it to brighten his way.

He finds them in the grass of the lane, sitting down like children, talking about Rebecca, of the farm before they owned it, and crying. Leslie plops down near them, the rut of the road on his tailbone. He tells them to watch the sky above the town, points to just over some dark trees. He smiles when the blackout is ordered; they can't actually see the town, but he knows the big lightbulb goes first and that there's more to come, sort of like fireworks in reverse, he decides. His mother and grandfather say, "Ooohhh!" when the rest of the town goes black, the night sky their only view. The two of them cuddle up together, the old man stiff as he tries to hold his baby. Leslie settles in beside them, ready for how long they will stay.

Lee Martin

Love Field

One night the baby died, and a few days later the mother, Mrs. Silver, came to Belle's house and said, "I want to talk to you."

Belle had been fearing this moment, because on the evening the baby had died, before she had known anything about it, she had put a card in the mail to the Silvers. "Congratulations on your beautiful baby," she had written. She had known that the card would be hurtful to the Silvers. The baby had come home from the hospital with jaundice, and it was obvious, even without that taint, that she was unattractive. Then Belle had heard the news of the baby's death, and she had felt stupid and mean. Ordinarily, she wouldn't have been so ugly, but so much had already happened before she had decided to send the card.

The story started earlier that summer when, each evening, she tied back the lace sheers at her front door so she could stand there, eager for a glimpse of the Silvers' first daughter, Naomi. "Sweet Naomi," she often whispered. "Funny little Naomi." She loved to say the name, her mouth rounding with the long *o* and then puckering with a kiss to the *m* as gently as the dusk that fell after the hours of blazing sun and curtained everything with its soft light. Belle welcomed the gaslights' yellow blooms on the lawns, the silvery ropes of water arcing from sprinklers, the last red of the sky shrinking in the west.

Then, with a flourish that delighted her, Naomi appeared. One evening she came in a bathing suit, her round little tummy pooching out, her feet covered with rubber flippers that slapped the street. Another time, when it was raining, she came on roller blades, a black umbrella held over her head.

With Naomi, it was always something. Privately, Mrs. Silver had told Belle that Naomi, who for eight years had been an only child, was having trouble getting used to the fact that she would soon have a little brother or sister. Sometimes Belle went to backyard cookouts at the Silvers' house, and there she saw Naomi bouncing on a trampoline, tooting a toy horn she clamped between her lips. "Oh, that's Naomi," her father said once, with a shake of his head. She went down the slide into their swimming pool, a bowling ball held in her lap. She stuck her arms out to her sides and spun 'round and 'round in her driveway, shouting something she must have heard on a television program. "My fellow Americans," she said. "I am an idiot."

"You're a pistol," Belle said to her once.

"That's me," said Naomi. "I'm a pistol-packin' mama."

She came to noodle around with the piano, the baby grand Belle had bought for her granddaughter, Irene. But Irene was in Hawaii now, and there was that baby grand, its mahogany cabinet gleaming. "So she'll play here," Belle had told Naomi's father when he had mentioned at one of the cookouts that Naomi had begun taking lessons, but, after putting in the swimming pool that summer, not to mention the fact that a new baby was on the way, he wasn't keen about springing for a piano, especially given the fact that this *was* Naomi he was talking about, who flitted about from one thing to another like a bee, delirious as it drank from this flower, and this, and this. "Your little Naomi," Belle had said. "You send her to me."

So she came each evening at eight-thirty, saving the piano like a last piece of candy, a treat at the end of the day. After water-balloon fights, bicycle trips, swimming shenanigans, and soccer games, she came smelling of chlorine and raspberry-scented sun block, and, when she was finally there, she gave Belle a hug, her cheek pressing into Belle's stomach—latched onto her, she did, as if she were dizzy with all the exertion of her day, and wanted now nothing more than these few moments with Belle, alone in the house where the old Regulator clock on the fireplace mantel ticked off the minutes with its pendulum, and the water garden in the atrium babbled, and the piano waited to sound its splendid tones.

In her own home, Naomi told Belle, after the baby had come, there was too often the noise of her crying. "Wah, wah, wah," Naomi said, opening her mouth wide and scrunching up her face in imitation of her new sister, Marie. "All the time. Wah, wah, wah. Please, just shoot me."

"She's getting used to being in the world," Belle said. Marie had only been home a matter of days. "I bet you fussed and fussed when you were that small."

"Oh, no," said Naomi with a grown-up earnestness. "I never cried."

Belle could almost believe it. Naomi seemed so convinced she could tame whatever was before her, it was easy to imagine her untouched by misery or distress even as she first settled into life. Nothing daunted her. Belle had seen her fall on her roller blades, go scraping over the street, and get up laughing. Once, during a thunderstorm, Naomi had sneaked out of the house to collect hailstones, and one of them, as big as a golf ball, had thumped her in the head hard enough to knock her to her knees; but she was up in a flash, shaking her fist at the heavens, shouting something Belle couldn't quite make out, but which sounded to her like, "Try it again. I dare you. Just you try."

Oh, Naomi was full of the most outrageous stunts. She put firecrackers in clay flower pots to see whether they would shatter. She climbed onto her roof one day, pretended someone had shot her, and fell backward, arms akimbo, onto an old mattress she had dragged out to the lawn.

The planet could barely hold her. At any moment, she seemed ready to escape its natural laws. But then she sat at the baby grand, and suddenly she was timid. She pecked at the keys, her fingers barely disturbing them, and the notes were faint in Belle's house, so faint they reminded her of the emptiness of that house now that Irene had gone, and she encouraged Naomi to play with more gusto. "A little zip, please, darling," she said. "Don't worry. You won't hurt it."

Irene had played like a house on fire; she had banged the keys with stunning chords and runs, had shot them with one finger the way Chico Marx had done in the movies. She had played ragtime, classical, jazz. Day and night, she had filled the house with music. Then, in the winter, she had gone, off to Hawaii instead of finishing her performance degree at the university. "Oh, Gran," she had said. "I'm ready for a change."

What could Belle tell her? She was merely her grandmother, the one who had given her a place to live while she went to school so her father, Belle's son, could save money on her room and board. He had lost so much on oil investments. Belle had even bought the baby grand with the last of the life-insurance money her husband had left so she could entice Irene into her home. "We'll be roomies," Belle had told her. "You'll have the piano, a room of your own, home-cooked meals. None of that cafeteria junk. You'll be on easy street."

In the end, it hadn't been enough. Irene had gone away with a boy who had told her there were humpback whales off the west coast of Maui whose mating calls sounded like notes played on a bass flute, and she had thought it would be marvelous to record them. "I'll always be able to play the piano," she had said, "but how many chances will I have like this?" Though Belle wished her smooth sailing, she couldn't help, after all she had offered Irene, but feel betrayed.

So she was glad to give Naomi the use of the baby grand and, when she had finished practicing, her favorite snack: a concoction called Dirt and Worms that Belle had seen Naomi's mother prepare, a mix of chocolate pudding and crumbled up Oreo cookies and strings of gelatin candy that wiggled like fishing lures.

"Like this," Naomi said, and she showed Belle how to grub down into the pudding with her fingers, pull out a worm, tilt back her head, open her mouth, and drop it in. "Gulp it down," Naomi said. "Just let it slide down your gullet."

"Goodness," said Belle. "I'll choke."

Naomi shook her head. "No, you won't. And even if you do, I know the Heimlich Maneuver." She stood behind Belle, wrapped her arms around her waist, and squeezed, her little fist driving into the soft flesh just below Belle's ribs. "Just like that," said Naomi. "You'll pop it right out."

When she finally left Belle's and started walking down the street toward home, she sang a song Belle had taught her, the same silly song she had taught Irene when she had been that age, "Mairzy Doats." Belle held the door open so she could listen to Naomi's voice drifting out of the dark, a thin, dreamy voice, as hushed as the notes she played on the baby grand. "Mairzy doats and dozy doats and little lamzy divey. A kiddlely divey, too, wouldn't you?" And, as the voice faded in the distance, Belle ached for the hours to pass so Naomi would come again.

Then, one night, she failed to appear. Belle waited by the door as the Regulator clock ticked and ticked. Eight-thirty passed, and then it was nine, and all she saw was the dusk turn to dark, and as it did, she became aggravated with Naomi, who had, she assumed, lost interest in the piano and forsaken her.

Well, as her father said, that was Naomi. Belle untied her lace sheers and let them fall across the glass in her front door. She turned back to her house, such a cavernous house now that she was alone. Her husband, when he had retired and built the house forty miles up the freeway from Dallas, had insisted on the two stories, the rooms and rooms and rooms they would need if their grandchildren came to live with them, as surely they would when it was time for them to attend the university. But all of them had gone to schools out of state, except Irene, who, like Naomi, had turned out to be a flibbertigibbet. Off chasing whales. The idea. As practical as the notion that their grandchildren would one day fill their house. Belle tried not to blame her husband, but there were times, when she felt the space of the house about to swallow her, that she couldn't help but resent him for dying—a heart attack while mowing their expansive lawn—and leaving her with so many rooms and so many days to wander through them.

It was nearly nine-thirty when the doorbell rang. Belle peeked out through the lace sheers and saw Naomi on the step, about to press the bell again with her nose. She held her hands behind her back, and leaned over. Belle opened the door, and Naomi jumped back with a scream.

"Lollapalooza," she said. "How about a little warning? I was just getting ready to ring the bell, Belle." Naomi giggled. "Get it? The Belle bell?"

At any other time, Belle would have thought Naomi's play on words endearing, but on this night, when she had waited and waited, she only found it irritating. "Don't be fresh," she said. "You're late."

"It was her fault," Naomi said. She pointed back in the direction of her house, and Belle saw that she had wrapped each of her fingers with rubber bands. The bands were scissoring into her flesh, cutting off the flow of blood, and turning her fingertips the color of pencil erasers.

"Whose fault?" Belle squinted out into the darkness, looking off to where Naomi was pointing. "Who are you talking about?"

"Yellow Baby," said Naomi. The doctors had told the Silvers to make sure the new baby got plenty of sun, plenty of vitamin D. "We kept her out by the pool until the sun went down, but she still wouldn't go to sleep. I sang and sang to her." Naomi gave Belle a shy smile. "She likes it when I sing to her."

"What did you sing?"

"The song you taught me."

"'Mairzy Doats'?"

"Most of the time it conks her right out. But tonight." Naomi rolled her eyes. "Oh, brother. She made me so mad I pinched her. Hard. Right on her fat old leg."

"Oh, you didn't do that?" Belle felt certain Naomi was exaggerating. "Tell me you didn't."

"I didn't," said Naomi.

"I knew you were playing the devil." Belle took Naomi's hand and led her to the baby grand. She sat beside her on the piano bench. "What will you play for me tonight? 'Twinkle, Twinkle'?"

"All right," said Naomi in a meek voice, and she began pecking at the keys.

Such a mouse, Belle thought. What was it about the baby grand that spooked her? "I can barely hear you," Belle said. "Can't you, please, give it more zing?"

Naomi lifted her hands from the keyboard. Her fingers, still wrapped in the rubber bands, were trembling. "Aren't I pressing hard?" she said. "I thought I was."

"You can't feel a thing." Belle felt her irritation return. "Look at your fingers. Take off those rubber bands."

"Oh, I can't do that," Naomi said. "If I do, Yellow Baby will wake up."

"That's nonsense." Perhaps on some other night Belle might have thought Naomi's superstition charming, but tonight the hocus-pocus with the rubber bands was merely a further annoyance. "That's just a game you've made up. How can you play the piano with your fingers like that?"

"I can't play the piano at all." Naomi put her hands over her eyes. "I'm rotten."

It was true that Naomi's playing, even though she had only begun her lessons, lacked the confidence it would need if she hoped to continue with it.

"You can't be afraid," Belle said. "The piano knows when you're afraid and it won't give you anything. Maybe you need to let it know who's boss."

"Like this?" Naomi brought her hands down on the keyboard, and the jumbled notes, the most forceful she had ever played, rang out with a vitality that delighted Belle.

"That's it," she said. "Yes, if that's what it takes."

Naomi was shaking her hands as if they were on fire and she

was desperate to put out the flames. "That hurt," she said. "I mean it really hurt. Yowza-wowza. I'm going home."

She tried to get up from the piano bench, but Belle grabbed her arm and pulled her back down. "You'll be all right. It's those rubber bands. Here, let me get them off you."

Belle tried to roll the rubber bands off Naomi's fingertips, and Naomi began to yowl. "Stop it," she said.

She tried to wriggle away, but Belle had her own finger between Naomi's and one of the rubber bands and it stretched out until it snapped.

Naomi's hand flew up to her eye. "You've hit me," she said. She jumped up and ran out of the house. By the time Belle made it to the door, Naomi was running down the street. "I'm blind," she was shouting. "I'm blind." And though Belle wanted to follow to make sure Naomi was all right, she saw neighbors opening doors, stepping out to see what the fuss was, and she couldn't bear the thought of passing by them, feeling their questioning eyes upon her, hearing her saying to them, with a wave of her hand, "Oh, you know Naomi."

The next morning, early, she called Naomi's house, and Naomi's father answered in his subdued baritone that Belle always imagined might be the voice of God. Mr. Silver held an endowed chair in Peace Studies at the university. It was his job, in his research, to figure out why groups went to war. Whenever Belle listened to him, she got the impression that he could tame any unruly force with merely a word. Any force except Naomi, for whom he had no answer.

"She has a scratch on her cornea," he told Belle. "Nothing serious. We'll keep it covered for a while."

"So she'll be all right?" Belle had spent the night imagining that she had maimed her forever.

"A scratch," said Mr. Silver. "She'll be Naomi in no time."

The musical lilt of the phrase, "Naomi in no time," reminded Belle of the baby grand and how she had encouraged her to play with more pizzazz. "She had rubber bands wrapped around her fingers," she said to Mr. Silver. "I was only trying to get them off."

For a while, Mr. Silver didn't say anything. Belle could hear the baby cooing in the background. She could hear the chirr of the swimming-pool filters, and she imagined Mr. Silver with the cordless phone, sitting by the pool, the baby snuggled against him. Finally, he said—and his voice was even more quiet than usual when he spoke—"That isn't exactly the way Naomi tells it."

"No?" said Belle. "What then?"

"She says you got angry with her." Again there were only the sounds of the baby and the pool filters, and then a thread of static on the phone as Mr. Silver cleared his throat. "She says you tried to slap her, and your fingernail scraped across her eye."

Now it was Belle who could barely find her voice. "And you believe her? You believe I'd do that?"

"In my work," Mr. Silver said, "I know that the truth is always somewhere between stories. One party says this, one party says that. What do we know? Only that we have trouble, and almost always each side is partly to blame."

"Those rubber bands," Belle said again.

"Who's to say why Naomi does what she does?" Mr. Silver chuckled. "Don't worry. She won't bother you anymore."

"If I could just talk with her."

"I don't think she wants to do that. At least not now."

"Just a few moments."

"Belle, I'm afraid I must insist."

She heard just the slightest tone of irritation in Mr. Silver's voice, and in that instant she knew what she had become: the old woman in the neighborhood whose granddaughter had left her alone, an object of pity, a burdensome test for the compassion of those who lived around her. She feared Mr. Silver would soon end their conversation. The thought of not being able to speak with Naomi—so badly she wanted to ask her why she had lied—while the rumor that she had tried to slap her spread through the neighborhood, left her desperate, and all she could think to do was to tell a lie of her own. "Naomi's right," she said. "I lost my temper. I feel just awful. Please, I must see her to apologize."

But already Mr. Silver had hung up, and all Belle heard was the hum of the phone line, which seemed to mock her confession, her admission to a crime she hadn't committed, all for the chance that she might once again see Naomi.

Belle, if she had to admit the truth, had never quite taken to motherhood. She had never gotten used to the feel of a baby squirming in her arms, the heft of it slung against her hip, and, somehow, she feared that her children had sensed her discomfort, knew it even now that they were grown. She thought it must be particularly true for Irene's father, who had left home as soon as he had been old enough to join the army. Now, though he lived in Houston, he rarely made the trip north to visit. He telephoned from time to time to let her know, in brief conversations, that he was well. Irene was as bad, throwing away her music studies for some wild expedition to Hawaii. Belle began to wonder whether the fault was hers. Did some lack in her, some inability to give herself wholly to people, end up driving them away? The night Irene packed her duffel for her trip to Hawaii, she suddenly turned from her dresser and threw her arms around Belle's neck. Belle stood there, surprised, afraid to return the hug, knowing that, if she did, she would never want to let go. "Do you have enough undergarments?" she finally said, cringing at the prim sound of the words.

One day, not long after Naomi's accusation, a letter came from Irene and a cassette recording she had made of the humpback whales. When Belle played the tape and heard the whales' calls, she felt something collapse inside her, some notion she had manufactured that it didn't matter a stitch to her what Naomi claimed. What was the word of a child to her, who had managed without Miss Naomi Silver and would do so again?

When Belle listened to the whales' urgent calls, she knew she was a fraud. In their groans and trills, and their bellows that rose to screams—what Irene, in her letter, called the "ascending phrases"—Belle heard her own need, and she nearly wept. She thought of all the nights she had stood at her door saying, "Naomi, Naomi." She imagined the first sailors to hear the whales' calls and how the cries must have pierced them to the quick, made the pitch and sway of their ship—this world at sea they had come to trust—seem foreign and perilous.

"The bellows are called bells," Irene wrote. "Like when a deer bays. He bells. Sort of a trumpeting sound."

The association of the sounds with her name stunned her, and it seemed then as if the whales were calling, "Belle, Belle, Belle."

She imagined Irene and her boyfriend on the boat they had rented, their underwater microphones dropped over the side, their headphones in place, as they listened to the swell of the ocean and then the whales' cries. Eavesdroppers, they were, listening to pleas and shrieks and whimpers, stealing this ancient and intimate language, not meant for human ears.

Sometimes, Irene went on to say, the whales swam up onto the shore and stranded themselves on dry land. The theory was that they navigated by using the geomagnetic field of the Earth, and when that field fluctuated, as it often did, they continued to follow a field of constant strength, a geomagnetic contour, no matter where it threatened to lead them. Often a beached whale, when towed back to the sea, would again swim to the shore, convinced it was moving in the right direction.

Belle's husband had been a geologist for an oil company, and he had explained to her the plates of the Earth's crust and mantle and how they drifted at various speeds and in different directions. At one time, there had been a single supercontinent, Pangea; then massive blocks of the Earth's surface separated. Some converged again; some slid past one another. The world of the here and now was only a fleeting manifestation of a grander reality. The land beneath their feet had started somewhere else. Perhaps two hundred million years ago the North Texas plains had been part of what was now Africa. Even as they spoke, he told her, they were drifting westward at one to three centimeters per year. "In the big picture," he said, "we're all moving."

Now she thought of the whales and their calls going out through the oceans of a drifting Earth. Most of their songs, Irene said, were audible to other whales nearly twenty miles away, and some of the low-frequency moans and snores could range over a hundred miles. Belle thought of Naomi and how she was only three houses away from her, but still the distance seemed too great for either one of them to close.

That night, and for several nights thereafter, her husband came to her in her dreams. Always, he was young. His black hair gleamed, and his broad chest flared up from his narrow waist. And in these dreams she, too, was young. They were back in their old house in Dallas, not far from the airport, Love Field. When jets took off, teacups rattled in the china cabinet, picture frames tilted on the walls, and the trapdoor to the attic rose and fell and banged against its frame as if spirits were tromping across the ceiling joists. "It's like someone just walked across my grave," she used to say to her husband, her hand at her throat. "Oh, don't complain," he would tell her, with a wink. "How can we go wrong when we live so close to Love?" It became a dear joke between them. "We're in the Love Field," they teased. "Oh, baby. We've landed in Love."

Now she lived in a neighborhood surrounded by pasture fields where longhorn cattle grazed and the blue sky stretched off to the horizon. Some evenings, she walked to the farthest reach of the subdivision and saw the land the way it had been before people had come to claim it: scrub trees, and clay soil cracking from drought, and grass turning to tinder—dry and burnt—under the blazing sun. How vast Texas must have seemed to the first settlers. So much room, a person could disappear if he wanted to, and perhaps no one would ever know.

One afternoon, though the heat was almost more than she could bear, she went for a walk so she could pass by the Silvers' house in hopes of seeing Naomi playing in the yard.

And there she was. She was sitting on the grass, her head

bowed, as she tried to lace up her sneaker. She was having a hard time of it. Her hair had fallen over her face, and she was poking the shoelace at the eyelet with no success. Finally, she let the lace drop from her hand. Her shoulders wobbled, and Belle knew she was trying hard not to cry.

Then Naomi looked up, and Belle saw the gauze patch over her left eye, held in place with strips of tape stuck to her forehead and cheekbone. At first, Belle could hardly bear the sight of Naomi, stymied, when she had always breezed through the world. Then Belle felt a stronger part of her drift toward Naomi's need. She was, after all the crazy stunts, a child who needed someone now to help her.

"That old shoelace is being a pill, isn't it?" Belle said.

Naomi nodded her head, and her bottom lip quivered. She picked up the shoelace again and held it out, inviting Belle to take it.

"Slip off your shoe, sweetie," Belle told her, "and I'll lace it for you. If I try to kneel down, I may never get back up."

Naomi kicked off her shoe, picked it up by the lace, and brought it to Belle. "I would have asked my mom to help me," Naomi said, her voice hushed the way it had been when she had come to Belle's house to play the piano. "But she's busy with Yellow Baby. She's always busy with Yellow Baby. I could just disappear, and she wouldn't even know."

"Oh, she'd miss you." Belle threaded the shoelace through the eyelet. She thought of Irene so far away in Hawaii. "Just like I've missed you."

"Me?" said Naomi, and Belle could see that her surprise was genuine. She had never known how much Belle loved her.

"I don't know why you lied, sweetie. You know I didn't hit you."

"No, you didn't," Naomi said.

"Will you tell your parents that? Tell them the truth? It was those rubber bands that caused all the trouble."

Naomi bit down on her lip. "I want to," she said, "but I can't. Then they'd know how wicked I am."

Just then, Mrs. Silver came out of the house with Marie in her arms. "Naomi," she said, "your father wants you to come inside now."

"Yes, Mother," Naomi said. Then she snatched her shoe from Belle's hand and dashed across the lawn.

Mrs. Silver owned a candy store. Belle had seen her commercials on television. In them, Mrs. Silver, a lanky woman whose teeth were too big, wore a tutu and tights and a pair of gauzy fairy wings. She carried a magic wand with a glittery star on its end. "At the Sugar Plum Cottage," she always said at the end of the commercials, "where being sweet to you is our business."

Belle walked across the lawn so she could get a closer look at the baby. "So this is the one," she said, letting her voice fall into the singsong rhythm she recalled other women using when they had admired her own baby. "This is the little sweetheart."

"This is Marie," said Mrs. Silver. She matched Belle's tone, an inflection that was identical to the one Mrs. Silver used in her commercials.

Belle peered down at the baby, who was, as Naomi had claimed, fussy. She was crying, her eyes clamped shut, her mouth open wide, her chubby fists waving in the air. "You're trying to tell us something, aren't you, little Marie?" Belle said. She was well aware that she was trying to curry Mrs. Silver's favor so she could broach the subject of Naomi and her lie. "We just can't understand what you're saying. No, we can't."

Marie was, in all honesty, sorely featured. Her head was too big, her eyes set too close together. Even without the yellow tinge to her skin, she was not, though Belle would never have said this to Mrs. Silver, a looker.

"She's . . . jaundiced," Mrs. Silver said, and the way she hesitated between the two words made it clear to Belle that she knew as well as anyone with two good eyes that her baby was far from handsome.

"Oh, that'll go away," Belle said. "What we need now is to get this sweetheart to stop crying."

And then Belle started to sing. She sang "Mairzy Doats," and the cadence of the song seemed to catch Marie's ear. She toned down her squall to an occasional whimper. "Maybe if I held her," Belle said.

She reached for Marie, and Mrs. Silver took a perceptible step back. There was an awkward moment, then, when Mrs. Silver tried to cover over the fact that she had just snubbed Belle. "Babies," she said, and her voice trembled with a phony laugh. "They're such a handful. I wouldn't want to trouble you."

Belle wanted to feel sorry for Mrs. Silver because she was a nervous woman, not such an eye-catcher herself, who owned a candy store and dressed in a fairy-princess costume to make herself feel pretty. Now she had a baby with jaundice and beyond that a face that people would remember for the wrong reasons. Belle wanted to offer her sympathy, but she couldn't manage it. Instead, she felt a rage start to rise in her because she knew that, when Mrs. Silver had stepped back from her, she had been announcing that she thought Belle dangerous, a crazy old woman who had nearly blinded Naomi. Let her hold the baby, Marie? Not on her life.

That evening, Belle wrote her message in the baby card, underlining the word, "beautiful," five times, satisfied with the irony. She had just dropped the card into the mailbox on the corner when she heard a siren's rising keen.

It was dusk, and she saw red light swell and pulse on the trees and houses as an ambulance turned down the street. She waited to see where it would stop.

Naomi's house. Naomi, Belle thought. Something's happened to Naomi.

But it wasn't Naomi at all. It was the baby, Marie. She had fallen into the pool. The word spread up and down the street. The pool. The baby. Marie. It was all anyone knew.

It was nearly dark by the time the paramedics brought her out to the ambulance. As they came hurrying through the Silvers' front yard, Belle saw, just for a moment, the baby's tiny hand, as the man carrying her slipped through the gaslight's glow.

Then Mr. Silver came running, barefoot and wearing swimming trunks. Mrs. Silver and Naomi dashed out of the house. They all got into the back of the ambulance, and its siren shrieked again as it sped away.

For a moment, Belle stood with her neighbors in the middle of the street looking at the Silvers' house. They had left the front door open, and she could see the lights burning inside the house and the slow turn of a ceiling fan.

"I suppose someone should go down there and shut the door," a man said. "And turn off the lights."

"I'll do it," said Belle.

"Oh, I can do it," the man told her.

"No." She stepped forward. "Please."

In the Silvers' house she went from room to room switching off the lights, letting darkness follow her. Upstairs, in Naomi's room, she noticed that a window was open. The screen had been popped out and was leaning against the wall. She felt the warm night air, smelled the chlorine in the backyard swimming pool. Her hand moved over the light switch, and then the pool lights cast the reflection of the water into the room. It spread over Belle and across the wall behind her. The blue tint of the shuddering light, rising and falling with the gentle motion of the water, caught her by surprise—how delicate it was, how wispy, like threads of smoke lacing the air.

She went to the window to close it. She looked down on the pool and saw a bright orange raft, the kind someone could inflate and float on, turned upside down. It was spinning in a lazy circle as if it had a slow air leak. As it swung around, she caught a glimpse of something settled on the pool's bottom: a dark shape, mysterious in the dim glow from the underwater lights. Then she smelled the scent of raspberries, and, in an instant, she remembered the sunblock Naomi always wore, and she imagined that what she saw on the bottom of the pool was a bowling ball. She pictured Naomi standing at the window, struggling with the ball's weight, balancing it on the sill, and then shoving it out into the air. Perhaps Mr. Silver had been on the float with Marie. He would have looked up just as Naomi yelled. Perhaps she screamed, "Look out below." Then the ball came crashing down into the water, and Mr. Silver, trying to shield Marie, let her slip from his hands, while Naomi looked on, stunned by what she saw.

Or maybe that wasn't how it had happened at all. Maybe, Belle thought, she simply needed to believe that Naomi had finally astonished herself, had wandered so far from the world she had found it again, had found her mother, her father, Marie, even herself, had felt the weight of their living.

One evening, not long after the funeral, Mrs. Silver came to Belle's house, the baby card in her hand. "You saw something in her, didn't you?" she said. "That day when she was crying and you sang to her. You saw something pretty in her."

Standing there with Mrs. Silver, the door open just a crack, Belle thought of her own son, and her husband, and Irene, and even Naomi, who would be a different girl now that she knew loss, who would more than likely remember Belle in the years to come, if she remembered her at all, as the old woman about whom she had lied the summer her baby sister had drowned. Belle imagined all of them standing together on the drifting Earth, all of them lifting up their voices, sending out their cries.

"Such a racket," she had always said when the jets had taken off from Love Field and risen with a scream over their house.

Her husband had made the same joke every time, yet she had never tired of it. "What can we do?" he had said with a shrug of his shoulders. "So little us. So much Love."

She thought of the joke again as she opened her door wider. "Yes, I saw it," she said to Mrs. Silver. "Your Marie was a beautiful child."

Ioanna Carlsen

Going Home

At the airport I have to make a phone call for someone to pick me up because my mother is at the hospital with my father, who has had a stroke. Next to me is a young woman also making a call; she turns to me, the phone dangling: "The ticket agent screwed up the connections—I'm missing my mother's funeral," she says.

I nod. "Maybe it's for the best," I say.

"No," she says, "I want to be there."

"You'll get there," I assure her, "don't worry."

As I turn away I see other women, ages thirty to fortyish, dressed in black, probably going to funerals, too. I glance back at the young woman talking intensely into the phone. I imagine her name is Charlotte and the funeral is somewhere in the deep Midwest. Afraid of missing it, she will not. And although she dreads arriving at it, she will attend it all the way there, and back.

Driving myself to the airport that morning I had my new blue truck on cruise control. As I was trying to figure out how it worked, it seemed to me that cars on a highway were like emotions—sometimes, in the left lane, they were going faster than I was. Sometimes, in the right lane, they were going too slow; sometimes they would come up on me, out of nowhere, sometimes I would see them up ahead and approach them for a long time. Sometimes the other cars seemed like other people's emotions, but mostly the cars were my own emotions—some of the cars were old and banged up, and some of the cars were shiny, expensive or cheap, and new. Manifesting outside these windows, on the surface of this blacktop, the cars appearing out of nowhere, the highway itself, were parts of me.

It didn't take long to figure out that in order to stay in cruise control I had to gauge the situation and change lanes ahead of time. The instant I got reactive, I was out of cruise control. The closer I got to the city, the harder it got to stay at the same steady speed because there were more cars.

The closer I got to home, the more emotions I had. When I got to the hospital my father did not know me, although my mother pretended he did. "He's dying," I said to my mother. She looked at me across his body in the hospital bed: he seemed already in his casket, sleeping so deeply she had to bring him back from long distances to force him to eat—I could see how far back he came and I was amazed.

"He won't die," she said, "I won't let him."

The hospital room became our home. The home I had just left had its children and its husband, and its wife and mother, who were me. But here, again I was the child; my intervening life barely existed, it seemed more like a dream. My father was her child now, too; my mother was still my mother, but also his—as a mother or a wife I was imaginary, and as a father so was my father.

No, he didn't die. How could he? She and I fought over it; you've got to let him, I would say. She would just ignore me. People would come in to test him for rehabilitation possibilities, and she would prompt him the way she used to prompt me from the back of the room at spelling bees, forming the letters with her mouth.

Now when I go home to see him, one more time each time, I'm glad she saved him; it gives us time to get used to it. I walk into the kitchen and put my bags down on the same green linoleum with the white swirling. The oven is new, and they have a dog—we never had a dog when I was growing up because my mother thought animals were dirty. But now that my brother and I are gone, they have animals. I know the drawers are full of things she never uses, which are as familiar to me as the photographs in the box with the broken hinge that she keeps in the closet. I know there is money in the bags of clothes there. I know there is jewelry hidden in other boxes under the bed. I know the altar is still in their bedroom with baskets of unironed clothes next to it, because she keeps the ironing board in there next to the exercise bike she is always nagging my father to ride. She doesn't have to because she has high blood pressure. The kitchen radio is on like always; the TV, like always, is on in the living room.

I set down my bags. My mother opens the dishwasher—which hasn't worked for ten years and which she never replaces because, since we kids are no longer at home, she has no reason to entertain—and throws in another plastic top from a margarine container. She never throws anything away anymore.

My father is sitting at the kitchen table fluttering in and out of the present like a leaf blown about by wind.

There are times when he just isn't here at all; the question is where, at those times, he is. Lost in the past, I think, as if it were a place—a room within this room, like Russian nested eggs.

When I am home he tells me stories from that place. In his particular case, it's an island, Greek. He sees the skirts of the old men swaying—he remembers being a little boy, teasing the old men who wore the Turkish-style trousers, called *vrachia,* that ballooned out at the hip; he's throwing pebbles at an old man, and then he sees the dirt road, the black skirt of the trouser swaying—suddenly, he tells me, it's as if he is actually there.

Whereas we can go out to dinner with old friends and the rest of us are chatting and he is not. He eats his food very slowly, head bent over his plate, as if engrossed not in eating, but contemplating it.

My mother, twenty years his junior, gives things to him: a glass of wine, a piece of bread. He ignores the wine, takes the bread and looks at it, turning it over, looking at her, as if to say, What is this?

After dinner someone asks him if he enjoyed his dinner. He looks up, startled. "No," he says.

Later we are at our friends' house, chatting, and suddenly he enters the conversation. We all look at him, the way you look at a person just entering a room.

The next day I say to him—"Why did you tell George you didn't enjoy dinner last night?"

"Did I say that . . . ," he says. "I wonder why."

"Well, you didn't seem to really be there during dinner," I start to say, and then suddenly, I get it, and I start laughing, saying, "but of course, no wonder you didn't enjoy it—you weren't there—it makes perfect sense, how could you enjoy it . . ."

We're both laughing now; he finishes the sentence for me, " . . . When I was someplace else."

We find this excruciatingly funny. My mother tries to pretend that it is not; she is annoyed with us and does not want to laugh. She cannot help finally smiling, because it is funny, but she doesn't like it. She doesn't like me getting into his oldness; she doesn't like me encouraging him to give in to being old.

It took him a long time to get old. But now he is being old with a completeness that takes my breath away. He reminds me of my grandmother, who was so old she died twenty years ago.

He takes his teeth out and doesn't like to put them back in. My mother pushes them at him across the table. He reminds her of my grandmother when he does not put them in. We call her the sergeant. "The sergeant wants you to put your teeth in," I tell him, and he laughs, and discreetly slides them under his napkin.

She is fighting the whole world, the laws of the universe, of life itself. He reminds me of my grandmother, and she reminds me of the Spartans at Thermopylae, doomed but resisting to the end; her love for my father is an idea she still has. One day I see him hobbling to their bedroom in the middle of the day. "I can't go on," he says to her, naming her name, "I can't," he repeats in the language they speak to each other, the language of their parents, their past, their lives branching off around it with all the things that are private between them, all the things I can't know.

But now I know something new. I know that just as she does not allow him to die, he lives only for her. It's a love story, the love story of the century, two merely human beings defying, for each other, for as long as possible, death.

I try to get the story out of her, their story; she has always been reticent, letting it out in little bits and pieces. I ply her with questions: Tell me when was the first time you . . . , tell me how did you know that . . . , tell me. "Why do you want to know," she says.

"Maybe I'll write about it," I tease her, "how can I make your story into a best-seller if you don't tell me?" She gives me a long look across the kitchen table, which she is now leaving, to go in and see how he is.

"Use your imagination," she says, and goes to him.

The young woman at the airport made it to her mother's funeral just in time. I can just see it—her father in a black suit, one of the pallbearers along with her brother. It is a hot day in early October in the Midwest. There is a haze over everything, and the small town her mother lived in before she died is far from here; only the family will go there, to bury her on the farm where her people are buried. But her father is ill; her father is having some kind of attack. Her brother stays behind with him and takes him to the hospital—they will follow later in the car, but she drives the hearse with her mother in the back up to the farm at Oscola; when her brother and father arrive they will bury her together. The cat will watch from the window; the dog will be locked in so it doesn't sniff the coffin. At the church she took the diamond earrings her husband had given her for Mother's Day and put them in her mother's pocket before they closed the casket. The diamonds in her mother's pocket glittered in the dark like living eyes as she drove her mother in her casket inside a hearse along the highways of southern Illinois, each farmhouse farther from the next in the dry October heat and the glazed sky.

At the farmhouse that she had grown up in, she had not the courage to open her mother's casket and look at her once again, alone now in this bleak Midwestern landscape she had always been trying to escape. She left her mother and found the key in the place it was always hidden, and let herself into the dark house.

Those few hours with the coffin in the car, between the church and this house that now was her mother's grave site, drove a wedge between her ordinary life and the present. She felt exposed, on some new threshold of her life, in an old house that was a new house. The furniture in this one was good as sold: the contents of its drawers piled up in the center of the living room in boxes ready to be taken away, the walls already showing holes where the paintings used to hang, the flowers already dying of neglect in the garden. She remembered her mother the last time she had seen her, standing here, just inside the doorway waving good-bye—her mother, grown stout, but still pretty, waving good-bye in her robe and wearing socks with her slippers.

Fear struck at her like a weapon; her legs were weak and she felt as if she had to go to the bathroom. She walked inside the house and let its emptiness ring through her as if she were a room with no one in it.

This empty room held her past. It was empty and yet full. It had all the familiar plates and chairs and tables and lamps she had grown up with; only the people were missing. Only the life was gone.

It was like stepping into an old dress, being back here, alone with her mother dead in the driveway. It was like the dress didn't fit right anymore, she wanted to take it off, sell it, give it away, but even if she could do any of those things, it would still be with her, in the closet of her head.

She sat down in the room. She sat on the couch as if she were testing it. If they did sell the house now, it would be empty for a while, then someone else would live in it. All their things would be dispersed: were the things their life? where was their life—was it inside these walls, was it in the cloisonné vase on the coffee table? Was it in the photographs in the box in the right-hand drawer of the kitchen chest? Was it in her, was it that now she was her mother?

Then she realized the phone was actually ringing and it was her brother; they had taken some tests at the hospital, their father would be all right, they would both be up next morning.

She sat back down on the couch in the complete darkness that had now overtaken the house, and the night was like a coffin closing over her face.

In the morning when she woke, she was her mother. She was her mother and she was making eggs in the same pan her mother always used, only wearing different clothes that were her own. Her hands went unerringly to the right places for everything she needed, her thought on the woman in the hearse in the driveway. She noticed how quickly the fire leapt into blueness and made the butter melt its heart out on the stove; she touched the silkiness of the glaze on the plate sitting attentively next to the stove.

That plate had all the time in the world, she thought.

She felt so alone it was like being in the Himalayas. The air was lighter than usual; she could just breathe it in. She was a dream, breathing.

The house was just the same as they had left it: the same plaid plates she still liked, the same green linoleum streaked with marbled white, the same dog bowl in the same corner—although many of the dogs who had used it were dead.

Outside the window she saw how the driveway curved around to the back meadow where, down below, at the foot of a small hill next to a pond, a little graveyard lay with the remains of three bodies: her grandparents, and a child born dead to her mother before she had been born. She saw how that road was her road, a road she was now on, that had no side roads; that now that she was on it, she would have to take it to the end. She heard how a bird outside the window was singing, It's your turn, it's your turn, over and over again. She heard how another bird answered at intervals, It's my turn, it's my turn, again and again. She saw how you can make birds say anything you want, and so she said to it, "Don't be afraid. Say, 'Don't be afraid'; say it again."

• • •

Her father looked so pale in the black suit. "You can take that off, Dad," she said, "it's only us now."

"No," he said, "not till after," and he burst into tears. She tried to comfort him, but he kept her away. She brought tea and bread and butter to the table with some ham; she was angry. He gave way to his grief, ignoring her. Her brother opened a beer, ignoring him. She watched her father, saying nothing, seeing how separate from him she was.

He pushed away her food, he pushed away her drink, and he hung down his head and his hands, looking down, toward the side. Then he put his arms down on the table like a protection, and dropped his head down inside them, and stayed that way, finally falling asleep there, grieving as if the world had begun and ended with his wife, ignoring his children—grieving for her as if she had been his life.

The next morning they buried her. They drove the hearse down to the place where they had paid a hired man to dig the grave. It was in line with the others. Her father insisted on opening the casket one last time. They had rolled it off the casters and it sat there beside the rectangular bed of the hole. They opened the casket and their father leaned into it, kissed his wife, and stayed there so long they had to pull him out. And when they did, he sobbed, a choking sound came out of him, and he fell back in, dead.

They couldn't believe it at first. At first they were furious like orphans abandoned at a crossroads. Her brother kept slapping his father's face, but she saw it was no use. "Terry," she said, "calm down, he's gone, they're gone, they've left, it's over." They sat down beside the coffin, their father still leaning into it, and they held each other and cried. They stayed there until they were both quiet.

"Let's go back in the house, Terry," she said, "and call the doctor."

"Why?" said Terry.

"We need a certificate of death."

"Then we're going to go through all this again—right?"

"Oh no, Terry," she said, "no, we're not. I'll tell you what we're going to do."

How she explained it to him on the way up to the house was how they did it. After the doctor came, the hired man came again with his son, and they buried her and put him in the ground next to her, the way he was, buried him like that, in the fetal position.

There was something comforting about the way the ground took him in. In this ancient, time-honored way, I imagined the woman at the airport, whose name I thought must have been Charlotte Irons, put her father into the ground beside her mother.

My father is older now than it is possible to be and still be, but he is. My mother brings him to visit us, old as he is. She will go nowhere without him, and he is upset if she is not around. His hands shake when he brings his fork to his mouth. Food spills down his shirt. He almost totters over every time he gets up from a chair. Getting him into a car is a drama, each leg lifted separately, the cane, the handle of the door, the door, each thing having a speaking part.

He shuffles when he walks, bent at the waist as if listening to something underground. The altitude is too high for him here, and he does not feel well. One day he comes in from being outside and sits down heavily at the kitchen table where my mother and I are shelling peas. He looks pale and waxen, something has happened to him. "I feel death coming closer," he says.

We all look at each other. I tell my mother to give him a glass of wine. She thinks I drink too much and encourage him to drink more than he should, but this time she gestures to me to get it.

"I don't want it," he says.

"Drink it," she says—the sergeant. I rub his shoulders, because he is crying, then I cry. My mother doesn't like it when we cry, but she cries, too. He drinks the wine, and my mother and I start making dinner, chopping, peeling, frying. My husband comes in and wants to know why we are all crying.

"He was outside and something happened to him," I say. "His death is coming closer, getting to know him like a friend."

"What does that mean?" My husband sometimes reminds me of my mother.

"He doesn't feel well," I say. My mother laughs.

"What was he doing outside?"

"Looking for things, he's always going in drawers looking for something, sometimes he goes outside looking," says my mother.

"What is he looking for?" I ask.

"Money," says my husband. This is very funny, because my father has always been a gambler, and one who lost a lot of money in his day—horses, poker, the stock market. He probably was looking for money; with one foot in the grave, he's still looking for money, and it makes us all laugh.

My father finishes the wine and he feels better. Nothing happens, again. Before they leave, my mother wants to know when I will be coming home again.

I am always going home, that's what she doesn't understand. I'm always just going home, driving to an airport, using cruise control for as long as I can, and then getting there, gaining on my parents, who are moving very slowly as I come up on them. He has a cane, she is smiling, and then, in no time at all, I see myself enveloped in the arms of the past.

Robin Bradford

Bob Marley Is Dead

She runs red lights to keep the baby happy. He hates for the car to stop. He tells her with a cry so loud they have a name for it. Doom-3 is a sudden fake cry, the closest thing to a whine a three month old can do. Doom-7 is red-faced frustration, no tears, that says you better give me tit, dry my butt, cut out the scratchy tag, or let me sleep *right now* or you'll regret it. But putting on the brakes, that gets you Doom-10. It's a full-body cry, red clenched hands, kicking feet, ugly face, tiny squinty eyes producing real diamond tears. *Keep the hell going!* So Rebecca guns the accelerator of the Honda hatchback and they bounce through the intersection. She glances at the cross traffic and when she gets to the other side brakes lightly to something closer to the speed limit. In the backseat Duncan coos at Wiggly Worm. Rebecca spies his glee reflected back to her in the rearview mirror. His brown hair sticks up on top and his dark eyes look just like Matthew's. He loves breaking the law.

She used to have time to stop. She remembers going to tai chi class wearing sweat pants and Matthew's baggy John Coltrane T-shirt. Her teacher, a Chinese man in his forties who looks like he's twenty, told her after class that in China the first thirty days following birth the mother is forbidden to touch water. The quaintness of this custom made her laugh out loud. She intended to give birth standing up. She planned to leave the hospital the next day. The first week she was doing dishes, putting clothes into the washer, cooking dinner, and designing the baby announcement on the computer. When he was talking to her that day beneath the pecan trees, Chang smoothed his shiny black bangs and stepped back a little as if in respect for her belly's life force. He said that childbirth is seen as a time to strengthen one's body and health, an opportunity to give birth to a new self.

When Duncan was born, Chang came over with a bright red box that looked like candy, filled with packages of dead mushrooms and other plants. He showed Matthew how to cook the herbs in the brown clay pot. Chang's girlfriend, a college student with waist-length blond hair, stroked the baby's feet with her knuckles while Rebecca nursed him, covering herself with the blue and pink baby blanket Matthew's dead mother had crocheted.

She drank the herbs, which smelled better than they tasted, for a few days. One time she nearly got the Chinese tea confused with the other tea the midwife had given her to soak her butt in. She wasn't used to healing or spending the day in the rocking chair by the window. She wasn't used to babies. Nothing prepared her for Duncan's sudden need, his irregular sleeping, his old-man good looks, the hundred expressions on his face, his yellow poos. Just the other day she discovered the half-finished box of herbs in the back of the cabinet where they keep the tea and cookie sprinkles and baking soda, and threw it out. Maybe she should have taken the Chinese remedy more seriously. Maybe she should have slept when the baby slept, like they say. Maybe then she wouldn't be going crazy.

Even on the worst days, Rebecca thinks once they get home from the post office and she is nursing the baby on the couch, having powerlessly endured his blasting cry while waiting unavoidably in the left-turn lane that led to their street, and racing up the driveway—even on the worst days, his feet are soft as flower petals, having never yet been walked upon.

While Duncan sleeps, she washes dishes, unloads and loads the dryer, starts another round of wash, brushes her teeth, and checks the time. Just as she's starting to sweep the kitchen floor the phone rings.

Hi, baby, Matthew greets her.

She can hear some kids joking in the background. Matthew teaches band at a nearby high school. When Duncan was two weeks old, Matthew went back to work. He would call once between classes and at lunch to check on her. She would cry into the phone and tell him that, like her, the baby cried all the time except when he was eating.

I'm sorry, sweetheart, he'd say. Then the school bell buzzed, leaving her alone again.

Reaching for the dustpan, she now rattles off the list of what she's accomplished, feeling tired just repeating it all.

Hey, I thought you were gonna take it easy.

Uh-huh.

You know, that thing about the heart getting the oxygen first before it pumps blood to the body . . .

Yeah, she replies. I forgot.

When she gets off the phone she turns on the stereo and lies on the couch. The music rolls over her body, a rock song with words she can't make out. She's too tired to change the station. Then a familiar one comes on, something that was always on the radio when she was pregnant. She remembers driving from work to the park for tai chi class, her belly making it impossible to button her coat, which didn't matter because she was hot all the time anyway. She would sing along; it was always on, a song about being young and leaving some guy and knowing it was right but still missing him. She'd sung it loud like the singer does, like it had to do with her, though she hadn't left anybody for years. Now when she drives she keeps the radio off and only sings when Duncan needs it. Once she sang "The Ants Go Marching One By One" in the elaborate style of an opera singer all the way up to twenty while they drove across town. Now she feels tears in her eyes hearing the song on the radio again, exactly the same as it was back then, while she is entirely changed. The black cat leaps from the rocking chair, landing with a thud, the chair rocking, and saunters over to her. Standing on his hind legs, he lays his thick velvety paws across her arm. She pets the top of his head and he jumps up next to her, lying on his back to have his vast belly rubbed. She rolls onto her side, the way she does when she nurses Duncan lying down. Purring loudly, the cat pushes rhythmically on her stomach with his paws, closing his gold eyes. She buries her tears in his soft head.

Her husband found Bob Marley, a mewing kitten crawling with fleas, when they were first dating. In fact, the cat was often the excuse for stopping by his place—just to check on him—though once they got there they quickly ignored the cat. Later, the fat little kitten joined them on the bed, rubbing his soft body on their naked skin. One day while Matthew was at work, Bob got loose. Matthew called Rebecca when he got home. Driving to his house she actually got tears in her eyes. They walked up and down the street calling—Bob-Bob-Bob-Bobby!—but he didn't come. They suspected the neighbor's dog, an ugly mastiff whose owner was always gone. They often saw him peering through the fence, growling, as if he were waiting for fate to deliver the black morsel on the windowsill. They stood by the fence while the dog barked relentlessly at them, looking for tufts of black fur or little white bones. Finally they went inside for dinner. While they were eating they heard a tiny scratching on the screen. When Matthew opened the door, Bob wound in, rubbing himself on their legs and the door frame. Now he is a twenty-pound tom, fixed, killer of mama cardinals and doves, and still walking in the winding, rhythmic way that had made Matthew name him after the greatest reggae star that ever lived, who died much too young. Just when Rebecca has forgotten all of this and is lying in her mind someplace deep among the repeating pattern of flowers on the couch, lost inside the soothing vibration of the cat's purr, the baby wakes crying. She sits up and the cat leaps onto the floor and licks his back. Everything begins again.

The next morning, on the way to the grocery store, the traffic slows to a stop. Duncan launches into Doom-7, threatening to go higher. Rebecca's shoulders hunch, her breath catches. She is a mother lion with a squalling cub in the back. She wants to scream, *Outta my way!* and ram through like she is driving one of those Big Trucks that has tires taller than she and can crush everything in its path. She takes a deep breath and begins the Duncan song. "Duncan, Duncan, you're a punkin . . ." it starts, to the tune of "Twinkle, Twinkle, Little Star." Duncan keeps right on screaming, cranking up to Doom-10 as they crawl forward. Just when she thinks they should just turn back, her lane finally starts moving. Eventually they reach the cause of the stalled traffic, an overturned white Explorer surrounded by vehicles with flashing lights. She averts her eyes so that whatever bad luck has fallen there will not land on her and her compact car and bawling baby.

Inside the store Duncan, lying on a blanket in the red plastic seat attached to the cart, is Mr. Giggly. As Rebecca pushes past the foil, mayonnaise, toilet paper, and lettuce, he bubbles with laughter. She fake-laughs back. She talks to him in the silly way she once reserved for Bob Marley, except that she doesn't feel self-conscious talking to the baby in public the way she has with the cat at the vet.

Is grocery shopping so funny? Is Hellman's mayonnaise so funny? Rebecca teases, pleasing Duncan deeply.

On weekdays, it is mostly old ladies shopping. The store is near a large apartment complex that provides subsidized housing for the elderly. It's also close to the blind school and a complex for variously impaired people. When they bought the house and moved to this more affordable part of town, they were amazed to see all sorts of people here shopping for groceries. A store employee described all the different kinds of cheese to a blind woman. A deaf couple apparently discussed brands of coffee. Slow, wide-eyed, smiling men and women who once were called retarded carefully added items to their shared cart, a twenty-something girl with long hair reminding them of the next thing on the list. But today the store is filled with old ladies. They overdress in out-of-style winter coats and knit hats or underdress in house slippers and knee-high hose. They are either friendly and interested or secretive and suspicious. The latter reminds Rebecca of her own grandmother who died before she and Matthew got married. When she helped her mother clean out her grandmother's house, they'd found years' worth of green rubber bands from the morning newspaper carefully saved in pickle jars and her good silver hidden in an old heating-pad cover deep in her linen closet.

What a *good* baby! a woman wearing a red scarf and red shoes and red handbag remarks now. She stops her cart and talks to the baby, telling him how good he is and then telling him about her son who had also been a good baby but was now all grown up.

He's not always this good, Rebecca interjects, realizing suddenly that she's already tired and it's only 9:30. He likes the store, she adds to try to sound more upbeat.

You like all the colors and lights and people, don't you, the woman tells Duncan.

Her shiny blue eyes hint of a younger woman's beauty. She holds out a stiff finger and Duncan squirms and tries to reach for it.

My son finally grew up to be an accountant, she continues to Duncan, her tone suggesting that it was an amazing occupation for a baby to aspire to.

Does he live here? Rebecca asks, warmed by the woman's patient attention.

No, he lives in California, she answers. But he visits often.

That must be nice.

Well, my husband has been sick a lot lately—actually, he's dying.

I'm so sorry, Rebecca offers, touching the woman's sleeve. She actually feels tears rise within her but she looks away and they are gone.

He's at home now, she says without sadness. My son's with him, but I should be going.

You take care, Rebecca says.

I wish I lived next door, the woman remarks, smiling and touching Rebecca's hand. It is a foolish, remarkable thing to say to a stranger in the pasta aisle. But Rebecca knows just what she means.

I wish you did, too.

Bye-bye! the woman says to Duncan, stroking his cheek. Bye-

bye! she waves to him. Then she repositions her handbag and pushes her cart past.

But bad luck does find them. When they pull into the driveway Rebecca is preoccupied. Now that Duncan is three months old and supposedly sleeping more and nursing less, she has been thinking it's time to take on some design jobs, building her own business at home. Matthew says to take it easy, but she's always worked, and it's not as if they can afford to live on a teacher's salary for very long. Right now things are slim, one meal out a week, not fancy, buying things for Duncan used when they can, buying nothing for themselves, putting off things like a new screen door and certainly a decent car. So when an old client she worked with at the firm called and needed a quick invitation for its annual gala fund-raiser, she agreed. Her desk is covered with papers from when Duncan was first born and they had to write down when he urinated and his bowels moved, and with borrowed baby books, half-written thank-you notes, and stacks of photographs. So when she pulls into the driveway, the trunk full of plastic bags, a huge package of size-small diapers, and a giant box of unscented laundry soap, Duncan peacefully asleep with his lips full and wet as if ready for a deep kiss, in her mind she is actually already at her desk, sorting piles, pushing the power button, retrieving the invitation text from an anticipated email, and selecting a kind of paper that will look lush but is actually affordable. She is not watching out for them.

When she puts the car in park she realizes that just before that she felt a slight speed-bump sensation as she accelerated up the driveway. A dark blur sweeps past the corner of her eye like a lost eyelash. She turns off the engine and gets out of the car, piecing together the possibly imagined event, following the cat's path around the house and into the backyard. She expects to turn the corner and see the cat lying open, red blood spilled across black fur. For a moment the world falls away—the baby, the car, the house, the partially designed invitation in her head, Matthew in his classroom just down the street leading the band in a jazz number they are preparing for the spring concert. When the cat sees her, he streaks across the yard into the bushes. Okay, she steadies herself. Everything's okay. And she goes back to get the baby in his car seat. She'll come back for the other things.

She tells Matthew when he gets home. Duncan is swinging back and forth by the kitchen table, pawing at a terry-cloth lion.

I'm not positive I hit him, she explains.

Well, did you feel something? Matthew asks.

I don't know. He just dashed across. Like he was chasing something.

Well, I'll take a look. He's probably okay. He's a tough guy.

At eight-thirty that night she finally turns on the computer. Matthew is petting the cat in the bedroom. The start-up hum reminds Rebecca of her old job: wearing short black skirts with loud, flowing blouses; the wonderful silence when everyone was working on deadline; the after-work get-togethers at the downtown brew pubs; her boss, an attractive woman with a daughter nearly Rebecca's age; attending the daughter's wedding with Matthew, themselves newly married, held at a mansion outside of town by a cornfield on a clear blue afternoon following a morning thunderstorm. By ten o'clock Rebecca's eyes hurt, but she's got the design, a simple layout with a font that is both witty and elegant. She chooses wine-red ink on a goldenrod stock with black flecks. She emails the client the design. When Matthew comes in, he's already naked for bed. She realizes she still has to do the envelope, but it's too late. Matthew is rubbing her shoulders and her eyes are closed. She reaches up to feel his stomach, his furry thighs.

How's Bob? she asks.

Well, I think he's very lucky, Matthew answers. They go in to look at the cat, sleeping on a towel Matthew folded up beneath a chair in a corner of their bedroom.

The next day when they get home from the post office, Duncan is Mr. Howler. Rebecca lifts the sweaty baby out of the car seat. On the couch she nurses him, house keys still in her hand. She has in mind a quickie to tide him over, but when she tries to pull him off, he screams. Still nursing, she manages to stand up from the couch holding the baby in one arm and walk into the kitchen, something she'd seen a friend with a baby a few months older do. Nursing had been so hard and painful at first that she never imagined that she'd be standing up doing it, too. She remembers her purse outside in the unlocked car and the stack of sample books she'd picked up at the paper store, but she can't go outside with her tit hanging out even though she is the only person on the street during the day. Often she walked out front with the baby and just stared up and down the street, looking for movement. The meter reader, a young Latino in blue shorts and T-shirt, and the mail carrier who drove up with a cigarette hanging in his mouth, were the only ones she saw. Sometimes the across-the-street neighbor pulled in for a quick lunch or to drop off their teenage daughter. When they saw each other they waved, but she'd never been inside their house nor they in hers. This moment, besides needing to get the things from the car, Rebecca realizes she is hungry, thirsty, and needs to pee. She manages to pour a glass of water and drink, but when she tries to get her pants down she accidentally pulls the baby off her nipple and he protests loudly. A quick decision, she places him in his bouncy seat and dashes to the fridge, grabs some cheese, and runs to the bathroom. She bites from the orange slab, leaving an arch of teeth marks, while she sits on the toilet, the baby wailing in the kitchen.

After Duncan falls asleep nursing, Rebecca runs outside and brings in her things. She makes lunch for herself and then lies down with the baby on the bed. He sleeps with them. The crib is attached to her side of the bed, and sometimes they move him over to it when they are feeling crowded, but whenever he wakes crying she pulls him back to nurse. Once, when they first brought him home, Rebecca woke to Matthew pulling the sleeping baby out from between their pillows. It was frightening to imagine that even when they were sleeping they would need to watch out for him.

Just as she is dozing off, the baby wakes and she lifts her shirt. He gloms onto her breast without even opening his eyes. Duncan's sucking joins them together in a way that reminds her of sex, body parts made for each other, finding each other, giving to each other. What does Duncan give her? Supposedly his sucking releases peaceful hormones inside her. She imagines them now, coursing from inside her nipples down her body and rippling in circles between her legs. Rebecca remembers that in the afternoon she has her three-month checkup with the midwife. She glances at the clock, notes when they need to get up, and shuts her eyes. Duncan's cooing wakes her thirty minutes later. He is lying on his back beside her, smiling at the ceiling and jerking his feet and hands. She scoops him closer and he smiles like she is Miss Universe and he is fourteen and they're in bed together.

Natalie, the midwife, works in a practice with several women doctors. Rebecca didn't see the doctor her whole pregnancy because everything went so smoothly. Natalie had let Matthew record the heartbeat on his digital recorder; she had traced Rebecca's belly with her hands, showing them how to feel Duncan's body folded inside; she had made suggestions like bringing lavender and rosemary oils to the hospital to relax and invigorate and having ginger ale and orange juice on hand after the birth to drink for quick energy. When the labor pains finally started, it was the last of Rebecca's perfect pregnancy. After twenty-four hours she still wasn't dilated, so Natalie said she'd have to do drugs. Finally, Duncan was born while one of the doctors stood by with forceps. Rebecca didn't get to see him at first, even though he was in the same room, because they had to clear his lungs.

Let me see him, Rebecca demanded, because her body was screaming for him the way it sometimes did for chocolate or sleep or Matthew—but a hundred times stronger. Can I see him? Is he all right?

He's beautiful, honey, Matthew said, standing between her and the group of strangers surrounding the baby.

They'll bring him in just a minute, Natalie said. The cord was wrapped around his neck, she explained, and it looks like he breathed in a little meconium. But he looks great.

Finally the nurse brought him, wearing a cheap blue cap. Rebecca took him partway under the blanket with her, both of them crying, while Matthew looked over her shoulder, crying, and Natalie stood at the foot of the bed smiling.

He's still a cutie, Natalie says now, taking Duncan wrapped in a blanket into her arms. How are *you* doing? she asks. Natalie is tall with graying, curly hair. She always wears dresses in bright colors like purple or aqua, not medical clothes. Around her neck she wears a gold cross with a purple stone in the center.

All right, Rebecca says, sitting on the examining table. Except I ran over the cat yesterday!

Is it okay? she asks.

Rebecca nods and shrugs at the same time.

Go ahead and lie down, Natalie commands. When Rebecca is settled, she takes the baby onto her chest and the midwife begins the exam.

All right, Natalie says just a moment later. Everything looks fine.

She picks up her chart and makes some notes.

How are your breasts? Natalie asks. Any soreness? Any changes?

Rebecca is smiling at Duncan, who is lifting his head up and grinning at her. Even though she was looking forward to seeing Natalie again, she finds it hard to keep shifting her focus from the baby to someone else.

Um, my left breast is sometimes sore, Rebecca answers vaguely. And it's kind of lumpy.

Let me see, Natalie replies. It's probably a clogged duct. We can massage it and that way it won't get infected.

Natalie rubs her hands together to warm them while Rebecca lifts her shirt and unsnaps her nursing bra. Duncan starts for the nipple and the women both laugh. Rebecca unsnaps the other side and Duncan latches on, sucking as if her nipple were her face or her soul.

Yeah, I'm feeling something, Natalie says.

Rebecca feels her fingertips softly massaging.

That hurt? Natalie asks, pushing harder.

Yeah.

I'd like Dr. O'Donnell to take a look, Natalie says. Do you mind?

Dr. O'Donnell was the one who brought the forceps into the delivery room.

Five more minutes, she had said then, laying the giant metal tongs on the sterile table with a clunk. That usually does the trick, she joked.

Now when Dr. O'Donnell comes in she goes quickly to the sink to wash her hands, while Natalie tells her about Rebecca. This time, when Rebecca uncovers herself no one laughs. The doctor examines her in the same gentle but quick way, the pads of her fingers working around Rebecca's breast. The feeling reminds her of Duncan's tiny, soft hands, patting her while he nurses.

Have you ever had a mammogram? the doctor asks. She is younger than Natalie and wears flippy skirts and linen blouses under her white coat. She has kids—Rebecca remembers seeing photos in her office once. Rebecca wonders how she does it—delivering babies at all hours, performing surgery, raising kids, and looking great all at once. Then she notices that her stylish wire-frame glasses are held together with tape and that makes Rebecca relax.

I've never had one, Rebecca says.

Well, this is probably nothing. I want you to use hot compresses—Natalie will show you what to do. But just to be on the safe side you should get a mammogram and a sonogram.

Natalie nods and writes in the chart.

Take care of that little guy, the doctor says as she heads to the door. I remember him. He's stubborn.

The cat is not all right. Bob Marley is sleeping more than usual. He isn't jumping or chasing or eating or going outside. Matthew takes him to the vet first thing Saturday morning and is gone a long time. Rebecca takes some of Duncan's newborn things that he's already outgrown to the consignment store. She saves the outfit covered with blue and yellow stars that he wore home from the hospital and the matching socks to remember how tiny he was. She goes into the store, which always smells like cigarette smoke even though she's never seen anyone smoking, wearing Duncan in the baby pack on her chest. He is facing outward with his arms and legs free. Rebecca thinks of it as wearing a very heavy spider around her neck. As long as she keeps moving, Duncan is happy. By walking back and forth past the shelves she finds a farmyard activity blanket. When you push on the cow, it moos. A real metal bell hangs by a red ribbon from the barn. A black-and-white cat is rendered in fuzzy fur. With the credit from Duncan's old clothes, the blanket, which looks brand-new, is only two dollars.

Where's the cat? Rebecca asks when they get home, handing the baby to Matthew so she can put down her things.

When Matthew holds Duncan it seems like the baby is only a cloud. He is so tiny compared with the six-foot-tall man who plays the shiny saxophone.

Still at the vet, Matthew answers, holding Duncan up so he can see himself in the bedroom mirror.

What'd they say?

Maybe internal injuries. They could do X rays but it costs a lot.

We can do it if you want, she says. I can take more jobs.

That's ridiculous. He was a little dehydrated so they're taking care of that and giving him some antibiotics. I'll pick him up later.

Okay, Rebecca says, hugging Matthew and Duncan. I hope he's all right. I'm really sorry.

We'll take care of him, Matthew reassures her. We'll see.

She plans to tell Matthew about the mammogram, but he is always busy with the cat. Matthew gives it an IV four times a day. He comes home at lunch to hang the clear plastic bag from the knob of the chair underneath which the cat lies all the time now. His black fur is already getting dull, but his gold eyes glisten and his purr can still be heard from across the room. Matthew expertly checks the clamp, unwraps a fresh needle, and attaches it to the IV tube. He lifts the fur on the black cat's shoulder and jabs the needle in without hesitating. The cat lies still while Matthew strokes his head and throat and the liquid slides down the clear tube.

You're so good at that, Rebecca observes.

I wanted to be a doctor when I was a kid, Matthew muses.

What made you stop?

Someone gave me a saxophone, Matthew jokes. And then there were my grades . . .

She has never kept a secret from Matthew before, but since she ran over the cat she can't come back with another problem yet. It's Matthew's turn. Plus the doctor said it was nothing to worry about. So when the day of the appointment comes, she calls the one person she knows who could watch the baby during the day.

Candice is a recovered alcoholic, twice divorced, once generously widowed psychotherapist whose kids are grown but haven't made her a grandma yet. She travels to San Francisco and New York to see plays and art exhibits. She works out with a trainer and frosts her hair. She buys her clothes at discount places and is always wearing a large pendant or clunky bracelets. Rebecca imagines she's a good therapist because when you talk she really listens. She even anticipates what you're going to say if you're having trouble saying it. She offers to watch the baby before Rebecca even asks. She says she is flattered to take care of him. Rebecca leaves a bottle of milk, though Duncan usually refuses it, and shows Candice how to rock the bouncy chair if Duncan wakes. She explains that going outside usually makes him stop crying. She shows her the diapers and tells her which way they go on. She leaves Candice rocking Duncan's bouncy chair with her manicured toe while reading a mystery she pulls out of her see-through bag.

Driving away from the house, Rebecca feels light, suddenly like her old self. She could pull into the parking garage downtown and walk into her old office and people would barely look up because, after all, she works there. Instead, of course, she drives to the new building by the hospital, past a statue of a giant woman holding a baby up into the sky next to a pounding fountain of water.

Everything is pink at the Women's Center. The carpet, the jacket of the retired volunteer who shows her to the inner waiting room, and the mats around the Mary Cassatt posters. The magazines are ones Rebecca would actually like to read—*Ms., Yoga Journal, Mother Jones*—and there is fresh-brewed hazelnut coffee. The volunteer opens a little fridge to reveal orange juice and half-and-half. But she hardly gets settled before the volunteer comes back to show her to the mammogram room. The technician, also in a pink coat, introduces herself and carefully explains what's going to happen. So that they can get a good picture, they asked Rebecca to make sure her breasts were empty. Even so, when the technician asks Rebecca to step up close to the hard machine and hold her arm like this, pressing her breast so hard against the metal that it feels like it's stuck in the proverbial wringer, a bit of milk seeps out. The technician wipes it away with a Kleenex before moving to the next shot. Rebecca notices a poem taped to the mirror, written from the point of view of the mammogram technician, apologizing for the necessary pain she must inflict to ensure your health.

The sonogram room has recessed lighting that the nurse dims before she begins. Of course, lying there next to the TV screen of a grainy gray mass that now is her breast, but could be her uterus for all she can tell, she remembers when they learned that the baby inside her was a boy. They hadn't tried to find out, but his penis was obvious even to them. Before she realized it, Rebecca was sobbing.

Boys don't *need* mothers, she said to Matthew. Not like girls.

No, boys need mothers *more,* Matthew said. Suddenly she remembered how fondly he recalled his own mother, who'd died of breast cancer when he was in college. The special egg-salad sandwiches she made him, the detailed Halloween costumes and dress-up clothes. He had wanted to marry her when he was five. His earliest sexual fantasies were about women who looked like her. Rebecca realized proudly that she would be that woman to their baby.

The nurse now asks her to lie on her side, applies a cold gel to her breast, and rolls the sonogram device under her arm and all over her breast, stopping to take still photos now and then.

Okay, she says. We're all done.

She hands Rebecca a pink hand towel to wipe off the jelly.

That was quick.

Your doctor should have results by tomorrow afternoon, the nurse says.

As she traces her way back through the maze of pink-carpeted hallways, Rebecca passes a woman with very short hair, wrapped in a pink blanket, sitting in a wheel chair. She is smiling at the nurse who is joking with her and pushing the footrests down so she can stand up.

She is going to tell Matthew. But she doesn't want to scare him. Whatever is happening with her, he will confuse it with his mother. That was nearly twenty years ago. Plus, there is no cancer in her family. Everyone lives until they're at least eighty.

The next day the cat seems worse. He's moved under the bed where he lies on the wood floor in the most inaccessible spot, beneath their heads. He is panting like a dog. The furniture seems darker and heavier with his breathing. Rebecca calls Matthew at work and says she thinks they should meet at the vet's at lunch to put him to sleep.

He's suffering, Matt, she pleads.

Okay, he says with resignation. Are you okay?

Yeah, but we should have done this days ago.

See you in a couple of hours.

She calls the vet and makes an appointment to euthanize the cat. But when she gets off the phone and checks again, the cat seems even worse. The animal no longer seems like Bob Marley or anyone she's ever known. A bad odor hangs in the room, not anything familiar, but she knows it is death. Her heart is racing. The cat will not make it two more hours. She must get to the vet now. Duncan has been patient on her hip all this time through the phone calls and the dipping down to look under the bed, but now he wants some attention. She is talking to him evenly and constantly.

Kitty is sick, kitty is sick. We're going to take the kitty to the doctor and say bye-bye.

She is also talking to herself.

Okay, now we are looking for the cat carrier. What did Matt do with it?

She spies the flat box she'd once gotten from the airlines under the bed in the study and kneels down to drag it out.

Duncan starts to cry, a dismal Doom-3, his forehead wrinkling, his mouth twisted up, his disappointment growing.

So Rebecca sings the first thing that comes to her mind.

Everything's gonna be all right. Everything's gonna be all right. Everything's gonna be all right. No, woman, no cry. No, woman, no cry.

The baby is blasting now so she sits down to nurse him. She looks up to see, amazingly, Bob Marley standing before her. He is staggering, swollen, a ghost of himself. He is making a raspy sound. He is slowly moving toward them. His eyes are blank. He looks completely strange, like something you would call someone to come get rid of.

Bob? she says in a high, sweet voice. It's okay, boy.

She looks down at Duncan to see if he's worried or scared, but he is happily staring at the light in the window while he sucks.

The noise startles her. It is so loud and painful and deep. She never knew a cat could scream. Bob Marley has fallen down on the floor. He is lying on his side. He is not moving. She knows immediately that surrounded by their things—her paintings, Matthew's mother's china, stacks of CDs and rows of books, the TV, a picture from their wedding day of the two of them nearly in silhouette kissing beneath an archway—and the walls of their house, and the dangerous grids of streets reaching north, south, east, west, and the empty sky itself, Bob Marley has died.

She calls the vet and cancels the appointment. Then she calls Matthew, who is in class and will get the message that she called when he gets out. Unless it's an emergency.

Is it an emergency?

No, Rebecca answers quietly.

Is there a message? the secretary asks.

Just say it's me.

She sits on the couch. Duncan coos and she tries to play with him while she thinks. Glancing out the window, she notices the neighbor's car. Maybe the teenage daughter is home sick. Maybe she's not very sick and they could watch Duncan while Rebecca figures out what to do next. She cannot leave a dead cat in the middle of the living-room floor all day. She has to step around the cat to get to the front door. Outside it is getting warm, there is birdsong and traffic. It smells like burning asphalt from a roofing job down the street. Far away she can hear an ambulance.

She walks across the street, into the familiar view they see from the living room. She unlatches the gate, walks through, and latches it again. She walks up the steps and opens the screen door. She knocks on the dark brown door. While she waits she looks across at their house, pale green with cream trim and overgrown rosebushes that never bloom. It looks like a nice place to live. She decides they must look like nice people. Not the kind that drive over their cat and let it die in pain a week later in the middle of the living room.

Just when Rebecca's about to give up and go home to call Candice, someone unlocks the door. Rebecca realizes that though this is the front door, the neighbors usually use the side door by the garage. They probably didn't even hear her.

The mother is a pale blond, shorter than Rebecca, and younger than her even though her daughter is a teenager.

I'm so sorry to disturb you, Rebecca begins.

No problem, the woman replies. The baby's gotten so big already! she adds.

They remind each other of their names and the woman, Martha, invites Rebecca in. The daughter, Amy, is sitting on the couch watching TV. She has her mother's blond hair and pale skin. They could be sisters, except the daughter wears much more makeup and shorter shorts.

He's so cute, she remarks in a high voice, and turns back to the TV.

The house is comfortable but dark. It smells like food, but Rebecca can't tell what it is. The phone rings and Amy runs to answer it.

Is she a junior or senior now? Rebecca asks. She goes to Matthew's school but he doesn't know her since she's not in the band.

Well, she was a senior, but she just got her GED because she wants to get a job. She's pregnant.

Rebecca is picturing the dead cat on her floor, so she's not sure she's heard right. Martha is smiling.

It's not what we had planned, but we're going to help her, she continues. She's due in June.

Well, congratulations! Rebecca says.

Amy bounces back in and now Rebecca can see that above her short shorts and long legs she is wearing an oversize T-shirt.

I just took some things to the consignment store, Rebecca says to the girl. But pretty soon I'll have some more. Would you like them? Amy vaguely nods, glancing at the TV. And Martha says that'd be really nice.

Finally, Rebecca gets to asking them if they can watch Duncan for fifteen minutes.

I have a very important phone call to make, Rebecca explains. It will just take a few minutes but I can't have the baby crying and there's no telling when he'll go to sleep.

Oh, I'd love to, Martha says. I took Amy to the doctor this morning and decided to take the afternoon off.

Amy scoots over by her mother on the couch and they both coo at Duncan. He thrills them with his smile. Rebecca always cringes when people interpret Duncan's moods and actions as if they were an adult's, but he really does look like he is flirting with these two blonds.

The cat's black fur is still warm, either from the sunlight falling from the window or from the life that was inside it for five years.

Kneeling, Rebecca sees that despite the complete stillness of this object, it really is Bob Marley. The cat's eyes are closed. There is nothing ugly or unbecoming in the cat's body now: his lush black whiskers, his pointy chin, the fine hairs that grow into fringe on the tips of his ears, his long tail draped in a curve below his feet, thick at the base and tapering into a paint brush. Once she had to give the cat a bath—he had a terrible case of fleas and she couldn't wait until Matthew got home. Bob Marley was still a kitten, but he was already big. She filled the kitchen sink at Matthew's house half-full with lukewarm water and got a beach towel and the flea shampoo. Bathing a baby was much easier than bathing a cat. Bob Marley had scratched her arms and even left a red line on her cheek, but when she finally lathered him, rinsed him, and pulled him out of the water by the scruff of his matted neck, his body was reduced to the size of a large rodent's, tail tucked between shivering legs.

Just as the cat had seemed to shrink then, now it seems to have spread like some gelatinous puddle from outer space. With her eyes closed, she wedges her hand beneath the cat's body against the wood floor. She doesn't have to try to lift the weight to know that it's too heavy and loose-feeling, like a large sack of shifting flour, to lift straight up and into the carrier. She will need to put her body into it. She stands, steps away. The radio is on softly, she realizes. She'd put it on after breakfast. They're playing a love song, something new and kind of jazzy, something you could slow-dance to. She glances at the neighbor's house. It's not on fire. It's just sitting there with the sun shining on it. The neighbor named Martha planted some calla lilies last year and the green leaves along the fence look good. They lined the new flower bed with limestone and that looks good, too.

A towel. She should put a towel in the carrier first so that when Matthew lifts the body out to bury it it will be easy. Rebecca remembers the roses that she splurged on at the store, and without hesitating pulls them from the vase on the kitchen table and lays them on the floor next to the carrier. The deep red petals will look beautiful against the cat's black fur. She chooses an old towel, a pink one that came with Matthew. It probably came from some old girlfriend. Maybe the one that lived next door to him and practiced the cello in the nude by the window. Good riddance.

Rebecca opens the carrier so it lies in two halves like a flat box and lid and drapes the towel across the bottom. She counts to five, just the way she does before she jumps into the spring-fed swimming pool they go to in the summer. The water is so cold, it is only by counting that she fools herself into getting in. Once you are in, you get used to it.

One, two, three, four . . . Rebecca takes a deep breath, holds it, and exhales. Five. In one swift movement she inserts her forearms beneath the cat, bows her body around it, and lifts its heavy weight up. She pivots on her knees and then she quickly places the burden on top of the towel. The cat seems to nestle into the box, the body still soft enough to adjust to the shape around it. Rebecca lays the roses across the cat so that the blooms frame his face. Then she drapes the ends of the towel, covering everything. She shifts jars and containers from the lowest shelf of the fridge, throwing a few things out, and finally there is room to slide the carrier in.

Just then, the phone rings. Rebecca quickly washes her hands and runs to answer it. She expects it to be Matthew, having finally gotten her message, but it is a woman's voice instead. Is something wrong with Duncan?—she'd given Martha the number.

Rebecca?

It is Natalie.

Dr. O'Donnell got the radiologist's report today, she says. It looks like there are some cells in your breast. They are precancerous.

Oh, Rebecca says, as if she understands what this means.

We would like you to see a breast surgeon for a biopsy. We recommend seeing Dr. Patrice White this week, if possible. Do you think you can do that?

This week? Sure.

Rebecca takes down the number.

We caught this very early, Natalie notes.

Uh-huh.

Are you okay? Do you want me to call Matthew?

No. I'm fine. I'll call him.

Okay. Keep in touch, Natalie says. I want to know what happens.

I will, Rebecca says, and hangs up the phone.

For just a moment she imagines hopping in the car and speeding down the street to Matthew's school, parking in the drop-off circle, pulling open the heavy blue doors, walking past the security sign-in, right down the checkered hall, to where the music is coming from. The classroom is built with risers in the floor so the back row, the drums, is higher. In the front are the girls, always girls, playing silver flutes, and in the middle, on the end, are the saxophones, droning, humming, screaming out the melody. Up front, against the dusty chalk board, the love of her life is waving his arms up and down, keeping everything together.

Instead, she walks across the empty street, past the lilies that she notices are just starting to unfurl their white blooms, through the gate, and up the driveway. She knocks on the door by the neighbor's garage, the door they always use, and waits to take back the part of herself that's missing.

Ann Beattie

Solitude

In 1981, my grandmother died. She was born in 1901 and lived to see the world become a very different place. At different times, she had believed in Herbert Hoover, General Patton, Art Linkletter, Art Buchwald, John Kennedy, Robert Frost, and Myron Floren. She never believed in Lawrence Welk, but she thought Myron Floren, with his accordion, was an underappreciated musical genius. She voted for Coolidge and for Humphrey. She opposed the war in Vietnam. She saw the Beatles and Ed Sullivan and thought it was much ado about nothing: just some limeys who needed a haircut, and probably a bath. Years later, when John Lennon was killed, she went immediately to church, though she was not a religious woman. All her life, she had been amazed that she had lived through her teens, so she was very sensitive to premature deaths. When she was seventeen, Grandma had gone to visit a friend in the hospital—a friend of a friend, actually, a boy who had grown up in an orphanage—and she had kissed his cheek before leaving, and later she learned that the boy had had the flu. The flu of 1918. He had had it, and she had kissed his cheek, then crossed the park with her friend, who later that month would become her fiancé. The next morning, after a night of high fever, the boy they had visited was gone. Apparently, the boy had looked very much like the boy who later became my grandfather, and it had made her wonder how it was that you came to love one person instead of another. They had the same cheekbones, she said. The same deeply hooded blue eyes.

When my grandmother died—unexpectedly, getting up to change the channel on TV—my mother was visiting her, in the parlor of Grandma's house on Rittenhouse Square. She had inherited this house, not from her husband, but from her husband's only son, her stepson Neil, who had died of an aneurysm soon after his fortieth birthday. Neil had never married. He left two horses in Kentucky to a friend from college. He left his collection of old Vuitton luggage to a former professor of Romance languages at the University of Pennsylvania. He left his house to Grandma. The week of her seventy-sixth birthday, Grandma was moving in, relocating from an apartment outside of Washington, D.C., in Crystal City.

Grandma's good friend Kitty May, who had been a hostess with her at the USO during World War II, had for years lived in the suburbs of Philadelphia. They loved to talk about the good/bad days in Washington when they had danced and sung for the boys. Together, they could still sing Billie Holiday songs in perfect harmony. They sounded hauntingly like Billie Holiday—or at least as she would have sounded if she'd been heard initially in stereo, singing slightly stepped-up versions of her songs. It didn't surprise my mother or me that Grandma would move to Philadelphia, but it surprised us entirely that she and Kitty May, reunited at long last, would get together, rehearse the songs they'd loved, and begin appearing at the Chester Hill Hotel cocktail lounge on Friday nights.

They were a sensation. I don't mean they were covered by the *New York Times,* but they were written up by the *Philadelphia Inquirer* and profiled in *Philadelphia* magazine. "Still crazy after all these years? I don't think so," one talk-show host said, and ended his program by broadcasting the two of them singing the triumphant ending to "He's My Man."

I listened to a tape of this program while recovering from a cesarean at Arlington Hospital. I had piles of work from the office and nothing else in the room except a clown made out of bronze mums from my coworkers, so I was delighted when my mother visited and brought me a tape player and the tape Grandma had sent of herself and Kitty May performing and being interviewed. I played some of it for my old college roommate, who brought me a bunch of foreign magazines that showed Japanese women smiling under umbrellas of real daisies, and scantily clad Scandinavian women pretending to be biting snakes. My husband, who had begged me to abort and who was immediately chastened once he had held the baby and fallen in love with her, came every evening after work and nervously monologued about the responsibilities of fatherhood in a manner that had become familiar to many people when Spalding Gray took it up. I was always exhausted when he left. My heart went out to him, but my incision itched and I was bleeding and it was clear I was never going to succeed at nursing my child. My mother had someone from La Leche call, but the woman had hiccoughs, and she traumatized more than helped me. Grandma called and told me to forget about breast-feeding and just give the baby a bottle. She also said my mother was driving her crazy because of her anxiety that the baby was three days old and still unnamed. This was before Rafe and I decided to call her Henrietta. What relative could take offense that the child was not named after her when we had decided on such an odd, specific name?

I could digress forever, as my mother often says. I could digress and tell you everything about everyone: the nurses; the doctors; the photos in their wallets; the gossip; how everyone's medical condition resolved itself, to the best of my knowledge. But this story isn't about me, or about those things: it's about Grandma—Frances Daphne Prendergass.

After she moved into Neil's house, and when she was already something of a singing sensation, she decided to rent a room to a young man who worked at an art gallery. At night, he waited tables at the Chester Hill Hotel. The man's name was Drew Soldener. He was tall and handsome—which I was amused to see disturbed my mother—and he had a way of charming people with his childish enthusiasm. "He's just glad to be able to make a living, and to look at some art, and to hear some music, besides," Grandma said, and instantly I realized the sort of bond she felt with Drew. What were we to say? The house was too big for her to keep up alone, crime was increasing, and nothing suggested Drew Soldener was an opportunist. In fact, he learned to drive and took her once a week to buy groceries, which he often cooked and always cleaned up. He was someone to drive her to work on Friday nights—someone she could turn to, as, of course, she did when rain leaked through the roof or when she discovered mice in the basement.

In 1980, when President Carter attempted the failed rescue mission in the Iranian desert, I got a call from Drew. He felt someone in the family should know that Grandma seemed to be losing her sense of balance. Though she had sworn him to secrecy, he had decided to break his word: in the last few days, she had fallen, stumbled, and complained of morning dizziness. Amid reports of burning helicopters, I fled the office and boarded Amtrak to Philadelphia. I had thought about calling my mother and taking her along on the trip, but had dismissed the idea almost immediately. My mother didn't like bad news and sometimes responded by becoming more of a problem than the person or situation you were worried about. She had the habit of listening to you only up to a point, then rushing to get her photo album so she could locate a picture of whatever person was sad, or ill, or acting badly, and pressing the page against her chest as if it were a heating blanket that would soothe *her.* Since his death years before, she had also slept with my father's framed picture underneath her pillow. Her devotion to him sometimes made me wonder if I was coldhearted. I loved my husband, but not only did I have no portrait of him, I had even vetoed, as too silly, a family-photo Christmas card. As the train clattered down the tracks, I thought of doing things differently: of being less autonomous; of commissioning an oil portrait of Rafe; at the very least, of taking the four pictures-in-a-strip from the photomaton we had mugged in on our first date off the refrigerator, where they had yellowed and faded, and framing them. By the time the train neared Philadelphia,

I had become truly sentimental: the way he tied his socks together so they looked like dozens of herringbone-patterned bows dropped into the laundry hamper; the heart he had outlined on the bathroom mirror with toothpaste last Valentine's Day. My Rafe was a kind, intelligent, sometimes perplexed man, who had married a woman who took washcloths to his finest sentiments. Although, on the other hand, there were times when I had taken charge and he had said that he would be forever grateful: the time I flushed the entire contents of the snail-infested, forever-burbling aquarium down the toilet; the time I got a job to prove that I would support us if he confronted his boss about the boss's drug dependency and ended up getting fired for his concern. The bottom line was that I thought Rafe and I were doing fine together. And—probably like my mother and like her mother—I never envisioned my time with him coming to an end. It seemed that as long as there was toothpaste, and he could squeeze it, that we would do fine without portraits, though I did think about preserving the picture strip.

At Thirtieth Street station, I got off and took a cab to Grandma's house, still unsure of what I'd say. I didn't want to get Drew in trouble unless it was absolutely necessary. I hoped, I guess, to notice something—*something*—that would give me an excuse to call the doctor. Everybody was crazy that day: the radio announcers; the patriotic cabdriver who saluted me when I got out; Rafe, whom I called from the train station. "You're in another city?" he kept saying. "Couldn't you have called me before you went to another city?"

If you drop in on people, you can usually expect a surprise. My surprise was that Kitty May answered the door and that Grandma was wearing an evening gown—she said it helped her get serious about singing—and silver mules. Kitty May had on a wig the color of alabaster that hung two feet down her back. Grandma's hair was in rollers. Rhinestone earrings dangled beneath the small pincurls above her ears. What was I supposed to say? *I understand you've been stumbling around lately?*

That afternoon, the two of them were rehearsing songs by

Blondie. They weren't forgoing Billie Holiday, but they wanted to keep up with the times, they said. I asked if they'd heard the shocking news about the aborted attempt to get the hostages released.

"It's not leadership we get now, it's madness," Kitty May said disdainfully.

Grandma shook her head: she'd heard, I decided, but had nothing to say. As I stood there at a loss—yes, why *had* I come?—Kitty May went into the kitchen to make tea. Grandma sat on the chair she always called Neil's throne: a Moroccan chair with mother-of-pearl inlay, padded with red velvet. She looked small and, of course, peculiar, though I had long ago stopped thinking of her as a little old lady wearing a housedress in her Crystal City apartment.

"I . . . sit in my chaaaaaair," Grandma sang, as Kitty May came into the room, carrying a tray with a teapot and cups and saucers.

"Fiiiiiilllllled with despair . . . ," Kitty May sang.

Then they both cracked up. They did sound remarkably like Billie Holiday.

"Oh, how I wish I'd had the pleasure to meet Lady Day," Kitty May said. "But once I started listening, I bought every record. Of course, I have Gorgeous George to thank for that."

"Who?" I said.

"You show your age," Grandma said. "Gorgeous George, the famous wrestler. He couldn't sing like Billie Holiday; he sang falsetto. But he knew all her songs, and he'd sing them to us while Kitty May fixed his hair, just to make us laugh."

"His hair?"

"'My locks, my tresses, pretty as dresses,'" Kitty May said. "He always mocked everything."

"Let us not speak ill of the dead," Grandma said. "Let us be proper old ladies. As I might have been. As I would have been if I hadn't had the good fortune to have a stepson as lovely as Neil, who left me his beautiful house and brought me back into the company of my dearest friend."

"Sentiment!" Kitty May said. "I take a tip from the Andrews Sisters: too much closeness breeds contempt."

"Grandma," I said, "you look a little pale. Don't you think so, Kitty May? You look pale, Grandma. Mother and I are worried about you."

Grandma and Kitty May looked at me, puzzled. They looked at me the way people probably looked at them when they started a set, before they were persuaded.

"Your mother has never had a day without worry in her life. I don't know how I raised such a girl. My only consolation is that one person alone cannot entirely shape another person's character. Your mother has never recovered from her father's death or from your father's heart attack. From the day your father died, she has never again looked forward. Tell me the name of one person who has ever done well without looking forward. And when she does seem to be looking to the future, she makes up the silliest scenarios or she assumes the worst because she's guessing in the dark. She's timid, I'm sorry to say. Imagine such a daughter being born to two adventurous people. She had nightmares about her father's death years before he even took up hiking."

My mother's father had died when he was forty-two, in an avalanche, skiing.

"What would she have wanted? Would she rather he'd died sitting in a golf cart, or with his feet up, watching TV?" Grandma said.

"It's too sad to think about," Kitty May said. "He was a wonderful, funny, noble man, always full of ideas."

"And truth is, fate, and fate alone, took him from us, though if it hadn't been for fate, I might never have married him but married his good friend, instead," Grandma said.

Kitty May peeked in the teapot, then put the top back on and served me, pouring carefully. "She would not have," Kitty May muttered. Then, as Grandma poured her own cup, Kitty May got up and pulled the front curtains closed, immediately turning on a table lamp.

As I watched them doing such ordinary things, I remembered the one time I'd seen them perform. Driving from Washington to Philadelphia with Rafe, it had started to snow. I'd brought Billie

Holiday tapes to play in the car as a sort of warm-up. We had listened to "Solitude" that night; it seemed exhilarating because her voice was so clear—as fragile and as soft as snow. It seemed to permeate the bushes and trees and fields beside the highway and to meld with the lights as we neared the city of Philadelphia. *They were good,* as I later reported to my mother from our hotel room: they were very convincing. Soon after they'd begun, people weren't staring at them, they began staring through them, to the past. It was as though they were hearing a shadow, touching a song. All the while, outside the tall windows of the hotel, snow flicked wetly against the windowpanes, reinforcing the idea that their voices were so transparent they must be true. Outside, everything was filtered through white.

Less than a year after the afternoon I sat drinking tea with Grandma and Kitty May in Philadelphia, Grandma was dead. Rafe stayed at home with the baby, because she'd had a fever the night before and was feeling miserable and cranky, and I drove to Philadelphia, thinking about the time I'd taken the train after receiving Drew Soldener's phone call, remembering how lost in thought I'd been, Grandma's dizziness having provoked a real loss of equilibrium in me so that, in my anxiety, I worried that I hadn't been nice enough to Rafe—wasn't that it?—and I had called him from the station, wanting to say something profound and romantic, but the minute I heard his voice, it was so reassuring, so absolutely normal, that I knew I'd fall apart if I began to tell him how much I loved him. I think I did say that I loved the orderly way he threw his dirty socks into the hamper, but he paid no attention to that because he was so surprised I'd left town without him. He often expressed consternation that the women in my family who were my role models (I found it endearing he thought of them that way) were either quiet and kept entirely to their routines (my mother) or did not consult with anyone about what he called "major decisions" (my grandmother). Maybe it was good that Grandma and I were so self-reliant, I had told him.

"Self-reliant!" he had said. He began to talk, again, of how astonishing it was that Grandma had sold the contents of her apartment and never mentioned it until the sale was over.

"Don't worry," I had said, shouting above the noise of the PA system in the train station, having suddenly figured out why he was so upset. "Don't worry, Rafe, I'm not ever going to leave you."

"But you just did," he had said, in the same hushed tones people once used when contemplating space travel. "You've gone to Philadelphia."

Later, in what I, at least, saw merely as an amusing moment, he was shocked, *deeply* shocked, that when I went into labor with Henrietta, I had picked up my bag and walked almost to the car before I realized I'd forgotten to tell him.

Now I was again in Philadelphia, and from the minute I parked and knocked on the door and threw myself into my mother's arms, I couldn't stop crying. Then, my pockets full of change, lint, wet Kleenex, and—damn!—Henrietta's favorite pacifier, we went to the funeral home and, the next day, to the service. After that, we drifted through her house, each of us silently wondering where to begin the task of boxing things or disposing of them. It was a relief when Drew Soldener appeared at the front window, peering in at the same time he knocked on the door. Of course he had the key, but he was being polite, knocking instead of just walking in. At the funeral, he had read a poem by Theodore Roethke called "My Papa's Waltz," which he had given no reason for reading, but which seemed, finally, appropriate. He had spoken fondly of Grandma. He had made no mention of Billie Holiday, no mention of Grandma's long life filled with so many changes, early and late. I wondered if his decision not to talk about Grandma as a singing sensation would have disappointed Kitty May. She had not been able to be there because, the month before, she had broken her hip.

For a while, Drew and I wandered through the house in silence. "Go through the ceramic ginger jars," he said. "That's where she hid important things." He raided the refrigerator. People would be coming to the house later that evening. We'd wanted to be alone for a while after the funeral, but it had also seemed important to ask Drew to join us. Until the last few months of her life, he'd lived in the house, trapping mice, combing out her hair, helping her balance her checkbook. He'd just gotten her to subscribe to *Entertainment Weekly,* he told us sorrowfully. He said it was going to be so sad, seeing the first issue drop through the mail slot. She had been about to subscribe to *Good Housekeeping,* and he had convinced her otherwise.

But he wouldn't be there to see it. Drew had moved to the suburbs, into the house of a friend, Leonard Jay. Leonard Jay was the same friend Neil had left his Vuitton luggage to. That past December, Leonard Jay had paid Grandma and Drew an unexpected Christmas call, and he and Drew had struck up a friendship. For a while, Drew told us, it had been the plan that Leonard Jay would spend one or two nights a week at the house, when he commuted into the city to teach night classes. But then, Drew said, shrugging, he had decided perhaps it was better to move himself. "It was too big a house even for me to keep up," he said. "I felt I'd taken on too huge a responsibility. I wouldn't have gone if she hadn't been so understanding. We both would have moved in if she'd really wanted that." He didn't sound as though he believed his own words. I nodded and agreed with him, though. My husband and mother and I had contributed very little; he had taken care of things for years.

As we walked through the house, talking quietly, my mother raised her eyebrows to me as Drew spoke of Leonard Jay; she kept trying to catch my eye, and I kept avoiding eye contact. Finally, she reached into her skirt pocket and took out a tissue to dab at her eyes. Then she turned and walked the other way when I followed Drew up the stairs. We looked into room after room, peeking in as though we couldn't be persuaded they were really empty. My mother could be so ridiculous: Why should she care if Drew got together with Neil's old boyfriend? It occurred to me that perhaps, if they had met years earlier, in the sixties, they might all have formed a commune, four eccentrics among many others: an old lady and her friend who sang

Billie Holiday songs in a hotel bar, and two men as adept at acknowledging the status quo when they had to be part of the workaday world as they were at changing into something comfortable—say, a kimono or an evening gown—in their off hours. Because that's what Drew, at least, had done: he'd begun to sing backup with Grandma and Kitty May during their practice sessions, dressed in one of their sparkling dresses, wishing himself on stage with them, but knowing he'd never dare do it. He explained this to me in a whisper as we toured the upstairs. Pushing back Grandma's closet door, he ran his hands over the padded shoulders, down the beaded rivulets of the bodices. "Forget getting into the shoes," he sighed.

As we neared the top of the steps, Drew cocked his head and said, almost in a whisper, "'Hold Tight.'" Though he had only been naming the song by the Andrews Sisters that had started to play, I gripped the banister as if I'd been given good advice.

Below us was my mother, who had just turned on the stereo, letting the last record on the stack fall into place on the turntable. We watched as the music started and she began to move, arms extended to embrace imaginary shoulders, dancing a deliberately improvisational, graceful waltz to a rather rousing song. The incongruousness of it jarred my memory instantly, so that suddenly I was standing at the top of another staircase—I must have been four, or five—watching my mother dance, in a way I now know she knew was seductive, with my father. He always dressed as Santa Claus late on the night before Christmas, in case I might awaken and tiptoe to the staircase to spy on them. It was amazing, I thought: all the women in my family who had lived most of their lives, through no choice of their own, with other women, without men. They had witnessed so many men dying prematurely—in wars, or with illnesses, or in natural disasters. And, though all those things might have happened in any time period, it occurred to me that their generations might have been the last to improvise by using the arts: playing a favorite song on the piano, reciting a poem, singing or dancing—all of which seemed preferable to endless talk and endless support groups as attempts to take tragedies in stride by pretending they were understandable.

And me? How was my life going to turn out, let alone the life of Henrietta? I'd never been able to carry a tune and had to concentrate hard to do a brief box-step with Rafe at someone's wedding reception. Maybe fate had been kind to me simply because I wasn't interesting enough. That night my mother had danced in Santa's arms, she had fed him a slice of orange or a cracked walnut, whatever I had left out earlier in the evening to be Santa's snack. I could remember her holding the food to his lips, which moved imperceptibly beneath the thick, white beard. It was so little time until he would die. She seemed to already know it was best to step lightly, to move close, not to end the dance.

The Writers

Dianne King Akers's stories have been published in *American Short Fiction* and *American Way.* She holds a BA in journalism from North Texas State University and an MA in education from the University of Texas at Austin. She has worked as a newspaper reporter, feature writer, editor, bookkeeper, social worker, nonprofit-program director, and (currently) grant writer. Akers lives in Austin, Texas, with her husband and son. She is working on the first draft of a semiserious, semicomic novel about middle age, sexuality, the war with Iraq, marriage, the current polarization of Democrats and Republicans, and the prevalence of obesity in America.

Richard Bausch is the author of nine novels and five volumes of stories, including *Selected Stories,* in the Modern Library. His work has appeared in the *Atlantic,* the *New Yorker, Esquire, Harper's, Playboy, Gentleman's Quarterly,* the *Southern Review,* and numerous other literary journals and anthologies, including the *O. Henry Prize Stories* and *The Best American Short Stories.* He was recently inducted into the Fellowship of Southern Writers. Bausch's novel *The Last Good Time* was made into a feature-length motion picture. *The Stories of Richard Bausch,* an anthology volume of forty-two of his stories, was published in 2003, and a paperback original of three short novels, *Wives and Lovers,* will be published in 2004. He is Heritage Professor of Writing at George Mason University in Virginia.

The most recent of **Ann Beattie**'s many books are the novels *The Doctor's House* (2002) and *Perfect Recall* (2000). Her articles have appeared in *Life*, the *New Yorker, Harper's*, and *Esquire*, among others. She has received the PEN/Malamud Award for Excellence in Short Fiction and is a member of the American Academy of Arts and Letters. She has taught at Harvard College and the University of Virginia, where she is the Edgar Allan Poe Chair of the Department of English and Creative Writing. She and her husband, the artist Lincoln Perry, divide their time between Maine and Key West, Florida.

Robin Bradford's work has appeared in *Boston Review, Quarterly West, Cimarron Review*, and *Brain, Child*, among other places. She received an O. Henry Award and the Dobie Paisano Fellowship for Texas writers. Her monthly column, Mother Load, appears at www.austinmama.com. Bradford works as communications and development director for a nonprofit affordable-housing organization. Born in Japan and raised in Oklahoma and Texas, she lived in Delaware and Rhode Island before settling in Austin. She shares a fifties house with her husband, Jim, their six-year-old son, Cope, and three cats and one dog. Being a mother—of a child over the age of three—is the best thing that has ever happened to her.

An assistant professor in the MFA program at Florida Atlantic University, **Ayşe Papatya Bucak** has published stories and poems in numerous literary magazines, including *Mississippi Review*, the *Literary Review*, and the *Ohio Review*. Her fiction has been short-listed for the *Mississippi Review* Prize and the Pushcart Prize, and she was a writer-in-residence at Hedgebrook Farm. She was born in Istanbul, Turkey, and now lives in South Florida.

Susanna Bullock lives in rural Missouri within sight of the house where her grandpa was born and the graveyard where most of her family is buried. Her first assignment for her high school students is "Tell me a story." A stack of books, a quilt project, and a blank legal pad rest beside each and every chair, couch, or bed in the house her grandparents built in 1953. She moves from one piece of furniture to the next in between responding to the writing of 157 students. Her friends and family, her cat Sam, housework, and her garden are all sorely neglected. She is editing a short-fiction collection and thinks about her novel during faculty meetings.

Ioanna Carlsen's poems and stories have appeared in *Poetry,* the *Hudson Review, Nimrod, Poetry East, Café Solo, Chelsea, The Quarterly, Field, Apalachee Quarterly,* the *Marlboro Review, Quarterly West, Alaska Quarterly Review, Columbia, Solo, Luna, Whiskey Island, Prairie Schooner, Confrontation, Mondo Greco,* the *Gingko Tree Review,* and the *Beloit Poetry Journal.* Her poems have appeared online in Poetry, Poetry Daily, and Poetry 180, a program of the Library of Congress. She holds a BA in English, and an MA in linguistics from the University of Illinois. She lives in the country in Tesuque, just outside Santa Fe, New Mexico, with a husband, Chris, and a dog, Toby, where two grown-up children, Clea and Tasio, reappear intermittently, and where she repairs and weaves chair seats, and writes when she can.

Herman G. Carrillo divides his time between San Juan, Puerto Rico, and Ithaca, New York, where he is an MFA/PhD candidate and instructor in the Department of English at Cornell University. His work has appeared in *Threshold* and *Other Voices* magazines, and is forthcoming in the *Kenyon Review.* Awarded a Sage Fellowship, a Provost's Fellowship, and a Newberry Library Research Grant, he was the 2002 Alan Collins Scholar for Fiction, the recipient of both the 2001 and 2003 Arthur Lynn Andrews Prizes for Best Fiction, a 2003 shortlisting for the O. Henry Prize, and a 2003 Constance Saltonstall Foundation Grant to an Individual Artist. He is currently completing his first novel.

Diane Chang was born near Shanghai, China, in 1976 and immigrated to the United States with her family at the age of three. She holds an MFA from the University of Michigan and, in 2000, received a Fulbright grant to work on her first novel in Shanghai, where she continues to live and write. Her stories and personal essays have appeared in *Green Mountains Review* and the *Asian Wall Street Journal.*

George Makana Clark grew up in Zimbabwe, of British and Xhosa descent. He received his PhD in English at Florida State University and currently teaches fiction writing at the University of Wisconsin-Milwaukee. Clark's collection of short stories, *The Small Bees' Honey,* was published in 1997 by White Pine Press, and his fiction, poetry, and drama have appeared in *Apalachee Quarterly, Black Warrior Review, Chelsea,* the *Cream City Review, Georgetown Review, Interdisciplinary Humanities,* the *Massachusetts Review,* the *Southern Review,* the *Southeast Review, Transition, Zoetrope: All Story,* and elsewhere. His work has been published in anthologies in the United Kingdom and the United States, and in translation in Argentina, Spain, Germany, and Japan. Productions of his plays have been performed in New York and California. He is currently working on a novel set in Zimbabwe and South Africa. Clark was awarded a 2002 National Endowment for the Arts Fellowship in Fiction Writing. He lives in Milwaukee with his wife and daughter.

Doug Crandell is the 2001 recipient of the Sherwood Anderson Foundation Writer's Grant, as well as the River City/Hohenberg Award judged by Booker Prize winner Peter Carey. In 2004 a memoir, *Pig Boy's Wicked Bird,* will be published by Chicago Review Press, and Ludlow Press will bring out his first novel. His essays and stories have appeared in numerous publications, including *Smithsonian Magazine,* the *SUN, River Oak Review,* and *Hawaii Review.*

Ronald F. Currie Jr. is a native of Waterville, Maine. His fiction has appeared in the *Southeast Review, Other Voices* (University of Illinois, Chicago), and elsewhere. He has received the Dibner Fiction Fellowship, a Pushcart Prize nomination, *Night Train* magazine's Firebox Fiction Award, and was runner-up in the 2003 World's Best Short Short Story Competition, judged by Robert Olen Butler. He has completed a collection of short stories and is at work on a novel entitled *Berklee's Book of Hints and Etiquette—A Life Primer.*

Junot Díaz is the author of *Drown.* His fiction has appeared in the *New Yorker, African Voices, The Best American Short Stories* (1996, 1997,

1999, 2000), and in *Pushcart Prize XXII.* He has received a Eugene McDermott Award, a fellowship from the John Simon Guggenheim Memorial Foundation, a Lila Acheson Wallace Reader's Digest Award, the 2002 PEN/Malamud Award, and the 2003 US-Japan Creative Artist Fellowship from the National Endowment for the Arts. He is an associate professor at the Massachusetts Institute of Technology and is a fellow at the Radcliffe Institute for Advanced Study at Harvard University.

Michael Frank's short stories have appeared in *Antaeus, Salmagundi,* the *Yale Review,* and other publications, and have been presented at Symphony Space's "Selected Shorts: A Celebration of the Short Story." A contributing writer to the *Los Angeles Times Book Review,* he lives in New York City and Seaview, Washington.

Nathan Long grew up in a log cabin in rural Maryland. He earned an MA in cultural studies from Carnegie Mellon, and an MFA from Virginia Commonwealth University, where he was the first Truman Capote Scholarship recipient. He has also received a Virginia Commission of the Arts grant to write fiction and a Mellon Foundation grant to attend the Salzburg Seminars in Austria. His stories and poems have appeared in *Indiana Review, Story Quarterly,* and elsewhere. He is currently working on a novel about an intersex child growing up in Ohio. He teaches English and creative writing at Virginia Union University and lives in Richmond, Virginia, with his Muppet Wolf Terrier, Gracie.

Lee Martin is the author of two memoirs, *Turning Bones* and *From Our House,* a novel, *Quakertown,* and a story collection, *The Least You Need to Know.* He is also the co-editor of *Passing the Word: Writers on Their Mentors. From Our House* was a Barnes and Noble Discover Great New Writers selection and also a selection of the Quality Paperback Book Club. His stories and essays have appeared in *Harper's,* the *Georgia Review,* the *Southern Review, Creative Nonfiction, Story, DoubleTake,* and *Fourth Genre.* He is the winner of the Mary McCarthy Prize in Short Fiction, the Nancy Dasher Award, the Lawrence Foundation Award, and the Jeanne Chapriot Goodheart Prize in Fiction. He has also won fellowships from the National Endowment for the Arts, the Ohio Arts Council, and the Texas Commission for the Arts. He is Associate Professor of English in the creative-writing program at Ohio State University.

Joyce Carol Oates is the author of many books, including the novels *Beasts, Big Mouth & Ugly Girl, Faithless: Tales of Transgression, Blonde, Broke Heart Blues, My Heart Laid Bare, The Collector of Hearts, We Were the Mulvaneys,* and *Zombie. What I Lived For* (1994) was nominated for the Pulitzer Prize and PEN/Faulkner Award for Fiction. "The Missing Person" has subsequently appeared in her story collection *Will You Always Love Me?* (copyright 1996 by Ontario Review, Inc.) Books of poetry include *Tenderness* and *Invisible Woman;* recent plays appeared in *New Plays* (1998). *(Woman) Writer* and *On Boxing* are among her nonfiction writings. She is publisher and editor, with Raymond Smith, of *Ontario Review* and Ontario Review Press. She has been awarded the PEN/Malamud Award for Achievement in the Short Story, the F. Scott Fitzgerald Award for Outstanding Achievement in American Literature, the Bram Stoker Lifetime Achievement Award in Horror Fiction, and the National Book Award. She is a member of the American Academy of Arts and Letters, and the American Academy of Achievement.

Jennifer Seoyuen Oh was born in Boston, Massachusetts, and was raised in Carrboro, North Carolina. She received her BA with high distinction in English from Duke University (2002). Her recent awards include the 2001 Short Fiction Prize in an international undergraduate contest sponsored by SUNY at Stony Brook, and a Benenson Arts Award to conduct writing workshops with AIDS patients in New York City. Ms. Oh is currently studying creative writing at Columbia University's MFA program.

Karen Outen's short fiction has appeared in *Essence* magazine, *conditions* literary magazine, and the *North American Review.* She obtained her BA from Drew University and now is attending the MFA program at the University of Michigan, where she received the Hopwood Award in Short Fiction. She has received a Pew Fellowship in the Arts, the

Pennsylvania Council on the Arts Fellowship, and the Rackham Merit Fellowship. She lives in Ann Arbor, Michigan, where she is working on her first novel.

Karenmary Penn, currently a Schaeffer Fellow in creative writing at the University of Nevada at Las Vegas, has published stories in *Gulf Coast, Pittsburgh Quarterly, Red Cedar Review, Willow Springs,* and *Indiana Review.* She was a 1997 Henfield Fellow, and she received two *Chicago Tribune* Nelson Algren Awards and a grant from the Nevada Arts Council. She earned an MFA in creative writing from the University of Arizona.

Margo Rabb grew up in Queens, New York, and now lives in Brooklyn. Her stories have been published in the *Atlantic Monthly, Zoetrope: All Story, Mademoiselle, Seventeen, Best New American Voices, New Stories from the South,* and elsewhere, and have been broadcast on National Public Radio. She received first prizes in *Atlantic Monthly*'s and *American Fiction*'s fiction contests, grand prize in the Sam Adams/Zoetrope short-story contest, and a Syndicated Fiction Project Award. She is completing a collection of connected short stories. Her series of young adult novels, *Missing Persons,* about two Jewish girl detectives from Queens, was published by Puffin Books in April 2004.

Nancy Reisman's short-story collection *House Fires* won the Iowa Short Fiction Award, and her stories have appeared in *Tin House, Five Points, New England Review, Kenyon Review,* and other journals, as well as in *The Best American Short Stories, 2001* and *Bestial Noise: A Tin House Reader.* Her first novel will be published in Fall 2004 by Pantheon. Reisman has received fellowships from the National Endowment for the Arts, the Wisconsin Institute for Creative Writing, and the Fine Arts Work Center in Provincetown, and she's currently the Helen Herzog Zell Professor at the University of Michigan. She lives in Ann Arbor.

J. Patrice Whetsell is a graduate of Oberlin College. She was an artist-in-residence at the Ragdale Foundation, the Headlands Center for the Arts, and the Vermont Studio Center. Formerly a lifelong resident of

New Jersey, she recently moved to Washington State, where she is working on her second novel and learning about the trees of the Pacific Northwest.

Monica Wood is the author of four works of fiction: *Ernie's Ark, My Only Story, Secret Language,* and the forthcoming *Any Bitter Thing.* Her short stories have been widely published and anthologized, read on Public Radio International, awarded a Pushcart Prize, and included twice in *The Best American Mystery Stories.* She has also written two books for writers: *Description,* a guide to technique; and *The Pocket Muse: Ideas and Inspirations for Writing.* She lives in Portland, Maine.

Acknowledgments

We are grateful for the intelligence and hard work of Paul Morris and Scott Allie, without whom the development of this book would simply have been impossible. Our hearty thanks go to our agent, Bob Mecoy, and to our Washington Square Press editors, Emily Bestler and Sarah Branham, for their faith in the collection; also to Sheila Levine, Doug Crandell, and Hazel for making it all connect.

We respect every author whose work is presented here and thank them sincerely for the opportunity to present their stories in *Glimmer Train Stories* and, now, here in *Mother Knows.*

As in all things, we must thank our whole family for their steadfast support in our endeavors, and especially our husbands and children for their wonderful love.